"*Libertyland* is a gripping po
readers with its relentless suspens.
This well-crafted novel is full of twists and turns, so you can
never tell what awaits in the next chapter, keeping you on your
toes till the very end. The narrative is a rollercoaster of political
intrigue and action-packed sequences that will have you on the
edge of your seat. The multifaceted characters and their intricate
connections further add to the story's complexity and realism,
making it impossible to put down until the riveting conclusion.

"However, what makes the story truly chilling is its
unsettling plausibility. As you read it you come to realize that
these events could easily happen in our world. A must-read
for anyone who enjoys suspenseful storytelling and thought-
provoking scenarios, *Libertyland* is a tour de force, leaving you
breathless and wonderfully disturbed."
—International Review of Books.

"Garrick Cripps, a lazy but charismatic professor, literally
charms the pants off Suzanne Dreyfus and gets her to write a
Liberation Manifesto to encapsulate his libertarian beliefs. She
does it as a joke, but is shocked to learn that Cripps takes the
worship of capitalism over all else seriously—deadly seriously—
and claims credit for her work in his quest to build an
organization that will replace the U.S. government with a cabal
of rich capitalists who will run the country like a corporation,
enriching themselves at the expense of everyone else.

"Nothing and no one will be allowed to get in Cripps'
way until he and his associates cross paths with retired Navy
SEAL Carson McReady. Cripps, in his plan to undermine
confidence in the government, and ultimately privatize it,
starting with the FBI, is willing to sacrifice innocent lives in
his quest. Unfortunately, one of the innocent lives is McReady's

son. The cabal of libertarians soon learn that there is something worse on their horizon than a government that gets in the way of them making profits – an angry Navy SEAL with a grudge to settle.

"*Libertyland* by Peter Sacks is a riveting story of good versus evil in which it becomes difficult to identify who the good guys are at times. It takes a deep dive into the dangers of too much greed and not enough accountability in our institutions that quite literally could've been ripped from recent headlines. But Sacks does this all without preaching. Nor does he let history get in the way of a good story that will keep you on the edge of your seat from page one to the stunning conclusion. I give *Libertyland* five stars and kudos to a master storyteller."
—Charles Ray, author.

"A seemingly harmless romance between Suzanne Dreyfus and another MIT alum, Garrick Cripps, evolves into a full-fledged plot to eradicate the government and redefine the meaning of liberty. When Dreyfus gifts Garrick the Liberation Manifesto, a satirization of freedom, for his fortieth birthday, an intended joke becomes the catalyst to a so-called movement that threatens the fabric of democracy.

"There are countless themes that run concurrently throughout the novel, whether that is the extent one will go for love, how humanity can be so fickle that it can be bought for a price, or what makes a killer. At a deeper level, the question of what liberty means to the individual is even more magnified through Garrick's callous outlook. In a nutshell, he believes that the capitalists are the victims, and the perpetrators are the underserved, disadvantaged communities and minorities who prevent the rich from getting richer. ...

"More or less, a high-stakes game of chess is taking place,

and the board is cyberspace. Garrick and his friend/crony Eurynomos have taken their billionaire status and manipulated everyone in authority, from judges to agents. In short, the survival of the government has the odds stacked against it. The end result is an electrifying and delightful experience for readers, yet one that is highly thought-provoking as they come to recognize that what is being shown to them is not necessarily reality."

—Mihir Shah, US Review of Books.

"Garrick Cripps always had libertarian beliefs, but Suzanne Dreyfus never fathomed the incredible damage that her college lover would eventually be capable of. Suzanne writes the "Liberation Manifesto" as a joke—something so ridiculous that it can't ever be reality. But Garrick disagrees. He takes it and runs with it, eventually creating a terrorist organization which seeks to overthrow the U.S. government and replace it with people whose only qualification is their immense wealth. It will take Suzanne, retired Navy SEAL Carson McReady, and cyber weapons expert Laura Cavendish to take down his dangerous ideology. ...

"In many ways, it's a cautionary tale. *Libertyland* expertly demonstrates the dangers that can happen when a delusional and powerful man starts to get his way. If you're looking for an amazing read that is thoroughly engaging and entertaining, you must read *Libertyland* by Peter Sacks."

—Pacific Book Reviews.

Libertyland
Peter Sacks
Copyright © 2024
Published by AIA Publishing, Australia
ABN: 32736122056
http://www.aiapublishing.com

ISBN: 978-1-922329-57-8

LIBERTYLAND

Peter Sacks

AIA PUBLISHING

ACT I
CREEP

Our progeny will build monuments dedicated to us. Saint Ayn. Saint Garrick. Lord Atlas. Saint Suzanne. Saint William. We are the very origins of the Church of Living Capitalism.

– The Liberation Manifesto

1

DO YOU TRUST ME, SUZY?

Suzanne Dreyfus had been skeptical of Garrick Cripps when they met at MIT in the early 1990s. Brash, handsome, smooth talker. Questionable work ethic as a research scientist but highly popular teaching undergrads. Suzanne had been aloof, spending most of her time alone. He sensed her isolation, and like a predator seeking the lone victim in the wild, he pounced.

They flirted. He mentioned his private dream of creating a libertarian paradise in America. She didn't take him seriously. Too far-fetched. Un-American, even. She teased Garrick and got him to laugh at himself. She saw his humanity. His kindness toward his mother who lived alone in Indiana. Suzanne and Garrick capitulated to one another. They had crafted their flawed alliance—Garrick with his narcissistic need to be adored, and she with her twisted desire to adore him.

If she had listened to her parents, she would never have met Garrick. Both Suzanne's father and her mother, a high school math teacher, were leftists who had met in Mississippi at a demonstration where Dr. King himself spoke. They kept preaching the practicality of going to CUNY: she could live at home and save money.

But Suzanne thought bigger. She had the brains to do anything she wanted. It was her time. MIT was looking for smart women to go into science, engineering, and math. She wanted to study astrophysics and join the faculty of a college somewhere in New England, to teach and to discover new planets and stars. She could meet a nice guy in Cambridge, a fellow scientist, and team up on big discoveries. But she also dreamed of having children and a pretty home in the suburbs or in the country. Get a dog. She wanted it all.

What happened? Love wasn't a choice. Nor was her lust and attraction to Garrick's cleverness and his insatiable thirst for power.

She was no longer little Suzy Dreyfus, the young head-turner from Brooklyn. Under Garrick's influence she questioned her beliefs. She loved her parents, but Garrick called them weak and naive. She remembered the one intimate conversation in Morro Bay years after leaving MIT. After a perfect afternoon of sex and slumber, Garrick revealed his true self—or, more accurately, the person he had become.

"Hope for the poor, Garrick."

"Screw the poor, Suzy. They're poor because they're incapable of winning."

"Education matters, Garrick."

"Only if you're intelligent enough to make it matter."

"Health care for all, Garrick."

"Where does it say that in the Constitution? The Founding Fathers never guaranteed a right to die later rather than sooner."

"Equal rights for all, my love."

"Nice in theory. But in America, we buy and sell rights

to the highest bidder, free from coercion. Get over it. It's called liberty."

In time Garrick's ruthlessness repelled her. And yet his hyper-confidence—the corollary of his ruthlessness—attracted her more. Suzanne could have had any man. She knew it—and so did Garrick. She often wondered if Garrick's badass attitude was an act to fortify his appeal to her.

January 2020 was the last time Suzanne had spent time alone with Garrick. She had moved to Boulder for a new job, but he'd flown her to his cottage in Morro Bay for the weekend. Garrick dropped the bomb that he was going underground until the "endgame." And it was Suzanne's job to work with their old friend, William—who now went by Eurynomos—and "make it happen."

"Make what happen, Garrick?"

They were naked after sex on the library sofa.

"We begin now."

"What the hell are you talking about?"

"It will become clear. I'm asking you to be patient."

"Why are you being so cryptic? You're messing with me, right?"

They talked for hours that day. Garrick soothed her, and she softened. They ordered in and holed up for another night in the cottage. They made love again, then enjoyed cognac and crème brûlée. Suzanne's mischievousness always elevated with her blood alcohol.

"Do you really believe?" She grasped her lover gently by his balls.

"I have to believe. My DNA, darling. You're making me hard, thinking about it."

"About what, exactly? My hands on your nuts?"

"My lusts. You know what they are."

"Money and power. Anything else?"

"And you, of course."

She clung to his nuts, squeezed tightly, then let go. She placed her fingers on his hard-on, teasing him.

She became more mischievous, carefully composing the words she knew would make him even harder. "Garrick, can I confess something to you?"

"Don't stop now, darling."

"You taught me to see the world differently. Without illusions. I fell in love with you for that. You seduced me with your ideas. You taught me how to find purity in a complicated, fucked-up world full of insecure people and impure thoughts. I fell in love with a devil who lusted for purity." She toyed with the tip of his cock, then spat on it.

"I love that, Suzy. Complexity is unnecessary. Our reality can be so simple and so pleasurable."

"And what is that reality for you?"

"That the strong shall prevail over the weak. Full stop. That simple idea turns me on. Makes me want to fuck you. Again and again."

"You think I'm weak?"

"You're one of the strong ones, Suzanne. I've always known that. But you tried to fight me at first, remember? You know, right after *The Manifesto*."

"What do you think of Lenny Bruce?" she asked, out of the blue.

"Lenny who?"

Her face tightened. She let go of his cock. "Garrick, listen to me. I always wanted us to be the way we were, before you became the one and only Garrick Cripps. I couldn't stop you, and I wouldn't leave you. An affair might have ended it, but you've always been faithful. Haven't you?"

4

"Always, darling. Look at you. What man would look anywhere else?"

"Good answer."

His cock had softened. She spat on the head and wrapped her mouth around it, sucking the blood from his brain, exploiting the gravity of natural law to engorge his dick with fresh fluid. She looked up, allowing her man to witness her adoring eyes framed by perfect breasts and stiffened nipples, and her wide mouth giving a pleasure greater than he'd ever given in return. But that was Garrick.

When she woke Garrick had vanished from his own home. She left Morro Bay in the morning.

She got home to Boulder, opened her suitcase, and found a note stuffed in her underwear.

From now on, you will deal with Eurynomos. Trust him. He's built for revolutionary work. You asked me if I was a true believer. To be honest, I don't know. But I know this: don't love me. Love the revolution. Garrick had closed with a question: *Do you trust me, Suzy?*

Suzanne showered and dressed for an evening out. But she wasn't going out. She slipped into a pair of black Christian Louboutins, and leafed through her closet and found a bright red wool coat, as if to cover her naked body in warm blood. Suzanne grabbed the note from her suitcase. The spikes slapped the hard floor as she walked to the kitchen. She opened the pantry and pulled out a fresh bottle of Campari. Not the candied Aperol. The Campari for its complexity, its herbal bitterness, and aroma of deep earth. Not a simple-minded Aperol cocktail at a Tuscan wedding reception. The New York City interpretation. A cool drink with sensuous purpose. She uncorked a chilled bottle of prosecco and mixed the drink in a fulsome wine glass, topping it with soda and

5

ice. She cut the lights then lit a small candle and placed it in a saucer. With a few strokes on her laptop, the Mark Coppey interpretation of JS Bach's *Cello Suite No. 1 in G Major* filled the darkened space.

She danced over the flame while ripping up the note, tossing the pieces into the wax-filled saucer. She threw another match onto the flame, amplifying the fire, as the prelude reached its crescendo.

Watching the burning note, her face contorted into a wicked smile. She lit a cigarette. Suzanne did not squat over the flame. She stood like a man, drink in one hand and cigarette tipping from her lips.

Celebrating the cello's burst of energy in her own private bacchanal, she sucked on the cocktail and raised her glass. She dragged on the cig and again pulled from the drink. She studied the burning paper for a moment, then spread her legs in a v-shaped stance, her clit above the fire. She touched herself. Again and again, until she came.

"Fuck you, Garrick," she screamed. Contemplating the art of revenge, she pissed with pleasure on the dying flame of paper and ink disappearing into a puddle of piss, cum, and betrayal.

2

THE ONE

January 2024

Carson McCready nosed his dusty BMW into the beachside parking lot and let Diego out of the back seat. He tossed a beat-up tennis ball into the surf and watched with pride as the young Lab bounded through the surf to fetch it. The dog's coat shimmered with drops of ocean and wet sand as he galloped back with the ball in his mouth and dropped it at Carson's feet.

The Lab continued to leap over the waves in a precocious display of athleticism. Carson tossed the ball once more with a little less force. The change-up threw off Diego's timing by a fraction.

A large male pit bull leaped into the frame. The pit moved in, not to play but to attack.

"Get the hell out of here!" Carson screamed.

A large man with a shaved head and a sleeveless leather jacket got into Carson's face. "Hey! Asshole. Leave my fucking dog alone. Rocker, get the fuck over here."

7

Carson usually backed off in dicey situations. Not worth going to jail and definitely not worth hurting the knucklehead. As a former SEAL, Carson knew how to diffuse conflict. Or, if need be, he could easily intensify it.

He met the red eyes of the man before him. "Show some respect to Dog Beach, buddy. Look around you. Rocker's fine. You are the problem."

"Fuck you."

"Look, I'm sorry for yelling at Rocker. My bad. It's over. No harm, no foul." Carson put out his hand. "Come on, man. I apologize. Let me buy you a beer."

He had barely finished the sentence when the pit's owner rammed his heavy boot at Carson's crotch. Carson grabbed the man's leg mid-strike and held it there. He could have busted the guy's knee with a hard twist, but someone came up from behind and landed another kick. Carson let go of the leg and the pit's owner kicked him a second time, this one slamming into his genitals. Carson spilled onto the sand, cussing and groaning.

"Son of a fucking bitch. Would you dumb bastards prefer a buttery Chardonnay instead?"

"Go fuck yourself, old man," said the one whose kneecap Carson had chosen not to snap.

A crowd was forming now, and they started booing Carson's attackers.

A boy who looked to be about ten helped Carson up. "I think your dog ran over that way."

He looked down at the boy. "Thanks, son."

"Hope you find your dog, sir."

He pulled out a few bucks from his back pocket and handed the money to the boy. "Get yourself a smoothie. There's a decent joint at the end of Dog Beach."

He hobbled down the endless shore, calling Diego's name.

~

A young woman had been out for a run and was just finishing her hamstring stretches. She looked up, hearing the vicious sounds of men and dogs—a pit bull attacking a yellow Lab and a man screaming at the muscled dog. She laughed when he mentioned the buttery Chardonnay.

She noticed the Lab running away and ran to catch up with the puppy, who was by then lollygagging and sniffing at shells and seaweed. She put one knee on the sand and called out, "Hello, baby. Come here, baby."

She turned around and saw the man limping in her direction toward the end of Dog Beach, where the canal divided Ocean Beach from Mission Bay. She could hear the man calling "Diego" again and again.

"Diego. Is that your name, pretty boy?"

Jane would have noticed Carson even without the hoopla. Or without the mystery woman paying her to follow him. The pay was good. Too good to tell the lady to piss off. She ran a clean business and relied on her good standing with the county to send them well-vetted job candidates. But the woman wanted this guy. The man running toward her, chasing his dog. He was no ordinary Ocean Beach dude. Mid to late forties. Tall with sandy blond hair, athletic legs, and tanned arms that resembled thick, taut ropes, he wore plaid shorts and a wrinkled blue shirt.

"In answer to your question, I'm Carson."

"What question would that be?"

"You said, 'What's your name, pretty boy?' "

She laughed. "I meant the dog. Are you okay? That burly

9

dude kicked you pretty hard in the gut."

"You saw what happened back there?"

"I did."

"Live around here?"

"I own a small recruiting company here in Ocean Beach. I match people with jobs. What about you?"

Carson took her in, trying to decipher the oddity of the tanned brunette's story. "What a coincidence. I'm looking for a job."

"What kind of job?"

"Good pay, not too challenging. Simple as that."

"You *must* be special," Jane said.

"Why is that?"

"Oh, you know. You want it all. Easy job and good pay."

"Hell, yes. I should be retired."

"How's that?"

"Navy until I decided I'd had enough. I want a job where I can put in my eight hours, go home, leave the job behind for the night, and have a normal, stress-free life. Not too much to ask."

Jane gazed at Carson. She reached into her fanny pack and pulled out a business card and a pen. She scratched out a note and held out the card. She smiled. "Can you control that temper of yours?"

"Temper? I tried to buy a guy a beer, and he kicked me in the nuts." He took the business card. "What's this?"

"Call that number and ask for Johnny Petit. He's director of human resources at San Diego County Jail. He's got an opening, and he hires a lot of ex-military. I have a strong suspicion you're the one he's looking for."

"The jail? To do what?"

"Just call him. I think you'd be perfect. I'll give him a

heads-up—what's your name?"

"Carson. Carson McCready."

"Give Johnny a call, Carson. Tell him Jane sent you."

~

Jane watched Carson trudge through the fluffy sand toward the parking lot. When he disappeared into the pool of parked cars, she pulled out her phone from her fanny pack and hit the dial button. A woman picked up immediately.

"Yes, Jane?"

"I found him. I told him he'd be perfect."

"Did he need any convincing?"

"Not really."

"Okay, good."

"Is that all? No background check, nothing?" Jane said.

"I've already told you that's unnecessary."

"Johnny Petit okay with that?"

"Petit knows what I tell him. He'll do a basic interview. You'll brief Petit. Stick to your script. When you're done with what I've asked, you'll receive what I promised. Now, lose my number."

3

MONEY TIME

"Carson McCready, let me introduce you to your new team members. I want you all to get off to a good start," Johnny Petit told the inmates.

Street slang gurgled through the dozen disparate prisoners.

Petit knew little about Carson. Only bits from Jane and what Carson had told him in the perfunctory interview. Retired Navy. Grew up locally. Needed a job to pay the bills. Petit stalled the usual background check, just as that mystery lady had told him to.

Petit turned to Buster, the guard standing at the door, then back to the inmates.

"Hello, guinea pigs," Petit said. "Welcome to our pilot telemarketing program. The higher-ups chose you from a pool of hundreds of convicted felons. For you lucky bastards this is an excellent opportunity, so don't fuck it up. Break up the boredom. Get your asses out of the yard. We're giving you the chance to do good for a change, to give something back."

"Give back, my ass," an inmate said.

Laughter.

12

"That's right, brother, we takin' it in the ass," came another voice.

Petit spoke over the snickering: "That buzz is the sound of the big machine of San Diego County Jail ramming your sweet asses. Smell that fresh paint? Your new beginning. The machine's gonna give you guys a break. Buster's got orders, so don't piss him off. Now, introduce yourselves to Mr. McCready and your fellow teammates."

Carson stood in silence, meeting Buster's eyes. The big guy was half-grinning at Petit's brief speech. Carson returned the smile while taking in the smell of the fresh beige paint. The absurdities, one upon another, reminded him of the military. Despite having never been in a civilian prison, this was Carson's comfort zone.

Petit turned to an inmate on his left. "Let's start with you."

Carson watched, not liking how it was going down. *Get boss-man out of the room. Get control of this thing.*

"Can I add a little something to the introductions, Mr. Petit? Matter of fact, I'd like to chat for a moment in private."

"Not a problem. Let's step outside. Buster, watch these boys."

Petit pushed through the door, and Carson let it slam shut.

"Johnny, I'd like you to leave me alone with my team for the rest of the shift. I'll take the reins."

"Sure about that, cowboy? These dudes are dangerous. You might want an experienced hand around. They could eat you alive, son."

"No worries. Got this handled."

"Okay, Carson. Don't say I didn't warn you. Be nice to Buster. If he likes you, he just might keep those cons from cutting you up."

"You might need to recruit my replacement already."

13

"Funny. That's no joke around here. Watch your ass."

Carson returned to the room and an unexpected silence. Like the first day of SEAL training. Actually, worse. A thousand times worse. His tadpoles wanted it—dreamed their entire lives wanting it even when they hated it. The hardships and relentless pain bound the men together. Gave them purpose. These inmates, however, wanted nothing except to get the fuck out of prison.

"Okay guys, as the boss said, I'm Carson McCready, and we're here to get this new telemarketing gig rolling. Help me put these chairs in a circle, and take a seat."

Again, the hushed sounds of prison slang amid the metal-to-concrete shifting of chairs. Angry sounds.

Carson turned to the guard. "Say, Buster, stand on the other side of the door. Please."

"Got orders, Mr. McCready."

"Go on, buddy. I'll take the flak."

"You got it, boss," Buster said as he closed the door behind him.

That shut everybody up.

"Okay, where were we? Let's go around the circle and introduce yourselves to your new teammates. I'll start. I'm Carson. Ex-Navy. Trained recruits for some of the hardest jobs in the military. I lead by example. I treat you fairly, and I expect the same in return. No more and no less." He turned to his left. "Next."

The man grimaced, like he'd just bit into a lemon. "Say what?"

"You heard me."

"I'm Montel. Served on the streets. Felony possession." Montel turned to the next inmate.

"I'm Tony. Man, fuck this."

14

Carson glared at him. "Buster!" he yelled, summoning him into the room. "Escort this man back to the yard. Next!"

Carson turned to a beefy white guy, head shaven, who stared straight ahead.

He frowned at the skinhead. "What's with you?"

"I ain't saying shit."

Carson looked down to gather himself. He stood and faced the men. "Let's get through this, shall we? I want to make some money today, and the sooner you guys quit acting like children, the sooner we make money."

Nobody moved.

"That's not a request. We doing this? Or should I bring the boss back in, this time with about five guys named Buster?"

More squeaking of chairs and angry voices. Carson pulled his cell phone out of his rear pocket, clicked three times, and a Neil Young song—"Only Love Can Break Your Heart"— filled the room. Its rhythm and Young's quiet, poetic twang startled everyone into silence at its beautiful absurdity in the face of chaos.

Now the inmates were listening.

"This is our Circle of Trust, boys. Whatever happens out there stays out there. Here, we are brothers. We leave all the shit out there. We make this fucked-up situation work for us, not against us. I don't give a shit where you grew up, what ink you got stitched on your back, or what tinge of white, red, Black, or blue your skin color is. What happens in the circle stays in the circle. Out there, well, you do what you got to do. In here no judgment and no gangs. Are we cool?"

Finally an inmate spoke, interrupting the sounds of men breathing and metal chairs rattling against the concrete. "It's cool, brother."

"And you are?"

15

"Terrell Smith, brother."

Carson turned to an enormous man who resembled a much larger Malcolm X, studious and smart in black-rimmed glasses.

The introductions continued until they reached two skinheads, Stompy and Boot.

"Hey, Stompy, no street names here. What's your proper name? The name your momma gave you."

Stompy stared at the concrete floor. "Mom called me James. James K. de Werdt."

"What's the K for?"

"Kennedy."

"Kennedy, as in the dead president?" Carson said.

"Wouldn't know nothing about that shit."

"Never mind. In here you're Jim. Big Jim."

Carson turned to the other holdout. "What about you, Boot? What's your real name?"

Boot looked down at his prison shoes, then up at the fluorescent lights on the ceiling.

"Come on, Boot. I'll look you up if I have to."

Boot rubbed his forehead as if in pain, and his mouth twisted into a weird grin, a cross between agony and futility. He finally blurted out: "Terrell fucking Smith. Mom called me Terry. Old man called me Dickhead."

Carson tried like hell to keep a straight face. A few Black guys nudged Black Terrell, the Malcolm X type with glasses, giving him shit. Carson's poker face remained unchanged.

Carson watched in amazement as the next few moments unfolded.

Black Terrell got up from his chair in a quick jolt of metal on concrete. He walked over to Boot. All the inmates stood, waiting for the worst.

Black Terrell and White Terrell squared off like prizefighters.

16

Black Terrell moved closer. "Ain't that something? Skinhead and an African in the same fucked-up place. Shake my hand, brother."

White Terrell's grimace relaxed, revealing a glimpse of an actual human being behind the mask. He put his right palm against Black Terrell's outstretched arm and hand, and they bumped shoulders, like professional football players after a good play.

Despite all the world's bullshit, there's still a common language there, Carson thought.

The room's energy drew back to Carson, who sat bemused, suppressing tears. Memories of his men on the SEAL team were creeping back. "Hate to break this up, boys, but it's money time."

~

Carson got home to his condo in Lemon Grove, still thinking about his new job. A casual trip to the beach with his dog had led to an interview at a high-security prison for a telemarketing sales manager's position, for which he had no genuine qualifications.

Before walking up the stairs, he checked the mailbox and opened a letter from his ex-wife's lawyer. Alimony and terms for visiting his fifteen-year-old son. Bills from two banks, both requiring immediate payment for overdue bills. And then another certified letter from the Department of the Navy. How many times must he relive and explain what happened that night in Somalia seven years ago?

That idiot politician from Kentucky. Nosy damned demagogue with a severe case of oral diarrhea and moral self-righteousness.

17

He stuffed the mail into the back pocket of his khakis then took Diego for a brief walk around the park, which was hardly enough to settle the knot in Carson's gut.

After retiring from the Navy three years ago, he had tried to keep his goals reasonable. Settling down, enjoying some solitude, taking the longboard to Tourmaline Beach—like the old days. Just stopping. Doing crossword puzzles over morning coffee. Taking Diego to the beach. Playing golf at Torrey Pines. Finding a simple job to make ends meet. Giving in to a sense of lightness and freedom. Like his days as a kid by the ocean, when he could breathe and splash as loud as he wanted. Not feeling the constant danger of his own breath, when merely breathing too loudly could get you killed.

He'd been out of work since mustering out, not counting his brief stint as a security consultant. For Carson that had been a transition gig to ease himself back into civilian life, as his commanding officer had advised him. Finding a normal life now seemed like a joke. The past was in the past, but Carson's past was an ornery bastard for whom lightness and freedom were apparently verboten.

He fixed a quick meal of beans, cheese, and a tortilla, washing it down with a cold beer. He flipped on the TV. He was just settling in when his phone lit up with a local number.

"McCready here."

"Carson?"

"Speaking."

"Johnny Petit. Catch you at a bad time?"

"I'm enjoying a cold beer and some Aztec basketball. What's up, Johnny?"

"Carson, just wanted to say I liked what I saw today. I'm hoping you'll stick with us. The suits really need this telemarketing deal to work."

Carson let a moment pass.

"What do you say, cowboy? Did I hire the right man?"

Carson hesitated, then remembered the bills piling up.

"I'm your cowboy, Johnny. I told you. I need the job."

"Glad to hear you say that. I'm happy as a pig in a tar pit."

Carson hung up.

On reflection the whole deal was weird. The beach. The dogs. The bullshit. Always the bullshit. But Jane, the headhunter, was helpful, and had brightened what had otherwise been a bad day at the beach.

At the job interview, Petit had peppered him with questions. Jane had told him about the fight.

"Why didn't you hit back? The guy kicked you in the nuts, for Christ's sake," Petit had said.

"I don't mess with civilians. That's why."

"Hell's that mean?"

"Always leads to law enforcement."

"In case you haven't noticed, plenty of law enforcement around here, McCready."

He told Petit most of the truth about himself. Forty-seven years old. Retired Navy. Taught basic training. Grew up by the ocean. He didn't tell Petit that he trained tadpoles, newbies in basic underwater demolition for the SEALs. Nor that he had reached the rank of master chief petty officer of a sixteen-member SEAL platoon and led off-book kill missions in Afghanistan, Iraq, Syria, and Northern Africa.

He told few people those facts.

After three years Carson still wasn't ready to talk openly about his time as a SEAL. Endless war. Comrades dead, or alive but in pieces. Too much damned trouble. Too many SEAL headlines and tell-all books. Some guys might enjoy embellishing war stories to new bosses. To Carson that was

19

like sticking your head up from the water's surface to get your mouth shot off. Big mouths always led to big trouble.

Now he was supervising a bunch of felons, many of whom were former or active members of some street gang in So Cal. He'd have to persuade rival gang members to play nice with customers, and with each other, in a relatively small space for four hours a day. He could do it. Carson could do anything. Just a matter of how much discomfort he was willing to handle.

4

JOSEPH MCCARTHY WAS A HERO

February 2024

Suzanne Dreyfus pulled a black wool scarf to her face to protect her perfect skin against the chill. She listened to the crunch of frozen snow under her leather boots. A slow but steady walk. The crisp air and winter sun felt good. Like in Cambridge years ago, walking beside the Charles River on the daily commute to her office at MIT.

She was dressed in urban black and tall matching boots, over-styled for Boulder's plethora of North Face and Patagonia. Suzanne was in no hurry to get to her office now.

She shut her eyes, feeling the warmth of the sun and a familiar tightening in her throat. A thought of Garrick. Strolling along the Charles had always led to Garrick. Never-forgotten emotions. The thought of him broke her smile like an icicle.

Suzanne kept walking, amused by the aspects of Boulder that Garrick Cripps had tried to convince her to hate. Entitled trust-funders from the east. Environmental leftists from

California. And coffee-house liberals from San Francisco and Seattle.

Boulder was Boulder, oozing a self-satisfied elitism. Classic architecture blended with the modern. Old western heritage recast to a soft urban chic—an urban forest. Mountains pressing on the town, enveloping a sense of collective self-centeredness. *We are Boulder and we're special.* Except that many of the town's "progressives" were actually full-on, trust-funded capitalists.

Her life was good enough. Better than most. She directed a faux environmental firm, a cover for an off-book program with the Pentagon. She had taken the job in 2000, allegedly for the movement—but also for Garrick, whom she had still loved until that fateful day of betrayal at Garrick's place twenty-four years ago. Years went by and the movement had stalled until Garrick came out of hiding and called a meeting at his Morro Bay compound in October of 2023. Garrick didn't even show, but she and William—who now likened himself to the underworld figure Eurynomos—hammered out a plan of action. Even that plan lingered untouched for a year.

Maybe, Suzanne had wondered, Garrick had finally seen the futility of his crazy ambition to dissolve the government of the United States, and finally abandoned his allegiance to an unworkable fantasy that amounted to all talk and small changes on the margins. After all, libertarians, ranging from the fringes of the far right to even the halls of the US Congress, had been philosophizing for generations about eliminating the government by spinning off its functions to the highest bidders. Endless, and relatively harmless, talk.

But that was her fantasy. Since the last Morro Bay meeting, Suzanne had heard nothing. She kept waiting for the other shoe to finally drop. Her gut told her the day would come, forcing her to carry on with her plan to eliminate the very movement she had inadvertently launched when writing *The Liberation Manifesto* as a satirical gift to Garrick on his fortieth birthday.

And on this day, the wait was over.

When the call came, she saw the 202 area code, and she braced for the terror, anger, and longing. She stopped, slipped off a leather glove, and hit the Call button. "Yes?"

"Suzanne."

"Who's this?" She knew exactly who it was—a familiar voice from the past. She rarely asked a question she didn't already know the answer to.

"Forget me already?"

"William? Or should I be calling you Eurynomos now?"

"You knew I'd reach out. Have you talked to Garrick?"

"I can't remember the last time I spoke to Garrick."

"Of course you can. I know you, Suzy."

"What do you want, Billy?"

"Are you still in the game or not? I need you to say it. Out loud."

"What do you want me to say? It's been months since Morro Bay. Garrick didn't bother to show up at his own meeting. I drank too much and hardly remember a thing."

"I want you to recite the enemies list, Suzanne. Do you remember the list?"

"You mean the list that Garrick etched into my once-gullible head?" Of course Suzanne remembered. She could play this game of submission to the man who liked to call himself Eurynomos—Garrick's short childhood friend, who they had jokingly called Little Billy back in the day.

Billy liked to play tough, but he didn't understand a

23

crucial truth. The list was not only The List but *her* list, the one she'd created for Garrick's public posturing. The list that defined his libertarian crusade when they were lovers at MIT. She had been young. Garrick had been persuasive—and strikingly handsome in those days.

But none of that mattered now. *Poor Garrick,* she thought. Strong, passionate, but incompetent in so many ways. Poor Billy. A servant to Garrick's overconfidence. Suzanne understood both men's weaknesses. Especially the one they shared as wealthy, middle-aged men who overvalued their masculine power over women. Suzanne had remained in the background. Beautiful, aloof, and useful for certain operations, while the movement's official leaders, the men, were achieving their self-styled greatness.

Her power was rooted in a secret. Such a dangerous secret that their inner sanctum—Garrick, William, and Suzanne— had tacitly agreed to hide it from the outside world, for if the secret were discovered, the movement would collapse under the weight of its own absurdity. But men will be men. Her power had always existed beneath their hubris, their unstated refusal to acknowledge that Suzanne held the key to the kingdom.

"I'll give you the list, Billy. Straight from *The Manifesto* itself: 'The enemies of freedom. Blacks, progressives. Ardent believers in the illusion of the democratic collective to ensure human progress. Socialists who run the education system and the government. It's time to take the country back.' Satisfied?"

"A bit robotic, but Garrick taught you well."

"Joseph McCarthy was a hero. Did I miss anything?"

Garrick's idol, Ayn Rand, was a Jew. Suzanne, too, was Jewish. But she had always suspected that both Garrick and Billy were closet antisemites. Suzanne had ignored it—and felt ashamed. She was useful. Like Ayn Rand was useful. Another clever, useful Jew to add intellectual heft to powerful capitalists and their political hacks.

"You were saying, Billy?"

" 'The Founding Fathers missed their opportunity to define America as the world's one true exception to the mediocrity that a soft society ensured.' "

"Is it number one on Amazon yet?"

"Suzy, that's what I mean. I'm not sure your heart is in this anymore. *The Manifesto* has been attracting a whole new generation of believers."

She played dumb. She played dumb a lot with Billy and Garrick. She pretended not to be bothered. But she *was* bothered. She wanted it all to disappear. But Billy's call suggested it would not disappear. He and Garrick needed her.

Fine, she would play the game. But from the moment of Billy's call, the other shoe would drop, all right. Her shoe. The one that she would press on Garrick's neck. While Garrick and Billy dawdled over the years and recent months, she'd been creating her own contingency plan that relied upon, by her own design, an ex-Navy SEAL named Carson McCready.

"Garrick was always an overachiever. Why are you really calling?" she said.

"I'll get to that. Have you heard from Johnny Petit?"

"Don't know the guy. Remind me."

"Petit. The human resources guy we recruited at the prison? Never mind. You know what we're looking for, right?"

"Regarding?" she said playfully.

"The new guy to run the pilot telemarketing operation at the prison. Dammit, Suzy."

"Oh, now I remember. Someone lazy and not too bright. But likable. That's taken care of, Billy. Exactly as I promised at the Morro Bay meeting. Are we done here?"

"Who is he?"

"Don't know and don't care," she lied. "You needn't worry about it. He's exactly what you wanted. Ex-military, I think."

"I'm just trying to understand where your head is nowadays."

"Is this Garrick or you talking?"

"Doesn't matter. We speak as one."

"I'm in Boulder, remember? I still work here. And you, William Wharton, can't question my commitment after all I've done for the movement."

"Calm down. I'm here to help you *help* the movement, assuming you're still with us. Which leads me to that bot. From what I gather, it's a killer. No known defenses against it, and it's smart enough to adapt to any conceivable threat."

"And you're referring to what?" Suzanne said, again feigning ignorance.

"That thing. God, Suzy, where's your head at? Garrick says the bot's passing every test he can throw at it. A young genius from Stanford is helping us. Professor Jonas Peterson, originally from Austria. Garrick loves him."

"I know exactly who Jonas is, you idiot. I put him in touch with Garrick, remember? And 'that thing' is called an algorithm. Anyway, I'm no longer involved with any of that."

"Everything is going according to script. We're totally anonymous and untouchable."

"So you say."

"Suzanne, your time in Boulder is ending. You could quit the Pentagon gig or take an extended leave of absence—I don't care. It's showtime, and there's an FBI agent we'd like you to contact. He's ready to cooperate, depending on how well you treat him."

"Who's the lucky bastard?"

"Darryl Cunningham, the Bureau's counterterrorism chief in San Diego."

"Was the FBI guy your idea? Or Garrick's?"

"I don't recall, actually. You really don't know, do you?" William said.

"What the fuck are you talking about?"

"*The Manifesto*? The original twelve chapters?" William said.

"What about it?"

"A thirteenth chapter surfaced. It details the endgame. It's called *Liberation Day*. The document first appeared on the dark web several months ago. Someone anonymously pointed it out to us."

"Hmm. Who would that be?"

"Doesn't matter. Your original twelve chapters unleashed the storm. The movement will forever be in your debt. But you stopped short. The thirteenth chapter guides us to victory, and it details every move," William said. "We find the right FBI agent who'll create a bogus threat assessment accusing a supposed Islamic terrorist cell of gangbangers and felons already in the jail as the culprits behind a certain cyberattack. It's all there, Suzy, in the thirteenth chapter that dropped on our doorstep."

"Stop, Billy."

"What?"

"I said stop. I wrote the thirteenth chapter. Just musings, really. When was Morro Bay?"

"It would have been last October."

"Right. After Morro Bay, I couldn't take it anymore. So I dropped that thirteenth chapter on the dark web and let fate take it. Call it one last gift from me to Garrick. I'm done. No more *Manifesto*. No more Garrick. Or you. This has already gone way too far. I've completed what I've promised, and more. I want a clean slate."

"You don't really believe that. We're so close. That thirteenth chapter details the endgame. How the US government as we know it dissolves, peacefully—no blood. Only temporary chaos while our people in Congress enact a new federal system owned and operated by the Society."

"So the Freedom Society can finally get out from under its rock."

"When the government dissolves, the Society will stand as a symbol of the most revolutionary libertarian movement the world has ever known."

"Not that I care, but where will Garrick be when all this goes down?"

"He hasn't told me exactly. Sorry, his call."

"Fine. But if you talk to him—as I'm sure you will—tell him I won't be around when he shows up."

"Come on. You and Garrick were never right for each other. He's a zealot's zealot. You and I, Suzy, we're the same. We have limits."

"Oh, really? I've never been comfortable with the extremists buzzing around us. The Austrians and their Nazi crap are over the top. Garrick is sucking up to the neo-Nazis in our own backyard—and vice versa. We don't need that. What's fascism got to do with making the world safe for capitalism?"

"Let's not get into all that now, okay?" William said.

"Where are you, anyway? Why don't we talk in person? I don't trust this."

"I'm somewhere. I'm sorry, Suzy."

"Are you with Garrick on the yacht? Put him on."

"Let it be, okay?"

Suzanne understood what was at stake. She was thriving in Boulder, yet she was trapped within a treasonous prison with no way out except to go to the FBI and cut a deal that would nail Garrick for leading a conspiracy to overthrow the United States government. William was asking her to seduce an FBI agent. Recruit him and bribe him if necessary. The irony was noteworthy. Create a capitalist state free from any hint of coercion. Priceless.

"You don't need me anymore. You two run the show, anyway."

"We need to finish what we started, Suzanne. Certain things need to happen, and you understand better than any of us how to do these things. We would pay well, of course. Our investors have remained steadfast—and generous. In exchange for your continued cooperation, the fuck-you money coming your way would be irresistible. You could quit the Pentagon and go buy a ranch in Montana. Whatever."

Suzanne stopped on the icy sidewalk. She had expected this. She waited. "How much?" she said.

"Ten million. For helping us see this through to the end."

"Define 'the end.' "

"Liberation Day, what else?"

"Which means what, exactly?"

"That thirteenth chapter is our guide. Precise details are still to be determined."

"Fifty."

"Fifty what?"

"Million, you moron."

"I can't go higher than twenty."

"Thirty, or you can find a new seductress for Agent Cunningham."

Suzanne clicked off with William and kept walking, mulling over the strange relationship they had developed over the years. To her delight the poor guy had grown to accept that Suzanne called him whatever the fuck she wanted. When they first met she had called him William, in deference to his prep school upbringing and wealthy New England family. When they became friends, she had called him Billy, or "Little Billy" because that's what Garrick called him. More recently she'd tease him using his latest pseudonym, Eurynomos, which she found insufferable.

She passed a young couple with a big golden retriever. They smiled, and she pretended not to see them. Seemed like everybody in Boulder owned a dog. Suzanne had no need for children, husbands, or dogs.

Once she had worked for the cause, but in reality, it was for her idiotic love of a borderline narcissist. As time passed he withdrew his love and caught a train deeper into extremism.

Now here she was again, the supposedly faithful woman recruited for the final phase of an angry libertarian movement that had started out ever so innocently.

As she walked on the icy sidewalk, she became teary, missing her family and the Brooklyn of her childhood. She wondered what her life would be like if she had stayed in New York and gone to CUNY. What if she had never met Garrick? Where would she be?

She might have ended up in Boulder anyway. Become a genuine all-American girl, following some crazy dream to live in Colorado, find a good man, and settle down into a comfortable life with a husband, children, and a dog. A tenured professor. A complacent member of upper-middle-class ignorance. Be like everyone else in her leafy neighborhood, who had no fucking clue that everything they assumed was true and everlasting could crash and burn at any moment.

She ought to turn herself in as a co-conspirator in planning a cyberattack on government computer networks. Guide the feds through the absurd plan to use a county prison as ground zero for the attack. The scheme sounded so far-fetched that the feds—the ones whom Garrick had not already bribed or threatened—would laugh her out of the building.

No, she would play along, just as she'd been doing for years. But this time the rules of the game would be hers. Eventually she'd talk. Tell the authorities how the movement began at MIT years ago. Strike a deal. Take a minimum sentence in a low-security prison with a living room and a TV, then start over. Get a second chance at a good life filled with trust and love.

Suzanne entered the vestibule of her downtown office building, wiping the snow and ice from her boots. She swiped her card at the gate and the door buzzed open.

Her receptionist, Darla, smiled. "Morning, Suzanne. How was your walk today?"

"Oh, the usual. Icy, but the sunshine felt wonderful."

"I admire that you walk to work every day, even in the winter. I should join you."

Suzanne stopped at the front desk. She removed her hat and gloves and turned to her young admirer. "You're an econ major, right?"

"I graduate in June. Why?"

"Have you ever read *The Liberation Manifesto*?"

"That book about capitalism and liberty?"

"Yeah, that one."

"I have, actually. My professor let me borrow her copy.

31

Interesting book. But odd. The author wrote it like some serious declaration of liberty and a celebration of capitalism, right? And all those right-wing politicians were raving about it. But parts of it were so off the wall I thought the author was joking."

"Joking?"

"Yeah. Like tongue in cheek. Satire. My very earnest professor disagrees. She says *The Manifesto* is one of the boldest defenses of capitalism of our time. The definitive answer to both Karl Marx and democratic socialism. I think she was quoting from a book review. Why do you ask?"

"Oh, I was just thinking about it this morning. I used to be friends with the author."

"Garrick Cripps? No way."

"I know a secret about that book that I've told nobody. You're the first. Keep this to yourself, okay?"

Darla mimed zipping her lips shut. "Do tell."

"The whole thing started as a joke."

"A joke? You're kidding. How do you know?"

"How? Because I wrote the silly thing."

"Then who is Garrick Cripps?"

"He's nobody, Darla. A damned fool who thinks he's John Galt."

Darla laughed as she parroted the opening line of one of Ayn Rand's most infamous novels: " 'Who is John Galt?' "

5

FREEDOM LIBRARY

Suzanne knew William had been testing her in that surprise phone call, suggesting that she might not be a reliable choice for the mission. Prudent of him. In fact, she wasn't reliable. Not anymore.

And yet she had never faltered. She'd always done everything Garrick had asked her to do, including taking part in the scheme that Garrick hatched at MIT in the early 1990s. All in for the Freedom Society and Garrick's mission to master the "technology of revolution," as he called it.

Garrick had been obsessed with cyber weapons. He fantasized about using AI technology to create a super cyber bot that would defeat all known cyber defenses. Suzanne had paid little attention to his longing, mainly because she didn't think Garrick was clever enough to create such a beast. Still, she had not resisted his risky, two-pronged plan: First, he found the raw talent in the students he taught as a computer science professor. Second, she took a job as chief scientist for a cyber warfare operation secreted in the Pentagon. She passed all background checks and had been relentless in talking her way into the highly sensitive position. Garrick sent the talented few from MIT her way and she set them up on secret Pentagon research projects, allowing the young guns to pursue their innovative ideas on cyber weaponry. Occasionally she spoke to Garrick about the research when on weekend trips to Cambridge or to Morro Bay, where Garrick had purchased a lovely home on the hillside overlooking the town and the bay. At first the exchanges seemed innocent. Just tech talk. But eventually she saw Garrick's scheme as mental assault of the highest order. None of his former students were aware Garrick was trying to suck their brainpower so he could invent algorithms in service of a conspiracy to destroy government computer networks.

One exception was Jonas Peterson who taught at Stanford. He had been one of Garrick's committed foot soldiers. Suzanne didn't know him well. Only knew that he was brilliant and came to the States from Austria. Garrick took a special liking to Jonas, which Suzanne attributed to the young man's ultra-conservative leanings. There were others too. Some cooperated with Garrick, but thankfully, most refused.

The best and brightest of all—the one Garrick cherished most—had been the hardest to get. Garrick gushed about the young woman's brilliance—and her apparent naivety.

Laura Cavendish came to MIT from Southern California as an undergraduate in the mid-1990s, graduating with a BS in Computer Science and Philosophy in 1999. She pursued her PhD at MIT. Garrick was annoyed that Laura had resisted his flirtations despite his charm. Suzanne's curiosity grew because Garrick was a hard man to ignore.

In February 2003 she asked Laura to meet her for coffee at a café in Kendall Square. Long gone from MIT, Suzanne hadn't met Laura but she had been mentioned by Garrick as a potential candidate for one of Suzanne's cyber projects at the Pentagon. She and Laura had traded a few friendly texts before agreeing to meet at a coffee shop.

Laura wore a thick white sweater that blended with her blonde hair flowing onto her shoulders. She held onto the steaming mug of coffee tightly.

"Don't you look like a genuine New Englander now? You're not in San Diego anymore," Suzanne said.

"I never realized this place could get so freaking cold. I'm getting used to it, though."

"No, you aren't. Be honest. Nobody gets used to this. I haven't, and I grew up in New York."

"How long are you in town for?"

"A few days. Appointments with several researchers. I'd like to include you in that category, if that's okay."

"Me?"

"Absolutely. Garrick has told me a lot about you."

Laura lingered over the mug for a moment, then met Suzanne's eyes. "I'm having a blast here. The department is first rate. I can't learn enough."

"To be honest I've had my eye on you for a while. You've certainly found your niche in cyber defense. Your work in AI looks promising. But Garrick has probably told you that already."

"Yeah, more or less."

"He's your adviser, right?"

"The department assigned me to him. It's worked out okay so far."

"Laura, look at me."

Laura raised her eyebrows. "What?"

"Do I look like a woman who tolerates any BS?"

"I'm sorry, I didn't mean—"

35

"No, no. You're fine. I'm just saying—I know Garrick. We've known each other a long time. He's got a unique MO."

"I'm not following you."

"Did he turn you on to his freedom library?"

"His what?"

Suzanne laughed. "I call it his freedom library. His list of books on libertarian philosophy that he tries to get his grad students to read, especially if they're pretty young women. Did he give you *The Liberation Manifesto* yet?"

Laura laughed and gently slapped her hand on the table. "Yes! How did you know?"

"Did you read it?"

"No. Heck, no. I politely declined. I don't have time for all that. I came here to learn computer science. I don't even have time to date."

"You minored in philosophy as an undergrad, right?"

"I did."

"Not my business, but do you mind me asking why? A lot of our graduate students studied math or a hard science as undergrads."

"Exactly. Guess I'm not most graduate students. I wanted to branch out. Have something to fall back on in case I got bored with computer science."

Suzanne scanned Laura's face. A pretty face. Untouched by trouble and trauma. Curiously, though, the face of a woman who was searching for something beyond the here and now. "Maybe that's one reason Garrick took a liking to you. As a philosophy student, you'd appreciate *The Manifesto*. You never read it?"

"I confess. The title intrigued me. I glanced through it."

"And?"

"Can I be honest?"

36

"If you didn't strike me as honest, I wouldn't be here talking to you."

"I found it strange. I couldn't take it seriously."

"Oh? Why is that?"

"Put it this way, Suzanne. I'm not a religious person. I'm trying to become a scientist here. Not a true believer. Garrick was writing for true believers. Besides, it was total bullshit."

Suzanne couldn't suppress a smile. "I can't disagree with you on that. Can I suggest something regarding Garrick?"

"Please do."

"Don't let Garrick bother you, Laura. He can be a pain in the ass. You might want to find another adviser. Your choice, but I don't see a suitable match between you two. I'll talk with some people if that would help."

"Oh, God, you'd do that? That would be a huge favor, Dr. Dreyfus. Thank you so much."

"Call me Suzanne, please. Just so you know, Garrick and I were together once. But we're just colleagues now. We communicate about promising new technology. That's about it. You and I should talk in more detail at another time. When you finish your doctorate, I might have a project or two for you to consider. If working with the Pentagon is your style."

"I'm open to anything at this point. I'd rather not work for corporate America."

"Let's set that up next time I'm in town."

"Cool."

"Excellent coffee, huh?" Suzanne said.

"The best. I love this place."

"May I ask you something personal?" Suzanne said.

Laura took a sip of coffee. "I don't see why not."

"Do you date at all? A million guys would love to take you out. Not all MIT guys are nerds. Then there's Harvard, if you're so inclined."

"Why do you ask?"

"Good question. None of my business."

"No, really, I'd like to know."

"My thought was this: if Garrick saw that you were with a guy, he might back off. Quit getting in your face about that libertarian stuff."

"Hmm. How do I say this?"

"I'm listening."

"To be honest, Suzanne, I'm still in love with a guy back home. I'm just not meeting anyone here who rocks my world, you know?"

"Don't tell me you're still in love with your high school boyfriend."

"I thought we'd gone our separate ways. We did. But I think about him a lot these days. I seriously doubt that he cares, because he's out of the country most of the time. I stopped trying to stay in touch."

"Then move on."

"I'm trying to. Why do you think I'm here?"

"What's this guy do?"

"He joined the Navy out of high school. Looking back, he should have come to MIT or Cal Tech. He's incredibly bright. He loves math and science. But . . ."

"But you pushed him away, didn't you?"

"You're right. I wanted to do this on my own."

"I get it. Do you regret coming here?"

"No, not at all. But I miss him."

"What's your guy's name?"

"Carson. Carson . . ." Laura smiled and shook her head. "It's funny. Carson always introduces himself by saying, 'I'm Carson. Carson McCready,' like he's James Bond or something. It's cute. Just a quirk he's got."

Suzanne noted Carson's name. A memorable name.

"So what's he doing in the Navy?"

"He became a Navy SEAL. I couldn't believe it. But when Carson sets his mind to something, it seems there's nothing he can't do. Navy's lucky to have him."

"Obviously you're in love with him. I guarantee he misses you too. Remember, you left. Write to him. Tell him how you feel."

"I want to. But I can't afford to be sidetracked now." Laura stopped, set down her coffee mug, and looked at Suzanne with more intensity than a moment earlier. "I'm on the verge of a technical breakthrough in my research."

"What sort of breakthrough?"

"I've discovered a way to code an AI-based algorithm that can penetrate all known and unknown cyber defenses."

"That's a bold statement."

"I know. I've gamed it out."

"That's Pentagon talk."

"I wouldn't know about that."

"You're sure?"

"About what, Suzanne?"

"That this algorithm does what you say."

"I need time. It'll take a year or more to test, retest, and then deliver something."

"Why are you telling me this?" Suzanne said.

"I'm taking a risk."

"I'm confused. Garrick told me you were working in cyber defense. That's what you dissertation project is, right?"

"Correct."

"Now I'm more confused," Suzanne said.

"Can I trust you, Suzanne?"

"This conversation is between you and me."

"My dissertation *is* on cyber defense. That's what I will publish. As you know, dissertations are public domain. I'm doing my own work on the side. It's secret. Garrick knows nothing about it. You're the first person I've told. I want to keep my research close until I'm ready."

"When will that be?"

"I want to protect my findings. Use my discovery for something good."

"I'm still not following you, Laura."

"I figure the best cyber defense is to create the ultimate offensive weapon."

Laura's words stunned Suzanne. Laura's research was Garrick's Holy Grail, a vital piece of his unlikely libertarian revolution. Was Laura working with Garrick after all?

"You write code like this in your spare time? No wonder you're single," Suzanne said.

"Yes. Please keep that to yourself."

"Did you know my dissertation was on artificial intelligence?"

"Of course," Laura said. "You worked on machine learning. Neural networks, to be precise."

"And?"

"I'm applying the concept of neural networks to cybersecurity."

"You know what I do at the Pentagon?"

Laura smiled. "I look innocent, I know. But when you asked me for coffee, I looked you up. I thought you'd be the perfect person to mention my research to and keep it on the down-low. Just between you and me."

Suzanne couldn't take her eyes off the young woman. "Why did you trust me?"

"You're a chief scientist at the Pentagon. I figured you get paid to keep secrets."

Suzanne frowned. Laura Cavendish was exactly the person Garrick had been looking for all these years. The connection between Laura's private project and Garrick's own Holy Grail to create the ultimate cyber weapon seemed too coincidental. She looked into Laura's eyes for any sign of deception. "You're positive Garrick knowns nothing about your private work?"

"Absolutely not. I've got a pretty good antenna for decent people. I don't like Garrick Cripps. They assigned me to him and we're stuck together. But I don't trust him."

Suzanne was surprised how disarming Laura could be. Just a natural in wit, intelligence, and beauty. Yet she was touched at just how innocent Laura had been in those days. In Laura, Suzanne saw both idealism and genius that needed protection and nurturing. Protection from predators like Garrick. Nurturing from someone who cared about her. The young woman had put herself in a dangerous situation and probably didn't know it. Laura was just bright enough to know that her work needed protection, but still innocent enough of the ways of the world to get herself into a lot of trouble.

~

In the months following the fateful Morro Bay meeting in October, Suzanne allowed herself one freedom heretofore forbidden: to entertain the idea of destroying Garrick and his cockeyed movement to replace the government with a stateless society. Garrick had been splitting his time between the central coast and Bermuda, where his yacht, *Liberty*, was docked. While he was absent doing god knows what, Billy was handing out orders and acting like a big shot. He tasked

Suzanne with finding the right "stooge" to supervise the telemarketing team at the prison.

What if, she wondered, she could fill the telemarketing job with exactly the opposite sort of man to what William wanted? A real leader. A thinker—retired or semi-retired—who never shied away from a challenge. Maybe former military. A man who could smell trouble from a long way off and wouldn't look the other way. A monkey-wrench in Garrick's scheme. A man who took nothing for granted.

Suzanne recalled her conversation with Laura about her ex-boyfriend years ago in Cambridge. She remembered he had joined the Navy right after high school and worked his way up an arduous meritocracy to become a SEAL. What was his name? Of course. Carson. Carson McCready, just as Laura had told her over coffee that winter day in Kendall Square.

Suzanne's hunt for Carson began in the archives of the *Navy Times*. After plugging his name into the website's search bar, she scrolled through many stories. One stood out: several years previously, a Navy SEAL named Davis Glover had got busted for the brutal killing of a Somali civilian in 2017. Carson's name jumped from the screen—he'd been the platoon leader during that operation. The senior senator from Kentucky had attacked Carson and his team for making a false accusation against Glover—who was the grandson of a Kentucky bourbon baron and a former fraternity brother of the hell-raising senator.

A later story in the *Navy Times* revealed that Carson, "who had been at the center of one of the most controversial incidents in modern Naval history, abruptly retired from the Navy at forty-four, after twenty years of unrivaled service." Based on interviews with former team members, an admiral, and a few captains, the profile described McCready as "highly decorated" and "a stellar leader," whose "unanticipated retirement was apparently related to the Somali incident."

Suzanne's research led to a story in the local daily paper that highlighted the controversy and the subsequent reversal of the Navy's decision to punish Glover. The article suggested Carson was forced out of the Navy to appease the powerful US senator. Carson had refused to be interviewed for either article.

Suzanne paid close attention to one detail: Carson had attended Torrey Pines High before enlisting. The article quoted a former administrator who'd been the principal there during Carson's time at the school from 1991 through 1995. He mentioned that Carson's graduating class comprised several remarkable students who would enjoy great success—educators, scientists, athletes, various local leaders, and others he didn't name, including "one young woman who'd won an important international science prize and later graduated from MIT."

Suzanne leafed through the yearbooks of Torrey Pines High online and found the graduating class of 1995. She spotted a group photo of the science and technology club and noticed one striking woman in particular with a beaming smile. Next to her was a boyish young man with messy blond hair and blue eyes. He had a devil-may-care grin on his face, and a slight tilt of his head and shoulders toward the girl.

Clearly, Suzanne thought when she first encountered the photo, even then young Carson McCready was in love with Laura Cavendish. Suzanne could see it in Laura's eyes too, self-assured that the faithful young man beside her had her back, always and forever

43

6

JUICE

Carson's team was buying and selling commodities like pros. Ten workstations were strung along the four sides of the telemarketing room, each one containing a computer, a phone, and an inmate dressed in prison greens. On this day in February 2024, several electronic items were on the block. Samsung forty-threes, state-of-the-art plasma TVs, routers, PCs, switches, cell phones, accessories, metal detectors, cables, connectors, do-it-yourself equipment, and cable modems.

"Hey man, Terrell here. Yeah, it's me. Dealt with you two weeks ago on that batch of lithium rechargeables. Got a truck load of 50-watt pro-series panels. Yeah, the solar panels you were looking for. Light up your life, man. Give me a number."

"One-twenty-five? Not a chance, man. I get two bills for these puppies, bro. This is Sunforce, not that cheap shit you get off Craigslist."

After a quick counter bid, the inmate whom Carson called Black Terrell had the buyer in his pocket for one-eighty-nine. The guys wasted no time. Deal or no deal. Write the invoice or hang up and find another buyer. To the casual observer, this was nothing less than an electronics commodity exchange, all happening in the bowels of the maximum-security branch of the county prison system. Notorious as the joint you'd never want to end up in, the facility southeast of Chula Vista showcased terrible food, hostile guards, and bad inmates. But to Carson none of that mattered. He didn't give a shit what the felons had done or whom they'd harmed. Carson looked into a man's character and lived life forward. He adopted the SEAL ethos of teamwork. Men sacrificed their needs and desires for the sake of the team. A single man was dead. A team of men kept each man alive.

~

After that day's trading—some six weeks into the job— Carson and Johnny Petit arranged to meet for lunch in the staff cafeteria.

"You're telling me you've never had a telemarketing operation here before me?"

"That's what I said. This is a pilot program. I thought I explained that to you."

"I don't recall that detail."

"Look, the suits upstairs wanted this to happen. Orders from my boss, Richard Heller. Matter of fact, that was Heller who came into the telemarketing room this afternoon."

"He didn't say much."

"Heller is low-key. Former Marine. All business."

"Why is the prison boss schlepping around the telemarketing room?"

"That guy runs the whole damned prison system in San Diego County, boss. He can go wherever he wants."

"But what do the suits want?"

45

"More 'cost-effective' prisons. Word's out that the county's maximum-security facility is the prison system's biggest money drain."

"And it doesn't look good that the worst criminals cost the taxpayers the most money," Carson mused.

"You got it. Bosses want a self-sustaining operation or some such BS. They got the idea from a consulting company back east."

Carson grabbed a french fry and soaked it in ketchup. "You're telling me this is a completely untested pilot program, and I'm the guinea pig?"

"Chill, cowboy. Your numbers are looking pretty fair. The suits like that. A lot."

"Is that so?"

"Yep. Heller liked what he saw. Told me so. But . . ."

"Here comes the other shoe."

"We need better. Heller wants to double the revenues by the end of the fiscal year. Doubling the revenues will cut the taxpayer subsidy to this joint to fifty percent. Commissioner Alvarez wants that number on the books by October 31. Then he can puff up for the November elections."

"What's the subsidy now?"

"Ninety percent, give or take."

"And you want that down to fifty percent?"

"You double your revenues with your team—that circle of trust or whatever bull-crap you call it—and we meet our goal."

"I need some juice on this deal."

"What the hell are you talking about, Carson? This is a prison last time I checked. No juice. No favors. No bonuses for felons."

"That 'bull-crap,' as you call it, is covering your ass and mine. We can kiss this whole deal goodbye."

"What sort of juice you talking about?" Petit said.

"I want a little extra for the guys. A point for every hundred extra each guy brings to the pot. We tell 'em they got it coming the day they get out. There will be strings, though."

"Hell does that mean?"

"The cons' exit bonuses will go to college scholarships. For them, their kids, or other kids who've grown up in the same shitholes as my team. My guys help the prison system become profitable. The convicts get a once-in-a-lifetime opportunity to turn a lifetime of shit into gold. Everyone is better off. We'll call it the San Diego Promise."

"You're messing with me, right?" Petit said.

"Tell me, where's the extra fifty percent go? My guys save your bosses fifty percent—and they get the commissioner re-elected besides. So what happens to the fifty? That's got to be several million, right?"

"Right back to the general fund. You don't know much about government, do you, son?"

"I know enough to know that politicians are always working a deal. You can't tell me that the suits haven't already tagged the fifty percent for somebody's pet project. I want assurance the dollars my boys save the prison system will go somewhere good."

"That's a high pony you're riding there, Bronco. Last time I checked, the commissioner signed your paycheck, not the other way around."

"I'll take my chances, Petit. You're forgetting that I don't give a shit. Talk to Heller. I haven't even told you the best part—for you."

"Hell, you say."

"Commissioner Alvarez is going to love it. The San Diego Promise puts him on the map. A great visionary for education

47

and public-private partnerships. He's a politician. He'll take all the credit, mind you, but the spoils of this brilliant idea will keep on giving down the line. A win-win for everybody. Even you, Petit."

"Okay, I'll talk to Heller. I'll set the meeting. You'll be there to argue your case. But, Carson, you're going to owe me big time for this."

Johnny Petit was fiddling with his phone, trying to craft a message to Richard Heller, when his phone lit up. It was Heller himself. Petit quickly tried to compose his thoughts.

"Rick, I was about to call you. What did you think about Carson's operation?"

"Impressive. Good hire, Johnny."

"I gather you called me about something you saw."

"Yes, as a matter of fact. As a division manager, you should be aware that our tech people have noticed something unusual in our computer network."

"I didn't get that memo. What's wrong?"

"Nothing yet. They tell me all systems are fine. But they're alarmed about the unusual activity."

"Not following you, sir."

"The tech people are detecting probes of our system. Somebody's scanning our system to detect its security weaknesses. These probes usually mean a prelude to an attack of some sort. That's if the probes find the weakness they're looking for."

Petit's ears pricked up, thinking about his private arrangement with Suzanne Dreyfus. She had told him to keep his mouth shut. Beyond that, he had no idea what she was planning.

"What kind of attack?" Petit asked.

"We don't know. Could be anything. Stealing data, planting malware to infect the system, seizing control of the network. Anything is possible."

"That's unbelievable."

"Yes. That's partly why I wanted to look at Carson's telemarketing operation today."

"You think Carson is up to something?"

"No, I'm not saying that. But the timing is unusual."

"You mean the probes started after we hired Carson?"

"Unfortunately, yes."

"Then I probably shouldn't ask you what I'm about to ask you."

~

Carson considered his proposal to Petit as he drove home to Lemon Grove. He had hoped the job would be a low-key gig under the radar. Do a competent job, survive, earn a paycheck, and live a simple, good life. Be a normal guy with a dog and a regular job. He slapped himself for ruining his dream right out of the gate.

Why the hell did I do that? he wondered.

Carson mulled over his weird habit of going with his gut. Taking advantage of opportunity whenever he could. The habit made Carson a force of nature as a SEAL platoon leader. An unstoppable force due to his single-minded focus on completing a clean operation.

He had grown tired of being unstoppable. The relentless pressure he put on himself was a big part of the reason he left the Navy. He wanted a life, not another mission. Yet here he was again. Seizing opportunities, making things happen, and falling into the same old trap. He couldn't help himself. The ability to live without complication wasn't who Carson had become in the Navy.

He didn't start out that way. As a kid he had lived in and around the ocean. Surfing, taking naps on warm sand, adventuring with his buddies to Blacks Beach. Checking out the pretty girls sunbathing nude among the black rocks. He grew up in light. The light of the beach, the ocean, and good friends.

He thought about Laura. Hardly a day had gone by when he didn't think about Laura Cavendish. A flicker of her smile lit up his neurons. Was Laura leaving for MIT the reason he'd changed? Why he'd become so driven to get things right and live up to an unreachable ideal?

Becoming a SEAL chief was the ultimate act of taking responsibility. But another part of him wondered if all these years he had been compensating for losing Laura, hoping that attaining superhuman qualities would win her back.

He turned into his parking spot at the condo complex and climbed upstairs. Diego greeted him at the door. He took the dog for a walk around the city park. Watched some young Latino kids playing soccer, then some older folks crawling back from the grocery store pushing a cart. Rush-hour traffic of the working class, coming home from jobs as laborers, maids, janitors, and retail clerks. They drove older cars. Some rode buses. All commuted dozens of miles to the opposite end of the county. They served, waited, dug, lifted, pushed, and scraped. And cared for the fancy people in the coastal communities. Carson figured he was among the few folks in the neighborhood who actually worked in East County.

Carson thought of his upcoming pitch to Richard Heller,

assuming Petit could get him a meeting with the boss. He tapped a few notes into his phone and worked out the math for his proposal. The numbers looked good. But would Heller have the guts to try it?

He climbed the concrete steps up to his condo, looking forward to a relaxing evening. He got a beer from the fridge and spilled his body onto the recliner, ready to watch some golf on TV. But then he noticed the letter on the end table. It had been lying there for several days. He didn't want to think about the Navy's instruction to schedule the meeting he'd been dreading for months.

He'd put it off long enough. It was past seven p.m. but Michael Denison would still be at the office. And Carson knew Mike wouldn't mind the call at this hour. They had grown up together in Solana Beach. They surfed and partied together. Then Mike went to college and law school while Carson worked in a surf shop and joined the Navy.

Carson dialed the number and Mike's assistant answered.

"This is Gloria."

"Gloria, I need to talk to Mike if he's still there. I know it's late."

"Who's this?"

"Carson. Carson McCready."

"Oh, Carson. Sure, I'll get him on the line."

A few moments passed, and Carson could hear Mike telling Gloria to call it a day and enjoy the fine weather.

"Carson?" Mike said.

"Yeah, it's me. I need to talk. I should have booked an appointment, but I need to get this off my chest."

"No worries, man. I can guess why you're calling."

"Did the Navy copy you on that last letter?"

"Look, Carson. I know you, and this shouldn't be

51

happening. The Navy is reaching."

"Should this crap concern me?"

"For the moment, yes, until I can clear this up."

"I'm done testifying. I told them everything. That idiot from Kentucky has no fucking clue what he's doing."

"You're referring to Senator Graybill?"

"Yeah. Has that guy ever served? Do you know?"

"No, the story is he wanted to join the Marines. But he got a medical deferment for flat feet or some shit. He chose politics instead."

Carson was pleased that Michael understood the case so well, particularly the code of honor instilled in a SEAL platoon. If someone is out of line, like Davis Glover was, the platoon itself deals with it. As platoon leader Carson took it up with his commanding officer, and that got the ball of military justice rolling. He testified. Ten of his guys also came forward. That's how it was done. Carson followed the protocol. The court convicted Glover. Now this Senator Graybill was pressing for a retrial because of a miscarriage of military justice at a time of war or some bullshit. Carson kept getting letters from the Navy, and half expected the MA to show up at his door and haul him off.

"I need this to go away, Mike."

"Graybill has no right to drag you back into this, especially now that you're retired. But he's a United States senator, and Davis Glover's a born-and-bred Kentucky boy. You know that. So here's how I'd like to handle this. I'll keep JAG occupied with legal papers for as long as possible. Up to a year. Graybill loses interest, and this goes away.

"If not, the Navy will call you to testify, and JAG will re-angle the case with more supposed evidence—whatever. I don't want you writing to the Navy, talking to the Navy, or talking to your old friends in the Navy. Don't talk to reporters. Talk to nobody. You did the right thing. Your platoon agreed, and so did a military court. Glover is a douchebag. Graybill is a demagogue who spends more time on cable news than passing laws. You're going to be okay, Carson."

"Thanks, but I've got one problem."

"What's that?"

"I can't afford you. You've done well, buddy."

"Maybe you should have become a lawyer, like your pop."

"That's funny, Michael."

"Al McCready was a legend for everyone but his own son."

"Because he did more pro bono than he could afford?"

"You're more like him than you even know. How you handled Glover. That shit is born, not bred, buddy."

7

ANOMALIES

The next morning Carson settled for one cup of Folger's Supreme. Any more caffeine would have sent him flying out the window. He prepared a plate of tasty scraps for Diego, placed the dirty dishes in the sink, and sped to work. Petit had arranged the meeting. Rick Heller advised he'd be in his on-site office by eight but he'd be available to talk at nine. Without thinking Carson knocked on his door at eight thirty, then barged in.

"I told you nine, McCready, and I meant it. I'm pre-coffee and it's too damned early for any demands. Take a step outside for ten minutes, if you wouldn't mind."

Carson found the civilian men's room and urinated the Folgers from his system. He waited seven minutes, then knocked again and entered the room. Carson saw Johnny Petit sitting in a chair across from Heller, sipping on a steaming cup of coffee.

"Have a seat, please. Tell me what you want to say," Heller said.

"Mr. Heller, I hear the bosses want my telemarketing

team to boost revenues. I'm okay with that. I'm more than okay. We work hard and we can work even harder. But I want to ask for something."

"Go on."

"Me and the boys want to start a new scholarship program for this city's youth. We want a percent of our extra effort to go to college scholarships for the very kids who would otherwise end up in this shithole someday."

"By shithole, I assume you're referencing your place of employment?" Heller asked.

"No offense. I love my job."

"How would this work?"

"Pretty simple. My team works their rear ends extra hard, and we promise them a college scholarship down the road. Either for the cons or their kids. We could open it up to other kids in the community later on."

"Okay. How do you propose to fund the scholarships? And we call them inmates, by the way."

"The cons, our inmates, are bringing in more revenue from their hard work, right? The county shaves a few points from its take to fund the scholarships. We'll call it the San Diego Promise."

Heller said nothing. He glanced at Petit who sat mute, and placed his coffee mug on the desk. He pulled out his phone from the top drawer, punching in numbers for several minutes. Finally he pointed the phone to Carson to show him a number.

"Do you see this number, McCready? Could you and your team promise us this number by the end of the fiscal year?"

Carson looked at Heller's calculation and got up. He walked around the room, doing calculations in his head. He pulled out his phone, punched a few digits into the keypad, and showed the calculation to Heller.

"You see this number, Mr. Heller? That is a reasonable number. It's a number that my boys can and will give you. I'll put it in writing. A business deal. That'll satisfy your revenue crunch from prison operations, and taxpayers will feel no pain."

Heller said nothing, but continued to stare at Carson's calculations on the cell phone. "I'll run this by Commissioner Alvarez. If you're right, the program pays for itself and Alvarez takes the credit. Are you okay with that, McCready? Your baby, but Alvarez gets the glory?"

"I've got no problem with that. None. I appreciate you hearing me out." Carson stood up, ready to end the meeting and go out into the hallway. Heller followed Carson out the door and stopped him.

"Okay, McCready. Tell me straight. What's your juice in all this? You've got your team covered. You've got the scholarships. I don't see you as a do-gooder. What do you want? Why are you here? To start a scholarship program for convicted felons?"

"And the kids. Don't forget the kids, Mr. Heller."

"That makes you even more suspect. Why do you want to help them?"

"To be honest I'm not sure why I'm here. Going with my gut. Feels like the right thing to do."

"The scholarship pitch is brilliant. Hope it works out. But I've got one more thing to ask you," Heller said.

"Shoot."

"Our tech people have detected some anomalies with our network. Somebody is probing the system for weaknesses, a prelude to a virus attack of some sort. You wouldn't know anything about that, would you?"

"Mr. Heller, I appreciate your help with the scholarships. But I have no damned idea what you're talking about."

Heller inspected Carson up and down, from his sharp blue eyes to his khakis and deck shoes. "You're retired Navy, right?"

"Yes, sir."

"Marines. Sergeant Major," Heller said. "It's odd, though. Happened not long after you started. Have you noticed anything suspicious with your team? Anyone acting strange?"

"Mr. Heller, they're all strange in their way. More so than most."

"Sure, sure. I get it. Sorry to put you on the defensive, McCready, but I had to ask. Keep your eyes open for anything. That means staff, guards, inmates, and your sister if you've got one, okay?"

"I'll keep my eyes open, sir."

~

Carson walked to the parking lot, considering Heller's warning about the cyber-probes. It was a warning, right? Even though he had had a friendly moment with Heller, the boss would watch him. Heller would watch the telemarketing crew, the guards, Petit, even the damned janitor. This wasn't Carson's problem to solve. That's why Heller and his tech team got paid the big bucks. But Carson knew a bit about cyberwarfare—although he would never volunteer to Heller how much he knew.

A cyberattack at the county jail, coinciding with his taking the job, was one more complication in a series of complications Carson was facing at the moment. All were beyond his control—even when he felt in control—as if his unconscious mind were running the show.

57

Carson left work thinking about his complicated life. He missed the exit to Lemon Grove and thought about turning around. But he kept going on the 8 West until he got to the 5 North exit. He let his body, eyes, and the steering wheel take him. He saw the exit to Torrey Pines Road and got off the freeway. He drove for a couple of miles until he reached the golf course.

Now, he had no interest in golf.

Sam, the bartender of at least thirty years at Torrey, saw Carson coming into the bar. He turned around and pulled a Spaten from the fridge. Not missing a beat, Sam set the beer bottle on the bar for Carson like he'd done a thousand times before.

"Carson McCready. Hey, what's up, man? Haven't seen you in ages. You still playing this silly game? I know you aren't here on business."

"Less and less, brother. Less and less."

"You should come around more. Other day someone was wondering, 'Where's Carson been?' Nobody had a clue. Where have you been?"

"Don't get over here much. I'm in Lemon Grove now."

"Lemon Grove? That don't sound like you, man."

"Yeah, well, you can't come home again. What they say."

"Suppose not. Good to see you, Carson."

Sam slipped away to help another customer while Carson enjoyed his Spaten. He wasn't sure why he'd come. The Beemer, his memory, old habits, and his hands on the steering wheel had brought him here as if on autopilot.

Sam returned with another beer, knowing that Carson never stopped at one.

"What about you, Sam? How you been?" Carson asked.

"Same old, son. I'm going on forty years here now, so

nothing much changes. Growing older. Seeing the doctor more than I care to. You know how it is. Though you're still looking pretty fair. How old are you now?"

"Forty-seven."

"You don't look it. Still hope for you, son."

"You know it, Sam."

"So aren't you gonna ask who was asking about you?" Sam asked.

"I figured some regular or an employee, right?"

"No, no. It was Laura, man. Your old girlfriend, right? We got to chatting. She was with a guy I didn't know, and your name came up. She was wondering if I'd seen you around. I had to say I didn't have any notion. She seemed surprised."

"Laura's here? She's back?"

"I got that impression. I asked the same question, and she mentioned she'd come back home to Solana Beach. That's how I heard it. I'm old and can't hear shit anymore, mind you."

"How'd she look? Was she happy?"

"Hell, Carson. All women under sixty look wonderful to me, man. That's how it goes. You'll see when you're my age. They all look good. So, yeah, I'd say she was looking pretty damned good. She was smiling, having fun with this guy, but who knows, right?"

Carson finished the beer and pulled out his wallet.

"Put that damned thing away. This is on me."

"You're still getting a ten out of this, and you know it."

Sam took the empty bottle and waved Carson off as he turned to help another customer. "Glad you're back, son."

Carson left the lodge and walked back through the parking lot. Laura was in town, and he had an excuse to look her up—he could ask her about the anomalies with the computer system at the prison. Laura had gone off to MIT to study artificial intelligence and cyber warfare after all. Before she left she had talked to him about her dream to create the ultimate AI bot. One that could defend the nation from any attack, from cyberpunks to nation states.

Laura would understand better than anyone what the probes at the prison meant. But he didn't know where she lived, who she was with, or what she believed. He had seen her just a few times after high school, when she had come home to see her parents and younger sister. After twenty-nine years since high school, he had become a different man. And no doubt she had become a different woman.

8

COURTSHIP

Suzanne Dreyfus answered the knock on the door then led her guest into a suite of four rooms that resembled the interior of a French country manor. The room included a sumptuous living area in which a Theodore Alexander sofa occupied the center, surrounded with end-tables of cherrywood, framed prints by French artists, and a glimmering-white faux fireplace. All the right stuff to signal she did not live or travel cheaply, despite her stated affiliation with the federal government.

As she had advised, Agent Darryl Cunningham had destroyed the burner phone. He took the straight route from the FBI's office in Mira Mesa to the oak-wooded town of Poway, home for him and his family for almost twenty years. She asked him to dress in evening attire—anything that didn't scream FBI.

Suzanne had told Cunningham she worked for a highly secretive military unit and had a proposal for the federal agent. Several dozen current and former high-level government officials had formed a task force to explore ways to make government off-book programs work more efficiently.

Sufficiently vague, and even plausible. But she'd done her homework nevertheless, persuading her boss, Col. McCabe Miller, to contact Cunningham's boss about the need for FBI and Defense to cooperate in investigating leaks on high-security cyber weapons projects of the type Suzanne oversaw.

She noticed his height, well over six feet. Around fifty with a graying beard and thinning dark hair. A gait that spoke to his time as a former athlete. He was nonchalant, as though he wasn't too bothered by much of anything. She brushed her hand over his forearm as he stepped into the room.

"There you are, Agent Cunningham. I'm Suzanne Dreyfus. I've been so looking forward to meeting you."

They sat down to drinks on the Theodore Alexander. He looked around the suite. "So where are the other officials?"

"You'll have to settle for me. We're a network, spread widely, and we've recruited some powerful individuals in and out of government who have committed to our cause. By the way, you look quite handsome in that suit."

"I don't do well with flattery, Dr. Dreyfus. What's your role in this cause?"

"No flattery intended. I act as their adviser."

Suzanne realized she was playing an all-too-familiar role in this encounter with Cunningham. The shtick was the same as always, but her intentions were not. Persuasion wasn't her motive now. She didn't care if Cunningham joined the conspiracy. No, this performance was to maintain her cover within the conspiracy. Play Billy's game. Recruit Cunningham. All according to Garrick's plan. Watch and observe.

Then seek and destroy when Garrick was most vulnerable.

"This isn't about cutting red tape from the FBI, is it?" Cunningham said.

"Correct. I want to explain everything. But, first, could

62

we talk a bit about you?"

"What do you want to know?"

"How you got to the Bureau."

"What is this, a job interview?"

"Sort of. Actually, yes. I work with people who are interested in you and how you can help us. It might be worth your while to chat with me. Informally, of course. Completely off the record."

"I don't know what you're talking about, but go ahead."

"I already know a lot about you. How the demands of your job were hard on your marriage, and how you and Debbie, your high school sweetheart, had two children who've become successful adults."

"What is this about, Dr. Dreyfus? I thought we were discussing security and enforcement matters."

"Yes, of course. But indulge me for a moment while I get to that."

"I'm a busy man."

"Bureau's been good for you and your family, hasn't it, Darryl?"

"That's a fair statement. We wouldn't be where we are without the Bureau. You still haven't answered my question."

"How did you and Debbie meet?" Suzanne asked.

"Please state your business, Dr. Dreyfus. I expected this to be an inter-agency meeting, not a one-on-one." He rose from the sofa and waved his hand around the room. "Matter of fact, this whole deal seems very odd. This grand hotel. On a government budget—supposedly. Doesn't look right."

Suzanne also rose from the sofa to face him. She stood five-ten, higher with heels. "I apologize for the confusion. And please call me Suzanne. Really, I am sorry. My clients are tight-lipped and meticulous. We simply need to get to know

63

you better."

Cunningham returned to the sofa, and Suzanne followed.

"What about you, Suzanne?"

"What about me?"

"What's your expertise?"

"Computer science at MIT. I met a professor there who had a profound influence on me. I started working for the Pentagon several years ago."

"Doing what, exactly?"

"I procure breakthrough technology for the Pentagon's use in weapons, computing, cyber warfare, and artificial intelligence. Top-secret stuff."

"Who's this MIT guy?"

"Dr. Garrick Cripps."

"Never heard of him."

"He stays below the radar. We were close once. I rarely talk to him now."

"I'm confused. All these names. You, Cripps. A guy named William. He contacted me, you know? Told me about you and some meeting I ought to attend."

"William reaching out to you wasn't random. He picked you."

Cunningham shifted his weight on the sofa. "Tell me more about you, Suzanne. Do you have a family?"

"The movement has been my family."

"Oh, so you're more than just a consultant?"

She met his eyes directly and waited a moment before answering. "I've worked closely with the movement for many years. Connections happen. And friendships." She could have said something more revealing, but she left him to wonder. Keep him off balance, igniting the male urge to hunt and conquer. Outdated, perhaps, but an MO Suzanne had mastered in more than three decades of dealing with male egos in male-dominated occupations. She could see Cunningham's mind trying to process her aura. Men hunted her instinctively, but they were unsure what sort of creature they were hunting.

Suzanne got up to refresh their drinks. She handed Cunningham a whiskey on ice. "How much did William tell you?"

"Not a lot. Said I'd be useful for an operation with national and international ramifications. Something about a new project to promote capitalism and freedom. Then my boss told me about the inter-agency meeting, and I had no idea William and my boss were talking about the same meeting. Until now. But maybe this meeting isn't that meeting. I'm still confused, and you're not helping much."

"I'll cut to the chase, Darryl. William singled you out. I arranged with my boss at the Pentagon for me to meet you to discuss security issues. Your boss had no problem with that."

"Then what the hell is this meeting about?" Cunningham said.

"William and his associates have San Diego in mind for one of their most significant initiatives, and he'd like you to play a key role in executing these plans."

"And who are 'they?' "

"A closely knit group committed to reforming the United States government."

"Reforming the government?"

"You have conservative values about property and liberty. Correct?"

"A lot of guys like me in the FBI. God, country, and family. Is that what your movement is about? What's the FBI got to do with it?"

"I'll get to the FBI's role. Correction: your role." Suzanne

65

smiled. "We are firm believers in liberty and the perfect beauty of the capitalist system. Tyrants, under the guise of government, force people to disregard their personal liberty and happiness. The movement holds that government must be eradicated for people to be free."

"Gotta say, Suzanne, that sounds treasonous."

"We are patriots, like you, Darryl. Defenders of liberty. And we're awfully pissed off that the American Way is being hijacked by socialists."

"As you know, 'patriots' is a loaded word nowadays. Your movement doesn't own patriotism. America has given my family a good life, and we're grateful."

"Drop the act, Darryl. I'm here to talk to the real you. Not the politically correct government agent."

"What's that supposed to mean?"

" 'Americans have become so accustomed to oppression, they don't even see it anymore, rendering them deaf and dumb to what shackles them. That's the evil genius of Big Government, destroying the human spirit and wrecking ambitions.'

"Sound familiar, Patriot Agent? That's your handle on one particular chat room, correct?"

"I'm sorry, but I shouldn't be talking to you. Are you OPR or counter-intelligence? Screw this," Cunningham said.

"I'm talking about the evils of socialism, Darryl, not conspiracies." Suzanne laughed.

"What's so funny?"

"Nothing, really. I just don't understand why you're trying to hide from who you really are."

"How the hell would you know who I am? I send bad guys to prison, and defend the country, including our government. I might not like everything about the system. But I'm not here

66

to blow up the damn thing."

Again, she laughed. "Hypocrisy is not your best look, Darryl."

"You're something else. One moment you seem genuine—a human being with a sense of vulnerability, even humility—the next moment you're an assassin. I went through a phase. I'm no longer involved with any of that chat room crap."

"Why not?

"It's bullshit and it's hazardous to my job security. You and your comrades are playing a dangerous game. You understand that, right?"

Suzanne moved closer to him. "It's a dangerous world, Darryl. You understand that better than anyone."

He stood abruptly. "You're a PI working for my ex, right?"

"Do you need some time to consider my offer, Darryl?"

"I'm going downstairs to the bar and having a drink. I'm going to let you think about the dangerous position in which you've put yourself. I might be in the mood to talk, even to listen to what you have to say. Then again I might not be in a real social mood at all. I might bring a posse of federal agents to take you in for questioning. You need to come clean. Tell me exactly what you want from me."

"I have a serious question for you, Darryl."

"You have three seconds."

"Let's say I have a very lucrative offer for you. Just you, and not your posse. Can you afford not to come back? Let's you and I close this deal."

~

When Cunningham left Suzanne's room, she poured herself another wine, slipped out of her heels, and sat back to go over the information about Cunningham she'd gathered from various sources. He was a tough guy. But that wasn't surprising for a federal agent with twenty-five years of service. Tough men just hid themselves better than weaker men. In the end they were rarely tough enough.

Cunningham had grown up in modest circumstances and had had a decent public education. His kids, growing up in Poway, were far better off than he and his ex-wife had been in small-town Indiana. That was obvious. He'd become a big-time federal agent. A guy who came from nothing and undoubtedly loved the FBI and what it stood for: protecting Americans and putting away bad guys. A guy deeply in debt who, she speculated, might throw his mother under the bus for enough cash. Willing to betray everything he stood for. She saw a weakness of character, a flaw in Cunningham's wiring. The large debt. Hooked on a government paycheck.

She freshened up, looked at herself in the bathroom mirror, and liked what she saw. She would scare the shit out of the hard-nosed federal agent, like she scared the shit out of most men. Sure, that hadn't been how she envisioned herself as a young woman—until she had realized her power. Tall, strong, and formidable. Smarter than most of her peers. And pretty. Uncommonly so. As a younger woman, she'd been determined not to use her looks to manipulate men. And yet men seemed to invite exploitation, deluding themselves to believe all beautiful women were theirs to pursue, catch, and conquer.

Cunningham knocked hard, twice. She waited thirty seconds then opened the door.

He walked into the room and remained standing. "You're fucking with a federal agent, Suzanne."

She didn't flinch, placing her fingers on a bottle of

Pellegrino. She twisted off the top. "I'm not surprised you're defensive, Darryl. Worked hard your entire life. Faith in the usual American institutions, including the socialist state that has taken care of you and your family for so many years. And what have you got for it? You're in debt to the tune of, what, about seventy, eighty grand?"

He stood erect. "I'm no socialist, and even if I were, that's none of your business."

"One thing you'll learn about us is we're willing to pay a fair price, free from coercion. We believe in freedom. You're free to walk away."

"Walk away from what exactly?"

"My client wishes to buy your allegiance to the movement's ideology, but that's unnecessary, really."

"You don't care what I believe?"

"The movement believes there's a market for virtually every aspect of human affairs. Even one's beliefs and morality—if the price is right. Am I wrong about that?"

He remained standing.

"Please sit. You're making me nervous, Darryl."

"I'm just a cop, Suzanne. Why me?"

"No, Darryl. That's where you underestimate yourself. A cop, yes. But a very special one. You can determine who is or isn't a national security threat."

"That's a reach. Those decisions are beyond my pay grade."

"I'm simply asking you to do your job in a way that benefits my client. In return for that benefit, I'm willing to make certain promises to you."

He said nothing.

"You haven't walked away yet. Would you like to hear my offer, or not?"

"Hold on a minute." He asked her to stand. "I'm a

cautious man, Dr. Dreyfus. Please indulge me for a moment and spread your arms and legs?"

"I'm all yours, Darryl."

Cunningham touched her arms, legs, and body. Normally, Suzanne assumed, the frisk was an act of power. An agent's assertion of authority. Cunningham seemed no different. "About that offer, Agent Cunningham."

"You're not wired. I'm all ears."

"May I sit down now?"

"You paid for the room."

"My offer is simple. You'll receive half a million dollars when the job is complete."

"Define 'complete.' "

"My client would like you to investigate a suspected terrorist cell in the San Diego County prison system. The prison has launched an internal telemarketing operation staffed by a few dozen inmates. A civilian manages that operation. Your professional opinion will be that this telemarketing operation is, in fact, a suspected Islamic terrorist cell."

"What the hell?"

"I can't say more. I need that threat assessment."

"Can you spell E-V-I-D-E-N-C-E?"

"Don't worry about the evidence."

"What, you're going to invent it?"

"We'll handle the incriminating materials," Suzanne said.

"What are you talking about?"

She reached into her handbag and pulled out a blue book with a cloth cover.

"Jesus."

"No, that's the Qur'an."

"Very funny, except it isn't."

"I need that assessment to suggest that this telemarketing

operation is a cover for an unprecedented sort of Islamic terrorist cell, secretly operating within the walls of the county prison system."

Cunningham sat down next to her on the sofa and helped himself to a glass of wine. "There's nothing there. That's a fact."

"Correct. Nothing of the sort exists in the United States."

"So this supposed evidence is a fiction?" he asked.

"Yes."

"Then what's my probable cause to go undercover? You just can't go around making up a story out of thin air. We have protocols."

"Of course. That's why you'll receive a Ragtime-P request from the National Security Administration to investigate this operation."

"There are about three levels of gatekeepers, plus a federal judge's signature, to get one of those approved. What makes you so special?"

Suzanne smiled, letting Cunningham's doubts simmer for a moment too long, until he got the message.

"Are you telling me you've paid off a federal judge?"

"I'm not admitting anything of the sort."

He glared at her. "Then what?"

"At our prompt you and your team will choose an appropriate place and time to make the arrests."

"Tell me the bigger picture."

"Our aim is to reform the federal government."

"So you say. Last I checked, that was Congress's job."

"The liberal elite and their friends in the media have had ample opportunities. They've failed. The movement won't." Suzanne touched Cunningham's arm. "What drives you? Greed or power? Love or lust? Security or liberty? What's your guiding light?"

71

"Crimes are crimes. That's my guiding light."

"Crimes are crimes—until they aren't. Change the facts, erase the crimes. We're in the fact changing business. I see that look. You're a cop. Facts matter to you. But once you understand that we have the power to change bad facts into good ones—and vice versa—you'll never doubt me again. You do believe in greed, Darryl. That's obvious."

"Don't go all Gordon Gekko on me. Fuck that. I want it in writing. In non-treasonous language, please. A business contract. And I want your media, as you call them, to absolve me when it's over. Put that in the contract."

"Of course, a business contract. That's all the truth anyone needs, whatever their politics." She had him. Like many men with scruples, Cunningham had a price. Even an FBI agent, a standard-bearer for justice and the rule of law, had a price.

"We are getting tantalizingly close to a deal," Cunningham said.

"Looks like we're very close."

"But I'm not there yet. I have a counter-proposal, the success of which will absolutely ensure my full cooperation, with results that I can guarantee."

"I'm not optimistic about complicating this deal with ornamentation," Suzanne said.

"I want a sit down with your friend, Eurynomos."

"William?"

"Yeah, he calls himself Eurynomos. I want to meet him."

"I don't see that happening. That's why you're talking with me right now, not some has-been billionaire."

"I take it you and Eurynomos don't see eye to eye."

"It's complicated, Darryl. I get along just fine with billionaires. I don't have to like them."

"Let's cut the crap, Suzanne. I need that meeting for my

reassurance. I'm ready to sign, but I want to be sure. You can understand that, can't you? Otherwise you're forcing me to help you. That's not capitalism—that's the mafia."

Cunningham got up to leave, and Suzanne walked him to the door. "I'll see what I can do, Darryl," she said. "I'm not a miracle worker, and my colleagues can be reclusive and mercurial. They're billionaires, mind you."

She noticed how Cunningham looked her over as he stood under the doorway.

He scoffed. "I doubt you'll have any problem, Suzanne. Your colleagues are men, right?"

Suzanne said nothing, waiting for Cunningham to leave.

"You know how to reach me," Cunningham said. "You've got twenty-four hours, or I turn this into a full-fledged investigation of you and your boys. Are we clear?"

~

Suzanne shut the door behind Cunningham and returned to the Theodore Alexander. She poured herself an unusually large glass of red wine. She listened to the rough recording in her mind of her words to Cunningham. She'd threatened, lied, flirted, bribed, and all but seduced the federal agent into cooperating with a treasonous scheme to overthrow the US government. She felt sick. She needed to get drunk and take a long nap.

If Cunningham followed through with his threat, she could go to prison for life. That is, if the Freedom Society hadn't already paid off decision-makers at several levels of the Justice Department and the FBI. Cunningham was clueless to all that, but now he was just one more pawn who didn't know they were one of many stooges in Garrick's conspiracy. Pawns who would look the other way. Suckers who would execute key aspects of the conspiracy, from phony threat assessments to eliminating any individuals who didn't cooperate or who were perceived as a threat.

Suzanne was among the pawns, but she was also treading a thin line between a good pawn and a bad one. Pawns were a double-edged sword. Pawns were good until they weren't. They were pawns because they could execute and look the other way. But what if they didn't? What if Johnny Petit squealed? What if Cunningham went public? The very thing that made them good pawns was also the thing that gave them power to burn you. They want more money, more power, more of your soul.

She took a serious gulp from the silly wine. Another sip led to another. Suzanne was as deep in shit as she'd ever been in her life, feeling alternatively depressed and exuberant that her plan was in full bloom, but the deeper she got into her own conspiracy the deeper her sense of hopelessness became. She didn't know how much more she could bear of this duplicitousness. But she had to own it. Either that or perish, with no reason to keep living.

The Manifesto. The fucking manifesto. She joked about it to herself. For years she had had herself a story that the gift to Garrick had been a joke among themselves. A gesture. A satire. Something to laugh about when they were old.

The damned manifesto was no joke. Her words had landed upon something in the culture that devoured it as if it were a long lost Eleventh Commandment from God, even if it contradicted all the other Ten Commandments.

"Thou Shall Take from the Poor to Give to the Rich, by any means necessary under the guise of liberty and private property." Would that be Suzanne's legacy, the everlasting commandment that would lay upon her grave? God help us, she thought, as she drifted away into sleep.

9

THE GOLDILOCKS PLAY

Setting up a meeting at Garrick's Morro Bay compound was more elaborate than scheduling a chat with the president of the United Nations. Suzanne met Darryl Cunningham at a private airport out in the boonies of Escondido. One of Billy's men met them at the Lear fifteen minutes before takeoff.

"Dr. Dreyfus, it's been a long time, girl."

"Hello, Jackson. Yes, it has."

"Don't suppose you need a blindfold."

"I know where we're going."

"Yes, you do. Nice to see you again, Doc."

Jackson asked, politely, if Darryl would mind putting on a blindfold.

"What is this, a drug deal?" Cunningham said.

"I'm sorry, sir. If I don't follow the procedure, I lose my job. And your watch, please."

"My watch?"

"Reduces the chances of you learning the location."

"Right. Why don't you just put me out for a few hours? Less hassle."

"We've considered that, sir. But recovery time is an issue, you know? Mr. Wharton—I mean Eurynomos—likes visitors to be alert."

Suzanne sat opposite Cunningham on the Lear. "Chill, Darryl. You wanted this meeting, remember? Do what Jackson says."

~

Suzanne led Cunningham to the opulent front door of Garrick's "cottage," which also served as the unofficial headquarters of the Freedom Society, overlooking the town of Morro Bay, California. By the time Jackson had removed Cunningham's blindfold, they were sitting in the darkened library, which smelled of lavender incense. They sat on a comfortable leather sofa beside a dimly lit end table, on which rested a wrapped cigar, a bottle of good whiskey, an empty shot glass, and a wristwatch.

Suzanne sat with Cunningham in silence for several minutes. She couldn't help but recall the last time she was on the same sofa after making love with Garrick all those years ago.

"That's not the Seiko I paid three hundred and fifty dollars for at Macy's," Cunningham said.

Suzanne poured two whiskeys. "Take the Swiss. It's yours. The cigar too."

He passed the cigar under his nose and lit it, enjoying the whiskey's warm buzz mixed with the earthy aroma of the Cuban.

A voice interrupted the silence. "I see you two have made the trip safely. Welcome, Agent Cunningham. I'm Eurynomos. Suzy, I wasn't expecting you."

77

She got up to give William a peck on the cheek. "I'd never miss this."

"Agent Cunningham, I see you've discovered the enjoyments we've put out for you. We're terribly sorry for the inconvenience. It was imperative that you come to us," William said.

"I'm here, aren't I?"

"Good. Suzanne says you have some questions for us."

"Who is 'us' exactly?"

"That will become clear. Again, what can I do for you?"

"I need to know what I'm getting into, or I won't make any deals."

"What did Suzanne tell you?"

"I understand you people are part of some secret group that wants to make the FBI look incompetent. Trust me, the agency has had its share of fuck-ups. Whatever you have in mind won't make a difference."

"We're offering you half a million dollars to execute the plan on your end. You will launch an investigation of the new telemarketing team at the San Diego County prison, suspecting the inmates are an Islamic sleeper cell waiting for instructions from their operators in Iran. Based on that brief investigation, you'll write a threat assessment recording and validating your case."

"You make it sound easy. Trust me, it's not."

"That's because you're thinking like an FBI agent."

"I am a federal agent, sir."

"True. But for this gambit to work, you need to drop the squeaky clean image. Loosen your tie. Become more comfortable with shades of gray, perhaps."

"I'm not following you."

"Hmm. I was afraid of that."

"I'm not a nuanced man. I deal in facts and hard evidence. I'm willing to listen, but please cut to the chase," Cunningham said.

"I understand. But consider my point of view. I don't know if we can put our faith in you. There's a lot at stake for us. We've trusted you to this point because I'm confident that you believe in liberty. You believe that government mustn't overburden our capitalists—the geniuses who make our way of life possible. If you don't believe that, we can part ways right now," William said.

"Fine. Suppose I do accept the title of libertarian. But I'm not a criminal, okay? Explain this shades of gray thing to me."

"Let me explain by showing you a pathway to success. In terms of counterterrorism, you're the boss, right? You'll need a trusted assistant who'll draft that threat assessment for your approval. You know what the assessment must conclude, and you'll provide rather powerful hints to your assistant to achieve that goal. Understand what I'm saying?"

"Okay. My assistant gives me what I suggest and I'm one step removed from the investigation, which provides me deniability. Then what?"

"Perfect, Darryl. You're getting it. Now once you have the threat assessment, which concludes that an Islamic terrorist cell is operating at the county jail, we're ready to go on our end."

"Ready for what?"

"I'd rather not get into that. Complete that assessment, and you'll have everything you need to make a high-profile bust of the terrorist cell," William said.

"That makes no sense. The public will think we've done our jobs. FBI heroes to the rescue, nailing the terrorists before they hurt Americans."

William smiled and set his whiskey glass on the cherrywood end table. "That's astute of you, Darryl. I neglected to tell you there will be an attack. Absolutely no violence. But an attack of sorts will occur, just as your threat assessment anticipated. Our media team will be relentless. We'll social media this to death, repeating again and again that the FBI's failure to stop the horrible attack is the most convincing proof yet that the US government has failed America. We'll have legislation drafted to eliminate the FBI and replace it with a for-profit corporation that you, Darryl Cunningham, will lead as the new chief executive officer."

"You're telling me this alleged Islamic terrorist cell is like Goldilocks? Not too violent, just violent enough to make the FBI look incompetent?"

"I like that." He glanced at Suzanne. "We'll call it the Goldilocks Play."

"What kind of attack?" Cunnigham said.

"I can't tell you that. It's better that you don't know precise details."

"Apparently you've thought of everything."

"We are serious people, Darryl."

"I can't say I've heard of your group. I found one item on the dark web that connects you to something called *The Liberation Manifesto*. Otherwise, you're invisible."

William glanced at Suzanne. "We like it that way."

"I need to know more about this movement."

"We are a society of individuals advocating for liberty and the end of government tyranny."

"And your membership includes?"

"We have no membership list per se. We've randomly assigned each of our members a pseudonym. Name us and you can investigate us."

80

"How's that work?"

"Only when I privately confirm one's membership does one know we've admitted him or her."

"No secret handshake?"

"Not exactly. We're always open to new members. Someone might recommend a friend or colleague to us, but only I can approve them. We promise members anonymity. No dues, nothing in writing. No headquarters, offices, or buildings, and absolutely no lists of members."

"What do members get from the deal? Why would they seek you out?"

"We call ourselves the Freedom Society, and we make a promise of liberty. Work with us, support us, spread the message of a government-free society, and be ready for the government, as you know it, to dissolve. We'll award our members the government assets that the socialists have wasted on useless federal programs. Nothing in writing. Everything in trust."

"Why would these uber-wealthy titans join you? They've already conquered America."

"Tell me, Mr. Cunningham, when in the history of human society has greed known any limits? Our members can be as brazenly self-interested as they wish—as long as they keep winning. If they lose, they're gone. We drop them. We help to ensure that they win."

"So they take a risk because you guarantee results?"

"We help our members maximize their prospects in the big game. We try to subdue whatever happens exogenously beyond their control. We minimize their risk."

"What's that mean?"

"Some kid in a garage could invent the thing that brings down one or more of our members. We work hard to ensure

81

our members encounter no surprises."

Cunningham's brow narrowed. "You want to suppress innovation?"

"The nation is entering a new era of capitalism. Our most successful capitalists—most of whom are members—must eliminate all risks and ensure their wealth and power lasts well into the foreseeable future. Forever, we hope."

"So owning the government is their guarantee?"

"We prefer to think of it as American citizens handing over their assets to an excellent manager. The invisible hand of capital seeking its highest and best use will create more wealth, not just for our members, but also more satisfaction for the people. Who needs mindless bureaucrats when our brilliant entrepreneurs are running the show?" William said.

"You're telling me I'm better off dealing with a low-paid clerk at the Justice Department instead of the career employee who gets decent benefits and a non-poverty wage? Not in your dreams."

"Darryl, you're a tough sell. You're assuming that the government employee who gets good benefits and respectable pay is better for the consumers of government. I challenge that notion."

"You don't live in the real world then, Eurynomos. Lose a few billion and then make that claim."

"Let's not go there, please. But I guarantee you we won't encounter any real counterrevolutionary opposition—except for the silly socialists and do-gooders on the margins. That's just the way it is."

"Frankly, Eurynomos, I don't see Americans buying into a society without a government. Public schools, Social Security, local fire departments, and cops. That's the government. Fuck, man. You and me both drive on socialist highways. I can't see this country being okay with capitalists owning all that. Can you? Be honest."

"Smell the aroma of that fine cigar. Taste that fifty-year-old Irish whiskey. It's seven-fifty a bottle. That wristwatch on the table that I want you to have, it's a twenty-five-grand work of precision. Those are the smells, tastes, and culture of capitalism, my friend, and Americans can't live without it."

"Even though most can only dream about it?" Cunningham said.

"And what's wrong with that? Remember, it's called the American Dream, not the American Guarantee. You work for what you get in this world."

"You're right. There's no guarantee of a good life for anyone in America. But people still need hope. I grew up working class. My dad was a beat cop who couldn't get promoted to detective because he didn't have a degree. I had brothers and sisters. Money was always tight. Actually we were probably lower-middle-class, but we were far better off than families that had almost no chance of getting ahead. Let's be honest. Gross inequality is capitalism's Achilles' heel. Some government gives hopeless people at least a chance to get in the game. Government is necessary. If we didn't have it, some Einstein would have to invent it. Just not too much of it."

William abruptly stood from the leather chair and crushed his cigar. "Excuse me for a moment, Darryl. Pour yourself another whiskey."

Suzanne was amused by the conversation. Cunningham made William squirm. Cunningham was relaxed, aided by the capitalist Cuban cigar and the finely aged Irish whiskey. Fifteen minutes passed with relative ease.

She heard footsteps entering the room and looked over her shoulder. It was Garrick. Obviously he wasn't on the yacht like

William had said. The sight of him made her heart leap and her stomach turn. She suppressed the urge to simultaneously smile at him and spit on him.

"Darryl, I have someone very special with me. Dr. Garrick Cripps is the unofficial chairman of our society. I've told him about our conversation, and he'd like to answer any questions you might have," William said.

In the dim light, Suzanne could see the familiar contours of an elegant man, now in his midsixties. Longish salt-and-pepper hair, a gray wool jacket over a pinkish shirt, and titanium eyeglasses with tinted lenses suggesting fine tastes and deep wealth. His voice was familiar, sonorous, and authoritative.

Garrick sat and turned to Cunningham, avoiding eye contact with Suzanne. "Darryl, I'm Garrick. I appreciate you being here to learn more about us."

"My pleasure."

"I couldn't help but overhear something you said to William a few minutes ago," Garrick said.

"Oh?"

"Your comments about inequality were fascinating. Could you expand on that?"

"Let's be real. Some are born better than others. Without something like government helping to level the playing field, we end up with two nations. One for the elites and another one for their slaves. Am I wrong?"

"Really? I'd say just the opposite has occurred in American history. An increasingly soft society that pays undue attention to the weak at the expense of the strong," Garrick said.

"I'll play devil's advocate here and say the capitalists have already won. I saw the private jet. I tasted the Cuban cigar. I've got a pretty good idea this 'cottage' as you call it is worth about five million. What are you freaking out about? Try to find a one-bedroom in south San Diego not infested with cockroaches for less than fifteen hundred a month. I'd have to sell drugs myself to pay for that. That's a soft society?" Cunningham said.

"Granted, capitalism can be tough on people. That's regrettable. But a tough society is a great society. That's all we want for America. Greatness, not weakness."

"You say you want greatness for America, which I take it means great wealth. I've got no problem with that. But what do we do with the losers? For the losers, the dream is all they've got, realistically. Take away their dream, and we're left with robots and slaves, not citizens. *The Fountainhead* or *Brave New World*? Which one is it, Garrick?"

"It's both," Garrick said.

"How do you mean?"

"Why does the American Dream keep working, Darryl? Why do people keep believing in the dream even though upward economic mobility has been steadily declining for decades?"

"I suspect you have an answer."

"Have you ever been a salesman?" Garrick said.

"No. Have you?"

"Well, yes. I invested in a robotics company, and we did very well. There's a sales technique shared by virtually all successful businesses, and it's commonly known as a 'bait and switch.' You know what that is, right?"

"Sure, a guy will promise one thing and actually deliver another thing that's not as good a deal as the one he promised," Cunningham said.

"Correct. Sounds innocent in a way because it's a commonly used term, right? But when you think about it, it's

85

really just an ordinary swindle. A con job. A shell game. Fraud. Hell, you know all this. You're an FBI agent. The gullible keep the dream alive because they're willing participants in the swindle. America—i.e., the media, entertainment, culture, churches, schools, the entire enterprise—promises the poor bastards a Corvette, but they're lucky to get a used Kia. They're grateful to live in such a wonderful country where people are free to keep dreaming about the Corvette. But fear works better than dreams."

"What's your point?"

"My point, Darryl, is that we can't lose. Keep the suckers fearful of losing jobs, health care, a roof over their heads, even the ability to feed their children. But keep pushing the dream like a drug. Allow the anger of failure to swell, like a cancer that eats at their souls. That's how the con works. If we don't get 'em coming in, we'll get 'em going out. We gather ardent believers and warriors, promising a new world liberated from the socialist scourge that tyrannizes them, keeps them down. Second, we promise a fountainhead of wealth that never runs dry. In the interim we'll piss off the do-gooders, but they'll be powerless to stop us. Future generations will accept a government-free society as a matter of fact. As a matter of survival. Yet they remain grateful because, in that alternative world, liberty, or the perception of it, is the *only* thing in true abundance. Anyone is free to achieve limitless possibility. Say that a million times. And a million more. An enduring *belief* in liberty is what holds our revolution together."

Cunningham got up to go.

"Are you leaving us, Darryl?" Garrick said.

"I need to get back to my real job, if you don't mind."

"Are you with us or against us? Are you a patriot? Or are you just another timid apologist for the socialist state?"

86

Garrick said.

"You're saying I can't be a patriot if I'm working for the government catching bad guys? More than enough hypocrisy to go around. Take you, Garrick, and your Freedom Society. Obviously you're smart people. You run with billionaires. You're all very well-educated and cultured. Accustomed to the best of everything, from Swiss watches and Cuban cigars to multi-million dollar homes. Speaking as an FBI agent, rich people like you definitely aren't on our radar as serious threats to national security. Weird as it may be, we think of you as the good guys. The pillars that make America work, like God and apple pie. But I wonder.

"Who does the dirty work? Frankly, the Bureau is paying a lot more attention to domestic troublemakers, and I'm not talking about labor unions or civil disobedience. White working-class terror, engulfed by racism and white power. Populism on LSD, otherwise known as anarchy. Not worldly, sophisticated, or well-educated. Not like you, Garrick. Most don't even know where MIT is. They call themselves patriots, just like you. They hate the government, just like you, probably for different reasons. A lot of these folks, more than I care to admit, are hiding in militant cells across the heartland, preparing for armed insurrection. The FBI has been asleep at the wheel since Oklahoma City. And now we're waking up to thousands of Timothy McVeighs, fully armed and poised to overthrow the government. January 6th was a dress rehearsal.

"And for what? Where's the damned tyranny you all talk about so much? The whole thing is a joke. Who are you fooling?"

Garrick smiled. "You know the answer."

"I'm still baffled. What do American patriots have in common with white nationalists and Nazis?"

Garrick held his glass of the high-class whiskey, then set it on the table. He took a deep breath and stiffened his demeanor. Cunningham had poked a hole in Garrick's polished facade. "Those people you're talking about are our friends, and they're not as ignorant as you portray them to be. Our movement has room for all kinds of patriots. We don't all think exactly alike. We don't all share the same tastes and economic fortunes. But we all share a strong sense of patriotism and a love of freedom."

"Come on. I don't buy that. A minute ago you said it was a con. You think you're special, above the riff-raff," Cunningham said.

"We're special because we're willing to pay a price for freedom. People like you and me, Darryl—admit it. We're driven by greed. Cold, hard greed is why people like us fight for our personal freedom. I'm being brutally honest. You see, I agree with you. Those who are less clever than us also pay a price, which is a beautiful thing to see. The unclever fight not for their freedom, but for *our* freedom, Darryl. They believe they fight for all Americans, bless their hearts. Truthfully, they fight for my freedom. For William's and Suzanne's. Yours, as well. They fight for the freedom of the Society and its members, who are empowered to exploit the very unclever people who paid the real price."

"And what price is that, professor?"

"The poor bastards pay with their own blood. And that's why people like us love people like them."

10
RAGTIME-P

"**G**et in here, Treadwell." Darryl Cunningham waved a document so his underling could see the imprimatur of an official NSA communiqué to the Justice Department. "See this, Treadwell? It's a Ragtime-P case via Big Brother. They've picked up some interesting chatter coming from, of all places, the San Diego County Jail. NSA has scanned the place for several weeks, and I'm told they're onto something. Hot as rats fucking in a wool sock, Treadwell. We don't know a lot of details, but that's where you come in."

Jason Treadwell sat down next to Cunningham's desk. "What's the theory, boss?"

"County started a new telemarketing program a while back, staffed by inmates themselves, and Big Brother believes it's a cover for a dangerous new type of Islamic terrorist cell. If this sounds weird, that's because it is. Clever as shit too, in my book."

"Are they serious?"

"It's the fucking NSA."

"Who's in charge of the telemarketing thing?" Jason said.

"You'll confirm all that. We know there's at least one inmate on the team who may have ties to an Islamic group. He's got a cousin who converted to Islam, and he's an important figure in one of the mosques in town."

Jason looked puzzled. "Really? So what's the play?"

"I want you undercover. Eyes and ears on this deal. Give me some theories."

"Right now? Or in a memo?"

"No fucking memos, Treadwell. Yes, now. Give me a working plan. No paper on this."

Jason avoided Cunningham's eyes and looked out to the Sorrento Valley.

"Still with us, Treadwell?"

"Darryl, I'm thinking. What about this: I pose as a reporter from some out-of-town publication, right? Can we arrange credentials? I go in like I'm doing a story on this great new prison telemarketing thing. An innovative way to use inmates to raise money for the prison system. Good PR for the county, right?"

Cunningham hoisted his feet on his desk, leaning back in his chair. "I like it—a lot. Set it up. We'll arrange proper credentials."

Jason stood at the door, ready to leave. "Okay then. Anything else?"

"This is emegent, readwell. The chatter we're getting suggests there may be something big in the works. Soon. You have no other priorities, okay?"

"I'm on it."

"Oh, one more thing," Cunningham said. He opened a drawer in his desk, pulled out a small blue book, and handed it to Treadwell.

"What's this?"

"What's it look like? That's the Qur'an, Treadwell. You've read it, right?"

"Actually, no."

"You're a counterterrorism agent, and you haven't even read their book? Never mind. Read it. Leave it on a desk at the jail. Be discreet."

"Whose desk?"

"Whoever's running the show."

"That's planting evidence, isn't it?"

"A two-thousand-year-old book anyone can get from Amazon is evidence? Just leave the damned book on the desk."

~

Cunningham left the building. He found his company Buick, wheeled through the parking lot, and drove methodically a few miles east on Sorrento Valley Road before stopping at a convenience store.

The routine was the same every time. The Sri Lankan who owned the store recognized him from among the thousands of anonymous souls who passed through this place. Cunningham picked out a disposable phone with enough prepaid minutes. He gave the clerk a twenty dollar bill and waited for his change, always the same fifty-seven cents.

He got into the Buick, then drove eastward. Waited for oncoming traffic and turned left onto a side street lined with small businesses, warehouses, and one nearby cell-phone tower. He pulled to the curb, turned off the engine, and rolled up the windows. Cunningham tore off the hard plastic wrapping from the phone, checked the battery, and clicked on the device. He got a signal and punched in the digits from memory. Let it ring two times. Hung up. Waited two minutes, then punched the digits again. Suzanne picked up after two rings. She answered with a simple, "Yes."

"I've sent the kid in."

"Good. Will he be okay?"

"He's okay. That's why I hired him. A puppy dog. He'll see what I want him to see."

"That better be true. What did you tell him?" Suzanne said.

"We've discussed this. I tell him what I tell him."

"You gave him the book, right?"

"Yeah, made up a story. It'll be in evidence, for what it's worth."

"Make sure Jason's threat assessment mentions it."

"You're not much of a cop, Suzanne. I get it."

"You know what this means, right?"

"It's for the greater good, blah blah. Don't worry. I'm all in."

"Have you decided which side you're on?"

"I'm on my side, Suzanne."

"I can't argue with selfishness," she said.

"I'd hope so. We'd be shitty libertarians, otherwise. You'll take care of me when this is over, right?" Cunningham said.

"Chill, Darryl. You're the man. The goose that laid the golden egg."

"What's the egg?"

"Revolution, silly."

Cunningham clicked off and tossed the burner onto the passenger seat. It bounced in the air and fell to the floor. Cunningham tried to reach it but the damned thing was already under the seat. Too bad. He'd get it later.

Too bad, indeed. That was Cunningham's go-to sentiment after the stranger-than-life meeting with Eurynomos and Garrick Cripps. The money was good. Better than good.

92

With half a million, he'd pay off his debts, get his son and daughter situated, and then he'd quit the FBI. Then a new nation without a government? He thought about the winners, and he thought about the losers. He had put Garrick on the spot asking about the American Dream, and the leader of the conspiracy came clean: the Dream was imaginary, a sufficiently believable story which would persuade the suckers to play the game just long enough for the winners to screw the losers out of their hard-earned wages. Oh well. Too bad.

And yet the losers were eager to shed blood for the very billionaires who screwed them in the first place. Cunningham saw the swindle for what it was worth. He both pitied and despised the poor bastards who would bleed for the rich.

If the poor bastards were that stupid, so be it. If those lousy billionaires could get away with the con, why not him? He'd bank the losers' patriotic contribution, all for the sake of "liberty." That's right. His liberty. Just like Cripps said.

ACT II
PENETRATE

Lies are transformative, enlightening the path to absolute truth.

– The Liberation Manifesto

11

THE JEWEL

It took the movers two days to fill Suzanne's new Windansea beach house with furniture and unpack her belongings from Boulder. She had arranged with her bosses at the Pentagon for an indefinite leave of absence.

"Family reasons" was the official rational for the leave, but her immediate boss, Col. McCabe Miller in Washington, tried to scratch the truth from Suzanne's lips.

"I've never known you to be anything but nose-to-the-grindstone," McCabe said. "Why now?"

Suzanne made up a story. McCabe had always treated her well. Never asked too many questions. Let her loose to procure talent and technology. Most of that bounty came from her secret arrangement with Garrick at MIT, and McCabe seemed not to care. He had never met Garrick, nor would he if Suzanne could help it.

Maybe the story was even true. A career reevaluation. Grief counseling. She grieved for the life that could have been hers until she had made the fateful wrong turn with Garrick. She could still explore the adoption of a child, even as a middle-aged woman.

Suzanne could no longer "have it all," as they say, but she still had time to create a family. Maybe get that dog she'd always wanted. Watch her adopted child play in the backyard by the ocean. Enjoy yoga on the beach. Try to be like she imagined Laura Cavendish to be. Healthy. Balanced. Open to the loveliness that life offered those willing to watch, listen, and learn. She hadn't seen Laura in several years. Not after she arranged for Laura to set up her AI lab at the university.

She wondered if Laura had reconnected with Carson. Suzanne mused about reaching out to Laura. But she dared not become personally entangled with either of her potential allies. Suzanne's first and only priority was to move the mission forward and bring Garrick to justice—irrespective of legal formalities.

She would be unencumbered by her personal wants and needs for the indefinite future, except for the small things that gave her pleasure. She had joined a gym in downtown La Jolla and bought a simple bicycle to ride to town. Windansea was only a few miles south, too close to drive and park, yet too far to walk to the gym.

One morning in early March, she rode her bike peacefully along La Jolla Shores Drive, passing a large church on the right side of the road. A very nice church, she mused. A welcoming feel, with a community center offering its members various social services in the middle of the week. She'd expect nothing less from La Jolla, California—as perfect a place as she'd ever seen.

As she rode past the entryway, a motorcycle screamed, dashing from the church's parking lot and cutting Suzanne off.

She swerved. The heavy bicycle tipped over, and she crashed onto the pavement. She screamed at the motorcycle's driver, an anonymous bastard covered in black leathers and a helmet. Emblazed on his black leather vest was an image of the US flag bleeding into the Confederate Flag, with the image of an AR-15 embedded over the top and the words The Second Keepers.

The rider didn't seem to hear Suzanne's shriek over the motorcycle's screaming four-stroke. He stopped fifty yards ahead, then curled back to where Suzanne was struggling to lift her bike and clean the dust from her shorts. Oh, she thought. He'd come back to apologize and help. Maybe a nice guy, after all.

He set his tall black boot on the pavement and sat undisturbed on the motorcycle.

She stopped and tried to see his face though the dark glass of the helmet. "What the fuck are you doing?" she yelled. "Help me!"

He didn't move.

"Are you Suzanne Dreyfus?" he said.

"Yes, why? Who in the hell are you?"

"Do your duty. Don't fuck up what you've started."

"Says who?" Suzanne screamed.

The rider didn't stop to converse. He took a sharp U-turn on the side of the road and sped off toward the town, leaving Suzanne on the shoulder, the handlebars of her bike twisted from the crash.

So this was how it would be. Somebody was watching her. Goons from Garrick's private militia, who called themselves the Second Keepers, a not-subtle reference to the Second Amendment.

Suzanne flashed back to her creation of *The Liberation Manifesto*, a one-off gift to her former lover, Garrick Cripps, that had begun in jest and evolved into this unthinkable mess.

99

Her bike helmet was twisted off her head from the impact of the fall, her chin cut and bruised from scraping on the asphalt, her neck throbbing in pain.

But the physical bruises and bloody scratches meant nothing compared to the brain-shock she felt from the cold reality of her own private Frankenstein. Now, decades after she'd created *The Liberation Manifesto*, Garrick's angry movement had landed, piercing the peaceful heart of untouchable La Jolla, California, the Jewel of America.

12

SOCIAL ENGINEERING

Suzanne poured a glass of wine and grabbed her copy of *The Liberation Manifesto* from her bookshelf. She scanned the chapter headings until she came to one called "Crime and Freedom." Suzanne skimmed the passage, remembering the winter day in 1992 when she had composed it in Cambridge.

She heard the doorbell. Jonas Peterson arriving on time, as directed. She set down *The Manifesto* and poured a full glass of the Caymus Cab. She handed it to Jonas as he entered. "Jonas, it's been too long."

"I love this neighborhood. Wish I could afford it."

She led the young Stanford professor to her back porch. "Windansea is lovely. Come."

Jonas took a seat on a white wicker chair facing the beach. Suzanne sat beside him, separated by a round wicker end table on which the bottle of Caymus rested. Jonas was wearing shorts, and she noticed his tan legs. His blond hair was closely cropped, like a young soldier or engineer. He sat upright and alert. Suzanne recoiled at the visage before her. A nearly perfect Aryan man—if perfect Aryan men were your thing, she thought.

"You're Austrian, if I remember correctly. Where did you grow up, Jonas?"

"I was born in Salzburg but grew up in Copenhagen. Have you been?"

"That little hippy place in the city. What's it called?"

"You're referring to Christiana," Jonas said.

"Right. I remember other travelers talking about it and how it reeked of hash. I had to check it out. I marveled at the hardworking blacksmiths. Odd place, though. No photos allowed, and yet the little economy was basically tourism. That's what tourists do, right? They take photos. I snuck in a few pics with my Sony automatic. This was way before cell phones, of course."

"I know Christiana," Jonas said. "A sort of libertarian paradise."

"Oh, really? I always thought of it as a commune, a communist utopia, if you will. Private property was abolished. Nobody pays rent, even. Remarkably the Danish government has tolerated Christiana for decades, legitimizing it as a 'social experiment.' "

"Perhaps you are right. I avoided the place myself. I had a cousin who lived there, if you can call such a nasty existence living. Then she grew up and became a banker. A perfect ending to one's childhood, I thought."

"I thought Christiana was quite pleasant. So what was your childhood like, Jonas? Did you go to university in Denmark?"

"I did. Received my undergraduate degree at an engineering school in Copenhagen. I'd heard so much about America. A land of possibilities and freedom. I came here and went to Berkeley for my PhD program."

"How did you meet Garrick?" Suzanne rarely asked a

question to which she didn't already know the answer.

"We were both attending a conference in the Bay Area. We hit it off, and he asked me to join his effort to create his super-bot."

"Now be honest. I know he's your boss, but what do you think of Garrick?"

"He's interesting. At first I thought he was crazy. Then we got to talking, and now I understand him completely. Dr. Cripps's efforts could make all the difference for any movement wishing to challenge the existing paradigm of quasi-socialist control of people's lives. I had similar ideas growing up in Denmark. So many aimless young people. Socialism was failing them. The state gives people so much. They have no incentive to work. I came to America because I thought Americans were different. You guys reject socialism like a reflex. I found that fascinating. Like a religious belief, even. Rightist political parties in Europe are changing the conversation, but I see America as the vanguard, doing away with socialism for good."

"Yet you came to Berkeley."

"Ironic, right?"

"Maybe not. I'm sure you worked hard in Denmark. You also got free health care. A good, inexpensive education. You paid higher taxes, but you and your family never had to worry about the basics. So what made you different?"

"Simple, actually. I admire people who work hard. Some people risk experimenting in ways that improve society. The people I admire don't set out trying to better society necessarily. But they help society because of their hard work. Just as Ayn told us. Same for Garrick's *Liberation Manifesto*. I assume you've read it?"

Suzanne took a long sip of the Caymus and set down her

103

glass. She had almost choked listening to Jonas's implicit claim that Garrick had worked so hard composing his masterpiece, *The Manifesto*. The very manifesto she, in fact, had written and given to him as a birthday gift. "Yes, I have read Garrick's master work. Many times. Tell me, Jonas, which part of *The Manifesto* most appealed to you?"

"So many passages blew me away, you know. Garrick's descriptions of the perfectly natural beauty—and brutality—of free markets, for instance. He writes about economics like a poet, you know? A brilliant man."

Again, Suzanne nearly spit out the Caymus while trying to hold back a hearty laugh. "And do you really believe what *The Manifesto* says?"

Jonas shifted his weight on the wicker, then took a sip of wine. "*The Manifesto* might seem alien, even abhorrent, to traditional values, but when I remove emotions from the equation, the words make logical sense to me," he said.

Suzanne smiled again. "But some people don't think as clearly as we do about free markets. Take the concept of the cull. How would you explain culling the excess herd as a key component of a free society?"

Jonas raised his near-empty glass. "This wine—what is it again? A delicious specimen of the Northern California grape. We can never rule out the blessings of God. I find genetics account for so much, don't you, Suzanne? If I may say so, you're a remarkably beautiful woman. I'd think you could have become a model."

Suzanne could see Jonas showing the blissful effects of the fine wine. She picked up the bottle from the table and poured. "Then allow me to refill your glass of this genetically perfect specimen. We were talking about the cull."

"Yes, of course. If I'm not mistaken, Garrick referenced

the economic utility of culling unnecessary individuals, those incapable of contributing to economic wealth. My life and yours are worth a great deal more than a homeless man's. How do I know this? The market proves it. It's black and white," Jonas said.

Suzanne tried to hide her astonishment. Jonas had adopted *The Manifesto*'s lingua franca as if he'd been born into it. When she had written the section about the "cull" in *The Manifesto*, Suzanne had meant to underscore the absurdity of pure capitalism when unrestrained by morality or social norms. Even Garrick, in those early days, had appreciated *The Manifesto*'s comic contradictions. He had been insightful, even prescient, noting that libertarianism, like most dogmatic enterprises, would eventually metamorphize from absurdity into tragedy. Jonas's enthusiasm was entertaining, and yet dangerously close to fascism. No, not dangerously close. It *was* fascism. She wondered about Jonas's ancestors from Austria. Were they Jew haters? Were they Nazis? How had young Jonas slipped so easily into such abhorrent beliefs? "Perhaps Garrick is taking Ayn's philosophy too far. Our movement is free from coercion of any kind. A society can't cull the herd without coercion, can it?"

"Most libertarians would probably agree with you. Neither Garrick nor I agree with most libertarians."

"What's that mean?"

"Culling the herd is still a radical idea, but we Europeans have experimented with eugenics in the past, as you know. We'll simply adapt eugenics to an economically logical framework. Allow markets to decide. Individuals would be free to pay a market-clearing price to stay alive and prevent authorities from the cull if they cease to be economically useful."

"What about your grandmother—if she could no longer

provide for herself?"

"I see your point. But I would that as a family unit, we would ensure my grandmother had accumulated sufficient resources to purchase her freedom, no? May I use your bathroom?"

~

Watching Jonas strolling to the bathroom half-drunk, Suzanne tried to suppress her contempt—for herself. Listening to Jonas, she saw first-hand what she and Garrick had wrought when they published the damned thing years ago.

As a scientist steeped in logic and rationality, Suzanne had intended her fifty-page pamphlet as a satire. A fun little project to give her brain a break from MIT's rigorous courses in mathematics and physics. She'd timed her gift for Garrick's fortieth birthday in 1992. She'd never written a satire. Nor did she even consider herself a writer. But she was a natural. She'd quoted the luminaries of libertarianism. Milton Friedman, Ludwig Von Mises, Ayn Rand, and many others. She'd poked fun at the oddities of the preciously dogmatic pseudo-science. Suzanne had made fun of the implicit belief that pure capitalism was the answer to virtually all human problems—not unlike an ill-conceived perpetual motion machine. She'd written with sylized letters with a thick black pen on parchment and bound the homemade book with a faux-leather cover, giving it the appearance of an ancient but decidedly skinny tome, like a comic book feigning sober analytical thought—in just the manner of the libertarian tracts she made fun of. When she finished her project at the Cambridge Kinko's, Suzanne smiled. Exactly the feel and look she'd wanted. The staff of the Harvard Lampoon would be jealous. She'd wrapped the handmade book in a brown paper bag and attached a birthday card that read, *For Garrick. May you always be inspired and delighted.*

Suzanne called it *The Liberation Manifesto.*

She had baked a chocolate cake, Garrick's favorite. They'd eaten the cake and drank champagne. And they had laughed together at the farcical tract.

"You wrote this, honey?" Garrick said.

"You like it?"

"It's freaking awesome. Damn, you nailed it. Who knew Ayn Rand could be so funny?"

"You may refer to me as Mark Twain, Jr., honey. I surprised even myself. Let's think of it as a reminder. A little oasis as we create our future. We'll live with intention. Live life to the fullest. But let's never take ourselves too seriously."

Garrick raised his flute. "To us, darling. To our lovely little oasis and what it stands for. To our future together." He kissed her. "I think we should publish it," he said, tipping back the rest of his champagne. "Keep the joke alive and see what happens. What do you think?"

"It's yours. Do what you want," she'd said, disappointed that Garrick would even consider such a thing.

From there her little brown book took on a life of its own. Garrick self-published just one hundred copies originally. He managed to get *The Manifesto* into the bookstores of most of the colleges and universities in the Boston-Cambridge area, including MIT and Harvard. It flew off the shelves. Garrick showed the book to his old friend, William Henry Wharton, whose father was an investment banker in New York.

"Garrick, this is absolutely brilliant. You wrote this?" William said.

"Well, Suzy . . ."

William interrupted. "Garrick. Look, my father would love this. He knows a few people. His Wall Street buddies get hard on this libertarian shit. I'll show it to him if you want."

"Wait, Billy. Does it strike you as funny?"

"Funny? How?"

"Never mind. Do what you want with it," Garrick had said. He'd neglected to tell Billy that Suzanne was the author of the book, nor that she wrote it as a prank.

William's father did know people, including the CEO of a small publisher of conservatively minded economics and philosophy texts out of Chicago. In fact William Wharton and the publisher were undergraduates together at Harvard College and were part of a closely knit group of college kids in the fifties who were enamored with Ayn Rand's novels.

By the early 1990s, *The Manifesto* had taken off. In today's world one would say the five-dollar pamphlet went viral, particularly on college campuses. Billy had been living in So-Ho, and he caught a train to Cambridge every weekend. Garrick and Billy were the core, while Suzanne helped out when she felt like it. They brainstormed at coffee houses and pubs over how to manage *The Manifesto* and the fire in the jar it had ignited.

In private Suzanne had implored Garrick to leave it alone. They'd taken a youthful joy-ride, and they'd had a blast. But it was time to move on and drop the illusion that *The Manifesto* could be anything more than a private joke, a loving birthday present, that she'd put together with spit and glue. She wrote the thing on a lark, and it represented nothing more than a young woman's affection for the man she would marry. As satire, *The Manifesto* had been her unstated plea to Garrick to stay grounded and balanced. "You're a scientist, Garrick. Don't allow your affection for Ayn Rand's fiction to blind you to just that: it's fiction, stupid," she told him.

One Sunday evening after Billy had left for Manhattan, Garrick and Suzanne were hanging out on the sofa of their apartment.

"Garrick, you haven't really bought into this crap, have you?"

"I know. It's silly. But a ton of folks obviously do. Why not take advantage of that?"

"Garrick, we know the truth. It's pure bullshit. It's not us. Okay, some idiots fawn over it. It's a game. People are so shocked they love it. Like watching a train wreck. It's a fad, babe. We're scientists and we have good careers ahead of us. I never intended that silly thing to go this far. I *am* the author, remember?"

"I haven't told you the best part," Garrick said.

"Huh?"

"Billy's father wants to form an investment group and launch a new organization. Sort of a think tank to do marketing and public relations for their beliefs, and we—you, me, and Billy—would be in charge. *The Liberation Manifesto* would be the ideological inspiration of the organization."

"Beliefs in what, exactly?"

"Capitalism and freedom. An organization founded on the belief that America is destined to be a nation run by capitalists, for capitalists. An organization that will make every effort to ensure capitalism survives forever and conquers socialism for good. Freedom is our mantra. We repeat it and repeat it forever, constantly, unforgivingly."

"Do they have a name for this magical enterprise?" Suzanne asked.

"The Freedom Society. A buddy of Billy's dad liked the name. Some rich whiskey guy from Kentucky. He's politically connected. The investors demand that they'll be completely anonymous. The Society's existence will be opaque. In addition to the Freedom Society's investments, we'll rely on sales of *The Manifesto* for revenue and to spread the message of freedom and capitalism globally."

"That's it? A cheerleader for global capitalism?" Suzanne said.

"Well, the investors expect more than propaganda. They're action-oriented. Our real task is to penetrate, creep, and undermine any organizations and institutions that stand to block our progress toward eliminating government and replacing it with a system of stateless capitalism. Basically like you laid it out in *The Manifesto*."

Garrick's enthusiasm at this crazy venture stunned Suzanne. "Just how much are these rich guys investing?" she said.

"The investors have promised fifty million to start. That's nothing for these people, Suzy. Once we launch and prove our effectiveness, the sky's the limit. Are you ready to be rich, babe?"

"Fuck." Suzanne took a moment to absorb the information. "Why haven't you told me all this before now? It's crazy talk, babe."

"Don't worry about it. Let's take the silly ride and see where it goes. I love you no matter what. If this goes down in flames, as I'm sure it will, we've got each other and the rest of our lives to be a normal, well-adjusted academic couple. You trust me, don't you, Suzy?"

He asked that question frequently. This time Suzanne didn't answer him directly. She scooched over to his side and kissed him gently on the lips, neither approving nor disapproving of what her lover was preaching.

Looking back, she kicked herself for not telling Garrick, in no uncertain terms, to choose: *The Manifesto* or her. She saw no future in the sophomoric game she'd been playing with Garrick. And yet she had let the game go on. Why? Because she was afraid of losing him? His relentlessness was like a magnet, against which she struggled to distance herself. His nascent drive for raw, almost sexual, power consumed him— and continued to alienate her. The big lie. Her farcical gift that became his infamous manifesto. Her own goddamned thoughts and words.

The investors wanted more than words. They always wanted more.

On the day Suzanne defended her dissertation at MIT in 1993, Garrick took her out for a lavish dinner at one of Boston's best seafood restaurants.

Garrick bent over the white tablecloth in the intimate corner of the restaurant and kissed her. "You look happy, Suzy. Congratulations, darling."

"I am happy. I'll take a few weeks then start my job search in earnest. Did I tell you Tufts is interested? The computer science chairman called me the other day."

"To your new career," Garrick said, hoisting his champagne glass. "I have another idea for you to consider. No teaching required."

"What idea?" she'd asked.

"How would you like to work for the Pentagon."

~

Suzanne cussed at herself. Her life's decisions that had brought her to this place, right now, watching Jonas returning to the back yard. He fingered the half-empty bottle of Caymus and refilled both glasses. She'd lost an epic battle of love and commitment to Garrick's narcissism. He'd succeeded in his quest while she languished in uncertainty and bitterness, schlepping in the gutter of the great American life she had dreamed of. She suppressed the urge to go volcanic with the young scientist sitting next to her. She quelled her lust for revenge for the sake of momentary efficiency. But just as Garrick had relentlessly built *The Manifesto* into an angry revolutionary movement, she would blissfully destroy it with equal intensity.

She put on a pleasant smile for Jonas. "I was with Garrick when he wrote it. I was his editor," she lied.

"Oh, *The Manifesto*? Garrick never mentioned that you had a role in his book," Jonas said.

"I suppose he wouldn't have. Garrick's the genius behind the movement. William is the operations guy. He gets things done. He knows powerful people who quietly contribute to our cause. People like you. Young men like you. We appreciate you for the important work you do."

"Thank you for saying that," Jonas said.

"Now, listen. Speaking of capitalism and crime, we need to talk about the cyber bot. Do you understand the big picture here?" Suzanne asked.

"I'm not sure what you mean."

"Let me map it out for you. You'll recall that I work for the Pentagon acquiring certain technologies for top-secret weapons systems. My main job is to identify promising AI applications for cyber warfare. Several brilliant researchers are under contract with the Pentagon to create cyber bots. Garrick has no association with the military, but he's benefiting from research by other scientists—you included. Some of these are defensive weapons designed to counter cyberattacks from

112

nation states, foreign intelligence agencies, or even rogue hackers. Garrick's is an offensive weapon. I have passed on many of the most creative techniques to Garrick. When you applied to my outfit for funding, my budget wasn't able to accommodate you. But I did give Garrick your name, which is why he hired you for his project. I hope Garrick explained all this to you."

"Are you saying that you've been spying on the government for Garrick?" Jonas said.

"Espionage is a strong word, Jonas. But if we fail we all spend the rest of our lives in federal prison, including you. What's wrong? You look shell-shocked."

"Garrick told me I'd be part of a team working under contract for the Pentagon. It all seemed legit, on the up and up."

"Guess he lied. Sorry about that. Maybe you should have asked more questions. Did Garrick also neglect to say you'd be responsible for launching the bot against our target network?"

"Suzanne, I'm no hacker. I'm an associate professor of computer science at Stanford University."

"How exactly are you helping Garrick?"

"I'm not sure what you're asking."

"Who authored the algorithm, you or him?"

"Neither. Actually, I'm not sure."

"Don't fuck with me, Jonas. Why is he paying you?"

"I had one job. Keep the algorithm secure and updated for future deployment. He told me, 'Don't fuck it up. It's a work of genius.'"

"Then who coded the original?"

Jonas fiddled with the wicker and avoided Suzanne's eyes. "I figured it was Garrick. But I never asked," he said.

"So you don't know who really authored it?"

Again, Jonas looked away. He forced a laugh. "Guess not. Garrick's got it covered. No worries."

"Oh?" Suzanne said, leaving the moment of silence to blossom into awkwardness.

After a moment Jonas raised his voice and sat erect in the wicker. "And Garrick is absolutely correct not to be worried. The thing is elegant, sharp, and deadly. I've scrutinized that code from top to bottom. It's a military-grade network killer. When we launch, that bot will melt computer networks like a nuclear explosion. The damned bot is scary."

"Oh?"

"Absolutely. I'm not sure Garrick understands just how terrifying it is. But rest assured, Suzanne. No reason to worry."

"That's it?"

"Correct. But I have a question. What's the target?"

"Garrick didn't tell you?"

"I'm clueless."

"Why do you need to know?"

"Well, knowing the full scenario would help me configure the bot and establish the method for launching it."

Suzanne reached to grab the bottle of Caymus, then realized it was empty. She looked at Jonas directly. "I'll explain the objective to you. But I need to be reassured you're absolutely certain you'll take this risk. Our movement will eventually take control of the Department of Justice, among the several functions of government we'll eliminate or privatize. A pardon is possible. Even then I personally can't guarantee that outcome. We do have an ace in the hole in your favor, though."

"What do you mean?"

"When we eliminate most government functions, the president of the United States will be unnecessary, correct?"

114

"I suppose so."

"However, the American people need an individual to play the role of president. A titular leader, like the monarchs we see in Britain and even in your homeland, Denmark. An Executive Committee of our combined corporations, all members of the Society, will appoint the president of the United States, who'll manage former government assets. We'll ensure that the Executive Committee will pardon you of any crimes. How does that sound?"

"I believe in the movement, Suzanne." Jonas set down his glass of Caymus. "I'd like to get to know you people better. I like Garrick. But you, Suzanne—you're a blank slate to me."

"Look, Jonas. I'm not here to be your friend. What you do with Garrick is your business."

"No problem. You can count me in, Suzanne. No worries. But you still haven't specified what you want, exactly."

"We need duplicates of the algorithm to be launched from several workstations at a government-run facility."

"Oh? What facility would that be?"

"You're kind of an idiot, aren't you, Jonas? Let me explain something. You'll know what you need to know. No more, no less. Understood?"

"Yes, I get it. Sorry."

"I'll put you in touch with a man called Johnny Petit. He'll take it from there."

"How many duplicates will you require?" Jonas asked.

"Ten to fifteen workstations, all running the latest version of Windows."

"That's not a problem."

"Are you going to tell Garrick about our conversation?" Suzanne said.

"I assume so. Why not?"

"Better that you didn't. Don't get into details. Just tell him you've been in contact with William about launching the bot and that it's all settled. I know Garrick. He hates logistics."

"William told me I'd be well-compensated for my efforts—in addition to what Garrick pays me monthly."

"How much did William promise?"

"Am I supposed to keep that private?"

"Jonas, you report to me now, okay? What did William tell you?"

"He offered a quarter million when I completed my end."

"Did he define complete?"

"No, he said I should talk to you about that. Which we've just done, right?"

"Correct. I will verify."

"Verify what?"

"That you've successfully launched the cyber weapon. What else?"

"Right, okay."

"Our arrangement includes your permanent loyalty. That means you leave no trace of my involvement. The same goes for William. You work for nobody except us, exclusively. And it means you won't talk to law enforcement, ever. You even wink at Google or the FBI and all bets are off. Your value goes to zero, and you know what *The Manifesto* says about humans having no value, right, Jonas?"

Jonas turned nearly as white as his shorts and shoes.

"Relax, Jonas, I'm kidding. We mustn't take *The Manifesto* too literally, right?" She rose from the wicker, and Jonas followed. "All that said, it's been a pleasure, Jonas."

Suzanne showed him out, but on the way to the front door she stopped and pulled an unopened bottle of the Caymus from a pantry devoted to her obligatory supply of fine wines.

She handed Jonas the bottle and reached up to kiss him lightly on the cheek. "Here's a token of our appreciation. Enjoy it in good health, my handsome young script kiddie."

~

Suzanne took a cold shower to rinse off the unpleasantness of the encounter. She had played Jonas to her advantage, but she was still groping for a way to protect herself and exact some reward from the movement that she had authored—even if she had intended it as a joke. She cringed at her own hypocrisy.

No amount of cold water could wash away the sick feeling in her gut. As the Pentagon's chief curator of cyber warfare technology, she could guess better than anyone who actually coded the attack bot in Garrick's possession. That realization came as no surprise. Garrick had obtained a copy of Laura Cavendish's algorithm. But how? Suzanne had always known that Garrick salivated over Laura's project, and Suzanne had tried to protect her from his prying eyes and sinister motives. Had Garrick hacked Laura's computer? Had Jonas Peterson done Garrick's dirty work and was now play-acting as Garrick's eager but not-so-bright assistant?

That mattered little now. The scheme was about to go live. If Laura, with Carson McCready's help, couldn't figure out a way to stop the very attack bot that she'd invented, then Garrick Cripps and his band of billionaires would rule a rudderless nation, and Suzanne Dreyfus would be forever remembered as the spy who helped him do it.

13

OVERKILL IS GOOD

"Okay, what've you got for me, Treadwell?" Darryl Cunningham barked at Jason without looking up from what he was reading.

"I spoke to Richard Heller and a guy named Johnny Petit. They showed me around. I saw the telemarketing operation up close."

"Okay, spare me the details. Do we need to worry about this shit?"

"I don't know. The evidence is inconclusive. It's a weird scene."

"Treadwell, is this a terrorist cell?"

"I told you, Darryl. The evidence is sketchy."

"Let me put it another way. What makes you think it *could* be a terrorist cell?"

"Well, Darryl, they're set up to do big trades on a lot of stuff. Moving product like you've never seen. They have the capability of buying and selling sophisticated electronic equipment and more. Hell, they could be selling this stuff to terrorists and not even know it."

"Who's in charge?"

"A civilian named Carson McCready. Ex-Navy. Low on the totem pole. He cut a deal with the prison bosses to raise cash for charity."

"What's charity got to do with the jail?"

"I know, right? I don't know what's in it for Carson, but it was all his idea. The higher-ups are taking all the credit, and it seems Carson's glad to let them have it."

"What about that Malcolm X guy? The one who has ties to Muslims."

"Terrell Williams? I didn't pick up any intel on him, except that Carson seems to trust him."

"Okay, we have felons buying and selling sophisticated electronic equipment to terrorists. We have a known Muslim associate as an important leader in the local cell. And this Carson guy is clearly doing charity work as a cover for the cell. That pretty well sums it up, right, Treadwell?"

"That's your call, not mine."

"Fucking hell, Treadwell. That's my conclusion based on your superb undercover work. With the help of our colleagues over at Big Brother, we've gotten inside a deadly terrorist cell, okay? Time is of the essence."

"Still, Darryl. What if we're wrong? Arresting them could embarrass the Bureau."

"Overkill is good. If we are wrong, well, we've done our jobs protecting American citizens."

"If you think so."

"Okay, write up your report, including all the critical information. The Islamic connections, the charity work as a cover for the cell, and that blue book. The Muslim bible. Did you leave the book?"

Jason smiled. "Dammit. I forgot it on Carson's desk."

"That's what I like to hear. This all adds up to a major threat, Treadwell. And use pictures. You took a lot of photos, right? Use them to document the case. Another thing. I told you not to leave a paper trail. But now you'll need some investigative notes to include in your threat assessment. Write up some notes, okay? Notes that support the conclusions of your report.

"Do that and we're good. I'd write you up otherwise. You know that, right? As you draft the threat assessment, think about surveillance and forming a SWAT team for the bust. We'll come down hard. I want a show of force."

"When and where, sir?"

"They *are* in jail, right?"

"Guess they aren't going anywhere," Jason said.

"Don't fuck this up, Treadwell. You're heading for a big promotion after this bust. Remember that."

~

After work, Cunningham got on the 5 South and beelined his way to an old haunt, a British pub on India Street between downtown and his office in Sorrento Valley. He was there to meet nobody. No meetings. No hushed conversations about momentous initiatives involving the Department of Defense and the FBI. No Suzanne Dreyfus around to bust his balls and his debt and his hypocrisy over his political beliefs. He was there for an ice-cold British Ale. He was there to think.

He'd avoided thinking about the deal he'd made with Suzanne and her allies, except to dream about the big money she had offered him. Privately he cringed at the crap he was laying on Jason. Kid didn't deserve it but a deal was a deal, and Darryl was a felon waiting to happen if he didn't pull this off

120

without a glitch. The guilty feeling was hard to ignore. He'd been a straight cop, a reliable and generous father, a good son to his parents back in Indiana. The scheme he'd gotten into was so out of character. Wasn't it? When large amounts of money and prestige are dangled before a guy, his real character is revealed. Despite his sterling self-image as the hard-core FBI agent, Darryl Cunningham was really just another schmuck. Another greedy bastard, no different from Cripps and that ugly Eurynomos guy whose real name was William. What the hell was that about? Was this all just a joke? Had his former fraternity brothers set him up for the grandest practical joke of all time?

By all rights he ought to turn the tables, haul the whole lot in for questioning, and charge those mothers with a conspiracy to overthrow the US government. But he couldn't, trapped by his own fucked-up experimentation with the "patriot agent" handle on sketchy underground chat rooms. He could plausibly claim the effort was job-related, that he had been doing research on domestic threats, just as a good counterterrorism agent should. But undercover work wasn't his assignment. His voyeurism wasn't by the book, and Suzanne knew it. She had him by the balls, ensuring his seemingly boundless cooperation.

14

PILLBOX

Upon Sam's news that Laura was back in town, Carson wasted little time in trying to locate her. He hadn't spoken to Laura's mother, Hilda, in many years, so the elderly woman's memory lapse didn't surprise him.

"Carson? Do I know you?"

"Hilda, it's me. From Torrey Pines High. Laura's old boyfriend?"

"Carson McCready? Is that really you? You sound so old, dear."

"Yeah, it's me."

"Where are you? How are you?"

"I'm great, Hilda. Listen, I don't know Laura's number, and I'd like to reach out to her, if that's okay."

"Honest to Pete, son. Of course you do. Let me find it."

Hilda returned with the number, and they said their goodbyes until next time which, hopefully, would be soon. That evening Carson wrote a simple, if mysterious, text that said, *Meet me at the Pillbox. Sat. Around noon.*

Carson got a return text that read: *Who's this?*

He didn't reply.

~

The next morning, Carson's brain cells lit up like a Christmas tree when he remembered his plan for the day. He toasted some bread, fried an egg, and combined the two for his version of a nourishing breakfast. He placed the dirty dishes in the sink, grabbed Diego's leash, and followed the dog's hard pull downstairs to the parking lot.

Before long the unwashed BMW carried Carson and Diego going ninety on the 8 West. He wasn't wasting any time because he wanted to be at the Pillbox in Solana Beach to catch Laura by surprise before her Saturday morning run, a habit she'd followed for as long as Carson could remember.

Carson was at the Pillbox by eight a.m. He turned the corner and walked through the park, which was already full of a Saturday crowd of families and children playing on swings and slides. He moved past the crowd and found the grassy bluff overseeing the beach. He sat down next to Diego on the grass and closed his eyes, listening to the sounds of Saturday, the beach, and the surf.

Carson melted into the grass and drifted off for several minutes. He woke up to Diego pulling on the leash and letting out a sharp bark, demanding Carson's attention. Carson opened his eyes as Diego pulled him toward a woman sitting in front of him on the grass. She appeared to be concentrating on her phone. Still waking from the nap, he momentarily forgot what he was doing there.

He looked at her back, recognizing her wild, sandy blond hair down to her shoulders like a surfer. Diego barked again. Carson hesitated, holding on to the dog who kept tugging him, and then Carson understood. He reached over to tap Laura on her shoulder.

"Hey, you."

Laura felt the touch, irritated that someone was interrupting her. She turned around and saw the dog leap toward her.

"Diego, I think that's your new girlfriend."

"Oh my god, Carson? What are you doing in Solana Beach?"

"Checking out the old neighborhood. Thought I'd bring Diego, and here you are."

"Was that you texting me last night? I figured you were someone else."

Carson stood and scanned the beach and the ocean. He breathed deeply, his chest expanding with each precious breath.

"Where are you living?" she asked.

He turned toward Laura and sat down on the bluff. Her smell. Laura's smell, with hints of the same sweetness of the cool breeze and blue ocean. "Lemon Grove. Getting used to it." He paused. "How long have you been back?"

Laura hesitated. "I'm sorry. I've been meaning to contact you. I'm at the university now."

"I didn't know."

"I've been incredibly busy."

Carson smiled. "I can't believe it's you. I remember the day you left for MIT. Broke my heart. But you knew that."

"Let's not go there, Carson."

"Just messing with you. I got married. Did you ever meet Kathryn?"

"I heard."

"Fucked that up. Long story."

Carson felt awkward. How to talk to a woman he knew

124

so well thirty years ago? Their lives had separated in full, and yet, he had always felt this day would come. Now that it had, he didn't know what to say.

"How's your kid?" Laura said.

"Michael is fifteen. He lives with Kathryn in Flagstaff."

"That's nice. Or maybe not."

"I'd like to see him more. Busy kid."

Laura got up off the grass. "I should get going. I need to be somewhere later," she said.

"No problem. I should have told you it was me in the text. I wanted to surprise you."

"It feels like you just dropped from the sky," she said.

"I know. I'm sorry."

Laura started to leave, and Carson wondered if it was the last time he'd ever see her. Diego sprang up to follow her. Laura leaned down to give Diego an extra scratch. "Such a sweet dog, Carson. You're very good to him, aren't you?"

Diego waited for Carson to speak to the other human or lead him to some new adventure.

"He's good to me."

As an old warrior, Carson thought he had a good sense for what might happen from one intense moment to another. He froze at the half-light of the proverbial Future and its grand plans. But Diego didn't care about fate. The Lab lived in the moment. Most naturally, the dog sought balance for the human soul he loved.

Upon prompting Laura to confront the still-point between her and Carson, the yellow Lab had already changed the future.

She stood to look Carson squarely in the eye. "Say, Carson?"

"Yes, Laura?"

"What are you doing Monday evening?"

"It's a holiday. I've got a day off. Playing golf at Torrey around one. Why?"

"Perfect. Torrey Pines Lodge. Six p.m. Does that work for you?"

"Shouldn't be a problem."

"Good. Let's do it. But Carson?"

"Yeah?"

"Try to change out of your golf clothes this time, okay?"

"Old habits, Laura. For you, though, I'll do my best."

15

TO OLD FRIENDS

After his golf game Carson ran up the hill to the lodge, toting his clubs on his back. He recognized the kid in the green kilt and handed him a five as the kid placed Carson's sticks in the luggage closet. "Enjoy your evening, sir," the kid said, opening the grand door to the lodge.

Carson looked around the bar, painted a golden hue by the diminishing sunlight coming through the ocean-facing window. The bar was not large. Carson surmised Laura had yet to arrive. Sam slapped the Spaten on the bar.

"I'll be outside, Sam. In case some pretty blonde comes in looking for me."

Sam let out a big laugh. "Go change, buddy. And at least comb your hair." Carson touched his visor and the hair sticking up. He laughed, then remembered his promise to change out of his golf clothes. Oh well. He was too late.

He took his beer outside and kicked back on the narrow deck overlooking the hotel pool. The last vestiges of the sun warmed his face. The after-round beer was ice-cold and perfect. After fifteen minutes, Carson believed Laura had snubbed him. He was about to grab another beer. If she hadn't arrived by the time he finished, he'd get the hell out of La Jolla and get his ass back to Lemon Grove.

It was then he heard a woman's voice behind him. "Sir, Sam said you could use another Spaten." Carson didn't turn around. He focused on a hang glider hovering over the ocean. He imagined himself in the cockpit, enjoying the freedom of the sky breeze.

Carson watched her hands as she set another cold bottle on the table.

"Don't recognize me in a dress?"

He turned around and saw Laura taking a sip of wine, her striking green eyes looking directly at him over the glass's rim. Her tanned skin glowed in the warm light.

"Wow, it's you."

"Come sit on the sofa under the heat lamp. It's pretty comfy."

Carson sat down, a reasonably friendly distance from his old flame. "I didn't know it was you. Lost in thought. Nice dress, by the way."

"Oh, thanks."

"You look fantastic."

"That's sweet, Carson. How's your beer?"

"Nothing on draft here. But I'll drink this."

"You really outdid yourself with the golf outfit, buddy. Play today?"

"My apologies. Couldn't be helped. Slow as hell today and didn't have time to change. Forgive me?"

"I suppose I can let it pass. Just this once. Who'd you play with?"

"A retired pop singer from Florida, a twenty-something software developer at Google—oh, and the CEO of a plastic

128

pipe maker in Minnesota. He's in town for the annual meeting of plastic pipe manufacturers. They were a hoot, actually. The hacks come to town wanting to play the tips and then . . . well, you know what happens."

The server interrupted. "Hey, you two. Get you another round?"

"I'm good for now. The lady will have . . . ?"

"Might as well bring another Pinot Noir, thanks."

The server returned with the drink.

"Aren't you two a fun-looking couple this evening?" She touched Laura's shoulder. "I love that dress, by the way. Enjoy!"

"I think she likes you, Laura."

"Oh, yeah?"

He raised his beer into the air. "To a fun-looking couple." Carson caught himself involuntarily noticing the lovely necklace resting on Laura's tanned skin, where the top of her breasts met the olive dress.

"How's Diego?"

"He's great. What about you? Any pets?"

"I have a cat. He's my buddy."

"A cool cat, most likely."

"You were always the cool guy, Carson."

"Which is why you ended up at MIT and I didn't?"

"Carson, don't put yourself down. You led SEAL missions to God knows where. I was the overachiever. But you always dusted me in science and math. I know that. I never understood why you never pursued that."

"You worked harder than me."

"No argument there. I worked my butt off. I think it was worth it."

They went inside and sat on the leather sofa facing the stone fireplace of the intimate bar.

"I love this place, Carson. I don't get here much."

"Another glass of wine?" Carson asked.

"I'm in the mood for whiskey."

"A fine idea."

Carson got up and returned with two drinks. He took Laura in as he sat down slowly next to her. The attraction remained. But her life was a blank slate. Who had Laura become? A scientist, but what about her life? He assumed she had never married. No kids. A cat. A boyfriend, perhaps? The guy Sam had seen her with at the bar? Now in their late forties, he felt like they were meeting for the first time. This wasn't high school anymore and yet, oddly, he wanted to be eighteen again.

"There is something I want to ask you about. Sorry, it's about bots, again," he said.

"Ask away."

He told Laura about the unexplained probes of the prison's computer systems. But as he brought it up, he already regretted doing so. Why did he need an excuse to contact the woman he had once wanted to marry? For that he needed no justification, so why confuse his feelings with a computer glitch he was reluctant to even care about?

Carson treaded carefully. "I've got this job, right? I'm managing a telemarketing gig at the county prison. A pilot program. Why they picked me, I do not know. Anyway my boss tells me his tech people are detecting a cyberthreat. They suspect someone is probing the prison's computers for weaknesses, as a prelude to some type of hack. Oddly, these probes started about the time I took the job. Is this something I should worry about?"

As he stated these facts, which he sensed to be pertinent, Carson felt that he'd left his masculine passions at the front

130

door and was overindulging in the nice guy, ex-boyfriend routine. He wanted to ditch the talk and make out. He couldn't take his eyes off her. Laura was older, but better. So much better that he could hardly hold himself back from reaching in to kiss her. The sophisticated beauty sitting close to him had replaced the pretty yet shy high-schooler he'd known so long ago.

So much for fantasy. Get a grip, he told himself. Be the damned adult he knew how to be so well. So well, in fact, that he had become weary of being the only adult in the room as a platoon leader with life or death on the line.

Laura did not divulge any emotions of her own and seemed unbothered by the information about the probes. "When did your boss tell you this?"

"Not long after I started the job. Why?"

"Have your computers slowed or been erratic?"

"Not that I can tell."

"Then let it go. Don't give it a second thought. Stay clear and let the tech people handle it. That's my two cents. But I wonder who would want to hack the county jail?"

Laura, being Laura, was asking the right question—one that Carson, uncharacteristically, hadn't attempted to answer himself. It was a damned good question. The probes were worth paying serious attention to, despite his urge to let all his worries go and just be with her again.

"You're right. Probably nothing. Thought I'd run it by you, just out of curiosity."

"I'll keep my ears open for any chatter, if that helps," Laura said.

Carson changed the subject. "I ran into Sam the other day. Says you were with a guy. Your boyfriend?"

"He works with me in my lab on the bot project. We

131

met a few years ago. We're dating, occasionally. Nothing too serious yet."

"Yet?"

"We'll see what happens when we both have more free time, after we submit the final product to my Pentagon masters."

He'd never known Laura with any other man except for him. It made sense she'd be seeing someone. The news settled in his gut, dampening any notion that he wanted to rekindle a romance. They could just chat, he told himself. Get to know each other again. Just old friends.

"I get that. Life happens. How was MIT, by the way?"

"That was several years ago—you know that, right?"

"How were your professors?" he asked.

"Mostly excellent."

"I would hope so, place like MIT."

"Yep."

"That's it? You had nice professors?"

Laura laughed. "There was one professor. I thought of him as my mentor at one time. But he was interested in more than mentoring."

"I'm not surprised."

"Anyway, he took an interest in me. Helped me a lot, for which I'm grateful. There was something sort of creepy about him, though. I can laugh about it now."

"Why do you seem to attract creepy old guys? Remember Mr. Young?"

"Our high school physics teacher?"

"He was taken with you, as I recall."

"No way! I don't remember that."

"You're too innocent, Laura. Or too focused. Probably why you didn't notice. But I did."

Laura grabbed her glass of whiskey and took a long sip.

Carson regretted bringing up her old innocence. Genuine, truthful, honest—Laura had always been those things. Innocent, however, no longer fitted. Worldly, confident, highly educated, accomplished. That was Laura Cavendish. And who was he? An old warrior who worked at the county jail. He felt the same old insecurities comparing himself to the woman who had left him for bigger and better things.

Carson hated the feeling. Around her, he was still vulnerable. As a SEAL being geographically and psychologically distant from her had cured him of his comparative deficiencies, his self-inflicted rationale of not deserving her. Part of him wanted to get up and leave. Get back to his hardened sense of invulnerability. He had become comfortable being a hard-ass in the military. That's the man he'd become. Feelings were so much extra baggage. Dragged you down. Made you slow. Made you vulnerable. Got you killed.

"This professor of yours. What was creepy about him?" he said.

"Let's talk about something else, Carson."

"Sorry I mentioned it."

"So what happened to you and Kathryn?"

"I can't believe you just asked me that."

"Oh, shit. Sorry I asked."

Carson raised his glass. "Here's to talking about nothing because everything is off the table."

"That's funny."

"Is that it, then? Part ways now and keep our years of accumulated shit to ourselves?"

"We know each other too well to be that sensitive, or that cynical," Laura said.

"That's the problem with getting older."

They each took awkward sips from their drinks and

said nothing.

Laura went first. She smiled. "Chill, Carson. Just relax. I can tell you're wound pretty tight."

"You can, huh?"

"I know you. It's been a long time, but I still know you, Carson McCready."

"Maybe you're right. I'm sorry. Old habits. I'm trying to be a regular guy again. Not that easy." Carson looked around the bar and the understated elegance of the surroundings. "I'm not used to places like this anymore. Being around all these nice-looking people like this. People like you. You've outrun me in the game of life, darling."

"Dammit, Carson, stop saying that. I'm still Laura. I may look like something new that you're seeing in your mind's eye, but it's not real. What happened to you? This self-pity act isn't you. It's not the Carson McCready I know. Just stop, okay?"

"You're right. It's not me."

A moment passed.

"Can I confess something?" he said.

"Of course."

"I'm struggling with normality. A square peg fitting into a well-rounded civilian life. Who am I now? The man I became as a SEAL, everything I've accomplished, became irrelevant overnight. Like the man I fought so hard to become suddenly doesn't matter. Like I'm used up goods that are no help to anybody. I fear that nobody needs me anymore. Nobody but Diego. He needs me. He keeps me going. My new job too, maybe. I'm trying there. Really trying to make it work."

Laura placed her hand over Carson's where it rested on the table. He could feel her warmth. Her honesty. This woman, though older and more sophisticated than she was thirty years ago, was the same Laura after all.

"If you ever want to talk, I'd like to listen, Carson. Don't hold back, okay?"

"I'd like that. I've never talked about much with anybody, actually. That would be nice."

"But now, I want to know more about Kathryn. And I want to hear more about that kid of yours. What's his name again?"

"Michael. Michael McCready."

"Sounds like a cool kid, McCready. Has to be. He's got you for a dad."

16

REGULAR GUY

The following evening Carson drove west on the 8 to El Cajon Boulevard toward San Diego State, where there were several dives and college bars. He found a dicey-looking tavern. The bar was darkly quiet and devoid of movement. Mostly biker types and laborers drinking in slow motion. Carson could tell he had been noticed. Most were hard drinkers with weathered faces, shit-kicker boots, and bad smoking habits. He took a stool at the bar and ordered a strong IPA. He gulped it in half, mindlessly watching a humdrum college basketball game on TV.

He had come to have a drink. He had come to relax. To try to be a regular guy who drank beer and talked to other regular guys about Aztec basketball and the Chargers. The contrast between military and civilian life underscored that he'd become a misfit around other civilians. Even after SEAL life, he scrutinized his environment from every angle.

He thought about Laura. What had happened between her and her professor that made her so uncomfortable? Was he reading too much into it?

If he hadn't been a platoon leader, he probably wouldn't care. He'd smile and let it go as an entertaining story, like regular people do. He wanted to forget his SEAL training. No need to be situationally aware at all times. No need to recall the arcane science of psychological operations to assess the expected behaviors of an enemy commander. And yet he clung to his skills. Skills that had served him well in battle.

But this was not war. The past was past. Life was more assured now that he was a regular guy. His battles were over. No worries, except for that phony senator from Kentucky trying to make a name for himself as the uber-patriot soon to be a candidate for president of the United States. Otherwise, life for a retired military guy on a predictable pension was simple. Survival was easy, and death a long way off. Lots of Torrey Pines golf left. Many beautiful days at the beach to play ball with Diego and then grab a Negra Modelo and a Mexican lunch across the street. That was freedom. Taking up hang gliding. Having a simple life with no bloodshed. That was all the freedom Carson needed.

He ordered his second IPA and stared at the flashing blue and red lights behind the bar. Nothing interesting here. Way too slow. But hang here long enough and things would descend into trouble. Trouble with one of the shit-kicking boots. He paid for the IPA and then noticed the bartender. Looked at her in the dim light. She looked different, but she was familiar. The petite blonde who sometimes worked the counter at his favorite donut shop in Lemon Grove.

"Becky? Is that you?"

"Hey, Carson. No maple bars and mega-coffee here, mister."

"How long have you worked here?"

"I've been part-time here since I was a freshman at State.

137

I graduate in June, and I'll probably stay here for a while. Easy money."

"Then why the donut shop?"

"Family business. I help."

"Family owns this place too?"

"Funny that you should ask. Dad owned it for years and his dad before that. A guy bought us out. Dude offered my dad a bunch of cash. Apparently he's very wealthy and owns a lot of dive bars. The sketchier the better."

"I've always wanted to own a bar. Something just like this. Feel at home in places like this."

"Can't say you fit in that well, Carson. No nice guys here. Donut shop's more your style."

"I'm almost offended."

"Don't be. I think you're a nice guy."

"Lost my innocence long ago."

He downed the IPA, left Becky a ten, and slipped out the door, feeling the eyes of the hard guys watching him leave. The door chimes rang as Carson pushed open the door, and he heard a familiar voice.

"Hey, Chief, what's up?"

Carson turned around. "Biff? What the hell. You look glued to that barstool."

"Just walked in. Didn't want to interrupt your convo with Becky," Biff said, winking.

"Live around here?"

"Just down the road. What the hell are you doing here?"

Carson took a barstool next to Biff Dickson, still stocky with a Navy crewcut and his toothy smile. Carson's second in command on his former SEAL platoon. They talked for more than an hour, laughing and reminiscing about their Navy days. Biff had retired and was coaching a semi-pro football team.

"No shit? Who do you guys play?"

"Hell, Chief, almost every town has a club. We play guys from all over Southern Cal. We beat San Bernardino last Saturday. Traveling to Torrance next weekend. We'll do a charity game here and there."

"These are adults? Where do you find guys who'll do that shit to their bodies?"

"Former college players. Guys who stopped playing in high school and still think they've got a path to the NFL. It's all a bunch of fun, regardless. Guys bring their wives, kids. Why, you interested?" Biff said.

"Not a chance. You any good?"

"You mean my team? Hell, yeah. We practice twice a week after work during the season. The guys use football to stay in shape and have fun. You'd be surprised, Chief."

"Hmm. I've got an idea. Just hear me out, okay?"

~

Carson got home at midnight. He took Diego for a quick walk, got ready for bed, and turned out the light. He lay in bed for ten minutes, nearly falling asleep, until his phone lit up with a new message. Carson wanted to ignore it, but he couldn't. He grabbed the phone, not recognizing the number. Then he opened the lengthy message and read it in the dark.

The message contained headlines and quotes from archived stories in the *Navy Times* about the tragedy in Somalia. Davis Glover, one of his men in the platoon, went berserk on a civilian, knifing him in the eyes and almost severing the man's head with several dozen jabs to his neck.

Carson read to the bottom of the text message.

Is this who you are, Carson McCready? You call this leadership?

139

If you work for Graybill, you can go fuck yourself, he wrote back.

No immediate reply. He tried to go back to sleep. His phone lit up again after fifteen minutes.

Stay tuned, the message said.

Carson flipped the phone onto the end table, feeling disgusted. Would the nightmare of Africa never end? Why wouldn't those bastards just leave him alone?

17

SLINGING JELLY BEANS

The telemarketing crew had half a container of cheap cutlery to sell. Steak knives and forks moved sluggishly until Carson ordered a fifty percent price cut. The cutlery was gone by four p.m.

Carson led the post-sales meeting with his team, summing up the day's gains and losses. The meeting was casual, friendly. White Terrell chatted with Juan. Black Terrell spoke in a low voice to a Mexican inmate. What started out as Carson's way to keep the peace on a potentially explosive first day with a crew of felons had evolved into a truly cohesive group of brothers.

The audio level of the conversation lowered to a still-point when the clock hit half past four--quitting time. The crew headed back into the yard with the general population of inmates, an irritation to Carson. His team would put old masks on and fall back into their respective gangs. *What a fucking waste,* he told himself.

As the group was breaking up for the day, Carson called out to Black Terrell. "I need to talk to you. Ask you a question."

141

Carson's level of trust with most people was low. Occasionally he couldn't even trust his own mother, and she was nearly dead. Couldn't trust the ex, and wouldn't trust the county bureaucrats. Carson wasn't even sure he could trust himself. He trusted Laura, but he didn't know if that was mutual. Oddly he felt he could trust Black Terrell, a man he barely knew. Carson needed to cut through the bullshit, and Black Terrell was just the man to cut it.

"What's up, brother?" Terrell said.

"I ran into an old buddy a few days ago. His name is Biff Dickson, and he's a former all-state quarterback from Ohio."

"Yeah, so what?"

"We served together in the military."

"Okay, cool. What do you want from me?"

"I want our guys to play a football game against Biff and his guys."

"Hell, you say. How you going to work that shit out?"

"That's why I'm talking to you. And after I talk to you, I'll talk to Johnny Petit in prison administration."

"What's your play?"

"I'm getting to that. First, are you at least open to helping me with this? It would mean a lot, and not just to me."

"I'm listening."

"I want to beat Biff and his clowns. To get the prison bosses to sign off, I'll propose it as a charity event for the inner-city scholarship program we set up a few months ago."

"More charity? For scholarships?"

"We'll beef up the San Diego Promise with a new angle. I want the guys on my team to get the scholarship money, you know, once you're out, or you could give it to your kids, nieces, or nephews for college. The whole team."

142

"Good luck explaining that. Looks suspicious."

"There's a reason I came to you first. 'Cause you're smart and you're a leader. Biff can be an ass, but he's an old buddy. This is good for everyone, including the brass. Whether we win or lose."

"Shit, man, this Biff guy could bring anybody. All we got is criminals and gangbangers."

"I want a tryout. We could open it up to the whole prison. Got to be at least a few dozen guys in this place who've played football. We'll find maybe twenty guys. A starting eleven and backup. After I talk to Petit, we'll set that up."

"Hell you want from me, then?"

"I need you to help me with buy-in from the guys. I want the crew to help us recruit players from the prison ranks. Spread the word. Get the guys to try out."

"What about you? You the coach?" Terrell said.

"I'm your quarterback."

Terrell didn't blink behind his Malcolm X eyeglasses. "You've played football?"

"Yeah, a little. I quit to play on the golf team. What about you?"

"I played some ball."

"Where?"

"All-state fullback, Stockton. You quit to play golf. I quit to sling Jelly Beans."

"What?"

"Ecstasy, Molly, etcetera. And pure blow, brother. How I ended up here. No more. Not here, not anywhere."

"How'd an all-state fullback get messed up with that shit?"

"Hell, man."

"Sorry, just wondering."

"I grew up on the wrong side of Stockton, okay?"

"So?"

"I shoved folks around and made good money on the street trade. Guns and blow, man."

"How did that work?"

Black Terrell stepped back and studied Carson. "What's this, man? Why all the questions? You a cop? Informer? You wired?"

Carson pulled up his shirt. "Hell no. Go ahead, check me out."

"Sorry, man. Just freaking me out. You're inside gathering intel for all I know. Your MO is weird. The circle, the scholarships, now a crazy-ass football game. You know that, right? You could be a crazy cop."

"I'm no cop. Just certified crazy. That is a fact, brother."

"Just checking. I trust you. I worked for a syndicate. This outfit hooked up with street gangs up and down California. They fed the proceeds into various so-called legitimate operations owned by the syndicate. Typical shit, man."

"Did the syndicate bosses ever get busted?"

"Fuck no, man. I couldn't squeal. Even if I could, I didn't know who to squeal on. That's how the syndicates worked."

"Hmm. So what about the Biff thing? You in?"

"I'm in. I'll spread the word."

"I'm grateful, my friend. Hey, come over here a minute," Carson said, walking to his desk. He picked up a book with a blue cover. "Any idea where this came from?"

Terell Williams—Black Terrell—towered over Carson. "That's the Qur'an. What about it?"

"Found it on my desk. Someone left it there or forgot it. Was that you by any chance?"

"And what if I did? Y'all might like it."

"How's that?"

"Well, it teaches good shit, man. Like follow your gut. Find your god your own way. Stay active for your fellow brothers and sisters. Don't blindly follow the powers that be. All good in my book. Hell, you already onto that shit, man. Why I like you and why I'll back your plan on that game. Trust me, we'll kill Biff and his college boys."

18

GREEN FLASH

Driving over the Del Mar bridge, Laura dropped into the flats at Torrey Pines beach. She had planned to go for a late afternoon run, but she couldn't stop thinking about Carson.

She pulled over to make a call. "Hey, it's me," she said. "What are you doing?"

"Tired. I could use a quiet night at home."

"Then I hate to ask you."

"Ask me what?"

"I'd like to meet up again," Laura said.

"Where are you?"

"State beach at Torrey Pines."

"Stay put. See you in forty minutes. Traffic, you know."

"Watch for a blonde on a log."

Laura got out of her Prius, slipped on a windbreaker, and started walking southward along the beach. She walked for a couple of miles, crossing rocks, ocean water, and sand, ending up at Black's Beach, where she could see the occasional nudist sunning on the warm sand. She found her own place against a giant log and sat down, listening to the ocean's many voices,

146

making it clear that life was still kicking and screaming to survive, no matter what. The sounds of life lifted her spirits. Yet she was fraught with uncertainty.

She looked out to the horizon. She thought of the Green Flash. How she never saw it. Growing up near the ocean, she had long known about the rare atmospheric event in which the setting sun over the ocean produced what looked like an explosion of green light, lasting only an instant.

Perhaps transcendent bliss was real if your eyes were open enough to experience it. Laura had never seen the Green Flash nor experienced transcendent bliss. Like seeing micro-life teeming on the beach by the ocean, you had to stop what you were doing to see it. You really had to stop and enter an unconscious still-point. Trying to see it made its absence more profound. Nature rejected your efforts, evading your desires when you wanted them most. She wanted clarity. What would come from her project with the military? What did Carson mean to her now? After all that was past, could she ever be closer to him than just friends?

She knew she had missed it, as always, try as she might. That, she realized, was the problem: the vast difference between looking and seeing. If you tried to see the flash, nature defied your efforts. For those whose minds were open to not seeing it, the horizon emitted a barely detectable greenish-yellow, which then disappeared in an instant. The Green Flash tantalized her, but had always evaded her. *Stop trying,* she told herself. But to stop trying was to try not to look, when trying itself was the impediment. Her eyes would see the flash only when she was ready not to see it.

She looked up and saw Carson jumping around logs and rocks to avoid getting wet. He got up to where Laura was sitting, slightly out of breath.

"I tried to get here as fast as I could. Where are we, Mexico?"

"Remember how we used to look for it but never found it?" Laura said.

"Look for what?"

"The Flash."

Carson sat next to her on the driftwood. "I remember. We never saw it together. But I saw it once, alone. After you left. I saw it. Before I joined the Navy. I don't think I ever told you this."

"No, you didn't."

"It was back when I was still an aimless kid. Some friends and I were out here, on this very beach, surfing at sunset. I came back to the beach with my board and hit the ground, exhausted. I lay there for a while. I was very sad. I missed you. I looked out into the horizon. The sun was going down fast, and I just watched. I felt numb and unhappy. Yet I never wanted my life to stop. I wanted to experience everything. Everything seemed incredibly precious to me. The earth itself seemed fleeting. Like the light could go out at any second. Everything—me, my family, my friends, even you, Laura— could disappear like we'd never even existed. And then I saw it. It's there, and then it's gone before you realize it. And then you doubt yourself. Did I see it? Was that my imagination? Seeing it, or thinking that I'd seen something that rare and beautiful, puzzled me for days. I needed something solid to hold on to. That's when I decided to join the Navy. Some guys have kids and families to hold on to, but that wasn't me. Not then. I had to experience everything from heaven to hell. I figured SEAL training would throw hell at me." Carson laughed.

"What's so funny?" Laura said.

"Becoming ocean-drunk in SEAL training put me on

148

solid ground. Strange."

"You pulled away from me, Carson. You let me go with hardly a word."

"What good would that have done? You were hell-bent on MIT. You had a big life in front of you. I wasn't going to stop you. The Navy was my way to let you go. No regrets. I wanted something so fucking intense that I could forget about you. Seeing the flash was my wake-up call. So utterly wonderful. Shocking, even. A new world had opened up for me, inviting me to experience life or even death in every way possible."

"I can't believe we're talking about this like it was yesterday. A lot of ocean has passed under that bridge, Carson."

"I know. Still a big turning point in my life. I'll never forget it."

"That explains a lot. Makes me sad thinking about those days. You've changed. I see that. You aren't as confused as most people I know. You know what you want and see things most people don't or don't want to see. That's why I'm having a hard time asking you what I want to ask you."

Carson slid closer to Laura on the driftwood. "What's bothering you?"

"I've never agreed with Garrick Cripps on anything that matters. I'm a scientific researcher, not a politician or philosopher. I don't make trouble, and I'm quite okay with that."

"What the hell are you talking about?"

"My old professor. You asked me the other night about my life at MIT. I didn't want to talk about it. But I'm telling you now, okay?"

"What about him?"

"I was afraid to push him away. He was screwing with my head. If you weren't nice to him, he'd make trouble. He went

149

over the line with me. I should have called the campus cops. Kate, my old roommate, warned me about him. She thought he was up to no good and kept her distance. She left MIT, in fact."

"Was he inappropriate with you? Did he touch you?"

"He tried. I told him hands off. But he kept at it in other ways."

"So what happened?"

"Maybe I'm reading too much into it. But he kept giving me books to read that had nothing to do with my work—or his. Books that had a particular point of view. All the Ayn Rand books. Then other books, really obscure libertarian tracts. Ayn Rand was like his hero. He hated the 'bloodsuckers,' as he called everyone who wasn't John Galt."

"Who's John Galt?"

"A character in one of her novels. Garrick tried to convince me I was one of the chosen ones who would lead us out of the, quote, 'wilderness of socialism.' He said I'd be a heroic figure in the movement."

"What movement?"

"Maybe movement is too strong a word. He was always looking for like-minded people who believed government was evil. Sometimes I'd see him cavorting with other grad students, mostly young women but occasionally a man or two. I wondered if he was working them like he worked me."

"Wait a second. I worked for the US Navy. You work with the Pentagon. How is that evil?"

"He might make an exception for the military. But according to Garrick, government in general takes the hard-earned assets from the creators of wealth and gives them away to those who don't deserve it."

"Who did Garrick run with in those days? I assume he

150

wasn't married."

"Why would you say that?"

"Married guys don't talk like that. Too busy paying the mortgage and taking the kids to school."

"You're right. He wasn't married. He was close to a woman named Suzanne, another former grad student. She got a job with the Pentagon looking for the best cyber-researchers to fund their developmental work."

"Close? You mean like lovers?"

"Yeah, that was my impression. She sought me out, in fact, for the work I was doing in cyber defense."

"You buried the lede. Garrick's help paid off. Big time."

"That's bull. I tried to ignore his cheeky side. At first the books and stuff intrigued me. I was young, impressionable. I read the books, or most of them, when I had time. I lost interest. I had my agenda, and it definitely wasn't libertarian politics. Basically I told him to fuck off and leave me alone."

"Was he good at his job?"

"I heard mixed reviews. Some of his colleagues disliked him. Thought of him more as a shrewd business type than an academic."

"So the strong deserve what they get and the weak deserve what they don't get. That's a meritocracy, right? That's America. Capitalism. You get what you achieve in life. Hell, that's your life, Laura. You worked hard and look what you've achieved."

"My path was paved for me. I realized that. With my advantages, a lot of young women could do what I've done."

"You think? Merit had nothing to do with your success?"

"Is that how the SEALs worked? Pure meritocracy?" Laura asked.

"Actually, no. Some were stronger than others. Others had special skills in areas the strong didn't. Above all the team

151

mattered most. We were all lost without the team. No matter how strong any one guy was."

"You were a leader. Does that mean you were the strongest?"

"God, no. I was a leader because I could lead. I could keep the team working as one. Without the team, there is no leader. Without the team, we're fucked. Pretty simple."

"Did you ever read Ayn Rand?"

"Never had the time for that. Why?"

"I read her book, *The Fountainhead*. It was like a comic horror movie. God-like beings pitted against bloodsucking socialist zombies. After that I never took Garrick's politics seriously. Apparently he wrote a book. *The Liberation* something or other. I had zero interest in it."

"Why are you telling me all this, Laura?"

"I'm not sure. You asked me about MIT, and I avoided the subject. I'm trying to be more open with you."

Carson picked up a flat round stone and tossed it into the surf, watching it skip through the water. "I'd be annoyed too. Especially if my boss was trying to drag me into a club I didn't want to join."

She didn't answer.

"What are you thinking, Laura?"

"Just thinking. Thanks for listening."

"Sure he didn't do anything to you?"

"I'm fine. Just still pisses me off that I had to deal with that crap."

"That's it? You just needed to vent?"

"I'm not venting. I'm just telling you about my life. Let's change the subject. What are you up to now?"

"Heading home. My body is tired. Me and my team are gearing up for this charity football game."

"What football game?"

152

"An event I'm cooking up. My telemarketing guys against this semi-pro team in town. I want to raise scholarship money for kids who don't grow up like we grew up, you know? I'm at a place where I can make a slight difference, and it doesn't involve a secret mission in Iraq or Afghanistan. I'm thinking, 'why not?' Why not exploit a fucked-up system to help the kids the system fucks up? Timing is good too. I'll bring my son over from Flagstaff."

"That's wonderful, Carson. If you're trying to impress me, it's working. You seem happy."

"I'm trying. Like I told you at the lodge, I struggle a bit trying to renormalize, if that's a word. My job is so completely different from anything I've done before. I'm not trying to force my life to be a certain way. Just let things happen. Be good with it. Day by day I'm feeling quieter, more accepting of who I am. Living life without others defining me. Some days not so much. But I'm heading in the right direction. On some days I'm blissful. So grateful for the life I've got. It took most of my life, Laura, but I'm feeling what it's like to be free. Or free enough. Nothing is absolute."

Laura moved closer next to Carson. "You deserve it. It's about time."

"How about you? Do you feel free?" Carson said.

Laura dug her toes into the moist sand. "Lately I've felt I've got the most freedom I've ever had. I've paid my dues. I've got to a place where I don't have to delay gratification any longer. My life is here and now. On top of my game as a research scientist, living here in paradise. But sometimes I'm not sure.

"You know me. I tend to see things positively. But sometimes that can blinker me. I miss a lot of stuff that is happening all around me because I'm too wrapped up in my

153

own thing to notice. I should be more aware of what's going on when I'm not looking. After all I am a cyber-security expert, right? Take Garrick. I've lost touch now and I wonder—did he give up the ghost or is he still harassing his grad students? Or worse, even."

"It's not your job to worry about him. Garrick may be a little confused, but he's probably just muddling along, an aging tenured professor about to go on Medicare."

"Oh my God, Carson, that's so perfect. Can you imagine Garrick on government health care? Just the thought of it would send him to the psych ward."

~

Carson arrived home exhausted. He took Diego for a quick walk around the park, then settled into his lounge chair, trying to find something to watch before going to bed. When the local news produced nothing of interest, he shut off the TV and stared at the blank screen, thinking about Laura. Spending time with her had shaken him—but in a good way, with feelings he hadn't experienced in years. He'd admit this to nobody, not even her, but it had taken only a couple of seconds to realize he still loved her, years after she had left him for a higher calling and a passion for science that exceeded her passion for him. He could still remember the bitter feelings. But seeing her now overwhelmed the past, like a tsunami washing over the pitifully small waves of ordinary life. They could still tell each other the truth.

Laura was fearless, despite herself. She broached subjects about the past that he'd buried. Things he'd archived in a memory vault that remained out of reach of his conscious mind. As he sat staring at the black TV screen, Carson realized that when his father, Alan McCready, had died from cancer in 1989, he was about the same age as Carson was now. Carson had been just fifteen when his father left him. In response Carson had crawled into a hole as if it were his own grave. Only surfing and Laura had been able to bring him back into the world—surfing alone at lonely beaches in the darkest storms, her beautiful light bringing him back from the brink.

Carson got up and poured a whiskey on ice. He missed his dad and he missed Michael, his fifteen-year-old son. Carson looked at his watch: 10:30 p.m. He frisked his body to find his phone, then hit Michael's speed dial. He listened to five rings and then a message. His boy's voice. Confident, strong. But still a kid, thank God. Carson clicked off, figuring Michael was sound asleep.

Carson got into bed and picked up a book he'd been reading for weeks. A book for tranquilizing him into almost instantaneous sleep. He was determined to get through the book, which he'd found at a used bookstore in Lemon Grove.

The sea had been Carson's youth and his lifework as a sailor. After retiring he had got the urge to read every book he could find about sea life. Books that he'd always known were there, but he'd never taken the time to dig into.

These days he was learning as much as he could about whales. He read fiction, essays, and classic scientific books about the magnificent creatures. He re-read *Moby-Dick*, about Captain Ahab's obsession with killing the creature that had taken half of his leg on an earlier whale hunt. In the end Ahab's selfish mission to take revenge on an indifferent leviathan destroyed the very means of his own survival—his vessel and every other human aboard. As a military strategist, Carson felt no pity for Ahab. Better to check the ego, know your limits. Don't play tough with an animal a thousand times more seaworthy than you.

Now he was reading *Leviathan* by Thomas Hobbes, written in 1651—nearly four hundred damned years ago. Despite the title, *Leviathan* had nothing to do with whales of the sea. Carson had got several pages into the book before realizing it was a philosophical treatise. At first the book had mystified him because he didn't understand how all its abstractions related to life as he knew it. Science and math were easier. Concrete. Measurable. Predictive. But the more of *Leviathan* he read, the more Carson realized he was learning about nature to the same degree as any scientific study. The science of human behavior in the collective.

Eventually Carson realized *Leviathan* matched up with his own life exactly. Hobbes's idea of individualism being tempered by the whole was an essential aspect of being part of a SEAL team. A means of survival drilled into his head from the moment he entered BUD/S training. Give yourself to the team, and someday, the team will save your ass.

Carson was fascinated by how his simple interest in whales had led to such intriguing connections about the complexity of human nature and survival. When he first read *Moby-Dick* in school, he hadn't appreciated what the book was really about. Certainly he hadn't known that a novel written in 1851, exactly two hundred years after *Leviathan*, would connect to his later life as a SEAL in the early twenty-first century.

As usual Carson was drifting off. He placed *Leviathan* on his nightstand, shut off his reading lamp, and let his head fall onto the pillow.

Carson was asleep when his phone rang at one a.m. At first he thought the beeping was his morning alarm, then he saw his son's name on the screen.

"Michael? Are you okay? What are you doing still up?"

"Dad, you called. I should ask if you're okay."

"I'm fine. I was asleep. You startled me."

"Did you want to talk about something?" Michael said.

"Is your mom asleep?"

"Yeah, I was with a friend. Just got home."

"A girlfriend?"

"Maybe. Why'd you call, Dad?"

"I needed to hear your voice, son. Are you okay with that?"

"Sure, why not?"

"I know it's late. Tell me what you're up to these days."

"Why the sudden curiosity, Dad?"

"I'm sorry. Just overwhelmed lately. Got a new job. Just Diego and me. I'd love to have you out here for a while, when summer comes."

"What would we do?"

"What do you mean? What we've always done. Go to the beach, eat some excellent food. You do miss the beach, don't you?"

"Not really. I'm getting used to it here. Flagstaff's cool."

"Like how? You mean school? Friends? Girlfriends?"

"I'm just living, Dad. Mom's doing good, in case you care."

"I'll pretend I didn't hear that."

"Although I was thinking . . ."

"What is it, Michael?"

"Could you give me shooting lessons sometime?"

"You mean with an actual weapon? Target practice?"

"Yeah, I guess. Mom met a guy who says he's a weapons expert, and I told him you were a SEAL, and he sort of chuckled like I was making it up."

"Wait, back up. What guy?"

"Just someone Mom met. Said he had a military background, like you. He didn't believe you were in the SEALs."

"Your mom didn't set him straight?"

157

"Not really. She doesn't like you, Dad."

"So I've heard. Don't take that to heart, son. She's hurt and it's mostly my fault. It's a lesson, son. Never let your job set you apart from your family. No matter what. When the job is gone, you've still got your family. Unless you were stupid and acted too late."

"Well, could you?"

"Could I what?"

"Give me some tips on guns and shooting and stuff like that?" Michael said.

"Sure, we can do that. Come see me. We'll have a good time. I'm putting on a charity football game. I'm actually playing quarterback. I'd like you to come."

"That sounds kind of cool."

"We'll make it happen, Michael. And other good stuff. You're fifteen. When I was fifteen, I was working at a surf shop. Stick to baseball. You're still playing ball, I hope?"

"I still play, yeah. I liked it better when you were around to see my games, though."

"When the time is right, I won't need this job. Then I'll rent a little place in Flagstaff."

"Really? It's not by the ocean, Dad. I don't see you liking this place. Anyway this guy Mom is seeing, he's teaching me some good stuff. He took me to the shooting range last Saturday."

Carson's breath stopped upon hearing this news. "You went alone with this guy?"

"Mom came with us. She shot some guns. She's pretty good, actually. His name is Dirk, by the way. He's kind of dorky, but he's pretty passionate about the military and being a patriot and shit. Showed me how to handle an automatic weapon. He said if my dad couldn't teach me, he would."

158

"Learning how to use a weapon is no damned game, okay? I'd rather you didn't go along with this Dirk guy. He strikes me as a wannabe. Stay clear of him. I don't want this idiot taking you down a path that's not who you are. Have Mom take you to a legitimate training facility. Just you two."

"Why's he a wannabe?"

"Trust me, son. A guy who knows his shit would never teach the teenage son of a new girlfriend about semi-automatic weapons. Your mom isn't showing good judgment. I'll talk to her later. And this Dirk makes a point of telling you he's a patriot. What did he mean by that?"

"Dad, I don't know. I never knew that was so complicated. A patriot is a good thing, right?"

"Absolutely. A wonderful thing. A necessary thing. Too many people throw that word around calling themselves this or that or the other thing, but it's just a word to them. A fashion statement. To be like the other guy and the other guy they hang with at the bar and the shooting range. Some are legit ex-military. But if a guy talks up war and violence, he's talking bullshit because that's a sure sign he's delusional or has no clue what he's talking about. You hear me, son?"

"I should go, Dad. It's late."

"Are we done talking tonight? I'd like to know how school's going. Flagstaff is great for the outdoors. Try hiking. Go skiing. Have fun. Meet friends who you have things in common with. I'm doing a lot of reading myself these days. I'd like to share some books with you. Then we can talk about some cool ideas. How's that sound?"

"Dad, did you ever think a guy like Dirk is the real deal and you're the one talking bullshit?"

Before Carson could breathe, Michael hung up.

159

19

PEANUT BUTTER SHOT

Carson lied to Johnny Petit and caught a plane to Flagstaff on Friday morning, allowing himself a few days to attend to the truth. Carson had told Petit his son had been in a car accident. Though the "accident" was a fib, the urgency was real. Get the facts and get Michael straightened out, or possibly lose him to an underworld of wannabes and weird fucks planning to blow up a synagogue or some shit. Was he overreacting? Probably. But Carson the former SEAL knew the type, and Carson the dad knew Michael's vulnerabilities. Carson scolded himself. His son could be at risk, and it was his own damned fault.

Carson didn't tell Kate, his ex, that he was coming—a bad move on its face. He de-planed, rented a compact Kia, and found a coffee shop where he could decompress and consider how to deal with Kate, who would or wouldn't allow him to see the child he technically had no right to see at that moment. He didn't want to barge in, but Kate being Kate would be bothered nevertheless, and he'd get defensive.

He fought the urge to see Kate as an enemy combatant

and himself as the invading force penetrating a high-security compound on a hostage recovery mission. Calling ahead would soften her, perhaps. Or perhaps not. A crap shoot, really. He got a hotel room and spent the rest of Friday looking around. A pretty, interesting town. Maybe a place he could retire for good before Michael graduated from high school. For now he'd wait until Saturday morning to go round, when Michael was likely to be home making plans for the day.

~

Carson knocked on the door of the townhouse on the west side of town. A newer place, modest but nice, in a decent neighborhood near tree-lined parks and schools.

He heard Michael's voice and his footsteps tromping on the floor. "I'll get it, Mom. It's probably Uncle Dirk."

"Uncle Dirk?"

The boy's face lit up. "Dad?"

"In the flesh. Come here, give me a hug."

"What are you doing here?" Michael said.

"I wanted to see you. Our last conversation didn't go well."

"Sorry I hung up on you. My bad."

"Forget it. I thought we could spend the day together, if you're free.

"We already have plans today, Dad."

"I'm here now, son."

Kate came to the door, out of breath.

"Mom, meet Dad. Dad, meet Mom."

Her brown eyes grew bigger and turned redder. "Who invited you, McCready?"

"Nobody, obviously. I invited myself. I'd like to spend some time with my son, if that's okay."

161

"No, it's not okay. We're fully booked."

"Look, Kate, I'm sorry. I should've called ahead."

"Damn you, Carson. Why now? What's the emergency?"

He glanced at Michael. "It's nothing," he lied. "I needed to see you guys. If it's too much trouble, I'll go."

While Carson stood at the door, an older Ram 3500 announced its appearance in the neighborhood, rumbling up the driveway and parking next to Carson's rental, rendering the Kia like a child next to the bright red monster on beefed-up tires.

Carson watched a guy who looked about fifty hop out of the truck, his legs bending against the force of gravity created from jumping from the truck cab onto the concrete. He rubbed his right knee. "Damn, gotta watch that knee. Old football injury."

The guy had stringy brown hair with an over-long beard and stood about five-eleven. Camo jacket, baggy jeans, and shiny black boots. Not exactly fit, but not unhealthy looking either. As the guy walked up the driveway toward the door, he locked eyes on Carson and stuck out his hand. "Dirk Chandler, buddy. And you are?"

"Dirk, I'm Carson."

"A pleasure. How do you know my friends here?" Dirk said.

Carson laughed and turned to Kate. "Oh, it's a religious thing. We used to go to the same church, right, honey?"

Michael laughed. "Dad!"

"I'm Michael's father and Kate's ex. My son told me about you."

Dirk took Carson's hand and squeezed hard. Carson figured Dirk worked with machines or heavy equipment and seemed proud of his manly handshake. Carson returned

162

the handshake, taking the guy's fingers and squeezing, just enough to give Dirk a mental pause. With no sign of emotion, he looked Dirk in the eyes with an unstated warning: *Do not fuck with me or my son.*

Dirk withdrew and turned to Kate. She gave him a light kiss. Dirk grabbed and squeezed Michael's shoulder. "We ready to head out, soldier?"

"Yeah, sure, let's go," Michael said.

"You coming, Kate?" Dirk said.

"I'll stay. You and Michael have fun. See you later, though, right? I'll make a big lunch."

Carson stood next to Michael and Kate. He noticed Dirk step back, his eyes giving away a weakness. Jealous of the old family unit together again, as if they were posing for a family portrait?

"What about you? Carson, right?" Dirk said.

"What about me, Dirk?"

"Why don't you come along." He chuckled. "You might learn something."

Carson glanced at Kate. "Would you mind?"

"Do what you came to do, McCready. I'm not stopping you. Just be nice, okay?"

Carson didn't like the predictable jab, but he ignored it.

Dirk was already standing by the truck door. He pulled himself into the driver's seat. "Now that's settled, let's go fishing."

"Where are we going?" Carson asked.

"To the lake, dude. Lake Mary. Michael's favorite, right, kid?"

~

Carson wasn't prepared. He was wearing casual shorts and soft tennis shoes that slipped easily on the gravel bank leading to the small lake. Wildflowers were blooming. Lake Mary was calm, except for a mid-morning breeze that ruffled the water. Michael and Dirk sat on outdoor chairs on the slope in the bright sun. Conditions for lake fishing weren't ideal. Better in the shade or amid the golden light during the magical moments before dark—where he and Michael could share feelings and thoughts. That was all he wanted. But this wasn't magic. The cheap folding chairs looked ridiculous on the riverbank. He envisioned his ass slipping off and pummeling him into the gravel. He sat on his haunches next to Michael while Dirk handled the rods and bait.

"So the kid says you were a SEAL or something?" Dirk said.

"Correct except the something. There is no something."

"Oh. Where'd you deploy?"

"What do you mean?"

"You know, who you fought. Where you served."

"I led a platoon. Direct-action missions to the Middle East and North Africa. Based in Coronado."

"That's California, right?"

"Across the bay from San Diego."

"I served myself. Badass shit, I'll tell you that. Never a dull moment."

"Lucky you. We sat on our asses a lot. Waiting, waiting, waiting, and then hell breaks loose."

Dirk handed Michael a rod armed with bright red fish eggs. "There you go, son. Knock yourself out." He turned to Carson. "Army Ranger myself. I went where the action was."

"No shit? What rank?"

"Master Sergeant, man."

"Michael didn't mention that."

"Platoon leader. Oorah!"

"Did you say Oorah?"

"Yeah, why?"

"You must have meant hooah. Oorah is Marines."

"I know that. Just messing with you, McCready."

"Ah. You got me there, Dirk."

Carson glanced at Michael, who had walked down the bank to a shady section of water. He seemed engaged. Carson had taken his son fishing a few times at Lake Cucamonga, east of the city, when he was just a boy. Carson wanted desperately to be alone with Michael; time was too precious to be bullshitting with Dirk. And the guy was a master bullshitter. Carson chuckled inside. Dirk's bona fides were suspect. A Master Sergeant who didn't know the army's war cry?

"Remember the peanut butter shot?" Carson said.

Dirk hesitated. "Sure. What about it?"

"Strangest alcoholic concoction I could ever imagine. One shot would fuck you up for hours. Remember?"

"Oh, yeah. I remember. Had my share of them fuckers. A kick-ass drink, for sure. Can't find 'em stateside."

That stopped Carson cold. What was with this guy? Why lie about it? Nobody who had ever been in the military could forget the infamous peanut butter shot, slang for the penicillin you took in the ass before boot camp. Carson had heard the needle was shockingly long. Everyone said "don't look at the needle." Carson looked anyway and was thankful he did. A life lesson. The medicine itself was soft and thick, hence the peanut butter metaphor. Once it was injected, Carson felt like a baseball was stuck in his butt cheek. Literally a pain in the ass that made tough guys cry. Carson didn't cry, but he couldn't sit for several days.

165

"How many would you have at a time?" Carson said.

"The drink? Oh, fuck me. Sometimes half a dozen, one after the other," Dirk said.

"Wow, you were a badass."

"I paid for it, buddy. My knees, man. You seen it."

"Thought that was an old football injury. You wouldn't have passed the physical with knees that bad."

"You got to understand something, sport. Brass exempted me since I was an excellent marksman."

Carson let the implausibility of that statement sink in. Time to cut the bullshit. "Do not gaslight me, Dirk. Just fucking stop, okay?"

"Say what, boss?"

"Lie to me. Really, I don't give a shit. But listen carefully, Dirk. Lie to my kid about what a badass you were in the army, and it won't end well for you. Not a threat. Just stating a fact. The army brass will knock on your door, and they'll officially shut you up. Are we clear?"

"Okay, okay. Don't get all sniffy, man. Maybe I fib a little. So what? I'm a patriot."

"A patriot, huh? What's that mean?"

"I'm all about my flag, my country, and my liberty. I'm free to say and do whatever I damned well please. This is America."

"Okay, so what do you actually *do* that's patriotic?"

"Look, man. A thousand guys just like me, right here in the Zone, brother. Arizona and every other state in America—a thousand more just like us. The military has mottos. Fine. We have our own motto. The only one that counts. 'Don't tread on me.' We ain't official military, but we're dangerous to those fuckers in Washington. We hate the damned government. We won't stop until we've crushed it and all the liberal bastards

166

running it. Our country will be great again. You did your patriotic duty overseas. Fine. My patriotic duty is to make the government suffer."

"And how do you propose to do that?" Carson said. He glanced down the shore to make sure Michael was out of earshot. He didn't want his son to hear this conversation.

"We train. We pray to Jesus. We acquire military-grade weapons and material," Dirk said. "We are not fucking around. Your boy, Michael? He's a patriot. He wants to join us. Guess he learned it from you. He's proud of you, man. Wants to be like you, a warrior, but you're not around much. I'm only showing him how to find what he already wants. I'm certain he'll be a leader in the movement one day."

Carson set down his rod on the gravel slope and stood. "Who appointed you as the sentinel of my country, let alone my son's career counselor? What truth will you die for? Because you will die. Trust me. You're a god-fearing, gun-toting patriot? That's all you've got? I see a hapless bunch of losers. You'd never survive Hell Week, let alone real violence against actual soldiers. War isn't a game. Or revolutions. Patriot? No, sir. You see patriots. I see whiners and crybabies. I know a hundred guys just like you. Blame the libs. Blacks. Jews. Mexicans. Muslims.

"For every misfortune you've suffered, it was a Black person or a Jew out to get you. I'm not saying your pain isn't real. I get it. But for fuck's sake, man, blame the right goddamned people."

"Hold on there a minute, buddy," Dirk said.

Carson ignored him. "You won't listen to me, but a piece of advice, anyway: do not fuck with the truth. It's not a motherfucking game, okay? A warrior knows that. Fuck with the truth, and the truth will fuck you right back, more deadly

167

than you can imagine. Face it, confront it. Live with it. Deal with it. Ignore it? Deny it? Make up a story? It's a free country, right? Truth, my friend, is a mean son of a bitch, and it's got zero tolerance for pretenders."

Dirk mumbled something that Carson couldn't make out while pulling a pack of Marlboros from his breast pocket. Dirk got up from the wobbly folding chair. Carson stood to face him but backed away a few feet, hoping to avoid any physical confrontation. Still, Carson had no choice. It was not time to be nice. Not time to be the emotionally neutral ex-husband hogtied by circumstances beyond his control. Now he could see the future. Dirk would become a bad influence on his son. Not might or maybe. Not harmless Uncle Dirk. The guy was no badass but he was a creep, a sheep of a man in camo covering himself in pseudo-patriotism. Let this go and the bullshit would only get thicker and smellier from here. Time to end this now.

"I'll only say this once. After today, stay the fuck away from my kid. Break off whatever bullshit relationship you've got with my ex. Trust me, she thinks you're a creep but she's too nice to tell you. She's vulnerable and wants the attention. Leave her alone."

"Fuck you, McCready. And what if I don't?"

Carson turned around to check on Michael before he responded. His son was standing in the trees behind them, apparently listening to at least part of their conversation. Carson's heart wanted to sink. Had he just made everything worse? Had he alienated his son even more? Had the whole trip to save his boy turned out to be a royal fuckup?

Carson didn't allow himself to linger on doubt. He was certain that he'd done the right thing. Michael might not understand why at the moment, but he would grow up, get

168

wiser, and know himself that his father had done right by his son.

In truth Carson hoped that his son would be special. Trusted that Michael would be smarter than Carson had been at fifteen. That Michael would learn sooner than Carson had learned about his own father. Alan McCready never took the easy way. Alan fought for freedom quietly, diligently, working twelve-hour days helping the poor, sick, and the old find their path to freedom. His dad had been no freedom fighter in the popular sense. He hadn't been Dirk's brand of patriot. He hadn't been a true-blooded American hero in ways that a true-blooded American teenager could understand. Carson hadn't understood any of that until Alan was gone. But Michael would get it, right? Michael would understand that becoming an expert with an AR-15 wasn't proof of anyone's manhood. He'd be precociously smart and wise enough to see through the bullshit.

Michael and Carson hardly talked when they got back to Kate's condo. Dirk had left, declining an invitation for the mid-afternoon lunch Kate had prepared. The family were together but said little while nibbling on the seafood salad.

"What happened out there?" Kate finally said.

Carson glanced at Michael, whose attention had turned to his iced tea.

He couldn't lie. And he wouldn't cover it up. But he didn't want to ruin Kate's lunch with the former husband and young son whom she used to call "my boys."

"Interesting and enlightening, Kate. Say, this salmon is wonderful."

"What did you think about Dirk?"

"Come on, Kate. Do you really care what I think about Dirk? The question is what do you think about him?"

169

"Carson, I can read your mind. You have a stake in this too."

"Fine. I don't think Dirk is a good fit for you or a good influence on Michael. I wasn't the ideal husband and I haven't been the ideal father. But you can do better, Kathryn. He's not even your type. There, I said it. For what it's worth."

"I knew you'd say that."

"Then why did you ask?"

"Just curious, okay?"

"Fine. When you seriously want to talk about this again, we can do that. But not now, okay?"

"Fine. But since when do you discuss anything involving me or your son?"

"Not fair, Kate. Come on. Let's drop it. I'm leaving today. I don't want to ruin everything. I'm enjoying your delicious lunch. Can we just try to be happy?"

Carson left Flagstaff angry and more uncertain about Michael than when he arrived. The trip had accomplished little apart from confirming that he had lost touch with his son, and the way to get him back wasn't clear. His only thought was to bring him to San Diego for the upcoming football game. Michael would enjoy that, and Carson would have the best reason of all reasons to make the game actually happen.

20

THE REAL GAME

Carson got home from work, picked up Diego from the sitter, and took him for a thirty-minute walk. He fed the dog then dropped himself and his whiskey into a lounge chair. He tried to watch some sports on TV but he felt unsettled, and it had nothing to do with work, his son, or football practice.

He fell asleep in his lounge chair and woke up an hour later. His phone flashed with the same mysterious number and a new message: *I know who you are.*

Carson glanced at the text and deleted it, avoiding whatever game the mystery sender was playing. He continued to scroll through the TV menu. His phone buzzed again with another message.

Did you hear me? the text said.

Tell me something interesting. I don't play games, Carson texted.

This is the game. The only game. The real game.

Who are you? Carson wrote.

That doesn't matter.

Is this Dirk?

Who's Dirk?

Okay, you're not Dirk.

Fuck Dirk.

Ok, Not-Dirk. What's in it for you?

Freedom.

You sure you're not Dirk?

Who in the hell is Dirk?

Never mind. You want freedom. From what?

Tyranny.

Right, 'Don't Tread on Me,' Carson wrote.

There's danger ahead. You won't see it coming.

Will I need to kill anyone? Carson texted, joking.

Unknown.

Take it up with the authorities. I'm busy.

Authorities can't be trusted. You've been set up.

Who set me up?

Freedom fighters.

Who are they fighting?

Carson waited several seconds for an answer.

They fight tyranny.

Don't fuck with me.

They fight for an idea.

What idea?

Liberty.

Don't we all?

Liberty for the few.

Now, that's tyranny. Carson waited twenty seconds for a reply, then texted again. *Why me?*

It's you or nobody.

I need a real clue, not bullshit.

There will be a cyberattack on government computer networks. Stop it.

172

I'm going to need more information.
The statement stands.
How?
Figure it out.

Carson hesitated before texting. It was a crapshoot. *Can Laura help me?*

Carson waited for an answer to his yes or no question.

A minute later, the messenger responded. *You have what and whom you need.*

You've given me nothing. Again, Carson waited while the messenger composed a reply.

Finally, the mystery person offered this: *Pay attention. Trust no one. Or your mission fails.*

~

Normally, Carson would have shut the messenger down and rid himself of the dubious conversation with a hard delete. In the past three years, he had received several anonymous texts—collateral crud stemming from the Somali affair. But after talking to Laura about her life at MIT, his internal sensor for possible danger ahead kept beeping in his head. He ran down the stairs to his car. Before reaching the on-ramp to the 8 West, Carson stopped at a Rite-Aid and picked up two cheap disposable phones with several hundred prepaid minutes. He ripped the packaging off one phone, set it up, and texted Laura's number. Carson wrote, *Must meet. Our midnight spot. It's me. Don't respond.*

173

21

A THOUSAND POINTS OF LIGHT

When Carson got to the top of Mount Soledad, he drove around the parking area looking for Laura's car. There were just a few vehicles and people around at that hour. All was dark except for a thousand points of light flickering as far as one could see, from the sea to the mountains, all visible from the highest landmark in the city where he and Laura had hung out as kids, kissing, hugging, and making out, just as teenage lovers did the world over.

By midnight he was still alone at Soledad. At twelve fifteen Laura's car slowly pulled into a parking spot near the memorial. She flicked off the car lights, and Carson heard the car door shut, filling the silence.

She wore white jeans and matching casual shoes. He watched her long legs stride up the hill and up the red steps until she sat down beside him. She jangled her keys and dropped them in a black handbag.

"Am I allowed to ask why you got me to drop everything and meet you here?" she asked.

"Nice to see you too."

"What's this about, Carson?"

"Some unexpected intel came my way. I'm not sure about the source, but if it's true, the information is alarming."

"Intel? Jeez, Carson. I'm a scientist, not a spy. What the hell are you talking about?"

"Garrick Cripps."

"What about him?"

"He's an accomplished guy, right? Professor at MIT. Well connected."

"Yeah, true. So what?"

"He can't be just a crazy old fucker as a professor at MIT, right?"

"I'm listening. Make your point."

"He went hard at you and, indirectly, helped you secure a huge cybersecurity project for the United States military, right?"

"True."

"That's a big fucking deal."

"I thought so. I took what he offered and ignored the other BS. Is this what you got me out here for in the middle of the night, Carson? To tell me he's an accomplished MIT prof?"

"Maybe he's more than your casual libertarian intellectual."

"You're still not making sense."

"I went to see my son, Michael, the other day."

"What's Michael got to do with Garrick?"

"I'll get to that. He told me something alarming on the phone. I flew to Flagstaff and met Kate's new beau, a guy named Dirk. Claimed he was ex-military, but it didn't take much to figure out he's a liar and bullshitter. He did scare me, though, and I told him to stay away from Michael or I'd have him arrested."

"Carson, the way your mind works is driving me nuts."

"Look, the guy, Dirk, fancies himself a badass warrior because he calls himself a patriot and runs with a crew of well-armed losers who think they can take down the damned government. I know these people. I saw it for myself. I had a troublemaker in my platoon who also ran with these same guys back in Kentucky. In the big picture, these dudes are irrelevant. But they're part of something even more menacing. I'm afraid to come out and say it because it would sound crazy to you."

"Spit it out."

"Here's the deal, Laura. You know this better than anyone. Revolutions don't need armies and tanks anymore. That's last-century shit. All the evidence points to information and propaganda wars. My point is that Garrick and Dirk are on the same team, but for different reasons. Dirk's bunch is naive. Their hate for the government is visceral, and they're blood-thirsty. Give 'em the slightest push and they'd follow almost any authoritarian asshole off a cliff.

"Now, Garrick. He's different. He'd push the Dirks off the cliff. Dirks don't think. They run off pure emotion. Emotionally, the world isn't adding up for them. They're lost and they don't know who to blame, so they're poised to lash out when someone like Garrick comes along to make 'sense' of their troubles. All in the service of Garrick and his cause. He's over-the-top anti-government, right?

"That's correct. But the Garrick I know would never shed blood for any cause."

"Exactly. He's an MIT professor, for God's sake. He's got the Dirks for that. He's the boss. He's in command."

"So tell me, what does Garrick want?" Laura said.

"What all authoritarians want. Power. He's greedy for power, and all this liberty and freedom shit is pretty makeup

176

to cover up that very ugly fact. That's his motivation. But guys like him don't need armies anymore. As a professor of computer science at MIT, he knows that better than anyone."

"Okay, so? I'm not convinced he's an authoritarian per se. He's an academic."

"Garrick could be working in cyber warfare, which would explain why he tried to cuddle up to you."

"I doubt it. A lot of researchers far more capable than Garrick are working with the military on cyber warfare." Laura stopped. She glared up at the sky.

"What's wrong?"

"Remember I mentioned a woman named Suzanne? Garrick's former lover who took the high-powered job at the Pentagon?"

"Remind me."

"I worked with her briefly when I was setting up my own Pentagon contract. Then we went our separate ways. She arranged everything, but I report to a project manager in terms of updates, deadlines, change orders, and such."

"Okay, so?"

"I'm wondering if Suzanne told me everything." Laura hesitated.

"What are you thinking?" Carson said.

"I suppose it's possible she could have fed 'intel,' as you call it, to Garrick about the military projects she worked on. Seems highly unlikely because I assumed she had broken away from Garrick. Plus she'd be breaking a half dozen federal secrecy laws."

"Call me suspicious," Carson said. "Being slightly paranoid was my go-to attitude in SEALS."

"You got to give me more than that, McCready."

"I put together a little profile of Garrick based on the stuff you told me and some other intel I haven't yet told you about."

"When did you do that?"

"After our talk at Blacks Beach. It's just a theory, all right? But it's based on a few assumptions that fit with what we know."

"Like what?"

"Okay, Garrick hates the US government, right? He hates all government. But Garrick is unique. Many people hate the government, but Garrick's hate is relentless. And he acts on it. It's not all talk."

"Why assume that?"

"Look how he went after you. It's unusual that a professor would risk his standing at the university by handing out political propaganda to students."

"Okay, so he's weird. He was annoying. That doesn't mean he's dangerous."

"Bear with me a second. Let's assume he would like to destroy the government and that he acts upon his convictions. What would he do? Hire special ops wannabes living in the outback of Montana and Arkansas? I doubt it. Or go the cyber route? Like you've said, he was no genius as a scientist. So he'd nurture other young scientists who were brilliant. Like you, Laura. Steer his protégés to the new and untamed field of AI cyber warfare technology."

"To what end?"

"Use your imagination."

"I personally know a half dozen MIT computer science PhDs were studying with Garrick around the time I was. Some of those also hooked up with Suzanne. I'm just now realizing how odd that was."

"It's not a coincidence. Why was Suzanne placing mostly MIT grads on those military projects? Just because she

178

preferred MIT grads?"

"Okay. Keep going."

"He's got a motive. Hates the government. Hates socialism. Loves capitalism. I mean *really* loves it. At some point he'll try to gain access to the technical breakthroughs in order to create the perfect algorithm that worms its way into government computers."

"Wow, Carson. You really believe he's playing that kind of chess, thinking several moves in advance?"

"Why not? Maybe he is brilliant, after all. He's got a formidable intellect. He doesn't apply his genius to software design or academics. That's not who Garrick is. He's a controller. A guy who needs to be in charge. He's not a creator, like you. He's the type who gets others to do what he wants."

"Okay, that fits."

"He'd like to get the intel directly from his protégés, but he doesn't bank on that. Like you, most are too independent and wouldn't drink Garrick's anti-government Kool-Aid. So he gets the intel indirectly. A mole in the Pentagon. How convenient that Garrick's former lover, this Suzanne, has this intel on how the attack bots work."

"That's still speculative."

"But look at the possibilities, Laura. With the right military-grade AI bot, Garrick could disable all government computer networks—his first step to bringing down the entire house. All it takes is one badass algorithm. Am I missing something?"

"I'm thinking . . . Garrick was up to something, maybe related to cyber weapons. Suzanne and he were close. But she never struck me as overly political or strange that way."

"What about the technology?"

"A single computer could launch a full-scale attack,

which could exploit weak spots in order to breach all critical interlocking servers in the government. But, Carson, if I say anything more, the feds would arrest me. You'd better be careful."

"You know me. I'm as careful as I need to be."

"I can't believe we are talking like this here, in the place we used to come to hide from adults," Laura said.

"We're still hiding. But now we are the adults."

Laura got up. "Let's do the loop."

They walked down the east side of the park, not speaking for several minutes.

"How would you do it?" Carson asked.

"Do what?"

"How would you launch a cyber weapon if your mission were to screw with government operations?"

"You mean something more sophisticated than a hack from a teenager's garage?"

"Yeah, a serious breach. Like something Russia would do."

"Ideally I'd find access to a local government operation with computing devices linked to the internet. That's the simple part. I'd have to coordinate the human operators at those desktops. They launch the smart bot simultaneously or in sequence. Best if they do so unknowingly. A mandated software update carrying the bot would do the trick."

"But a dozen operators spread across several local departments would work?"

"Sure, but the logistics of pulling that off are more difficult."

"Right. I see that . . . What are you thinking? You've got that blank look you get when you're trying to figure something out."

Laura turned back to Carson. "You never really told me about your new job. You're a government employee, right?"

180

"True."

"How does prison telemarketing work?"

Carson looked at her quizzically. "It's not rocket science. I work with anywhere between twelve and fifteen inmates on a shift. The guys are like commodities brokers. We've got a stack of items we've already traded for—could be anything from hairspray to jump drives—and then we need to offload it. Not all that different from a commodities exchange since we have nothing but the paper that says we own it. My guys are connecting with buyers and sellers around the world. They're damned good at it too. I assign the commodities to the various inmates and make sure the deals turn a profit."

"That's a little strange," Laura said.

"Doesn't seem strange to me. It's just how we work."

"It's just the jail, right? But the terminals connect to San Diego County, which connects to the state and the federal governments. County officials pretend it's a closed network, walled off from the other government entities, but it's not that simple. The right bot can slither from one network to the next, stealthily and seamlessly."

"And your bot could do that, I presume."

"Yeah, I designed Nessie as a network protector. But if I flip the proverbial switch, she can become a network killer as well. Using principles of AI, she seeks weaknesses, responds to countermeasures, and launches attacks and counterattacks with far more speed than any known countermeasures."

"Who is Nessie?"

"The code name of my bot. Keep that to yourself, please."

"So no network is safe?"

"Correct. In attack mode, Nessie would be devastating. A dozen Nessie bots infecting government computer systems, for example, would disable the government in a matter of minutes.

181

No human intervention could prevent total destruction."

Carson was incredulous that Laura had possessed such a killer mindset.

"Why are you looking at me that way?" she said.

"Sorry, I didn't realized you were that steeped in cyber war, because the consequences could be devastating for either side."

"Which is why I wanted to create the most dangerous cyber bot that I could, Carson. Nessie is defensive. She's a guardian. Just don't piss her off. I think of her as the ultimate peacekeeper."

They kept walking.

"Carson, how'd you get that job, anyway? You've never done that kind of work. You're way overqualified for that, aren't you?"

"Probably. Well, definitely. But I was looking for something simple, without a lot riding on my shoulders. I'd had enough responsibility in the Navy, so I thought the prison job would interest me. I could work my shift and have a life afterward."

"Sure, I get that. So you got referred for an interview and they hired you, just like that? Did you tell them you were a former SEAL?"

"Not a chance I'd open that can of worms. SEALs have gotten too popular, over-hyped. I didn't need that baggage following me around at a new job. I told them I was ex-Navy and I trained newbies. It was unusual, though."

"Why?"

"I'm at Ocean Beach with Diego, right? I won't go into the whole thing, but I had an issue with a guy's pit bull attacking my puppy while we were playing ball in the surf, minding our own business. I got into a minor scuffle with the pit's owner, and Diego ran away and ended up at the far north

182

end of dog beach. I run after him, and there's this young lady who saw what happened. She caught up with Diego while I'm limping down the beach, and she held him until I got there. Turns out she's a job recruiter who helps the county scout for job applicants.

"I mention that I'm looking for a job, and she tells me to contact the hiring manager at the county, a guy named Johnny Petit, and I go to the interview. He's asking me these questions like he's not sure I'm the right fit. I'm wary at first, then I sort of try to sell myself because I need the work, right? So, unbelievably, he offers me the job. I reported for work the following morning."

"Just like that, huh?"

"Yep."

"That is an odd way to fill a government job. You just met the recruiter at the beach and then she talks you up to Petit, right? Or you wouldn't have gotten the interview. Did they interview any other candidates?"

"Not that I know of. I got the impression they were in a hurry to hire someone."

Carson suddenly placed both hands on his head, pulling on his hair. He bent over at the waist and hissed. "God fucking dammit, McCready."

Laura put her hand on his back. "Carson, what's wrong? Are you okay? Take a breath and calm down."

She wore a fanny pack stuffed with a bottle of water. She pulled the bottle from her pack and handed it to Carson. He took a few sips.

"I should have known. Something wasn't right. Fuck, Laura. Was I hand-picked for this job and didn't know it?

"You probably should've asked more questions. That's not like you. So you let your guard down for a minute. You're probably overthinking this because you have a paranoid side to you now. I can't remember you being like that."

"Okay, so I'm not a total dimwit. Let's assume I wasn't picked on purpose. Petit needed to fill the job and he got me by accident. Just a guy on the beach who's also an ex-Navy SEAL and platoon leader who ran super-dangerous direct-action missions in the Middle East."

"Sounds okay to me. Why not?"

Carson stopped suddenly and faced Laura. "Fuck. Laura, I *was* picked. The prison is the key to the whole thing. Somebody wanted me for that job."

"What makes you so sure?"

"The intel I told you about. I got a strange text last night. Here, let me show you." Carson pulled out his phone from his jeans pocket and scrolled to the mystery text. "Look at this."

Laura scanned the text and read it out loud. " 'There will be a cyberattack on government computers . . . Trust no one.' "

"See what I mean?" Carson said.

"Stop, Carson. Think it through. Why the prison?"

"Supposed I'm Garrick, the self-appointed freedom fighter. I need the prison. Why? Because I need the felons. I need them because they're bad guys, right? Why do I like bad guys? Because they do nasty shit. But who am I? I'm the guy who wants to fuck things up. Maybe bring down the government. There's the technical aspect of the operation, but also a psych-ops aspect. I need a story to pin the attack on the cons. I've already got a head start. They're bad guys, right?"

"Then what's the most plausible story to pin the attack on prisoners?" Laura said.

"Think about it. What shakes up Americans when nothing seems to shake us anymore? Situation normal, all fucked up.

184

Nothing matters. The big shots make up stories, and people just buy it. We've become that cynical. What makes people give a damn? What excites the survival instinct? When we can't find food. When someone points a gun at our heads. Seeing a pool of blood next to a child's body. When a thief steals the TV on Super Bowl Sunday, or when New York gets blown up in the sequel to 9/11."

"But, Carson, Garrick doesn't see himself as a terrorist. He sees himself as a well-intentioned bourgeoisie professor who thinks government is the road to serfdom. That's all."

Carson saw a bench and took a seat. Laura followed. He could feel her shoulder touching his.

"Garrick doesn't want to be a terrorist, but he's probably capable of thinking like one," he said.

"I suppose we all are after 9/11."

"Exactly. Nobody likes terrorists, especially Islamic terrorists. That's a story our mastermind would buy into, and one most of us buy into whatever your politics. That story still fires our survival instinct—even years after 9/11."

"So our evil genius wants everyone pointing the finger at dudes in orange suits locked up in a high-security prison," Laura said.

"But they're not just guys in orange suits, Laura. These are bad guys, remember? Plus they're mostly brown and Black. How does the outside world see brown and Black guys locked up in a high-security prison? Who or what scares people? Most Americans aren't too upset when an antisemitic white punk fires an AR-15 into a crowded synagogue. That's considered par for the course in a society driven by gun violence.

"But Americans draw the line when a foreigner— particularly a dark-skinned man with brown eyes and a suicide vest—threatens us on our land. That's an invasion. That's what prompts Americans to retaliate. We catch the bad guys, send them to Guantanamo, and pretend all is A-OK, right?"

They walked on toward the Soledad parking lot and got to Laura's car. She clicked the driver's door to unlock it, and Carson opened it. She slid into the driver's seat.

"Well, then it's simple, Carson."

"Simple?"

"Yeah. According to your anonymous tipster, a cyber war is coming, originating from the very county jail you work at. You know what you gotta do."

"What's that?"

"Don't sleep."

22
SECURITY UPDATE

Carson finally fell asleep at two thirty in the morning, but the disinterested alarm jolted him awake at six a.m. He stuck to his usual routine and got to work by eight. He tried to normalize his emotions, knowing he couldn't talk to anybody at the jail about his worry that a disgruntled MIT professor might launch an unprecedented cyberattack against the US government—bizarre as that sounded. He trusted no one. He cycled through the motions of the day, then went to the scheduled practice with his team for the upcoming charity game.

His arm was rusty. If he threw hard, he could feel the shoulder pain. He'd have to work up to it. So he threw hard enough for practice. Hard enough to let the boys know he could throw.

He was sore but he felt good about the bet with Biff Dickson. He told Biff that night at the dive bar, "That's right, Biff. You'll have an edge. I'll be lucky if I can find guys who aren't in jail." Carson grinned.

"Earth to Carson," Biff replied. "They *are* in jail."

The game was scheduled for early June—about thirty days away. Carson would throw hard then, when the arm felt ready. Then he'd throw very hard. He'd throw the bomb. And he'd already picked the guy he'd throw the bomb to: Antoine, a guy from the yard who tried out. Like Carson and like Black Terrell, he quit football in high school. Grew up in rural Alabama and ended up in San Diego with the Navy. Mustered out and wound up on the streets. Got busted stealing a car. The real all-American story. But now Antoine had something to prove. He was fast as a rabbit on steroids.

After the first few days of tryouts and practice, Carson was pleased. After a week of tryouts, Carson had found twenty guys who were decent.

"They may outclass us, but they won't beat us up," Carson told Johnny Petit. "No way Biff Dickson will find tougher guys than mine."

Black Terrell was hands down one of the best fullbacks Carson had ever seen. He could run into a truck and suffer only minor bruises. White Terrell, the skinhead, was large, fast, and had good hands. A solid choice for tight end on offense and linebacker on defense. The two Terrell boys would make a formidable line-backing team. White Terrell looked mean as freaking hell. And Black Terrell, the spit image of Malcolm X behind his fat black glasses, looked gentle and studious.

~

After practice Carson wandered back to his office to finish up some paperwork before heading home. He ran into Johnny Petit in the hallway.

"You look like a dog, McCready. Sure you and your boys will be ready?"

"No promises, man. But we might surprise some people."

"Gotta say, Carson. We watched those Biff guys practice the other day—me and Heller. Those boys look pretty damned good. You sure about this?"

"Have you heard the term 'shock and awe,' Petit?"

"Yeah, who hasn't?"

"Biff's guys won't know what hit them. I'll say no more."

"Are you serious? Our guys are full-time inmates. Biff's guys actually play for a living."

"I would not call beer money playing for a living, Johnny."

"Okay, Carson. Fine. Heller told me to give you guys a chance to bail now and save face. I'll tell him you told me to go fuck myself. Is that about right?"

"Yeah, I like that, Johnny. Tell Heller that. And tell him to call me if he needs any more convincing. A white flag isn't in our playbook."

Petit looked down. "Something I need to tell you."

"What, Johnny?"

"Heller's getting push back from the county council. They don't like the idea of our gangbangers getting a day off for a football game at Aztec Stadium."

"Christ, Johnny. I thought this was all settled."

"Alvarez likes it. But a couple of other commissioners are asking questions. So are the lawyers. Liability issues, supposedly."

"Fuck, Johnny. My guys have their hearts set on this game. Everybody wants this."

"Don't panic yet. Heller's presenting the case before the county council next Thursday. He's in. So's Alvarez. But thought you should know it's not yet a go."

"Should I tell my team?"

"Your call." Petit turned to go. He stopped and turned

189

around. "Oh, McCready?"

"Yeah, Johnny?"

"Forgot to mention. Come in an hour later tomorrow. We're updating the computer system, and the IT guys won't work in the same room as the inmates. We'll hold the jailbirds until the IT guys finish."

Carson stuck his key into the office door and clicked it open. With everything on his mind, Petit's talk about a security update got Carson's undivided attention. He was halfway through the door. He looked down, then met Petit's eyes.

"What's the update about?" Carson asked.

He watched how Petit's eyes wandered leftward. A tell?

"Remember those strange probes of the system we were getting a while back? Time for another computer security update."

"Another one? We've already updated all our machines."

"The Big Machine speaks and I follow. All I know, cowboy."

~

Carson drove home, thinking about Petit's unusual directive to report late to work in the morning. Yes, another computer security update was plausible, but the last one was a comprehensive overhaul of all computer software and security systems. The tipster's warning—*Pay attention. Trust no one*—rattled his brain.

He didn't want to bother Laura. But he alone wasn't capable of stopping whatever mess Petit could put into motion. Carson figured he had until midnight to figure out a plan and execute it.

He called Laura and skipped the formalities. "This is getting real."

"Actually, I'm glad you called."

"Oh? Why's that?"

"I had a dream last night. I dreamed that some mystery person was warning me about something."

"Are you making fun of me?"

"No, I'm serious. I wanted it to be a bad dream. But when I looked at my phone this morning, it was all real."

"You're not messing with me?"

"Unfortunately, no. They told me I'd been hacked, whatever the hell that means."

Carson didn't reply.

"Say something."

"Laura, whoever contacted you also knows who I am. Where I work. They know I was a SEAL. A notorious one with a well-documented history. I'm not sure what they don't know. They warned me about a cyberattack, right? Someone who's hell-bent on fighting tyranny. Now, I've got even more troubling news."

"What?"

"My boss is telling me to clear out tomorrow morning because of another security update. We just did a big one several weeks ago. Makes no sense."

"Are you suggesting your boss is involved?"

"Someone's got to him."

"More speculation."

"Look, Laura. If I'm right, then we don't have much time. I think Petit is on the move tonight or early next morning. We usually start the day at eight, but he told me to come in at nine. All telemarketing trading delayed an hour, and Petit says the IT guys refuse to be in the room with the telemarketing boys."

"Listen to yourself, Carson. Now your boss is involved, and suddenly he's connected to Garrick and the plot of the century! Why don't we leave it alone and assume everything is normal? At worst someone is pranking us. Sounds more rational than beating ourselves up about this. Besides, protecting America isn't our job."

"You're resisting the irrational. I know. It's confusing. You're right to doubt what doesn't seem logical. But we can't ignore this, Laura. The tip I got doesn't name Garrick. But it points in his direction. It confirms our suspicions. Will you just listen to me a second?"

"I have never not listened to you, Carson. Except when you were telling me you quit biology class to study shop so you could shape your own surfboards."

Carson cringed. "Well, I saved a lot of money, and it was more fun than mitochondrial DNA."

"Whatever, Carson. Spit it out."

"Okay. Let's assume a cyberattack is imminent. You're the expert. What can we do *right now*?"

"I still think it's a prank and this is all speculative. But I'll play along and put it back in your court. If you were to think like a SEAL for a moment, what strategies neutralize an enemy attack?" Laura said.

"Is this a quiz?"

"No, I want to make sure we're on the same page."

"At a minimum we'd have sufficient firepower to at least match that of the enemy. But we worked based on overmatch. We always operated from the perspective of superior planning and training and far superior firepower. Running up the score wasn't a problem for us."

"But if you operated from the paradigm of neutralization, not defeat, simply matching the enemy is sufficient. That's the new paradigm of AI cyber defense. It's smart and efficient. Humans aim to destroy, but a cyber bot learns to neutralize with the least effort possible."

"The cyber bot?"

"Yeah, the bot that will neutralize the malware or whatever kind of attack it encounters. You asked me what we can do right now. I have an idea based on what I think could be coming. We'll create a mirror image of the attacking algorithm and launch her into the computer network. Because the attacker would be facing an equally capable foe, the aggressor would game-out the likely outcome and rationally conclude further attack is no longer worthwhile. Zero sum. Game over."

"How do we get from here to game over?"

"That's the rub. Obviously I don't have time to create an anti-bot from scratch, so I'll do something that represents a huge risk, both for my freedom and for the security of the computer networks."

"I don't like the sound of that."

"If this is happening—and that's a big if—then I have to make some huge assumptions. I'll assume Garrick is behind the attack, just as you figured. I must also assume that Garrick is probably using a version of the attack bot I've designed for the Pentagon. My own Nessie. I have to assume that Suzanne, or someone else, provided Garrick with insider knowledge of what I was creating for the US government. If all that is true, that means Garrick has a military-grade cyberweapon in his hands, bought and paid for by American taxpayers."

"My God. That's a lot of assumptions."

"I know. But in this puzzle we're putting together, my assumptions fit with the whole theory, right?"

"True. But if you're wrong about one piece of it, the cyberattack becomes unstoppable, right?" Carson said.

"I once told Suzanne that my ultimate goal was to design the perfect defense against the ultimate attack bot. I designed

Nessie for the Pentagon as a killer bot that could defeat any threat. Luckily I know Nessie inside and out. I'm certain that I can mount a defense against the most intelligent bot in the world, because I created her."

"Give me the bottom line, Laura. We're running out of time."

"We'll launch a mirror image of Nessie to preempt whatever attack Garrick might be cooking up. Let's call her Baby. She'll attach to Nessie and neutralize her. Nessie games out the outcome and sees no way forward. I see no other way to stop her."

"What if it doesn't work? I still don't understand what makes Nessie so deadly. And what if Garrick is too clever?"

"Now's not the time for a deep dive into how artificial neural networks work, Carson."

"I've heard of the concept. That's what Nessie is based on? The way a human brain learns?"

"Yes, but with the ability to sift through billions of data points in milliseconds. That's how Nessie learns to dominate. With sufficient training, she has learned to neutralize any threat that human computer operators have ever encountered since the beginning of computing technology.

"But Nessie has never learned to defeat her mirror image, an equally capable foe. She can't because it's impossible. That's what I'm banking on."

"But Baby could still fail if Garrick has anticipated your countermeasure," Carson said.

"I can't rule out the possibility of failure. Garrick could have anticipated the countermeasure I'm trying to create. I doubt it. But if he has thought of it, then Nessie, my own creation, would blast through government computer networks like wildfire. The US government, as we know it, would no longer exist."

23

HIGH CRIMES AND MISDEMEANORS

Showing up at the prison after working hours would not be a good look. Out of time and out of place—a setup for no fucking good.

Since taking the job at the county's most dangerous prison facility less than a year ago, Carson's routine had been a basic case of following rules, an effortless practice for a guy who'd spent a career in the Navy. Ready to work at eight and stand the fuck by. Ready to leave by five and punch out for home. Hours between five and eight were blackouts. But tonight would be different.

Going solo was one option. Suiting up and creeping in. Breaking into or overcoming a fragile spot of the prison, locating the dark and empty telemarketing room, and launching the anti-bot via fifteen jump drives. A thirty-minute job assuming no SNAFUs. Bad assumption. A ridiculous idea for several reasons, not least of which was that prison guards would surround him in seconds, and out of sheer practicality, he couldn't shoot or physically disable them. Option two: he'd adopt a familiar profile. His "girlfriend," Laura, would re-route the guards' normally guarded mentality as a nice and pretty surprise.

He called Laura. "Don't take this the wrong way, okay?"

"What?"

"We're going to a prison full of guys."

"We?"

"Please. I need you. But you might be the center of attention. You okay with that?"

"I thought about it. You're right. I'm the beauty *and* the brains of this operation."

"Well . . . yes, that's true. The odds of this operation going south are formidable. Any advantage . . ." Carson paused.

"Spit it out, mister."

"It's a given that I need you to prevent a fatal fuck up on the technical end. But I also need you to disarm the enemy. Are you okay with that?"

"Disarm? How?"

"Mentally. Emotionally. Oh, never mind. I shouldn't have said anything."

She said nothing for several seconds. "Don't worry, Carson. I've got this."

~

Carson had the basic elements of the plan worked out by the time Laura arrived at his apartment at half past seven on Friday night.

He opened the door and came across as skeptical. "Wow."

"Wow, what?"

"Never mind. Did it work? Is Baby ready?"

"I wouldn't be here if she wasn't. Where's your bathroom?"

She walked to the toilet and emerged ten minutes later.

196

"Eye shadow was a bit thick. How's it look now?" she asked.

"Just be yourself. Trust it."

"Are you nervous, Carson?"

"Hell, yes."

"That explains your cheerful attitude."

Diego followed Carson to the kitchen. Carson grabbed a bottle of water, spread a handful of kibbles in a bowl for the Lab, and handed the bottle to Laura. "I'll make up some story about forgetting my phone in the telemarketing room and how you wanted to keep me company. Sound good?"

"One problem. I've got to monitor the attack. I'll need my laptop. It's in the car."

"When's the monitoring start and stop?"

"From the moment you insert the jump drives. I've instructed Baby to launch itself on the email server. When or if Petit—or whoever—launches Nessie, I'll get data as she attaches to apps and memory. What networks it hits and where it ends up. Baby will lie dormant in the network until she recognizes the attack. At the point of recognition, Baby will attach to Nessie, and we hope, neutralize the aggressor."

"How and when will we know it's working?"

"I ran some limited tests. Baby performed well against Nessie in my simulations. We won't know for certain how well until twenty-four hours out. If we launch Baby as soon as possible, she'll counter-attack the moment she recognizes Nessie. Understood?"

"I wish you could explain the details of how all this works, but we don't have time. I'll have to trust you."

"Carson?"

"What?"

"Can you just relax and maybe take for granted that I'm on your side? I'm sorry if I've come across as skeptical. I can't help it. But I trust you. I always have. You know that, right?"

Carson said nothing. He reached out his thick hand, worn and rough from years of doing hard things in hard conditions, and delicately touched Laura's face. Her skin was soft and cool. At that moment he wanted to kiss her. Undress her and take her into a bedroom that hadn't seen a woman in years, least of all the woman he'd always loved who was here now, not for intimacy, but to risk everything because he'd convinced her to follow him into an abyss.

She touched his hand lingering on her face and moved toward him to touch her lips to his. Gently. Not teasingly, but as a reflection of their past, present, and future. At that moment Carson knew that they were now bound together by trust and fate for as far as he could see. Carson McCready could predict most futures, but this one refused to give away its secrets.

Laura kissed him then picked up the beer bottle. She took a satisfying gulp. He liked what he saw, Laura smiling and looking confident. He couldn't question her technical know-how, but he looked for signs that she could handle the inevitable psychological heat of the mind-game they were about to play for real.

He grabbed the water bottle from her fingers. She seemed calm enough. Perhaps calmer than him, but he never let his anxieties show in public, before or during an operation. This was no deadly gig. Piece of cake, actually. But the consequences of failure weren't just a missed target in a tight perimeter of cause and effect. Failure now could be catastrophic, and they both knew it.

"Right, okay," Laura said. "You insert the jump drives. I'll pretend I'm playing Minecraft on my computer while you're saving the world."

Carson turned to Laura with a serious expression. "I'm going to pretend I'm just on another mission and you're working on another routine cyber project. If we end up saving the world, for just a while anyway, I'll be happy. But I won't dance in the street and pat myself on the back."

"No, but I would have a double shot of whiskey."

"And I'd join you. We're alike, Laura. We do this because people like us do what's necessary. I've known this about myself all my life. And that's why I've always loved you. You see a lost dog and you save it."

"Why do some people act and others don't, I wonder? To save ourselves? Blind faith?"

"Faith in ourselves. Trust in our own good judgment. To save ourselves from a world we could not bear to live in. The hate, mistrust, and cynicism. When folks don't stop the car to save an animal suffering on the side of the road. Where bystanders do nothing when a mugger slugs an old man at the ATM. When cops stand around in hardened vests, afraid to take down some dumbass with an automatic weapon who's mowing down six-year-olds in a school house."

"Is that it, we need more heroes?" Laura said.

"Maybe being a hero isn't as hard as people think. I believe humans are hard-wired to be heroic—for one another, for human survival."

"You really think so? Seems that the modern human is motivated by fear above all else."

"You're the scientist, Laura. How do you think humans have survived this long? When we stop being heroic, the species dies. That's my take on human evolution. If we're devolving, as you say, that means our heroic nature is vanishing. The driving force of our collective survival may be going extinct."

Laura said nothing for a few moments, mulling what

Carson had said. "In that case, we better start evolving, again. I'll drive."

~

When they arrived at the prison gates, Carson had two words on his mind: Redirect and Amplify. Being out of sync with his usual time and place concerning the county jail, he had to overcome any suspicions among the guards that he'd gone absolutely nuts between the time he left work at five p.m. and when he showed up at midnight. Divert the guards' attention from himself to Laura and amplify her presence relative to his. In this performance Carson would be the bit player. Laura was the star.

They rolled in at 12:15 a.m. Buster was manning the front gate. Laura rolled down the driver's window, allowing Carson's torso to lean over her chest. The guard's frown softened when he heard Carson's voice coming from the passenger seat.

"Hey, Buster. Late shift tonight?"

Buster bent over to see him. "Carson McCready. You out of your mind? You don't clock in until nine. What I heard. Go home, man."

"What can I say. I love my job. Hey, buddy, this is my girlfriend, Johanna."

Laura gave Carson a sharp look. Buster mumbled something into his walkie-talkie attached to his chest pack. He turned to Laura. "Nice meeting you, Ma'am. You keeping this crazy in line? I got to say, you're way above McCready's pay grade."

"The man's incorrigible; what can I say? Nice to meet you, Buster."

"What the hell are you doing back here, Carson?"

Buster asked.

"Forgot my phone in the T-Room. Thought I'd come bust it out of jail and give my lady a quick mini-tour if that's all right."

Laura glanced at Carson with a hint of skepticism and smiled at Buster. "I know it's a big favor. I'd be grateful. Though he loves his phone more than me," Laura said.

Carson noticed how her golden blonde hair shimmered in the bright lights of the prison gates. Even Carson was mesmerized at her ability to shoot the shit with Buster, who now seemed uncharacteristically bashful. Then Buster seemed to realize he was still on guard-duty. His face turned from friendly to cautious. "Let's see what we can do. I could just have a guy bring it out."

Carson leaned in. "Seriously, buddy, no worries. I should have called ahead that I was bringing a guest. I hid the phone somewhere in that clutter. The guy wouldn't likely find it."

"I was looking forward to seeing the jail," Laura said.

Buster pressed the walkie-talkie button and mumbled more words surrounded by static noise. He walked to the front of the vehicle holding a yellow pad, about to jot down the license plate number.

Buster spoke into the mic. "Guess who I found trying to break in? No, man. It's Carson. Brought his girlfriend. Drives a white Prius, license number . . ."

More static and mumbled words coming from the other end. "Don't worry about it?" Buster asked. "Okay. Good. They're coming through."

Buster moved around to the driver's side. "You two are good to go. Don't mingle too long."

"Sure you won't get in trouble? Isn't there a prison rule?" Carson said.

"Case by case. Staff members are usually okay. As long as you're not gonna leave contraband or spring a con out of jail. We know you, Carson. You're okay. So's your girlfriend."

"We're balls to the wall. Owe you one, brother."

~

Carson led Laura through the slammer and down a fifty-foot hallway that reeked of Global Industrial. They passed the staff coffee and TV room and turned the corner. He shoved open the squeaky metal door to the telemarketing room, which prison janitors had recently neatened up and de-cluttered. The room's chairs obediently hugged computer terminals in a straight line against the wall.

Laura slung open her laptop. While she punched keys, Carson went to work booting up each of the desktop computers and waited for Laura's instructions.

"Go down the line and insert one drive at a time. Then go back to the beginning. At that point, you'll see a thumb-drive icon on each screen. They're identified with numbers one through fifteen. Click on each drive icon one by one and wait."

Carson said nothing. He worked down the line until he reached the last computer, with an elapsed time of five minutes and thirty-five seconds. He stood next to Laura as she monitored each jump drive from her computer screen. Carson watched as the crazy-looking computer code flowed like a never-ending river through her monitor. They watched and waited for nine minutes and ten seconds, resulting in a total elapsed time of fourteen minutes and forty-five seconds for the entire operation. Carson placed his hand on Laura's shoulder and squeezed lightly once.

The black phone on the wall next to the door lit up and shrilled twice quickly. Carson slid down the concrete floor to answer. He heard Buster's voice, unusually formal. "Mr. McCready, Johnny Petit coming your way," he said, then hung up.

Carson saw Laura coming toward him, moving her lips. "Who was that?"

He said nothing, gesturing with his hand to stay calm. They both looked toward the shut door when they heard men's voices laughing and joking. Carson slipped off his shoes and gently clicked the door lock.

"How much longer?" he whispered.

"About sixty seconds. What should I do?" Laura asked.

"Remove your shoes. Mess yourself up like we've been making out."

Laura looked puzzled.

"Quickly, he's coming in," Carson said.

Laura tussled her hair and smudged her lip gloss. She folded her laptop and shoved it into her handbag. She withdrew each jump drive one by one, starting with number fifteen at the far end of the room. Carson followed her lead, starting with number one, and they met in the middle. The doorknob wiggled.

"Hey, Carson! You in there? What's going on?"

Laura was working down the line, shutting down each computer in an orderly fashion. Carson realized they were out of time. They'd have to abort or improvise. He whispered. "Laura! Leave it."

He felt in his right front pocket. "Fuck!"

"What's wrong?" Laura said.

"Forgot my damned phone in the car."

Laura ran to her handbag. "Here."

203

Holding Laura's phone in his right hand, Carson slung open the door and saw Johnny Petit staring at him.

Carson grinned and held up the phone, almost shoving it in Petit's face. "Found it, thank God. How are you, Johnny? Hey, meet my girlfriend."

Laura meandered over to greet Petit.

"Nice meeting you, Ma'am."

"Petit, your face is turning red. You okay, buddy?"

"I'm getting the McCready tour, Mr. Petit. Carson has said so much about the prison I wanted to see for myself. Hope that's okay," Laura said.

"Sorry. Forgot your name already, Miss," Petit said.

Laura glanced at Carson. "Johanna."

Petit scanned the room. "Everything good? Why are those computers still on?"

"My fault, Johnny. I got messy today. Getting that football game planned and all. SNAFU City, brother." Carson turned to Laura. "All right, babe. Are we done here?"

"Sure, honey." Laura reached out to shake Petit's hand. "So very nice to meet you, Mr. Petit. I finally get to put a face to the stories Carson's told me."

Petit's face relaxed. "Good stories, I hope."

Carson interjected and touched Petit's arm. "Nothing but, buddy. Nothing but."

He took Laura's arm and started for the door. He stopped and turned to face Petit. "Why are you here, Johnny?"

Petit looked sideways, as if searching for something beyond the wall. Something to say. Carson noticed. One whale of a tell.

"I get it. You're an open book."

"Hell's that mean?"

For effect Carson waited a beat. Then two, watching

204

Petit's reaction. "Women are like that," he said, glancing at Laura. "Go to jail with you one minute. Kick you out of bed the next. And here you are."

"Ah! Your girlfriend came to the jail. Guess you're not getting lucky tonight either, McCready," Petit said.

Carson turned to Laura. "What do you say, darling? Am I getting lucky?"

"Honey, you're doing just fine in the luck department."

24

DEBRIEF

In a hard rain, Carson and Laura drove back to his place in Lemon Grove. They said nothing to each other for almost fifteen minutes. The clock on the dashboard read 1:55 a.m.

He glanced at Laura as he drove. She stared straight ahead, giving nothing and taking nothing.

"That was interesting," Carson finally said.

Laura said nothing.

"Are you okay?" he asked.

"Don't feel like talking right now."

"Know what you mean."

Ten minutes later, Carson pulled the Prius into the condo's parking lot. Rain was still splattering on the windshield. "Let's go up."

"Carson, I should go. It's late."

"You're not going anywhere tonight. It's cold, dark, and it's going to rain all night. You're exhausted. We both are. I'll sleep on the couch."

"You're not getting lucky tonight, if ever, okay?"

"I've got no problem with that."

They got up to the apartment, and Diego greeted them. Carson took the dog for a quick walk and pee. When Carson returned he found Laura lying on the couch with two whiskeys on the coffee table.

They clinked glasses and Carson plopped down next to her, both facing the TV set on the wall.

"Want to watch something?" Carson asked.

"Not really. Happy just sitting."

"I hear you. Decompression feels good."

"That was intense, Carson. I was afraid of saying the wrong thing."

"What are you talking about? You saved our asses."

"How did I do that?"

"You charmed the hell out of Buster and Petit. I was awestruck."

"You were right about Petit."

"Unfortunately, yes. My tipster wasn't wrong."

"You handled it. Think he suspects something?" Laura said.

"I couldn't tell. You saw what happened."

"Petit looked guilty as hell." She pulled her laptop from her case, cranked it up, and took a sip of the whiskey. She clicked keys for about a minute and watched the screen for any sign that Petit had launched the bot. She looked up and grinned. "It's working."

"What's working?"

"My program is searching the internet for signs that Nessie is traveling. We'll know in a few minutes. Now we wait."

Carson touched her hand as they sat in silence, sipping the whiskeys and petting Diego, who had hopped on the couch with them.

"Is this what a hard-core SEAL team looks like?"

"Wish it were. I might have stayed."

207

"Why did you leave? I assume you were good at your job."

"You want to talk about that now, Laura?"

"Why not now? We're passing time, waiting. Tell me what you've been doing all these years."

"Honestly, Laura, I found what I loved leading a SEAL platoon. The assignments kept getting bigger, more consequential. Never got bored. But shit happened that should never have happened. All the training in the world can't prevent human stupidity. I tried to shake it off, but then I got demoralized. The proverbial last straw."

"Are you allowed to tell me what happened?"

"I shouldn't. Most of it is classified. One of my guys killed an innocent Somali civilian. Cold-blooded murder. Our guy knew better. Power got to his head. We're trained killers. But we kill with purpose in the defense of the United States. We're damned good at our jobs, and we police ourselves. That's the military code of honor, and it's passed on generation after generation. Just takes one asshole to fuck it up. Put it this way: he showed his true colors."

"What exactly did he do?"

"Besides almost severing the civilian's head?"

"There's more?"

"Dude was a special nutcase. Unfortunately he's not alone in the military these days. The political bullshit in America spoiled a good soldier. White nationalist shit. Somalis aren't white and they're not Christian, right? I told him I'd nail him for insubordination if he mouthed off about that crap around the team. But on his own time, he whispered to other guys on the squad. He boasted, you know? How the patriots back home in Kentucky were planning something big, and he was giving them, shall we say, 'technical assistance.' "

"This guy was in your platoon?"

"I blame myself for not coming down harder. With the backing of the team, I reported the incident in Somalia, and it seemed like justice would be done until some Kentucky senator went cowboy on us, filed to get the motherfucker pardoned. That good senator is screaming to re-open the case. Pro-military is good. But some of these fucking politicians hide behind Old Glory for their own self-aggrandizement. They prey on people's ignorance. The 'take names and kick ass' crowd. Get the good senator on a mission with us. Put his life on the line. Give him a come-to-Jesus moment when he realizes this is not a fucking game. His politics don't mean shit to me, all right? The betrayal we felt was ruinous. In my platoon, morale went south. What the hell were the guys supposed to depend on? What was the code of conduct? When the politicians throw out the rules, where does that leave us?"

"You're angry, Carson."

"Yes, I'm angry. On our next mission about six months later, another one of our guys, with similar motivations, did something questionable. Thank God he didn't shoot the captured combatant in the head, but he sliced him up pretty good. Ruined the man's face. And for what? It was criminal and senseless. Judge me right or wrong, but I couldn't go through with it again. I was done. The day we got back to Coronado, I filed my retirement papers."

"Sorry that happened to you. But it's all past now, thank God."

"Never really goes away. I'm scarred, Laura. I try to keep a lid on that anger. I've been in therapy. But I'll never be the guy I was before. When you knew me best."

Laura touched his face with her hand. "You're a good man, Carson. I know you. Your resilience. You see the best in

209

people. That's who you are."

Carson got up to take a piss. Laura opened her laptop to inspect the progress of the competing bots through the internet. At least ninety minutes had elapsed since launching the Baby algorithm.

Carson returned to the living room with a smile on his face. "That piss felt exquisite. A good piss is a sign of how much tension you've been carrying around. And your hunger level after. I could never eat before a mission. Now I'm famished. How about you? Let's see what I can dig up in the kitchen."

"I'm happy for your exquisite piss, honey. I might have slightly more important news though."

"So I'm your honey now?"

"Old habit, McCready."

Carson sat down next to her. "What happened?"

"Baby is working. She's killing the attack."

"How do you know that?" Carson asked.

"I saw it with my own eyes. It's clear that Petit—we presume—launched Nessie from the desktops after we left. But he was too late. My data are telling us the unvarnished story. As an AI Baby thought on her feet, so to speak. Once she launched she detected no threats. She didn't travel. She simply lurked on the outer fringes of the network. Once Petit launched Nessie, however, Baby recognized the threat and instantaneously attached itself to Nessie's algorithm. Like an antibody attaching to a virus." Laura reopened the laptop and pointed her finger at the evidence.

"See here? That's Nessie's self-generated code right there. As an AI itself, Nessie reconfigured its code to counter Baby's defense. Both algorithms immediately recognized a nearly infinite number of potential moves, all leading to stalemate.

210

Nessie saw no advantage in reconfiguring itself further so it just stopped."

"How does it just stop?" Carson asked.

"Better to say it's lying dormant. Nessie sees no move until it sees some advantage. I see no route forward for this attack. Nessie will remain dormant in the network."

"For how long?"

"Until somebody comes along and recognizes what's happened and comes up with new technology to destroy Baby—technology that I'm not aware of. For the foreseeable future, we're safe. I'm ninety-nine percent confident of that. Not only that, we have just confirmed something vitally important."

"You guessed right. The modifications worked," Carson said.

"Exactly. And so we can be almost certain that Garrick is behind this." Laura laughed. "The bastard exploited my creativity to bring down the government and create his libertarian paradise."

"How's that?"

"Garrick fancies himself the creative genius who creates the wealth that everyone benefits from. He sees himself as John Galt. But Garrick took from me to create wealth for himself."

"So Ayn got it wrong?" Carson said.

"I'd say so. She was writing about an idea. The real world ate her idea and barfed it up."

Carson got up. He walked to the kitchen in bare feet and returned with another whiskey bottle. He filled both glasses, picked up one to toast, and sat next to Laura, who remained glued to her laptop.

Still glaring at the screen, she took a long sip of the whiskey and set it on the coffee table. Sitting beside her,

Carson dropped his head to his knees and rubbed his head and his eyes. He looked up and saw Laura smiling.

"No doubt in my mind. This was Garrick's handiwork," she said. "His or whomever he hired to help him. I was able to pin-point exactly where Garrick had altered Nessie's code. Clever move. I'll give him that. I matched the change on Baby and she neutralized the attack."

"In technical terms Baby just ate Nessie's lunch, right, honey?" Carson said.

Laura smiled. "Technically, yes."

They sat in silence for several minutes, enjoying the whiskey. Carson put his arm around Laura's shoulders. "You are amazing. You figured that out and acted with the pressure of the whole damned country on your back, and nobody even knows it. Not yet, anyway."

"Oh, they will. Garrick will. Trust me."

"Then congratulations to us. But . . ."

"What, Carson?"

"An enemy fueled by passion won't give up that easily. He'll return to attack again. In the Middle East, we fought true believers. The Russians fought the same and lost after three decades. We fought and lost for a few decades more. Garrick is a true believer. He fits the profile. He's been at this for years, and he hasn't gone away. He's tried to recruit you and other would-be disciples for years. You really think he's done? Baby has given us time to figure out a defense for the next attack. That's where we're at."

"I was hoping for a Hollywood ending. But it feels like the other shoe has to drop," Laura said.

"I'd like to get back to my work, especially our charity stuff. Honestly, that's all I want. Now this BS has to be first priority."

212

"What do you have in mind?"

"Now's when we need outside help, Laura. We got lucky this time."

"What about getting the FBI involved?" Laura said.

"They could take forever. We don't have time."

"So maybe we could help them. We design an AI bot to locate Garrick's private documents and records, then feed them to the FBI. We uncover secrets and merely point the authorities in the right direction."

"You mean anonymously, right?"

"That's right."

"They'll track us down. They'll bring us in for questioning, so I don't see the point. Besides, doesn't the Bureau have tools like Baby and Nessie already?" Carson asked.

"No, they don't. Not yet, anyway. The military is way ahead of law enforcement on this technology."

"Laura, stop. Are you insane? We can't use military technology without explicit permission from the Pentagon, no matter how righteous the cause."

"It's not as risky as you think. The right bot can cover its tracks. I'll code it to evaporate its zeros and ones into a digital black hole so nobody could trace it to us."

"Feeding intel to the FBI makes sense. But we've got to be super careful. We can't assume they're all good guys with a moral compass."

"You would know better than me. But I have one suggestion," Laura said.

"What's that?"

"We've got to find the right agent, correct?"

"That's our hope."

"This sounds sexist, I know. But I'm fairly certain she's a woman," Laura said.

"Oh?"

"Women are born to question authority, unlike men, who fall in line more easily and fall for the propaganda. We're more practical. We're mothers. When's the last time you lied to your mother and got away with it?"

Carson picked up his whiskey from the coffee table. "That's a pretty bold statement."

"You think I'm wrong?"

Carson considered the question and chuckled.

"What's funny?" Laura said.

"I'm realizing the irony. Men possess superficial power, but women are dangerous to the status quo. And men know it. Men pretend to have a moral compass. Women actually do. So, yeah, I agree. Our agent is a woman, and she's unbreakable."

"I'll go with that."

"Just one catch."

"What's that?"

Carson laughed. "The deep state."

"Oh, that. What exactly is it?"

"The civil service employees who make government work. The experts in the rank and file who don't take ideological sides because that's not their job. They execute laws and regulations under exact rules and lines of authority."

"Then why do they call it the deep state?"

"Because civil servants are a permanent part of the infrastructure that makes government work. Deep, right? Can you image a government where every employee gets fired every four years when a new president takes office? It would be chaos. I say thank God for the deep state."

"Nice civics lesson, Carson, but why do we care?"

"I'm saying we can't expect miracles. We get what the

system will give us. We want justice, right?"

"Of course."

"Then we're at the mercy of some lowly civil servant who keeps her head down, follows the law, and in order to keep her job, just does her job. To me that's a form of justice."

Laura looked at her watch and sighed. "How tired are you, Carson?"

"I'm dead. Why?"

"I say we're on a roll. Let's brew some coffee and keep working. Get this done. Otherwise I won't sleep."

"This could take all night, darling. After we find the right agent, then we have to find the dope on Cripps."

"Where do we start? The FBI must have a tip line, right?" Laura said.

"No doubt they do. But do we want to go over the transom and get lost in the shuffle? We'd be one in a million tips, and I doubt any glassy-eyed assistant would seriously consider what we've got."

"Because it would sound crazy."

"Exactly."

"We need an organization chart," Laura said.

"Try starting with the Department of Justice."

Laura clicked away on her laptop and brought up the Department's website. "Oh, shit. I don't think so. This place is gigantic. I wouldn't know where to start."

"All right. Let's reverse the order of our tasks. Let's find the dirt on Cripps, and that information could help us narrow down whom to talk to at Justice or the FBI."

"Love it." Laura reached into her handbag, pulled out a data stick, and stuck it into her laptop.

"What are you doing?"

"What we talked about. I'm going to modify Nessie's

algorithm to crawl all public records and hack into all private records involving Garrick Cripps. We'll start there. If we don't turn up anything, we'll go to the dark web.

"Don't we have to sort the records by some parameters?"

"Yes, we could. We probably should in order to get the best results. What should we sort on? What parameters?" Laura said.

"Criminal records. Court documents and cases. Corporate filings. Shit, the list is long. How fast can Nessie do this? How smart is she? Can she give us items with the highest probability of persuading an FBI agent to investigate? Or do we have to make that call?"

"Nessie will take time. Then we, mere humans, will have to scan her results and see what she turned up. I could modify Nessie's algorithm to maximize probabilities, but that would take days to code. Should we wait another week?"

Carson got up and walked to the kitchen. He turned around, looking inquisitive. "You still like cream and one Splenda, honey?"

"Only when I'm not tired and pissed. Fucking Garrick. I hate him. Coffee, black. And no damned Splenda."

ACT III

DESTROY

Natural law is to human capitalism what evolution is to nature itself. To the extent that our sense of God is reflected in natural law, pure capitalism is, in reality, the human being's most concrete expression of God himself.

– The Liberation Manifesto

25

IS MISSISSIPPI NECESSARY?

To: Amy Watson, Agent, Office of Professional Responsibility, US Department of Justice, Los Angeles, California.
Re: A conspiracy to overthrow the United States government
From: Concerned Citizens

Amy Watson almost choked on her morning coffee after reading the tipster's introduction to this odd court transcript. Apparently whoever sent it believed she could save the world from a terrible conspiracy out to destroy the country—a big stretch since Watson's charge was to investigate misconduct within the Justice Department, including wayward FBI agents. She'd be right to wonder, *What the fuck?*

A Madison County District Judge named Earl Brooks presided.

~

Adam Markov, Attorney for the Plaintiff: Could you please state your name and your affiliation?

Defendant: I'm Dr. Garrick Cripps. I'm the CEO of Phrygia Solutions.

Markov: Please tell the Court the nature of Phrygia's business activities.

Defendant: We're engaged in several businesses related to making governments operate more efficiently. I believe you want information about our division that contracts with state labor departments to manage their UI claims.

Markov: So when someone gets laid off from a job, your company determines whether the person gets an unemployment check.

Defendant: That's correct.

Markov: You mentioned that your company helps governments operate more efficiently.

Defendant: True.

Markov: Are you aware of a document called *The Liberation Manifesto*?

Defendant: I'm aware, yes.

Markov: Are you the author of this document?

Janet Creighton, Attorney for the Defendant: Your Honor, I cannot see the relevance of this. My client wrote it years ago, for heaven's sake, and it has no bearing on this litigation.

Markov: This document, Your Honor, speaks to the Defendant's general frame of mind in relation to the corporation and its mission to make governments more "efficient," as he describes it.

District Judge: I'll allow it, but get to the point quickly. You may answer the question, Dr. Cripps.

Defendant: Yes, I am the author of *The Liberation Manifesto*.

Markov: So it's true that you wrote in this manifesto, "The

perfect economic system is pure capitalism, the one and true result of which is the survival of the greediest and the most powerful," correct?

Defendant: I have a way with words, don't I?

(Audible laughter)

Markov: I'm sure we're all impressed by your wit. What did you mean by that statement in *The Manifesto*?

Defendant: Basically that the strong must prevail over the weak.

Markov: And why is that?

Defendant: For the nation's survival, the strong must prevail. Otherwise the weak will drag us all down into a perpetual state of poverty.

Markov: Is that all you have to say about that passage in your manifesto?

Defendant: Pretty much. That's my opinion.

Markov: You also wrote: "The vigorous thrust and thump of truth and progress is the Big Bang of the capitalist machine marching onward, and that machine will be impeded only at the collective peril of all humankind." Also from your manifesto, correct?

Defendant: I'm proud of those words.

Markov: This also comes from *The Manifesto*. You wrote: "When our revolution is complete, the bottom-feeders will have no place in our society."

Creighton: Your Honor, this line of questioning is getting us nowhere but to a late lunch.

District Judge: I'll allow this. But let's get to the point, shall we, Mr. Markov?

Markov: Dr. Cripps, does that sentiment also apply to the state government of Mississippi, your client in this case?

Defendant: I don't understand the question.

Markov: I'll make it simple for you. Is the state of Mississippi necessary?

Defendant: Necessary?

Markov: Would you like me to repeat the question?

Defendant: I can find no credible evidence that the state of Mississippi is necessary, no.

Markov: And that is because?

Defendant: The state ensures the perpetuation of the weakest, cheating the strong of their natural rights and liberties. Again, my opinion.

Markov: Then you would agree that plaintiff's unemployment claim to the state is fraudulent because the very existence of the state is contrary to natural law?

Creighton: Calls for speculation.

Defendant: I'll answer that. Yes, my opinion is that the state's existence is fraudulent. That is unrelated to whether the plaintiff's claim is fraudulent, which it is.

Markov: According to your algorithm, you mean.

Defendant: That is correct.

Markov: Dr. Cripps, what percentage of UI claims in the state of Mississippi did your firm classify as fraudulent?

Defendant: Depends on the county. The average is about seventy-six percent, I think.

Markov: Meaning that just one-quarter of all UI claims in the poorest state in the nation were legitimate, according to your system. Correct?

Defendant: Congrats. You can do arithmetic.

Markov: Do you know what Mississippi's unemployment rate was last year?

Defendant: I don't know.

Markov: According to the US Bureau of Labor Statistics, the state's unemployment rate last year averaged ten point two percent. Some counties were more and some less. Does that sound about right?

Defendant: Those are your facts, not mine.

Markov: They are also the state's facts, correct?

Defendant: Yes, but . . .

Markov: Thank you, you've answered the question. Are you aware that the plaintiff lives in Holmes County and filed a UI claim in that county?

Defendant: I'll take your word for it.

Markov: According to the algorithm developed by your company, a county's unemployment rate and per capita income together account for about ninety percent of the differences in claims designated as fraudulent, correct?

Defendant: I don't understand the question.

Markov: Okay, I'll simplify it. Taken together, joblessness and poverty predict ninety percent of fraudulent claims in your system. By your definition fraud goes up the poorer a county is, correct?

Defendant: I can confirm those are the variables used in the algorithm.

Markov: Your company's algorithm is biased against poor people, correct?

Creighton: I object, Your Honor. My clever opponent is seeking the gift of confession to claims that remain in litigation.

District Judge: Your objection is sustained.

Markov: Mr. Cripps, would it be fair to say that Holmes County ranks as one of the more economically depressed areas of Mississippi?

Defendant: Probably, yes.

Markov: Let's get back to those fraudulent claims and the variability among counties. What was your algorithm's denial rate for Holmes County last year?

Defendant: I don't know that number. That's what I have accountants for.

Markov: In fact, state records show your company classified eighty-five percent of unemployment insurance claims in Holmes County as fraudulent claims, correct?

Defendant: So you say.

Markov: You don't know? You base your business model on that information.

Creighton: Argumentative, your Honor.

District Judge: Overruled. Counsel has stated a fact already in evidence.

Markov: By the same token, approximately what was the per capita annual income of Madison County?

Defendant: Obviously people are better off there.

Markov: Please answer the question.

Defendant: I am not aware of that specific fact.

Markov: According to the Department of Labor, Madison County's per capita income that year was $58,604, correct?

Defendant: Again, I do not dispute that you are quoting from an official document.

Markov: Indeed, I am. So you probably know my next question. What was Madison County's unemployment rate last year?

Defendant: I'm guessing less than Holmes County's seventeen percent.

Markov: According to the Department of Labor, it was seven point two percent—correct?

Defendant: Yes, okay.

Markov: Now, even as out of touch with the Mississippi labor market as you seem to be, you must know your company designated as fraudulent just twelve percent of UI claims in

224

the relatively wealthy Madison County. Are you aware of that statistic?

Defendant: No, I am not.

Markov: Are you aware of the general pattern that poor counties, with the highest rates of unemployment, have the highest denial rates in your system, while the richest counties with relatively low unemployment rates have the lowest percentage of denied claims?

(Defendant: Inaudible exchange with the attorney)

Markov: I'm sorry, I did not hear your answer. Would you like me to repeat the question?

Defendant: No, I am not aware of that pattern.

Markov: Your Honor, I'd like to submit as Exhibit B an audio file of a telephone conversation between the plaintiff and his associate one year prior to the launch of the defendant's company. The conversation speaks to the defendant's state of mind regarding the questions before the court.

Creighton: Objection, Your Honor. We have received no information about this alleged conversation.

Judge: Mr. Markov?

Markov: If the defendant's counsel had bothered to read our brief, she would know that the audio file is in the public record, submitted in a similar lawsuit against the firm in another state.

District Judge: You may proceed.

Markov: The audio begins with the defendant asking his associate, a man called William or Billy, a question. The first voice you hear is the defendant's.

District Judge: Okay, let's hear it.

(Attorney Markov plays the recording:)

"Billy, what do you think about unemployment insurance?"

"It should be eliminated. Weaklings dependent on the

state guarantees the survival of weakness. There's no such thing as involuntary unemployment. The weak remain jobless by choice."

"Right, of course. But we've never been able to get rid of it entirely. It's too popular. Workers think they need it and politicians don't dare get rid of it."

"Agreed."

"So what if we were to spin off a company that managed unemployment insurance programs for states? It's an easy sell. We meet with the right politicians and bureaucrats and make them a promise."

"What's the promise?"

"We promise that we can save states hundreds of millions a year."

"Sounds too good to be true."

"Help me out on this, Billy. I can design an algorithm that rejects, say, ninety percent of all first-time UI claims in counties with the highest unemployment rates, warning applicants that their claim may be under scrutiny for criminal fraud."

"I like how you're thinking, Garrick."

"I thought you'd appreciate this. So each claimant receives a letter from the state deeming that his or her claim is suspected as fraudulent, a felony subject to a minimum fine of, say, fifty thousand dollars, plus a prison sentence of no less than thirty-six months. Something like that. Over the top."

"Empty threat. They'll just appeal the decision."

"I disagree. First, the algorithm produces an automated letter that tells the claimant nothing about appealing shit. Second, I figure only two out of ten would appeal. It would scare the crap out of the remaining eighty percent. They're poor or near-poor and not savvy about their rights. I've calculated that a large state, like California, would save half a billion in the first year. Billy, the political appeal of such a feat is incalculable."

"Brilliant. But there will be pushback. Especially in liberal states."

"I would expect so. But the windfall to state revenues will allow states to make political deals with the economically powerful, who will drive public opinion. That's how it works."

"That's brilliant, Garrick. It's a freaking money-making machine, I'll give you that. What do we call it?"

"Phrygia Solutions."

(Sounds of static, shuffling, and glass)

"Holy hell, that is why I love you, my friend."

(End of Audio)

Markov: Let's shift away from the phone conversation for a moment.

Defendant: It's your cross, counselor.

Markov: What were the company's revenues from its Mississippi operations last year?

Creighton: A fact not in question, Your Honor.

District Judge: Overruled. I'd like to hear this.

Defendant: I don't recall exactly.

Markov: Then I'll answer it for you. Your Mississippi contract was worth fifty-five million dollars last year.

Defendant: I'll take your word for it. Sounds about right.

Markov: Let's back up a minute. Who is this associate of yours whom you call Billy?

(Defendant consults with his attorney.)

Defendant: A business associate.

Markov: What is his role in the company?

Defendant: William Wharton is the executive vice president for external affairs.

Markov: Approximately what is William's annual salary

227

at the company?

Defendant: I don't know right offhand.

Markov: It says here in a court filing related to a similar lawsuit in Michigan that William's annual salary was five and a half million last year. And your base salary, Dr. Cripps, was twenty-five million, correct?

Defendant: I would imagine so.

Markov: For the record, please tell the Court what other businesses Phrygia operates.

Defendant: We provide global solutions to state and local governments throughout the country.

Markov: What sorts of "global solutions" as you call it?

Defendant: I told you. We work with government entities to help make them more efficient. We work with prisons, hospitals, fire departments, and police departments, to name a few. We also work with local garbage-collection services.

Markov: How does that work? How do you help make these government entities more efficient?

Defendant: The way we'd make any enterprise more efficient. We recommend ways to cut costs and expand revenues.

Markov: You mean making these government units more profitable, like a business, correct?

Defendant: More or less.

Markov: Now, Dr. Cripps, has your company ever consulted with state or local court systems like, say, the very Madison County District Court in which this trial is being held?

Creighton: Objection, Your Honor. I cannot see the relevancy of this question.

District Judge: Agreed. The question is not allowed. The objection is sustained.

Markov: But Your Honor, I'm trying to establish the

fact that Dr. Cripps's company has consulted with the state of Mississippi Courts to raise revenues and reduce costs, including this very court, which calls into question the court's objectivity on this matter.

District Judge: Nice try, but overruled. Your client sued, and this is the proper venue established to hear that action. You may proceed.

Markov: What about the federal government, Dr. Cripps?

Defendant: What about it?

Markov: Do you or have you consulted with any federal government departments to make them more "efficient," as you call it?

(Defendant consulting with attorney.)

Defendant: I believe we have submitted a proposal with the Federal Bureau of Investigation, but I don't know what came of that.

Markov: To which FBI department was that proposal directed, Dr. Cripps?

Defendant: William handled that. I can't tell you specifics because that effort is classified under FBI regulations, I believe. Southern California perhaps.

Markov: Can you be more specific?

Defendant: Los Angeles, San Diego. I let William handle that.

Markov: William reports to you, the company president, does he not?

Defendant: Yes.

Markov: And yet you can't confirm specifics of William's work on a proposal that would be worth millions of dollars to your company? You don't strike me as that naive, Dr. Cripps.

Creighton: Your Honor! I object to this innuendo.

District Judge: Objection sustained. Mr. Markov, please

stick to the facts of this case.

Markov: I'm trying to establish a pattern, Your Honor. Dr. Cripps's company has clearly manipulated state and government operations throughout the country to make them look and act like private enterprises seeking to maximize what amounts to profits to his company—at the expense of said agencies and citizens.

My client's lawsuit alleges that in Mississippi alone, Cripps's company has redirected hundreds of millions from taxpayers to pad his profits and cheat citizens of their rights. Cripps has discovered how to skim money from his acts of piracy to enrich certain government officials that go along with his scheme. It's odd, Your Honor, that administrative expenses in the state of Mississippi's UI system have risen twenty-five percent since his firm has taken over the management of UI claims. The same holds true for the Mississippi Department of Courts and Justice. District Judge salaries alone have shot up thirty-five percent since Phrygia Solutions took over the administration of the court system, including yours, Your Honor.

Now we find that the same company is making overtures to the FBI. For these reasons, Your Honor, I will file an objection with the Supreme Court of the State of Mississippi arguing that the state cannot guarantee my client an unbiased venue in which to hear his complaint. I will also seek redress with the US Department of Justice if it comes to that. With that, Your Honor, I rest.

District Judge: As you wish, Mr. Markov. You certainly have not helped your client with this outburst. Miss Creighton, do you have anything to add?

Creighton: No, your Honor. Other than to say in my twenty-five years of practice, I've seen nothing remotely like this, an attorney's baseless accusations against my client, simply because Dr. Cripps helps America by helping himself. That's called America, Your Honor. My client has done nothing illegal unless this court were to declare that capitalism is illegal. And we all know how silly that would be.

~

Agent Amy Watson's life had just become a lot more complicated. She shut her computer and cussed at herself. Normally she would have deleted the message from her computer and called it a day. But this one was different, a hot piece of gunmetal lurking inside her laptop, taunting her, invading her, pointing her in an alarming direction.

Somebody had anonymously sent her this email knowing she was internal affairs at the Office of Professional Responsibility overseeing the Justice Department, including the FBI—the very federal agency this Garrick Cripps fellow had apparently targeted for one of his corrupt business deals. Somebody in the agency had gotten mixed up with Phrygia Solutions, despite its reverse Robin Hood-ism, taking from the poor to bribe government officials and line the pockets of Cripps and his gang.

But the most pressing question lingered. How did all this nasty business relate to a conspiracy to overthrow the government, like the tipster said?

231

26

MIGHT BE SOMETHING THERE

Amy Watson specialized in two things particularly valuable to undercover work. She was an expert at psychological profiling and analysis, which was not uncommon in her profession. But, uncommonly, she had also studied theater and playwriting in college, then got her MFA in acting. Amy's theater background gave her an advantage in undercover work, and virtually none of her male counterparts could claim similar skills.

Amy was special in another way too. When a girl grows up on a farm twenty miles from a small town in North Dakota, she misses a lot of the junk spewed out by mass-produced, standardized culture. That always made Amy seem a bit odd.

Amy was just herself. Low-key, quiet, and, in some people's eyes, a bit on the mousy side. So just being herself made her a master of disguise. When she wore glasses and put her hair up, she looked like a modest worker bee on an electronic assembly line. But when she let her straight blonde hair down to her shoulders and wore some nice clothes for an evening out, she looked like a model on a Vogue magazine cover. In short she had a face and personality that were custom-tailored for disguise and a mind that tolerated no bullshit.

Amy lived in Pomona but most weekends she looked forward to going south to San Diego and spending a few days in Crown Point, where she owned a small condo on Mission Bay. On this Friday in early May, she got to work in Los Angeles and composed a classified email to David Green, her boss in DC. She attached the transcript of the lawsuit in Mississippi.

Amy wrote, *David, read this. I'll call you later.*

She left LA at six and got to her Crown Point condo by ten thirty, an arduous trek in weekend traffic. She changed into jeans, removed her shoes, and gave herself a full pour of Chardonnay.

Amy walked barefoot to the beach on the cool sand. Just as she was about to stick her feet in the water, her phone buzzed from the rear pocket of her jeans. She removed the phone while taking a few steps back and sitting on the pillow-soft sand. It was David Green.

"David, we can talk tomorrow. It's late where you are."

"Nice idea, Watson, but then you send me this goddamned shit, which I just opened."

"Sorry for the trouble, David."

"Any idea why'd they send it to you?"

"I don't have the slightest. What's protocol on something like this? Is this ours or counterterrorism?"

"Good question. Looks like both. Let's treat it as a tip. Let's assume it came to us for a reason. I'll give you five days of due diligence, then file it. Where are you?"

"My beach house."

"You mean that little condo in San Diego?"

"It's Crown Point, and it's on the beach."

"Right. My mistake. We must pay you too damned much. Did I tell you I'm retiring in two years? Getting too old for this crap."

"Are we trying to catch bad guys or what, David?"

"Fine. Let's think this through."

That was David Green's way of saying he'd take the tip seriously. Actually at forty-two, Amy too was thinking about early retirement, which she hadn't yet disclosed to David.

"You first," Green said.

"A William Wharton, who works for Garrick Cripps, contacted the FBI somewhere in Southern Cal for an odd business proposition. So we have this company that rips off taxpayers to pad its profits and pay off government officials wanting to privatize the FBI or some shit. I've never heard about this. Have you?" Amy said.

"Agreed. Let's go down the list at the decision level. Let's start with LA. How's Lancaster doing? You two talk much? Frankly I never liked the guy after Guantanamo. Duplicitous bastard, depending on which politician he's sucking up to."

"I didn't know he was that political," Amy said.

"More than most. Fact is he's the Special Agent in charge of the Los Angeles field office. He earned it. A big deal. Took over after five years in Washington. I beat him out of this job. We were both finalists. Don't remind him. I need you two to get along."

"I've had my moments with Lancaster. We don't talk regularly. Not one of my favorites. But he's on top of the FISA shit," Amy said.

"All right. We'll assume Lancaster is okay. Neither of us likes him much, but we know who he is. Ambitious but not dangerous. That leaves us with Bill Anderson in San Diego," Green said.

"What's your impression of Anderson?" Amy said.

"Bill's rep is outstanding. Known for his counterterrorism work. Hired a hotshot named Cunningham from the Midwest to lead the counterterrorism unit."

"I met Darryl Cunningham once at a meeting in San Diego. Do you know him?" Amy asked.

"Cunningham? Never met the guy. As you know, San Diego's another planet for me."

"So you've said."

"What do you know?" Green asked.

"Hotshot is right. Cunningham is the best there is. Outstanding leader. Great agent. Gets things done quickly. Won't drag out an investigation. If there's no case, he drops it."

"What else? Where's he from? How'd he grow up?" Green said.

"Midwestern boy. Working class. Athletic scholarship. Came to us from graduate school at Purdue. Studied economics. Married his high-school sweetheart. Two kids. One's a doctor working overseas. The boy is still in college. Oh, and the divorce. She left him. She has no real skills. There's alimony of about five grand a month. And debt. The daughter's medical school cost him a few hundred grand. The son, not so much. But the kid's still on dad's payroll," Amy said.

"How much debt?"

"Seventy-five thousand in credit cards and unsecured, plus a fancy house in Poway. Still owes a half a million on the house."

"You know I was joking about your vacation condo. Truth is we can't pay people what they're worth, let alone enough to pay the mortgage and send the kids to school. Opens folks up to pacts with the devil. Cunningham is a risk. I don't like

235

the profile," Green said.

"What should I do?"

"Has he filed any recent threats on Guardian?"

"I checked. Nothing in the works. But you know how reliable that system is."

"Chief of counterterrorism with no threat assessments in the hopper? I find that strange. Who's his chief assistant in anti-terrorism?"

"A young agent named Jason Treadwell. Five years out of Quantico."

"Your memory is still sharp, Amy."

"I know our agents. That's my job."

"Start with Treadwell. Leverage the kid. Scare the shit out of him if you have to. Who knows? There might be something there. I'm going back to bed."

27

OPR

On Monday morning, Amy performed a background check on Jason Treadwell's hobbies and learned that he played co-ed softball for the O'Brien's Pub team, which was scheduled to play its next game that coming Wednesday in Kearny Mesa, a working class community several miles south of downtown San Diego.

In truth she was on a limb. Her evidence of wrongdoing was sketchy. But she'd never be able to persuade a judge for a probable cause order without getting to Treadwell and finding out what he knew.

She remembered Greene's words. *Scare the shit out of him.*

Wednesday at six, Amy was on the road. She slid north on the 5 from Crown Point, got off on 52 West, and found her way to O'Brien's small, crowded parking lot. She drove around the corner and parked in a rare spot on a side street next to a car dealership. The pub had a good buzz going from the regulars, including young professionals, semi-professional drunks, and a variety of sporting types.

Amy sipped on a beer and kept a subtle eye out for the

237

agent who matched the Bureau's house photo of Treadwell. Within thirty minutes, a guy entered the bar who fit the description. About thirty-five, six feet tall, slender, dark hair. A merry group of three men and four athletic-looking women came along behind him. One of the blondes touched Treadwell's arm.

She watched Treadwell and his pals having a good time— drinking, eating bar food, and laughing about the softball game they'd just won. Jason got up and walked to the men's room. Amy punched in his cell number. She had certain powers to investigate any FBI agent in her jurisdiction. But the agents had rights too. For a relative newbie like Treadwell, Amy's opening move would be a bit of a reach, but it was effective. Talk to him like she was pissed. Persuade him to cooperate with her because she was the best in the business. Show empathy, as needed. The target was Cunningham, not Treadwell, and she would remind him whenever she was losing control.

Amy dialed the number.

"Jason here."

"Jason Treadwell?" Amy asked.

"Yes, this is Jason. Who is this?"

"I'm in the bar. I'm an OPR investigator at Justice, and we need to talk. Don't call anyone. Meet me outside on the street across from the car dealer. Go out the back way. I'll go out the front and come to you."

Amy clicked off. She left her three-quarters-full beer on the bar and walked out the front door. She went around the corner toward the car dealer and found Treadwell standing in a shady spot by a chain-linked fence in the back. A Mexican cook in a white bib was having a smoke, taking a break. The cook looked at Amy listlessly as she walked toward Jason.

Treadwell looked shell-shocked. Amy flashed her badge for three seconds and stuck it back in her light jacket. "Special Agent Amy Watson, Office of Professional Responsibility. Walk with me, and keep your mouth shut until I say otherwise."

They walked for two minutes before Amy spoke.

"I've been watching you, Jason. So closely, in fact, that I'm opening a criminal investigation."

"What crime? I can't talk to you. Call my boss," Jason said.

"I think you know what I'm talking about. It's about your boss, Darryl Cunningham. You need to tell me what you've seen and heard."

"I need a lawyer. I don't like your tone," Jason said.

"Tell me what you know, Jason. My boss is David Green. Do you know who he is? He's the director of the Office of Professional Responsibility. The United States Senate confirmed him for that job. You would do well to cooperate. Your career with the FBI is on the line. And that's the least of your problems," Amy said.

Treadwell searched his pockets for a smoke. Amy pulled a pack of Newports and a lighter from her bag. Jason took a cigarette, lit it, and took a long drag.

"Can't believe I'm smoking. I quit, you know. I play softball now."

"That's too bad. You'll get back on track. Just like you'll get your career back if you tell me the truth," Amy said.

"I can't help you, sorry."

Amy opened her jacket to reveal a holstered service revolver. "If you insist on being evasive, I'll take you to Los Angeles and we can talk there. Your girlfriend might miss you."

"I'm just doing my job."

Amy took his arm and guided him toward the parking lot. "All right. Let's go."

"Wait. There is something that has struck me as odd."

"Now's your chance."

Jason glanced around the area. The cook was still leaning against the fence, apparently on a break, smoking a cigarette. "Can we go someplace more secure? This makes me nervous."

"Follow me to my car."

Amy opened the passenger side door and let Jason in. She swung around to the driver's side, slammed the door, and cracked open the windows.

"Okay, now we can breathe. I promise there are no listening devices in here. Talk to me, Jason."

"I shouldn't be telling you this because it's classified. Darryl asked me to open a counterterrorism investigation. We got a referral from NSA."

"What kind of referral?"

"A Ragtime-P. One of San Diego County's high-security prisons could unknowingly be harboring an Islamic terrorist cell. Cunningham asked me to check it out and provide a threat assessment. I'm following chain of command. Doing my job. Why finger me?"

Amy stopped in her tracks, realizing she had stumbled into something far bigger than anything she had expected. She struggled to maintain her composure. She opened the driver window another six inches. She lied. "Why do you think I'm here, Jason? Go on."

"Cunningham believes there's an Islamic cell holed up in the county jail poised for some kind of attack."

"Have you drafted a threat assessment? What's your recommendation?"

"Investigation's inconclusive. I need more time. My gut tells me Cunningham is reaching. He wants this bust to come down, regardless."

"Regardless of what?"

Jason rubbed his eyes and wiped the sweat off his brow. "What do you want to know, Agent Watson?"

"When did Cunningham ask for the threat assessment?"

"About a month ago. Make it look thorough, he told me. Honestly I can't imagine why he'd want to execute a fraudulent bust. Makes no sense," Jason said.

"Are you making this up? Do not fuck with me."

"I'm serious. He gave me an order to go in. I went to the prison under the guise of a journalist doing a story. I watched the telemarketing operation for any clues."

"You're telling me Cunningham wants to bust a suspected terrorist cell operating within the confines of the county government, but you're not convinced it's real?"

"I know. It sounds crazy. But if it's a terrorist cell, he's done his job. If not, then he's still done his job. Overkill is better than missing something and all hell breaking loose. FBI let it happen, blah, blah, blah. That can't be good for anybody."

"Any idea what's in it for Cunningham?"

"He's a career guy. Worked his way up. Ambitious as hell. You tell me," Jason said.

"Do you know anything else about him? Personal stuff?"

"Not really. He keeps to himself."

"Dig deeper. He's acting oddly, right? What does he like to read? What are his hobbies? Who does he hang with?"

"I really can't say. I don't know the guy outside of work, and that's fine with me."

"Why is that?"

"We're not friends. He treats me like his slave. He's intense."

Amy studied Jason, then reached over to poke her finger at his arm. "You better not be playing me, Agent Treadwell. The second I suspect anything irregular about you, then you

241

become my next target. I'm not taking you to LA—yet. You're going to cooperate with me to get to Cunningham. I believe you're highly motivated to do the right thing. Correct?"

"What if we're wrong and he's on the level? Cunningham will shit all over me if that happens."

"Not to worry. He'll never know. You're working for me now."

"That's debatable. I've got rights. What do you want from me?" Jason said.

"Act as if nothing is abnormal. You'll wear a wire. You'll effectively work as a double agent, reporting to Cunningham and to me. Follow his orders, record him."

"A wire? You're nuts. I won't get through the front door," Jason said.

"I'll handle that. My boss will clear it. Cunningham won't suspect."

"Is that it?" Jason said.

"Do you have concurrent notes, anything?"

"He told me no paper trail except for my write up of the threat assessment. That's a formality. We do everything else face-to-face."

"Okay, you need to get him to repeat those orders on the wire, because they're highly irregular."

"You must think he's stupid. Or I'm stupid."

"He's stupid, all right. I'm withholding judgment on your mental capacity. But you belong to me. You'll do what you need to do."

"And what would that be?"

Amy pulled the wire from her bag. "Wear this at all times. I'll be monitoring it. And do whatever it takes to break into his damned computer."

When Jason returned to his office the next day, he saw a note from Cunningham on a red Post-it pasted to his desk: *Let's talk. Bring the draft of that threat assessment.*

Jason froze. He'd been fiddling with the draft threat assessment for a few weeks and kept putting off its completion. His heart wasn't in it. The whole deal was being cooked up, and he couldn't imagine why Cunningham was fudging facts in this dangerous game.

He wasn't ready to confront Cunningham now, if ever. But he had little choice now that OPR was involved. He secured the wire under his dress shirt, ensuring the device was tight and invisible. The threat assessment he promised hadn't gone beyond his private notes. He grabbed his notepad and pen and walked down the hall to Cunningham's office. As he entered Cunningham was speaking to his assistant, Margie.

"Sorry to interrupt. How's it going, Margie?" Jason said.

"Hello, Jason. Doing okay. You?"

"Thanks, Margie," Cunningham said, her signal to leave the room. He turned to Jason. "Shut the door. Is that your report in your hand? Let me see it."

"Boss, I need to clear up a few details before giving you the draft."

"Shit, Treadwell. We discussed this."

"I wanted to be sure."

"Sure about what exactly?"

"About what we talked about before."

"You tell me what you think we talked about, Treadwell."

"I thought I heard you say that you needed me to play up the plausibility of the terrorist cell operating in the county prison."

243

"Play up the plausibility? What kind of crap is that? You know that's not how we do things, Treadwell. We're the nation's leading law enforcement organization. We're a model for ethical police work. I can't believe I just heard you say that."

"I'm sorry, boss. Guess I misunderstood you."

"Just do your job, Treadwell. I'll expect your final report in forty-eight hours."

~

Jason left the building and walked to the cafeteria. He grabbed a ham sandwich and an iced tea, then stepped outside to have lunch on the outdoor balcony. He devoured the sandwich and washed down the food with the cold drink. He pulled out his phone to call Amy Watson. Wrong phone. He placed the company phone back in his suit jacket and pulled out another mobile, his private phone. The sun's heat beat down on his face. He grabbed the empty bottle of tea and pried one more sip.

"Watson here."

"I did what you asked."

"I know. I heard the wire."

"Now he's the model Bureau guy who would never consider submitting a biased threat assessment. He must have gotten tipped off that he was under suspicion," Jason said.

"This makes no sense," Amy said.

"I know."

"Did you tip him off? You must have a tell. What was different?"

"I don't know. Look, he's an experienced guy. You tell me."

"Who the hell is protecting this guy?"

244

"Somebody in the Bureau who knows what you're doing. Has to be."

"I was thinking out loud, Jason. I couldn't care less about your opinions. We need access to his computer. All his devices, if possible. We need to know who he's talking to. No way he's on his own in this."

"Can we get a warrant?"

"We don't have probable cause, Jason. I was hoping you would firm that up today. No, you'll have to break into his computer. Get what you need. Leave no trace. Then I'll convince a judge as an emergent matter of national security. Only way."

"I can't do that, Amy. It's illegal."

"You can and you will. A judge is one thing. My gut is another thing altogether, and my gut's usually right."

"But you don't have anything yet."

"I have you and what you've told me. Honestly I thought Cunningham was working a side gig on something else. But what you've told me is far more alarming. I'm assuming you're being straight with me. Are you?"

"I am. I don't like what Darryl is telling me."

"You should have reported him earlier. You know that, right?"

"Probably. I feel bad about that."

"Jason, another question. You don't have to answer it but I need to know, okay?"

"Spit it out."

"Who was the blonde on your arm at the bar?"

"That was Angela, why?"

"Angela who?"

"Angela Belford. We work together in counterterrorism. She's new. Six months on the job, I think."

245

"Hmm. I haven't met her. Are you two close?"

"That's against the rules," Jason said.

"That's right. I'll ask again. How close are you with Angela? Professional colleagues don't hold hands in Irish pubs last time I checked."

"She's a friend. A good friend. In case you haven't noticed, counterterrorism agents can't trust many people. We work together and like each other. We offer mutual support. That's it."

"Did Cunningham hire her?"

"Yeah, why?"

"Do me a favor, Jason."

"What do you want?"

"Watch Angela. Tell me if you see anything suspicious, big or small."

"Now you're messing with my personal life, Amy. What did I do to deserve this? Angela is an excellent agent and a decent person. And, now that you've threatened me, what really do you have on Cunningham? What's he done wrong except to ask me to write a threat assessment based on intel he got from NSA?"

"Tell me more about that."

The line was silent for a few seconds.

"I thought I explained that. The threat assessment was predicated on a Ragtime-P request from NSA. That's all he told me," Jason said.

"You really aren't very smart, Jason. Neither is Cunningham. Before I talk to any agent under suspicion I do a records check. I find out exactly what orders, requests, threat assessments, documents, etcetera., the agent has on file in the system. I checked Cunningham, and I can ensure you, he received no intel from NSA about a suspected terrorist cell."

"I wasn't aware of that. I didn't think he was lying to me. He's tough and intense, but still a decent guy, I thought."

"In case you haven't noticed, Jason, there are no more decent people," Amy said.

"What the hell does that mean?"

"Life boils down to two kinds of people, and decency isn't even in the equation: those who play for money, ego, and power—and those who aren't in the game. Welcome to the game, Agent Treadwell."

28

CLEANING UP AFTER LITTLE BOYS

Suzanne was on edge. Jonas Peterson had arranged for Petit to plant Garrick's bot in the fifteen computers in the telemarketing room of the prison. She had waited forty-eight hours for the attack to play out and determine how far it had spread and what networks it had wormed its way into. Or not. If all went as planned, the *or not* side of the equation would blow Garrick's mind.

She holed up at her Windansea home, scanning news reports and intelligence sources to find any news of the attack over the weekend. There was nothing. No comments from local authorities or the FBI. Nothing from national computer security experts.

Petit had launched the bot on Saturday in the early hours. By ten a.m. Monday morning, Suzanne got Billy's call. He was both furious and sarcastic. She felt like Seinfeld saying hello to Newman.

"What the hell have you been doing, Suzy?"

"What the hell are you talking about, Billy?"

"Jonas Peterson, our whiz kid from Austria, told me he

248

tried to contact you."

"Why? We spoke just a few days ago."

"Perhaps you've noticed. Garrick wanted chaos. Betsy didn't deliver a whimper."

"I told you, it's called Nessie, Billy. How long have you known?"

"Jonas notified me within hours of the launch. He swears he gave Petit the right disks. Petit must have fucked it up. I called him and threatened his ass. Then there's you. Well, you must live the good life in La Jolla because I can't find you when you're needed."

"Where are you?"

"I'm in DC, why?"

"Imagine that. I moved here to handle this, and you and Jonas are talking shit behind my back. I've been on pins and needles all weekend. Nobody told me anything. And now you're blaming me for someone else's fuckup, and you need me to clean it all up? You're pretty predictable, Billy."

"Apparently Nessie fizzled right out of the gate. It's your job to anticipate that shit."

"Or, perhaps, it's Garrick's job to be competent. Or Jonas's job not to fuck up his end. And whose idea was it to use Johnny Petit for such a critical operation? He's a flunky."

"Jonas is one of the best," William said.

"Garrick hired him. They're both incompetent."

"Dammit, Suzy. Can you say something positive for once?"

"Where did you find Jonas, anyway? Did you even check him out?"

"I can't add anything to what you already know."

"You can't or you won't, Billy?"

"We have partners in Austria who sent Jonas to Stanford to work on cyber warfare projects. When we asked for help, they lent us Jonas. He's on the team—in more ways than I even know. Garrick has been spending a lot of time in Austria."

Suzanne considered how much to reveal about the operation gone bad. Now that she knew exactly why it had failed, the irony was too good to keep to herself. Laura, the woman who had stopped the attack, had created the Nessie super-bot that Garrick had banked on to bring down the government. Who better than Laura herself to figure out a way to stop the attack? What did that make Garrick but a fool? "So you're saying Garrick and Jonas were perfect? You know what that means, right?"

"You tell me, Suzy."

"It would appear that someone at the county jail pre-launched software to defend against the attack. Maybe the county's technical experts. Apparently Nessie was not as flawless as Garrick thought. "

"Nessie is bulletproof. That's the whole point."

"Really, Billy? The evidence suggests otherwise." She resisted setting him straight, despite her desire to see his reaction if he learned the truth. "Look, Billy. I'm caught in the middle trying my best to clean up after you little boys. You're wasting my time. I'll speak to Garrick directly."

"You know Garrick is lying low on this. I can hardly get to him myself these days."

"Have him call me, please."

"What if I don't?"

"No, you won't worm out of this. Neither will Garrick."

"Or what, Suzanne?" William said.

"Or what? I won't spell it out for you. Get a clue, Billy. My patience with this cluster is wearing thin."

~

Garrick's cyberattack had failed thanks to Carson McCready and Laura Cavendish doing what they did best—Laura solving cybersecurity problems and Carson acting without fear. Suzanne poured a glass of wine and congratulated herself. Garrick, the Grand Poobah himself, had to be fuming about now.

Laura's talents shined above all. Fortunately she had rejected Garrick's ideological pursuits, but he had used her anyway, borrowing heavily from Laura's work in artificially intelligent bots. Suzanne had helped him, and she could talk to no one about the guilt she felt now.

Had she been honest with herself, she would have known what sins Garrick was committing years ago by asking her to take the job at the Pentagon. Suzanne saw what Laura could create—a once-in-a-lifetime technical achievement. And yet Suzanne had provided Garrick an unsecured copy of Laura's algorithm, a felonious breach of federal law.

How much of her obsequiousness was explained by unrequited love? Or was the explanation something deeper? She had always needed to be seen as the smartest in the room. The brilliant woman who could do anything—even steal secrets from the US government—and not get caught.

But now she came to terms with her fuck-ups. Helping Garrick steal from the government wasn't the real Suzy Dreyfus, the girl from Brooklyn with decent parents who gave a shit about others less advantaged than they. Suzanne stopped trying to feel guilty. She *was* guilty, and there was no sense debating that.

She abhorred magical thinking in herself and others. She was a scientist, a problem solver. And solving problems wasn't a matter of blind faith or ideology. Did he believe the Freedom Society could outsmart science itself? To outsmart science one

251

had to out-think the best practitioners of science. Garrick was a sloppy scientist, allowing ideology to replace facts and hard evidence. Jonas was equally patriotic to ideology.

Laura couldn't care less about ideology. She had no agenda. Her agenda depended on what worked versus what didn't. She represented the best of science, and the Pentagon was lucky to have her. Suzanne took some solace in that.

Her logical, practical side had planned carefully: decimate the movement and sever Garrick's ability to lead it. It had taken years of misdirected devotion to a hollow man. With Garrick out of the way, perhaps she could lead a revitalized movement to bring about real freedom. Universal freedom. Freedom *and* justice. Because without justice, freedom was a null set. Freedom and justice, the yin and yang, composed the Judeo-Christian universe in synchrony.

She had never cared what her parents thought of her as an adult but right here, right now, Suzanne finally saw with great clarity: her parents were hardly bleeding heart liberals. They were practical people who worked hard for what they got. And yet they thought about something more than their individual well-being because one's well-being was a result of an interactive force that transcended individualism.

She could remember her father's voice: "Suzy, dear, I am well because you are well."

Suzanne thought of her father's words whenever she felt down and needed cheering up. Joe Dreyfus did that for her. Dad was a scholar in his heart. A computer programmer for the city as his vocation. A gentle soul who reminded her.

We. Family, country, society.
I and Thou.
We are not alone.

Suzanne had been brought up well. Why had she gone

252

so wrong?

As a child she had been clever, yes, but had also had a wicked sense of humor that led to her occasional acts of benign mischievousness. She got it from her father. Her dad was sharply political and culturally astute. He was fond of Woody Allen movies, Mort Sahl, but he liked Lenny Bruce best.

"Who's Lenny Bruce, Daddy?" Suzanne asked when she was ten.

"A funny Jew the establishment hated. God, they hated Lenny."

"Why did they hate him?"

"Lenny's a truth-teller. He made fun of hypocrites, religious bigots, and the idiocrasy. He spared nobody. If he weren't a comic, he'd be a rabbi. A hilarious and occasionally wicked rabbi. But a good rabbi because he could not tell a lie."

She could almost hear Joe Dreyfus's voice talking to her now. The way he would have said it had he known about her present struggles: "Suzy, you tell that Freedom Society to go fuck itself."

29

SHOT OVER THE BOW

William Wharton, a.k.a. Little Billy, took the secure call at thirty thousand feet in the company's Gulfstream. According to the phone-tracking program, the call had originated in Nassau, then been rerouted through Omaha. It had come to this. Garrick's familiar voice went back decades. His tone was urgent and blunt.

"Billy. Where are you? We need to have a brief chat," Garrick said.

"I'm in the air leaving Washington. Why?"

"I'd like you to divert the flight. Come see me. I'm on the yacht."

"You sound tense. What's wrong?"

"What's wrong? Everything's wrong. Years of planning just went down the drain, Billy. Between you, Suzanne, and Jonas, I don't know who to trust. You're all fucking incompetent."

"Have you talked to Suzanne?" William said.

"Never mind her. We'll talk here. I'm off the coast of Nassau."

Two hours later William stepped off the plane at Nassau

International and caught a sea-shuttle to the yacht. A deckhand dressed in white Bermudas and tan shoes reached over the brass rail to help William climb the stairs to the ship.

"Dr. Cripps is waiting for you, Mr. Wharton. Follow me to the main deck, please."

Garrick was sitting in the luxurious shade beneath a canopy. He ordered his old friend a drink, an iced vodka and soda.

William removed a large white sun hat and eased into a deck chair. "Why am I here, Garrick?"

"Besides the obvious?"

"I don't know what to say. Everything went well on our end. The plan was flawless."

"Then what fucked us? Never mind. You're clueless."

They watched the deckhand setting two chilled glass of vodka and soda on a linen-covered table.

"I'm a businessman, Billy. New voices are coming to us, which will only amplify our ability to grow and penetrate mainstream America. It's incredible what's happening. Countless politicians in Congress and the states are repeating our talking points."

"Such as?"

"You know. The usual stuff. Socialism must die, free markets will resolve virtually all public problems, and so on. Remember that white paper we did on applying market principles to voting rights? Even that is catching on."

"Garrick, after all these years, maybe it's high time you and Suzanne kiss and make up. She'll know what happened to Nessie. Besides, we wouldn't be here without her."

"I don't want to talk about Suzanne. Maybe you don't know this, but she never was a true believer. But we'll be okay. I'm sure of that. American society is finally catching up with us. More than half the members of Congress are born-again libertarians. The younger ones have taken our lead and they're dismantling government from the inside. It's a beautiful thing to see. Public health and welfare. Environmental regulations and oversight. The entire federal government is eroding, and states can't afford to replace what our people on the inside have legislated away, even if the states wanted to—but most don't anymore. Our ideas about freedom have penetrated government that deeply, all the way down to city council meetings. Who knows what's next?"

Garrick continued to preach while William listened. "Luckily for us, average Americans have been blind to the libertarian elephant in the room growing larger every day, town by town, district by district. Just the other day, a southern senator boasted that the elderly in his district would willingly sacrifice their remaining lives for 'appropriate compensation.' So Grandpa signs his own death warrant, and he's free to add funds to his estate—tax-free.

"Medicare and Social Security debt, solved. We can't change people's passions and beliefs, but we can invent incentives that change people's behavior. Racism and bigotry? Also solved, when the free market is allowed to work its magic."

William stared blankly at Garrick. "Come again?"

"Oh, never mind, Billy. You get the point."

"Then how will Phrygia fit?"

"Our ace in the hole. Phrygia will become a major player in transferring government-held assets to our private partners and investors. We're already positioned to do just that with the work we're doing with state and local governments. We'll continue to exploit Phrygia on the federal level."

"I still worry," William said.

"You get paid to worry and spray perfume on the shit that

256

comes down, and it's my job to turn the shit into gold. We'll be okay, trust me."

"I always have, Garrick. You're right. I get paid to worry."

Garrick studied William's face. "You're not telling me something, Billy. Your face is an open book."

"Had a chat with FBI Director Fletcher a few days ago," William said.

"Good. We needed to tie up loose ends with the Bureau."

"Another front is opening at OPR in Washington. Some bitch called Amy Watson in LA has her sights on our man, Cunningham. We don't know who tipped her off. We're scrubbing him. We still need Cunningham, right? He's got an official threat assessment as the foundation for busting the cell at the county jail. That was the plan. Make the FBI look like a bunch of clowns missing in action when terrorists attempted to hack the government. Asleep at the wheel in their brand new, one hundred and thirty million dollars facility in San Diego, courtesy of US taxpayers. I assume we are on point with the plan?" William said.

"No arrests yet. Tell Fletcher that," Garrick said.

"Garrick, Nessie failed. We hoped it wouldn't but it did."

Garrick slipped off his deck shoes, revealing white feet in contrast with his golden brown legs. He refilled their drinks. "I'll admit. The idea was elegant. But I'm out of patience. We were already supposed to begin the asset transfers with FBI and Justice, right? We're behind schedule. Our investors are impatient with our progress. We need something more emphatic than a failed cyberattack to ignite a populist uprising."

"You're killing me here, Garrick. More emphatic?"

"Something guaranteed to ruin the Bureau and get the masses riled up."

"We had a good plan. A plan that led to the next plan. We

257

creep, we penetrate, we destroy from the inside. That was the goddamned plan, Garrick."

"That's still the plan. It's valid in the big war. In this battle, I want an extra something. Cunningham's fine. He'll get that threat assessment on the record, which sets up a rather delicious table for us—if we need it."

William didn't react. He raised a brow and took a long sip from his drink. "What are you thinking?" he said.

"I want the government's domestic security service to feel the pain. I want them to fail miserably, utterly, completely. I want the public poised to revolt. Cunningham has set the stage, but the bust itself will stand down and stand by. No busts until I say so."

"And when will that be?"

"When I get my shot over the bow," Garrick said.

"What the fuck does that mean?"

"I'm not going to spell it out for you."

"We agreed no violence. Just gross incompetence. We pile up examples of federal ineptitude and grow the public's disenchantment. That was the goddamned fucking plan."

"Don't you get it, Billy? We won't have sufficient traction. We need an aggressive statement, now. Simply busting a suspected terrorist cell changes nothing and leads to nothing."

"We made promises. To Cunningham. To Suzanne, even. You may not trust her right now, but you've got to give her the respect she deserves. Remember our pact. She created *The Manifesto*. Fuck, she created you, the Garrick Cripps that millions of believers now follow."

"I'll handle Suzanne. As for promises to Cunningham, are you referring to the deal to make him director of the for-profit federal security service?"

"Of course. We made the man a fucking deal. We're

capitalists. We make deals, free from government control and coercion. Don't tread on us. Live and let live. That's liberty, Garrick. That's what we stand for. That's who we are."

"Billy, I've woken up. I've created a new vision. I call it postmodern liberty. A vision that meets our moment in history. The Enlightenment is dead. That's indisputable. There's no right, and by implication, there's no wrong. There are no rights. There is no justice. Democracy is a choice, not a dictate from the Almighty. Therefore we can choose something else because history demands Libertarian Nationalism. Patriotism imbued with pure capitalism. Where everything is for sale—at the market-clearing price that allows us, the highest bidder, to take the property and lives of others as dictated by the market. Period."

"I've never heard you talk quite like this, Garrick."

"There is no liberty unless you pay for it. Some have it, most don't. Anything goes. Everything is possible and true. My choice. Your choice. I say it's true, therefore it's true. Nothing matters unless value and wealth make it matter. Not love, not freedom, nothing.

"One thing never changes, and its value lasts forever: those possessing the power to shape the story of the world, and those who have nothing to say, nothing to eat, and nothing to know. Those who can't afford life have just two choices: become a slave to the highest bidder, or die. That, my friend, is liberty."

30

GOD'S WORK

William drove through late afternoon traffic to a leafy neighborhood in Bethesda, a gated community of Washington politicians and power brokers. When he reached his destination at a neighborhood park, he called one residence of the exclusive enclave.

"I'm here. Can you take a walk?" William said.

"Give me five minutes. The bench in the southeast corner, under the trees."

He was known as Agent X. He was not among the most generous benefactors to the Society, but strategically, X was priceless. Agent X came through with cold precision, whether the task was to remove a pesky federal agent who got in the way or make key phone calls to certain local police to set up a secure location for an "event." For the Freedom Society, an "event" was a tactical operation to support the evolving mission objective to Creep, Penetrate, and Destroy certain American institutions that thwarted economic freedom. These operations were known as CPD Events. It was William's eye-opening coup d'état that the society's key player in CPD events was nobody less than a former director of the Federal Bureau of Investigation.

William saw Agent X walking across the grass into the shady area to where he sat at their usual meeting spot. Agent X took a seat next to William, breathing noticeably. They hadn't seen one another in more than a year.

"I thought you'd take up golf in your retirement," William said.

"Who has time for that? I'm always working—for you, it seems. I've got a question. What the hell is your name nowadays? I heard you call yourself Euro-something."

"Eurynomos. From Greek mythology, a flesh-eating creature from the underworld. I don't expect you to call me that. I think of it as my stage name, for intimidation purposes."

"You're shitting me, right?"

"Never mind. Don't worry about it."

Agent X looked puzzled. "Okay, I won't."

"I hope you know how much we appreciate what you do for us. That's why I need you, brother. We're still brothers, aren't we?" William said.

"Of course. Speaking of brothers, how's Garrick? I rarely hear from him."

"Garrick is Garrick."

"Where is he?" Agent X said.

"Somewhere on his yacht."

"Lucky guy."

"I worry about him. His zealotry is dangerous."

Agent X turned sideways on the park bench, facing William. "Why am I not surprised? Dare I ask why you're here?"

"He needs you for a CPD event in San Diego."

Agent X didn't answer for several moments. He looked

around the park, taking in the sunny day in Bethesda. "You bastard, we go back a long time," he said.

William looked away, watching a young couple meandering through the private park. They glanced at William and Agent X, two older, distinguished men sitting on a park bench together.

"I often think of those days. Seems so long ago now," William said.

"Yeah, good old Ronnie Reagan. We were rookies in Congress. Then, Newt. That fucker made us relevant again. Remember?" Agent X said.

"It meant everything to us. We were firebrands. When you told me you were an ex-cop, that got my attention. Congress was a stepping stone. I knew you'd become someone special," William said.

"From beat cop to Congressman to retired director of the FBI. Not your usual career path."

"As long as you believed, it didn't matter what your resume looked like," William said.

"I've got to admit, I wouldn't have voted for me. Had no fucking clue what I was doing, Billy."

"Affirmative action for red-state dirt farmers, Bible thumpers, and ex-cops, right?" William said.

"You know it," Agent X said.

William was waiting for the right moment to get down to business. Agent X was talkative today.

"Frankly, I'm surprised at how long Garrick's San Diego plan has been in the works for. You could be the most patient man I've ever met," X said.

"I let Garrick be Garrick. It's worked out so far."

"He'd be lost without you. And Suzanne. Especially Suzanne."

William said nothing.

"I never really knew why you chose me and not someone else. We all spoke from the same playbook," Agent X said.

"I sensed something special in you."

"You foresaw me becoming director?" Agent X reached into his jacket and pulled out two cigars. He handed one to William and tore off the wrapper on his. William reached for a lighter in his jacket pocket. They lit the cigars and sat in silence, enjoying the aroma.

Agent X puffed on his cigar, saying nothing.

"You know about the charity football game, right?" William said.

"What game?"

"Okay, I'll back up. You know about our plan to frame a non-existent Islamic terrorist cell at the San Diego County prison for a major disruption to our national security, igniting a popular uprising against the government. Correct?"

"Of course. I've been briefed on the plan, Billy."

"What you apparently don't know is that the guy running the telemarketing gig at the jail has turned out to be a do-gooder. He's arranged a football game between prison inmates and a semi-pro team in town. Garrick wants to disrupt this game in a significant way. We'll need tactical support. A minimum of ten to twenty men, fully briefed and loaded. Plus transport and logistics. And one highly effective explosive device."

"Seems like a lot of firepower for a piddling football game."

"It's bigger than you think. That guy we got hired at the prison, Carson McCready, is like a force of nature and for some damned reason he gives a shit about poor inner-city kids. We didn't expect any of this crap, and I blame Suzanne for that. Anyway the local press is predicting maybe ten to

263

fifteen thousand people. Politicians, dignitaries, even the damned governor might show up. A socialist circus. It's a big fucking deal, and Garrick knows it. And if we get this right, Garrick gets to pin the attack on the very same, quote, 'Islamic terrorists' at the jail who launched the failed cyberattack, all under the FBI's nose."

Agent X said nothing for several moments. He took two quick puffs on his cigar. "Now's when I need a stiff drink. Did you bring a flask, Billy?"

"Forgot. Are you in or out?"

"Why not leave it to the populist mob?"

"You're joking, right?"

"Yeah, I'm joking. That's why I love you guys. You don't let amateurs do grown-up jobs. A Timothy McVeigh or something else?"

"We don't want to flatten a city block if that's what you're asking. Something that causes a big ruckus. A shot over the bow."

"What does Garrick want?" Agent X said.

"Exactly that. A statement, a dramatic one."

Agent X inspected William's eyes. "What aren't you telling me?"

"I'm telling you what I'm telling you."

"Shit like this can go wrong. Way wrong. We can initiate an event but then our ability to manage it gets iffy, very quickly. Does Garrick realize that?" Agent X said.

"I don't completely trust Garrick's tactical judgment these days. I want to be effective, not suicidal. I believe Suzanne is with me on that. You're right, my friend. The wrong moves could decimate the movement."

"I should speak to Garrick myself, Billy."

William set down the half-smoked cigar on the arm of

the wooden bench, the dull-green paint of which had nearly peeled off. "I'm not stopping you."

"Are you with Garrick on this?" Agent X said.

"Garrick's stability is a question mark. We had a good plan. Now he's suddenly changing it. He's been an effective leader—until now."

"What the hell are you saying, Billy?"

"We've got to remix the ratio of ideology and pragmatism. If we find the right balance, we'll make the FBI look foolish. And down the road we'll also make other government institutions look grossly incompetent. As we amass political power, the White House will have no choice but to cooperate with us. The political damage to the socialist state will be incalculable. Our people in Congress will pick the low-hanging fruit. And that's just the beginning. We'll let Cunningham carry on with his threat assessment. And you, my friend, will eventually direct the privatized national security service—if you're still interested."

"You come to me to carry out Garrick's orders, and yet you don't agree with him? You sound like you aim to push Garrick out."

"Garrick and I go back a long way. I'm doing the job I committed to for a friend. I told Garrick he was wrong about San Diego, but he wouldn't listen. I'm passing on the intel to you. Do what you want with it. I'd understand if you wanted to back out."

"Billy, I have to be honest. I'm not sure I can trust you. You've burned too many bridges."

"What's trust have to do with it? I don't trust Garrick. I don't even like the guy any more. He's become a real asshole. Look how he's treated Suzanne. But he's my friend, and damned if he hasn't been a brilliant tactician. I never thought he was capable but look at what he's done. He's got the FBI in his pocket. He's got Cunningham who's poised to bust a ragtag crew at the county prison for possible terrorist activity.

"After this upcoming CPD event in San Diego, the bust will come down, but it won't matter. The FBI fucked up and we're all the worse for it. I can't argue with Garrick's passion. I do argue with his morality. But as libertarians we don't legislate morality. It's a free country. I believe in freedom, and so do you. I've made my choice. You make yours."

Agent X's cigar was down to a half, which he smothered on the arm of the park bench. "You're right. Trust is worthless. But this is how it's going to work, Billy. I'll burn down the fucking house if I'm being jerked around."

"What's that mean?" William said.

"I agree with Garrick on this. We must act in the right proportions. You want no violence. I think we're way past that point. Garrick wants a Goldilocks, not a Timothy McVeigh—but not a pretty show of fireworks either. Besides unpredictability, we face several potential threats. Amy Watson comes to mind first. And her boss, David Green. They're very good at their jobs, and they're patriots. The real kind, not the brand. We're in a race of time—we need to do this before Green and Watson know enough to bust us. I don't need your promises about the money, Billy. I want it all, up-front this time, and I want it in my Cayman account by midnight. Then we get it done. Are we clear?"

"Thanks for the Cuban, by the way. It's delicious," William said.

"Are we clear, Billy?" Agent X repeated.

"Sure, we're clear."

"I might want something else," Agent X said.

William turned toward his old friend. "What's with the

hard-ass routine?"

"When it's over, I want a promotion. CEO of the new Corporation for Justice. What we now call the Attorney General."

William sat back and pulled smoke from the cigar. He looked straight ahead. "Not an easy sell. Director Fletcher is in line for that job. And then there's your past. The reasons they fired your ass. You'll be the director of the new FBI, and you'll be happy about it."

"It's a new game and all the rules have changed," Agent X said. "If the Society wants my help, then give me what I want."

"What about Fletcher?" William said.

"Billy, please. Fletcher won't be a problem. I know too much."

31

YOU'RE STARTING TO SOUND LIKE A COMMIE

Suzanne packed an overnight bag and drove downtown to meet William, who had checked into a swanky hotel on the Bay. She told William she didn't want to be alone—a guise to keep a close eye on him during the final hours leading up to Liberation Day, which aptly coincided with the day of Carson McCready's football game.

At eleven a.m. Suzanne arrived at the hotel. She said a quick hello to William then excused herself to the bathroom. She took her time, soaking in a delicious blend of fancy soaps, creams, and shampoos, letting forty luxurious minutes pass in the steamy bathroom. She came out of the ensuite in a plush white robe and lay n the bed. A bottle of Perrier-Jouët in an iced container rested on the bedside table, inviting her to sip from the good life to which she'd become accustomed—a life of fine wine, international travel, and pricey hotels.

"My God, you look beautiful this morning," William said.

He rose from the sofa and came to the bed with two empty flutes. He carefully opened the bottle and took his time filling the flutes with the precious liquid. "Here's to Liberation Day."

Suzanne raised her flute to touch William's with a slight clink.

"Thanks for coming, Suzy. You've made my day even more luscious." He raised his glass again. "To us."

Suzanne followed suit. "Who is us, Billy?"

"You and I—and the movement, of course."

"And Garrick?"

"Of course, and Garrick."

Suzanne sipped on her champagne. "Just thinking out loud. What would happen if Garrick were no longer in the picture?"

William feigned surprise, but she could see in his body language that Little Billy wasn't especially shocked. Perhaps he harbored similar notions. "That's hard to imagine. This is his baby."

"Let's be real, Billy. Something could happen to any one of us. Could we survive without Garrick?"

William looked at her, apparently bemused.

"What are you thinking?" she asked.

"Look, Suzy. Let's not speculate about that. We'll get through today and see what happens."

"I'm not even sure what Liberation Day means anymore."

Just then William's phone buzzed.

"I need to take this," he said, turning away from Suzanne.

She didn't recognize the voice at the other end, but she figured the man was older, maybe in his seventies. A drinker and a smoker, judging by the raspy voice. The volume was up so loud Suzanne could make out every word. She wondered why William wasn't turning the phone's speaker down. She stepped away toward the Bay window with her back to William, and listened.

"Are your resources in place?" William said.

"The team is originating from obscure sites around the country, including small-town police forces and sheriff's offices. We've redirected those resources to a port in Mexico and then back into the United States via the Port of San Diego. All under an entirely legal import/export exchange."

"Personnel?"

"Twenty-five men blended into the civilian population approximately five days ago. They'll convene near the stadium disguised as maintenance workers and cable guys."

"Okay. Good," William said. He forced a laugh and turned toward Suzanne. She sipped on the flute of Perrier-Jouët, her dark hair silhouetted against the huge window and the big sky.

"What about Cunningham?" the voice said.

"We have the threat assessment. It's official. He's promised to be at the game, ready to make the bust."

William glanced Suzanne's way, then hesitated. His voice lowered. "Frankly, I wanted you to be aware of something."

"What?"

"Be wary of Cunningham."

"You hired him to bust the alleged Islamic terrorist cell, and he faked the threat assessment you wanted. Right?"

"Yes. We needed Cunningham's threat assessment. But Garrick changed the plan and Cunningham's allegiance could be questionable, depending on what happens at the game."

"He still doesn't know about our plan?"

"No, and I think his cooperation is contingent. As long as we come through on our end, he'll bust the terrorists after the game. But he knows the truth. If he thinks we're jerking him around, all bets are off."

"I'm not worried. My team will overmatch any FBI tactical team Cunningham brings to the party."

"God help us. We don't need any dead FBI agents, okay? Make sure of that," William said.

"Understood."

"Okay, the game. Have you scouted the attendees?" William said.

"You were right. It is a big deal. Commissioner Alvarez; Anthony Jones, the president of the university; county officials; state legislators; educational leaders; teachers, principals, and parents. Probably kids too. They'll be rooting for Carson McCready's ragtag crew of felons. Imagine that, Billy. School children who, by all rights, should root for the San Diego All Americans, will instead cheer for a freak show of felons and criminals.

"Alvarez will take the stage before kickoff. He'll preen at the podium. It'll be a socialist shit show while real, hardworking Americans get the shaft."

"Are you running for office again?" William said.

"I can talk the talk. And I know how political criminals think."

"Political criminals? We're American revolutionaries. That's what this is about—always has been," William said.

Suzanne stretched her back and neck, as if performing a yoga routine. She stood there for several minutes listening, looking out at the steel-blue water of the Bay that seemed frozen in place, like a dark blue popsicle dotted with tiny yachts and sailboats.

"Let's cut the bullshit, Billy. For once."

"I'm not going there with you."

"Just say it."

"Are you drunk—again?" William said.

"You grew up with a silver spoon in that revolutionary mouth of yours, William Wharton. Why didn't you follow your father to Wall Street and steal from the poor legally?"

William sighed. "Not now, okay? We had this figured out."

"Yes, now."

"God dammit. What's your point?"

"Look, I grew up poor, working class. I scraped for dimes and quarters. I put myself through college. I became a working-class cop, and I got lucky. I found a political mentor who had connections in Washington. That was you, Billy. I made it with luck and hard work.

"I feel privileged to have had the chances I've had. I'm with the movement. But I'm not a hypocrite. So let's cut the crap." The voice was getting angry now.

"My God, you really are drunk. You're sounding like a broken record—again," William said.

"Only way I can look myself in the mirror sometimes. We're self-righteous motherfuckers who preach liberty and freedom for us, not for the unlucky fucks who really need it. We don't give a shit about them or the country. We do give a shit about our money. A privatized FBI could be very bad for the country. I know that. You know that. But it would be good for us. Very good, indeed."

"That's the genius of capitalism," William said.

"Good, then let's not fool ourselves into believing we're in this because we believe in the welfare of the goddamned country. I know who I am and what I am. I want it all, and I can't help it. But I won't pretend I'm overcoming a tyrannical government for my personal freedom. This is still America, last time I checked."

"Since we're being honest, you and I both know why

you're no longer at the Bureau. You were an alcoholic, and you couldn't keep your dick in your pants. That was a nice speech just now. But you're heavy with baggage. You need us as much as we need you. So get off your high horse," William said.

"We've been friends a long time, Billy. You know my vulnerabilities and I know yours. Don't think for a minute that, as director, I wasn't onto that scheme of yours and Garrick's years ago. Your tax-evasion schemes. That company of yours that stole unemployment insurance from all the poor fucks."

"Come on, man. We're in the middle of a CPD event, okay? Save me the bullshit and tell me what you want."

"Okay, I'll spell it out for you. I turned a blind eye then. But I've got you by the balls now. Fuck with me like you're fucking with Cunningham, and I'll hand your balls to you on that silver platter you grew up with. When I'm satisfied with the outcome of the event, I'll get the ball rolling on the legislative end. Before long the FBI as you know it will be history. And I'll get my job back with six-figure annual bonuses. Never doubt me on that."

William clicked off. Suzanne turned around to face him. He smiled thinly at her and refilled the flutes. "Sorry about that. An old friend touching base."

"Who was it?" Suzanne asked.

"One of our oldest members. I let him talk and I pat his head. He's fine."

"Didn't sound like just touching base. Who is he, Billy?"

"He's an old drunk with too much time and way too much money. Half-crazy and likes to act like he's still relevant. We rib one another. We go back years. Served together in Congress. He . . ."

Suzanne interrupted. "Don't waste your breath, Billy.

273

That was X, wasn't it? What the fuck are you two up to? Never mind. I'm heading downstairs for some fresh air."

"Want company?"

She looked at William standing in his white robe, his expression an unlikely blend of hope and anxiety. Suddenly he seemed like Little Billy again, the kid whom everyone teased for being awkward with girls, overly polite, and too solicitous of the cool kids.

~

Suzanne got to the hotel bar and bummed a cigarette from a guy sitting two bar stools down. She'd have it later, but for now she pretended to light it and inhale the phantom smoke. The big moment, Liberation Day, had finally come. Judging by the conversation she'd just overheard, Garrick and his gang were about to enter the abyss, risking the future of the movement to which he'd given half his life.

For what? To prove Garrick could lead a movement he was now about to destroy? It was her manifesto, not Garrick's, and certainly not Billy's or Agent X's. Her manifesto to safeguard or do whatever she fucking well pleased with it. She caught herself daydreaming. *Oy vey.* Even she, the creator of the idiotic tract, was taking her authorship too seriously.

She'd miss Garrick. The sex, the power. Even his ruthlessness. She wouldn't miss the man whom she had once loved. The man with whom she nearly had a child all those years ago in Cambridge. The child would have been born nine months after Garrick's fortieth birthday. They had made love that night, after she'd presented her gift of *The Manifesto* to him. She wanted the child and her half-crazy lover. But Garrick had turned cold at the thought of a family.

274

She left the hotel and headed to her home in Windansea. She flopped onto the wicker outside. Her body wanted to stop. To reset and forget it all. She dozed off. She daydreamed. The unthinkable truth. Garrick's end was clear and unobstructed. He had rejected her, their would-be child, everything they had ever dreamed of. His trajectory was clear. Now he had made his final choice to leave reality behind, and with that, his own sanity.

~

Suzanne awoke in a panic. She was out of time. Years of going along for the ride, doing nothing, had collapsed into a state of emergency.

She looked at her watch. It was a long shot. Still a few hours from kickoff, she tried to contact Carson and warn him about the possibility of trouble. Her message was never answered.

She warned Cunningham too, and waited for his return call. She got on the Five North and drove east on the Eight through Mission Valley. She got off the freeway a few miles from the stadium. She parked on a side street in a pleasant neighborhood.

She continued to wait—for what, she didn't know. Her mind gave in to an overpowering sense of immobility. She shut her eyes and drifted, unwillingly, into sleep. She was afraid to sleep, but even more frightened to stay awake.

32

WOULDN'T IT BE NICE?

On that same morning, Carson shaved, put on some nice clothes, and cranked up the BMW. First stop, the airport. Kate had relinquished and agreed to allow their son to visit Carson for a few days. Carson's heart skipped a beat as he saw Michael coming through the gate. The boy he used to carry on his back, his green eyes now nearly meeting Carson's as they hugged. The boy grinned and held onto his father for several intense seconds, and Carson felt his warmth and loving nature—the Michael he'd always known but feared he'd lost in the move to Arizona. New friends, new life, and apparently, a new father figure.

Carson was prepared for the worst, and Michael gave him his best.

"What's wrong, Dad? Why are you crying?"

The father wiped his eyes. "Michael boy, you've gone blind. Maybe I'm happier than hell to see you."

"That's okay, Dad. I'm happy too."

They walked to the car, and Michael stopped on the curb under a palm tree. He needn't say what his happy eyes revealed. "I forgot how good this air felt, Dad."

"Come on, son. We'll have plenty of time to smell the fresh air. We'll go to lunch later, after the game. First we're heading to Solana Beach."

"What's in Solana Beach?"

"You'll see."

~

Carson stopped at the car wash then cruised to Solana Beach in just twenty minutes, driving ninety most of the way. He stopped at Safeway's flower section and picked out a decent array of springtime flowers. Then he slowly drove the next few miles toward the ocean.

He found Laura's two-story townhome with her Toyota Prius parked out front. Its customized California license plate said *IBOT*, a too-obvious reference to her working life. He knocked at the door. He heard feet bouncing down the steps. Laura answered the door out of breath, dressed in running clothes. She looked surprised, as if she were expecting someone else. Her look startled Carson. He felt embarrassed. He hadn't told her he was coming over.

"Carson, I was just about to go on a run. Oh, you brought Diego! And who's this handsome young man?"

"Laura, meet Michael McCready. My son."

"I won't tell you who you look exactly like because I don't want to embarrass you, Michael," Laura said.

Michael turned to his dad and gave him a slight punch in the arm. "That's okay, I've heard it before."

Carson held the flowers behind his back, now feeling that giving them to Laura was a completely silly idea. He wanted to toss them into the bushes.

277

"Are those flowers you're holding behind your back, Carson?"

"Oh, these? Yeah, thought they were pretty."

She stood in the doorway. "Come in, you idiot. These are beautiful. Thanks." She bent down from the top step to kiss him on his forehead.

Carson and Michael, holding Diego on the leash, followed her upstairs and watched her cut the flower stems and place them in a vase. She filled the vase with tap water and used her teeth to rip open the packet of plant food. She fed the plant and turned to Carson. "Would you like a beer? You seem tense. What about you, Michael? I have juice."

"Sure, juice is fine."

"Yeah, it's game day, and I'd love a beer."

"I've got this West Coast IPA in the fridge. I heard it's good."

"That's fine. Thanks."

She uncapped the beer and Carson took it, watching Laura move about. So much had happened lately. He would have felt uncomfortable being there, but Michael made it right, somehow. He took a mouthful of the cold beer.

"I'm glad you stopped by. We needed to talk."

"How are you doing?" Carson said.

"It's odd. I feel shell-shocked. Like I know something happened, but I can't wrap my head around what. Kind of in a daze," Laura said.

"Have you heard anything? Any blowback from anybody?"

"Not a word. What about you?"

Carson glanced at Michael. "Son, you okay? We won't be long."

"Sure, Dad. I'll take Diego out for a minute. Okay?

"Hold him tight. He's getting strong and likes to

chase squirrels."

"Got it, Dad."

Carson watched the boy and dog bound down the stairs onto the street. He turned back to Laura. "You're certain about Baby?"

"As certain as I can be. Unless Garrick coded a time delay for another attack, we're clear. We stopped it, Carson."

"Is that possible? A time delay?"

"Of course. Assuming Garrick knows what he's doing. Knowing him, he's probably got someone smart on the payroll."

"Hmm."

"Are you okay, Carson? You've hardly touched your beer."

"I'm fine. Just nervous about the game, you know. It's gotten big. I'm hearing several thousand could show up. And Michael, of course. I'm thrilled he made it."

"That's unbelievable. Several thousand?"

"Yeah. Why I'm nervous."

"Sure you are. It's a big deal," said Laura.

"I also feel like something is weird, unsettled. Petit has been quiet. He's hardly looked me in the eye the past few days. He says he's excited about the game but he isn't acting like it."

"How do you mean, weird?"

They heard steps outside. Michael helped himself inside with Diego in tow. The dog was breathing hard, his tongue wagging. Laura filled a bowl of water for the dog and set it on the kitchen floor near the back door.

"That was quick," Carson said.

"Your dog missed you, Dad. He got all nervous and started whining."

Laura touched Carson. "Finish what you were saying."

"It's just a feeling. But a familiar feeling. Like I'm on a

mission. We've made the first move in and fired a thousand rounds in a matter of a few minutes. We're pumped and ready to finish it. But there's uncertainty. We halt. We don't breathe. Nothing but quiet. And dark. I want survivors, captures. I don't want a massacre. I can hear one drip of water coming from cracks in the concrete building. We're like pieces of a living organism. Every one of us is feeling the same thing at that moment, and everyone has an uncontrollable urge to stop breathing. We're trained to breathe, slowly, steadily, without effort. Just as the surroundings can't get any quieter or any blacker, the fury descends, and hell busts lose, and we must finish the thing. That's what I'm feeling. Like we're waiting for the hell, and it's almost certain to come—and, what's worse, I have no clue how to finish this thing except to jump on a boat or truck and go to wherever the bad guys are and do my job."

Laura didn't move. She sat spellbound, finally getting a glimpse into Carson's former life as a warrior. She had known his job was intense but she had never understood how intense until now. Carson was no ordinary man. He never would be. Yet he was trying his damnedest to become a regular guy in extraordinary circumstances.

Laura stepped over to where Carson was sitting. She wrapped her arms around his neck and held him for several seconds. "Breathe, baby. Just breathe. There's nothing to fear. Have a wonderful game. Play well. Play your heart out like you always have. Help the kids. Soak it up. Nobody can take that away from you. Spend the rest of the day with Michael. We'll follow up with that agent, tell her what we know. Try to make everything right. You're so used to planning for the worst you've forgotten what it means to live in America. How lucky we are. You don't have to be a SEAL anymore."

Carson hugged Laura. "Wouldn't that be nice?" He got up

and touched Michael on his head. "Check this out, son." They all stepped out to the deck overlooking the town of Solana Beach. The ocean was a deep blue that morning. "This is what it's all about, right, Michael?"

"It's amazing, Dad." He laughed. "I hate Flagstaff."

"I thought you loved it."

"Not really. I tried to talk myself into it."

"This is your home too, Michael. You were born here."

Carson raised his beer bottle as if to toast, then handed it to his son, who grinned at the unexpected gift. "Drink up, kid. Help me finish this."

Carson turned to Laura. He put her hand on her waist and inched closer. He kissed her gently at first, then with more passion, which she returned in kind. He whispered in her ear. "I love you, Laura. Always have. Always will."

She whispered, "I'm not going anywhere, McCready." She turned to Michael. "All right, you two. See you after the game? Maybe lunch later?"

"We'll be famished. How about Los Olas in Cardiff? Remember, Michael? You always loved it there."

"I remember, Dad."

~

Carson and his son drove along the Coast Highway, joining the light Saturday morning traffic. His last words to Laura rang in his ears, igniting memories from his own youth. He glanced at Michael, consumed by the fresh ocean air whirling past the speeding car. Carson opened the sunroof. He slipped a CD into the car stereo and hit the play button. He needed to hear the opposite of the anxiety he felt. He drove fast, feeling the cool morning breeze off the coast and listening to

"Wouldn't it be Nice?", his favorite Beach Boys song. It was the same tune he had played and replayed after Laura had left years ago.

He and Michael sang along, the magical tune bridging the generations of men and women, boys and girls, young and old—all seeking freedom. American freedom. From time immemorial to now, nothing had changed. And yet everything had changed.

As the song played out, Michael turned to Carson. "Back at Laura's. I never heard you talk that way about what you did, Dad. You know, about the Navy and all those months you were gone from us. So you were scared. I never knew that."

"Yes, son. I was scared. Fear came with the territory."

"But you did it anyway. Because you were brave?"

Carson glanced sideways at his son, who'd never shown such interest before. That was okay. Now Michael was old enough to maybe understand what he was about to tell him. "Fear is powerful. One of the most powerful human instincts. As strong as love and sometimes stronger. I'd do anything to keep you safe, no matter how scary the monster I'm fighting. But there's something else too. Duty. I loved some of my guys in the platoon, but not all of them. It's more that I loved my platoon—the whole platoon as a unit—as much or more than I loved any single man in it. As their chief, it was my duty to protect the platoon. Guard it from all the bad that fear creates. Being over-confident was one. Hate was another. All ignited by deep gut-wrenching fear. Love first, son. Do your duty second. That was my prescription for dealing with fear. Hopefully you get to a point where fear doesn't enter the equation. You love, you do your duty, and you act. It's not bravery. Why put that pressure on yourself? You do what you promised. It's not complicated when you think about it."

"But most people don't think about it," Michael said. "If they don't promise anything, they don't have to act, right? They don't have a duty to do anything because they never committed to anything."

"Sounds like you have some experience with that."

"All the time. People are flaky, Dad."

"Like who?"

"Girls, sometimes. Friends flake out. I thought it was just California that was like that but it's everywhere now. Even Mom's friend, Dirk. I thought he was a good guy. But I heard what you said to him in Flagstaff. He never came around again after that.

"And I'm thinking, what a flake. Says he's a patriot and all that. He talks about taking his country back, but who's he taking back from? Me? You? It's stupid. I don't get it. I was proud of you, Dad. What you said. I am proud of you. You deserve to hear that from me because I'm your son. Sorry, I'm just blabbing now."

Carson kept driving, trying to eek a smile through the tears wetting his eyes. He reached over to scratch Michael's head. "I love you, son."

"I love you too, Dad."

"We'll have fun at the game, won't we?" Carson said.

"It's gonna be great. Then we'll go to Las Olas, right? And we'll see Laura. She's pretty cool, Dad. I like her."

Carson smiled. He didn't deserve such happiness right then. Yet everything in the world seemed bright and fine and all okay. After all the bullshit, there was still hope. In the past, as a platoon leader, he had often thought he could predict the future. That's what a leader learned to do. He could smell his environment and all its details, and he could see what was coming over the horizon. Now it seemed different. His

283

happiness overcame all fears and all doubts about the future. For once in his adult life, Carson McCready was blind in that moment, and he didn't care.

He scratched Michael's head again. "I can already taste that enchilada."

33

LIBERATION DAY

On a brilliant Saturday afternoon in June, the charity football game between the ragged San Diego County Prisoners and the polished San Diego All-Americans was about to start.

The miracle was that Carson's game was even happening. A week before the event, the county commission had gone into a last-minute emergency session to discuss the game's risks and security issues. Neighbors near Aztec Stadium had been frantically calling commissioners about felons and criminals in their midst. The university president and Commissioner Alvarez pleaded the case for the game. They promised free tickets to neighbors and stated they would be willing to extend the San Diego Promise scholarship opportunities to all qualified families in the vicinity.

"It's only right," Commissioner Alvarez promised. "We'll double-down our efforts to secure the game from any and all mishaps and misdeeds. But I promise we've covered our bases. The governor will be there. Elected officials from the entire region will be there. This event will make our community proud, our state proud, and hopefully, our whole country proud. I hope you can all be part of it. Come to the game. Come to enjoy and stand as witnesses to this event—the first of its kind anywhere in America. With your help, it won't be the last."

With a unanimous vote, the motion to cancel the game was defeated.

By 1:45 p.m., fifteen minutes before kickoff, nearly ten thousand people had filled Aztec Stadium, including many from the surrounding neighborhoods. A high-school band played marching tunes, and a local celebrity sang the national anthem. The mood was festive, with beer suds overflowing plastic cups, the smell of fresh dogs on the grill, and the sounds of electric anticipation filling the stadium.

Carson stood by the fifty-yard line, waiting for the coin toss. He watched as an entourage of officials entered the stadium. State, local, and federal officials; the governor of California; two members of Congress (one red and one blue); the president of the local campus of the state university; several members of the state legislature; and San Diego County officials, including Commissioner Johnny Alvarez and Richard Heller, the director of county prisons.

The governor came onto the field, accompanied by two security agents. He spoke briefly about the importance of higher education to the state and the "beauty" of convicted felons giving back to their communities with college scholarships for needy kids. The governor said he was honored to introduce County Commissioner Alvarez "who played a pivotal role in making this incredible event possible."

Alvarez came to midfield. Carson joined Richard Heller as they walked to the microphone. He felt odd in his football gear, wearing number twelve, walking with Heller in civilian clothes. *This is surreal,* Carson thought as his mind flashed

286

to the contrast between where he had been a few years ago as a warfighter to where he was now, wearing a football suit, walking with his boss toward midfield. Carson watched Alvarez taking the microphone from the governor, who stepped aside to listen.

Carson had heard Alvarez would make a speech, but he didn't know what to expect. As Alvarez spoke Carson grew impatient with the proceedings, itching to get on with the game. He scraped his cleats through the white line on the green grass. As expected Alvarez took more credit than he deserved.

"When we hired Carson McCready, we asked him to be creative at his job heading the county prison system's first telemarketing program, through which we raised money to offset the taxpayer subsidy to our prisons. I'm happy to announce that with Carson's help, my team and I did just that, and in the process created an unprecedented college scholarship program, funded from telemarketing revenues, for the children of San Diego."

Alvarez continued. "We knew things would be different when we first saw Carson's Circle of Trust at work, a ritual he and his telemarketing team did every day after their shift. To me, the Circle was a sign of cohesiveness and teamwork, a rarity these days. With that, allow me to introduce Carson McCready."

Carson stepped forward to get the microphone as Alvarez was receiving a polite applause. Carson didn't care who got credit. That was hardly the point of the scholarships. The kids were the damned point. *Let's get this over with,* he told himself.

Then, as Alvarez was handing Carson the microphone, he looked directly at Carson and said, "Thanks for what you've done to help give to the children who wouldn't have had a fighting chance otherwise. Win or lose, you're a hero, Carson McCready."

The ten thousand fans erupted in joy, and Carson didn't know what to think. Alvarez was giving away at least part of the limelight.

Carson smiled broadly while giving Alvarez a slight bow. He took the microphone and thanked the commissioner. Carson looked up at the audience in the stadium as he spoke off the cuff.

"Who would have thought that a prison could be more than a prison, a place that could help people who are down on their luck and could use a break? I sure didn't. But I'm now a believer. Kindness really does go a long way."

Alvarez stepped forward and asked Carson to tell the fans a little about how the scholarships worked. When Carson had finished, Alvarez again stepped forward. "Any thoughts about today's game, Carson?"

"I know what everybody is saying about our chances today. We're a ragtag bunch and we're up against a polished, semi-pro team. Of course we know our odds are long. We know we are physically out-manned. But, I'm telling you, we have something special here. We know why we're playing today. We know what's at stake. We know who we're working for. We know we're not the All Americans. But we also know this: we're working for the children."

Again the audience roared. Carson got a standing ovation before a single pass was thrown. Whether the felons won or lost the football game, they had already won the larger victory: the hearts and minds of the ten thousand people in the stands. By the opening kickoff, magic filled the air, as if the fans could not be disappointed regardless of the outcome.

Late in the second quarter, the Prisoners were down twenty to nothing. Carson had problems connecting with his wide receivers. They weren't accustomed to the pressure of performing on such a large stage. Carson had played a lot of football in his youth, but he was rusty. He threw behind the receivers several times. His fullback, Black Terrell, was the Prisoners' only offensive weapon during the first half. Their defense was under continual strain because the offense couldn't hold onto the ball long enough to put together a sustained drive. Biff Dickson's All Americans seemed unbeatable, deflating the hopes of everyone rooting for the underdogs.

When the Prisoners returned to the field for the second half, Black Terrell's skin had turned a reddish hue. The tight end, White Terrell, naturally had red hair and light skin, but he turned a bright, burning white, even hotter than red. The guys who were down twenty points were ablaze with a horrific energy. The ten thousand seemed to feel the terrible force, and they lit up when they saw the Prisoners sprint onto the field.

From the first snap of the third quarter, the level of violence on the field rose threefold. The visage was at once horrible and fascinating. American football is a violent game, and the violence increases with the size and quickness of the players. But size and speed aside, the Prisoners played with an animal-like intensity. They flung their bodies through the air to block and tackle. They played uninhibited by normal human fears. They weren't playing for their lives. After all, it was just a game. And yet it was not just a game, Carson realized.

The Prisoners were playing for something you couldn't

touch or feel or see. Playing for something they could only imagine. Something bigger than any single man or team or government or point of pride. They were playing to defy. They were playing to refuse. They were playing for an idea.

It wasn't liberty that they fought for. Liberty was something people of power yielded to other people, for a price. The Prisoners fought for the thing given to them at birth. The innate human desire to seek freedom. So true, yet so abstract. Freedom. A common word so overused it had lost all meaning.

The Prisoners were not fighting for their release from jail. Not that kind of freedom. Their fight was for the freedom to lend their spirits to the people they loved, expecting no love in return. The prisoners had not earned love. They had spent lives destroying love, ruining lives, wrecking things.

As human beings what was left for them but to fight for the freedom to love? The prison was not a place to show love but a place to nurture hate. The Prisoners harbored no ideology, no righteous indignation, no sense they were victims of a system gone foul. The system was theirs. They owned it. They chose it.

Carson's epiphany was the ten thousand's epiphany too. Love was all the Prisoners had left to give. To watch the unbelievable fight on the field for the freedom to love lifted the ten thousand, elevated their souls, gave them something one can only imagine—but the imagination was sweet and powerful and could move mountains.

Carson felt like a different player. He transformed from mediocre to magnificent. Found his timing. Threw bullets. Bombs. Easy lofted throws to a moving target. One target was a smallish guy who played wide receiver. Antoine. Ex-Navy. High school dropout from some southern state. Lived on the streets after he mustered out. Got in trouble and wound up in prison. Carson had found him and put him on the team. Carson saw things in people. He felt their essence. Antoine dropped the first two passes, but Carson kept throwing to him, kept trusting him. He threw to him a third time. He dropped back and scrambled to the right, and then he looked across the field to the left and the kid was all alone, running back to the center near midfield.

It looked like a mental error. Carson violated a quarterback's cardinal rule. Don't pass across the field. But the All Americans were fooled. Nobody on the field believed Carson's arm was that strong. Except for the kid. Except for Carson.

The pass flew forty yards to the left and sixty yards downfield while Carson kept moving to the right. A physically improbable, if not impossible, move for a man his age. The stadium went silent, watching the pass fly, like slow motion, through the air. The play was shocking for its blatant disregard of the attainable.

When the clock stopped, the San Diego County Prisoners had defeated the All Americans 27-20. The ten thousand started dancing in the bleachers and a tsunami of them ran onto the field, overwhelming the security guards. It was pandemonium. The crowd chanted in rhythm, "The-San-Diego-Promise. The-San-Diego-Promise." Again and again the ten thousand grasped hands and chanted.

And then nothing. The fine balance point of silence between the finite and the infinite. A hissing sound, the air of life sucked from the stadium. A thousand chants turned to screams, and Carson flew for what seemed like a thousand miles before landing hard on the green grass. A last image of Michael. Laura smiling at bright flowers. *This is how it ends,*

Carson thought. On American soil, in his own hometown. The Timothy McVeigh blew through the stadium with the roar of a hurricane, and for all purposes of thought and practice, of dreams and reason, America was dead.

~

Suzanne jerked awake to a thunderous crackle, as photons and electrons were bolting and clashing through the same oxygen she tried to breathe. She got out of the S-Class and saw smoke billowing into the sky. She watched in disbelief for several minutes, then heard her phone buzz in the car. She reached over the driver's seat to pick up her mobile resting on the center console.

"Where are you?" He was almost crying, speaking hysterically.

"Darryl, what the hell is happening?"

"Headquarters ordered us to stand down. I was ready to go in with my tactical team. A big show of force, like we planned. We let the game go on. Then with about fifteen minutes to go, I got the order from Rick Anderson, my direct at regional."

"What did he tell you?"

"He says, 'we're good, Cunningham. No need to hang there. It's Saturday. Take the rest of the day off.' So I told him about the threat assessment—signed, sealed, and delivered."

"Then what?"

"Well, by then, I'm pissed. I cussed and wondered what the fuck was going on. Then he tells me the stand-down came from Director Fletcher himself. Can you believe that shit?"

A moment or two passed.

Cunningham finally spoke. "Where are you, Suzanne?

Did you know about any of this?"

"I should go, Darryl."

"I asked you a question. You need to tell me."

"My God, Darryl, what have we done?"

ACT IV
RESIST

Our progeny will build monuments dedicated to us. Saint Ayn. Saint Garrick. Lord Atlas. Saint Suzanne. Saint William. We are the very origins of the Church of Living Capitalism.

– Garrick Cripps

34

DESTINY

Just as he turned around to hug Black Terrell in celebration, Carson heard the blast, louder than a thousand fighter jets taking off at Miramar. Deafened, he watched the pandemonium fly through his frame of vision like a Picasso mayhem. An adult body tossed like a stick through the air. A child cut in half, her blond head bouncing along the green field, half her body crushed under a slab of concrete. Black Terrell bent over, pleading with White Terrell to wake up. "Wake up, brother, get your ass up, man! We won, brother! We won, you motherfucking white bastard."

The bedlam turned into a silent movie that Carson watched until a rescue worker strapped him on a stretcher and hauled him away. He remembered the panic, horrified that medics were carrying his ass to a military hospital.

Carson's brain was fuzzy when he woke. Pain coursed across his back and legs, down to his toenails. He felt his head and

297

touched his nose and eyes. Then he remembered. A football game. Michael standing on the sidelines, mingling with the other players. The joy of seeing the guys on the crew playing their hearts out. Then: nothing.

He tried to get up, but tubes were attached to his chest and arm.

He pushed the call button for the medical staff. "Where's my son? Why am I here?"

A young medical assistant dressed in white rushed in, swiping the curtain with a loud *swoosh*. She checked the monitor for vital signs as Carson gasped for breath, his skin drenched, his heart rate soaring. "Talk to me, sir. Do you know who you are?"

"I'm Carson fucking McCready and my son is missing. Why isn't he here?"

Carson continued to rage, mixing nonsense with an innate sense that something had gone terribly wrong.

Three medical staffers hurried through Carson's privacy curtain. "You're having a panic attack, Mr. McCready," a nurse said. She inspected Carson's recent medical history. "Not surprising given what you've just been through. The doctor is on her way, okay?"

Carson closed his eyes and waited for the doctor in silence, except for the beeps, chimes, and distant voices of the hospital's constant buzz. He forced himself to take several deep breaths and felt himself returning to normal. That wasn't him yelling and screaming like a lunatic. He felt better. The pain meds were happily interacting with the nerve endings in his body and mind.

Michael would arrive any moment. The doctor would show him in and smile at their joyful reunion. Carson couldn't wait to tear off the hospital gown and get the hell out of here. He hated hospitals because time stopped in hospitals. Time stopped and time ended in hospitals. They'd get out of here, and he'd let Michael drive the Beemer. Take the Coast Highway up to Oceanside and grab a beer and some lunch. Catch up with him about life back in Arizona.

Somebody knocked twice before whisking into Carson's space. A woman about his age with shortish, pitch-black hair wasted little time. "Mr. McCready, you're looking better. I'm the surgeon who worked on your arm and hand. Nothing broken, but the tendons in your arm got smashed up pretty good. We'll send you home with some pain meds, but other than that, I think you'll live. Thank goodness. That was an awful mess."

"Where's my son, Doc? His name is Michael McCready. I took him to the game. He was by himself. I haven't heard a damned thing. Why isn't he here?"

"Your wife hasn't contacted you yet?"

"Ex-wife, and no. I'm in the dark here."

"The social worker neither?"

"I'm not repeating myself. What the fuck is going on?"

~

When the attending physician revealed that his son had died in the stadium bombing, Carson turned to darkness. He felt nothing. Despite the pain from his injuries, he felt no pain. No love for another soul. Full of hate toward the world. He thought about Laura for a minute. He thought about Diego. He returned to nothing but his grief. He couldn't cry. He couldn't move.

He ripped the PICC line from his arm and tried to leave in his hospital gown. He pushed an orderly. He fell to the concrete floor and whimpered helplessly. The hospital sent a grief counselor, and he couldn't speak. He saw his life until that moment and hated every choice he'd ever made. Fucking, goddamn motherfucking hell. Why? His conceited bullshit talking bravery and heroism to his child, a boy who had worshipped his dad despite the years of insecurity and loss of a family life. All bullshit because it was all for nothing.

What did he have left but hate? Hate for the megalomaniac who killed his child. By the time he had grieved for several days in the hospital, Carson had no questions left. No mysteries to solve. Michael's death answered all questions, resolved all mysteries, explained all the evidence presented in the court of universal justice.

He'd gone through the stages of grief. He blamed his life, himself, especially life as a SEAL, regretting every important decision he'd ever made because it had all led to this. Nothing was worth this. His ability to predict the future was a fraud. A "skill" restricted to transactional happenings that were barely beyond the moment at hand. No man can predict the future. Not even the great SEAL platoon leader, Carson McCready. His own conceit had killed his son.

But, in the end, would he have done anything differently? Should he not have missed his son? Needed him to be there in San Diego? Was the game itself wrong, even if had become so vital to his sense of right and wrong, of justice itself? Where had this sense of justice come from? His father, the quintessential man of law and justice? The military? His very own DNA? Justice came at a high cost. Last time, it had been the end of his career as a SEAL. This time, the life of his child.

Fuck justice. And yet he couldn't live without a just world. Wherever it came from, that sense of right and wrong under the laws of the universe was imbued in Carson's soul. He couldn't imagine a life otherwise. To be without justice would be to live the life of a robot or a slave. A human being's will to live implied the insatiable urge to see right from wrong, and no human being was immune. No man or woman or child was above that law. Not a single one.

~

Carson floundered for several days after leaving the hospital, his life busted into a million little pieces. Each day Diego pulled him along to the city park where they sat under the shade of a gigantic tree. He avoided the eyes of most people in public, fearing they'd recognize him from the TV coverage.

A few days after coming home from the hospital, Carson picked through the large plastic bag in which the hospital staff had stuffed his belongings. He found his cell phone and yanked it out. Several messages and calls had filled the phone. He looked for anything from Laura. She had called him immediately after the game and then three more times while he was in the hospital. Why hadn't she come to see him? She'd left no messages or texts. He tried to reach her but her number was out of service, and her messages got returned as undeliverable.

According to news reports, an unidentified black-ops squadron had swooped in with ultrasophisticated weapons, placing black bags over the heads of the surviving inmates at the football event. Local authorities had made no comments about the fate of Black Terrell, Antonio, or any of the others. That meant the feds had taken over the case. Local officials redacted most details about the bombing from official police reports.

Few media outlets, except for publications on the left

fringes, deviated from the common storyline: FBI malfeasance had opened the door for a deadly terrorist attack on American soil. The "terrorists," allegedly led by a Black man named Terrell Williams, were placed in military custody enroute to Guantanamo Bay, Cuba. Constitutional rights, such as habeas corpus, were suspended, even for the American citizens sent to Gitmo.

Then, Michael's funeral. Kate wanted to take his body to Flagstaff, but Carson insisted he be buried where he grew up. The ceremony took place atop Mount Soledad, one of Michael's favorite places as a kid. Like father, like son. As folks spoke in somber tones, Carson's mind drifted. He preferred to allow images of his son to flow through him, soothing him. Three-year-old Michael on his back as they tromped on the beaches of Coronado, the boy reaching around Carson's shaved head with his chubby little arms. Michael at six, grinning and dripping vanilla ice cream from his mouth at the white shack at the north end of Ocean Beach. The family's first dog, Ki-Ki, a hairy mutt that tolerated Michael riding his back while fondling the dog's ears and nose. The images softened Carson. But for Michael's lingering aura, Carson felt he'd erupt in a fit of anger at any moment.

～

Two weeks after the bombing, Carson walked to the old donut shop down the road from his condo in Lemon Grove. He ordered his usual large coffee and a donut, and sat at the corner table near the window. He sat quietly, sipped on the coffee, and scratched his mental calculations out on a napkin, searching for a way to get from where he was to where he needed to be.

302

He heard the bells clang on the donut shop's front door. An old woman, stooped and wearing an old dress, chatted with the cashier. She took a table across from Carson. The cashier brought her coffee and a maple bar.

Carson tried not to make eye contact.

"Hello there, young man," the old woman said.

Carson gulped down the coffee and donut. He got up to go.

"Don't leave, please," she whispered. "I know who you are."

"Then I really must leave," Carson said.

"You don't look so great."

"Who in the hell are you?"

"Calm down, Carson. You contacted me. You sent me and David Green a letter. Remember?" The old woman spoke in a whisper. "I'm Amy Watson. You tipped us off about Garrick Cripps. You and your friend, Laura Cavendish."

"How would you know that?"

"I'm an investigator. Not difficult to put the pieces together. I know most of it. Still foggy on some details. We started with Garrick Cripps and worked back. You provided us with some useful information. Much appreciated."

"Didn't do much good, did it?"

"Why were you so reluctant to come forward? If you'd come to us directly, we might have stopped it."

"Who's us? It's hard to tell anymore."

Amy glanced around the shop and lowered her voice to a near whisper. "My ex-boss, David Green, and me, for starters. Your Garrick Cripps tip led us to a William Wharton, a.k.a. Little Billy, in the District of Columbia. Both are associated with criminal enterprises in several states, including the guns and drugs trade in Southern California. Wharton's tracks led

303

us to a woman, Dr. Suzanne Dreyfus. I see that astonished look. How do we know this? Your coworker, Johnny Petit. He's saying you and your team had nothing to do with the bombing. He's in police custody. The conspirators can't afford for Petit to testify. They'll push him to finger you for a deal."

Carson looked Amy up and down. "Why are you dressed like that? You're not that old, are you?"

"Good eye. No, I'm not. I'm an undercover agent, and I've gone to ground."

"Why are you here then? What do you want?"

"To warn you."

"A little late for that, right?"

"You're in danger. Laura too. The higher-ups in Justice have been co-opted in the conspiracy, and they want to nail you and Laura as co-conspirators in the bombing. They'll twist the evidence to make both of you look guilty. The conspiracy runs from an FBI counterterrorism agent named Darryl Cunningham back to William Wharton and then to the head, Garrick Cripps. You and Laura pose a danger for Cripps."

"Seems that you know a lot. But you're still a federal agent, and I'm a suspect."

"I know a lot from my gut and how the pieces appear to fit together. I've got a problem, however."

"What's that?"

"I can't prove a conspiracy in a court of law. Not yet. Maybe never. That, and I'm up against the entire Justice Department acting like it's on Cripps's payroll. This isn't a surprise to you, is it?"

"How do you mean?"

"You didn't put me on Garrick Cripps's trail for nothing. How did you know about the attempted cyberattack on government computers?"

"I thought that was covered up. There was nothing on the news."

"My boss, David Green, got a heads-up from a former colleague. I won't say who. But this guy would know. He's one of our only leads."

"Who is he? Or she?"

"The investigation is ongoing."

"Fuck that."

"Well, how did you stop it? I heard it was some kind of super-bot," Amy said.

"Long story. I received some anonymous intel. Laura figured out how to block it. She works with the military on cybersecurity. That's all I can say, for Laura's sake."

"How did you know to point me to Cripps?"

"Laura knew Garrick. She was his student at MIT. We put the pieces together. Turns out he's a diabolical wing-nut out to destroy the government. Like I said, we got some help."

"What kind of help?"

"I got a series of anonymous texts warning us. I think Cripps has been planning this shit for years, maybe decades. We expected the cyberattack, but not exactly how it would work. Not until I realized Cripps was planning to use my telemarketing computers as a gateway to crash government computer networks.

"We thought we'd foiled the plot, but we didn't expect Cripps to be a madman. I should have seen it, but I missed it. Fuck, everyone missed it, you included. Cripps appears to have gotten help from a tactical team of unknown origins. I seriously doubt that San Diego is the end," Carson said.

"We don't know yet that Cripps was behind the bombing."

"Come on, Agent Watson. I don't buy that."

"I'll give you this: it appears that Cripps has built an

anti-truth machine that's becoming almost impossible to stop. Have you heard of the Freedom Society, by chance?" Amy said.

"Can't say I have."

"I don't know much. It appears that this society calls the shots. Powerful and secretive. I suspect Garrick answers to this cabal of billionaires. And he's not the only one. Half of the FBI leadership is playing along or playing dumb. Headquarters ordered Cunningham, the region's top counterterrorism agent, to stand down just before the blast," Amy said. "We could have stopped it, but didn't. Now the government has blood on its hands."

"Why are you here talking to me, Agent Watson?"

"As a federal agent, as an investigator, I deal in facts. I'm highly motivated to get the truth out, but Cripps's misinformation machine will mold public opinion before we can tell the people what really happened. The clock keeps ticking, and we don't have the traction we need to inflict lasting damage on this damned conspiracy.

"That's why we need your help, Carson. David Green is working his sources and assembling a team. I'm working mine too, and I'd like to convince you to join us. We can't find Cunningham. According to the FBI, he's on medical leave. He could be dead for all I know."

"You people can't seem to decide what side you're on. What about you, Amy? Who's side are you on when you're not interrogating me?"

"Don't you fucking mess with me, McCready. Just don't. I'll fight this evil for as long as it takes to destroy it. And it is evil. Make no mistake. The insidious destruction of our country from the inside, disguised as an attack from foreigners and international terrorists. Doesn't get much worse than that."

"Okay. I believe you. But you can see my point. Federal agents have lied in the past to entrap an innocent suspect. What makes you special?"

"Listen to me carefully, Carson. We can't trust anyone in the administration, including the Attorney General and the Director of the FBI. They've all been bought or frightened to death of defying the conspiracy and the powerbrokers behind it."

"Then we're fucked," Carson said.

"The whole damned country is fucked. You've got skills that could help us. I know about you. Ex-SEAL, nearly famous. That Kentucky senator, Graybill, is now piping off that you were the guilty one in that incident years ago, the one in Africa, and now accusing you of masterminding the San Diego bombing to get back at the Navy."

"Masterminded a bombing in which my own son gets killed?"

"I know. The bullshit is flying. Legally and institutionally, we're in terrible shape. Green and I have discussed this. We might have to resort to other, more direct measures, on a case-by-case basis."

"Are you saying what I think you're saying?"

Amy didn't reply, allowing her silence to speak volumes.

"I'm not in the game."

"I could approach others like you, and they'd tell me to go fuck myself. You know that. They'd listen to you. I'm betting they'd even follow you. I know what you did as a platoon chief. I know what you tried to do at the county prison. You're a goddamned hero, McCready. Like it or not, you've spent your life preparing for this. If there really is such a thing as destiny, then this moment right now is yours."

"You tell me—what's my destiny?"

307

Amy put down the Styrofoam cup of coffee and turned to meet Carson's eyes directly. The old-lady outfit disguised her youthfulness, yielding a rare combination of exuberance and wisdom. "So you're okay with what happened? An attack by domestic terrorists on American soil doesn't bother you? I know you're not that jaded, McCready. As a man, as a father, as someone who served your country with dignity? All that goes down the rathole?"

"Agent Watson, you need to shut the fuck up. I lost my son. Garrick Cripps and his gang killed my child. I have a pretty good idea about my destiny, and that's my business. You and your team of investigators can go about your own business. You're a law enforcement officer, but now you can't even uphold the law because the law is dead.

"I was a trained killer for the American government, and I had the authority to go after terrorists thousands of miles from home who'd fucked with my country. I have no authority now. I have no deniability. I'm a free man. Destiny? I don't give a shit about that, never have.

"My dad was a civil rights lawyer. Did you know that? If he gave a damn about destiny, he'd never have given his life to the poor fucks who needed help the most. If he cared about destiny, he'd have hooked up with men like Cripps and his gang. He'd have worked his ass off to make the strong even stronger and the rich richer. If underdogs believed in destiny, the so-called American Dream would be pure bullshit. Just a slogan. Because destiny is for kings, not peasants."

"I don't believe that," Amy said. "The poor can believe in hope. Hope can lead one to fulfill their destiny."

"I won't sit around and hope good things happen. My father taught me that. And now I'm realizing I'm okay with it. In this world, you act or don't act—for good or for evil. They

308

say there's no truth anymore because everything's just a shade of gray. Now truth is what you claim it is. Bullshit. Not in my world. Not now, not ever, will I succumb to lies disguised as truth. I know exactly what happened, and Garrick Cripps won't bullshit or gaslight his way out of it. I'll do what needs to be done, destiny be damned."

"So you'll work with us?"

"No. Especially not on this. From now on, I work for myself. No authorities to be accountable to. No Navy. No FBI. And no fucking freedom societies. On this, I play by my rules."

"What rules are those?"

"That 'the strong shall prevail over the weak.' I read that in the so-called *Liberation Manifesto*. High time to make Garrick Cripps eat his own bullshit."

35

YOU ARE A REVOLUTIONARY, RIGHT?

Suzanne showed up unannounced at Garrick's doorstep in Morro Bay. She smelled the brittlebush and birthroots in bloom along the stone pathway leading from the street to the architecturally wonderful main entrance adorned with brass fittings and a feeling of invincibility.

Garrick had always had a personal gardener and a handyman to maintain the facade of perfection. His staff now included two large men in suits who stood by the front door. A cozy life Garrick had made for himself in the heart of the central California coast, and yet he needed a pair of goons to protect him.

"Could I see some identification, ma'am?" one guard said.

"Don't *ma'am* me. Tell Garrick to get his ass out here to greet me like a gentleman."

Suzanne waited while a bodyguard stepped inside. After several minutes Garrick came to the door wearing a Hawaiian shirt and flip-flops.

"Thought you'd still be on the yacht."

He stood at the door for several seconds, saying nothing.

310

Suzanne sensed confusion, perhaps even the beginnings of senility. "Early flight home, Suzy."

Suzanne looked around the cottage as if for the first time. "So bourgeois, Garrick. Not exactly the home of a revolutionary. You are a revolutionary, right?"

"Oh, Suzy, be nice. I'm glad you came. What can I get you to drink?"

Suzanne removed her jacket and followed Garrick to the kitchen, taking a stool at the breakfast nook. She noticed how the bald spot on the back of his head had gotten bigger, a not-so-pretty contrast to his over-long, graying hair.

"Whiskey and ice okay?"

"I'm not staying long."

Garrick handed her the cold drink and sat next to her, looking into her eyes. She saw through his act of pretending that she was his one-and-only point of interest.

"I hoped you'd come back eventually. Even after our last conversation. That did not go well for me."

"Right, it's all about you. Blowing up a football stadium, killing public officials, children and their mothers and fathers, then framing innocent men for an act of domestic terrorism?"

"I have no idea what you're talking about. Besides, they were hardly innocent, Suzanne. They were convicted felons. Why would it matter? Guantanamo or a high-security prison in America—all the same to those losers."

"You have a rationale for everything, don't you, Garrick?"

He stood and slammed the glass on the stainless-steel countertop. "Why so angry, Suzanne? This should be a time of celebration. I've got a nice champagne chilling."

"Are you liberated now, at last? Or just inebriated?"

He turned toward her and folded his hands together, as if he were a pastor of a church and delivering a sermon.

311

"Inebriated with joy, Suzy. Magnificent things are coming to us, to the entire world. Unlimited wealth and liberty are imminent, without the yoke of government holding us down. I'm proud of you, Suzanne. For all the work you've done to get us here. History will remember you as a great leader. Our progeny will build monuments dedicated to us. I envision a sort of sainthood for us. Saint Ayn. Saint Garrick. Lord Atlas. Saint William. And last but not least, Saint Suzanne. We are the very origins of the Church of Living Capitalism."

Suzanne put down her drink. She stood and started clapping. At first soft and then harder and louder, rising to her feet and clapping back, almost touching Garrick's nose. She remained standing, meeting his eyes. "Save the speech for your favorite cable news channel. You fucked us. For good. I don't know how we get out of the mess you've made."

Garrick put down his drink. He lifted his chin toward the ceiling and puffed out his chest, as if to recover a sense of power that was fast slipping away. "Suzanne, I thought I knew you. *The Liberation Manifesto* was yours, but you never took credit. You stayed in the background but always came through whenever I needed you. I've never really thanked you for that. Well, I'm thanking you now, Suzy."

"I left you. I'm sorry for that too. We'll start over."

Suzanne looked at Garrick and pitied him with all the sincerity of the woman who once would have done almost anything for him. "I'm sick and tired of your words, Garrick. Words, words, and more words. You're a man of words. But a man whose words don't matter because you're a liar. I know two things for sure. One, you just killed nearly a thousand people in San Diego, including the son of a former Navy SEAL named Carson McCready, and two, you won a target on your back that will follow you for as long as you're alive.

312

Mark my words, McCready is going to hunt you down and he's going to kill you."

"I know about McCready. I have a source of power that he can't match."

"Power? What power?"

"The power of hate. There's no end to the amount of hate people like me have for people like McCready and countless other do-gooding sons of bitches."

"I know your game, Garrick. I know you too well."

"What game?"

"You hate the sort of people who do good just for the sake of doing good. Kindness doesn't compute for you. You hate yourself for being that way, but you can't help yourself."

"There's always an ulterior motive, Suzy. This much I know for sure. Humans are greedy bastards. Always have been, always will be. Get over it. I prefer to live in the real world in which nothing is guaranteed, including life itself."

Suzanne stared blankly at Garrick then pulled out a recording device from her coat and held it in the air for Garrick to see. "You are officially on record for confessing to an act of domestic terrorism and mass murder. If I don't get what I want, this recording goes live."

"What do you want?"

"I want what I deserve."

"Deserve? Are you kidding? That's a word socialists use. But tell me, Suzy, what do you deserve?"

"I want you to step down. Announce your retirement to the membership. Sail away on that yacht of yours. Or do the right thing and turn yourself in. I don't give a damn. We'll issue a joint announcement to our members. I will become the fresh face and voice of the new movement."

"What new movement?"

313

"Under my control, the movement will be divorced from Nazis, private militias, white supremacists, radical libertarians, and the so-called Freedom Society. A movement devoid of you and everything you stand for."

"Is that all, darling?"

"One more thing. You'll announce that I am and always have been the author of *The Liberation Manifesto*, and I will make it abundantly clear that my stupid little gift to you was meant as a joke. I will confess that everything I wrote was a lie."

"Now you want to take credit?" Garrick said.

"I don't need to take it. The authorship is authentically mine, and I can prove it."

"How?"

"Are you kidding? Fight me on this, and you'll lose."

"I'll be seen as a fraud, and that would hurt the both of us. You'll end up destroying the movement and all we've built," Garrick said.

"I'll let you down easy. We'll promise a new manifesto, a serious one, that updates and supplants the original." Suzanne snickered. "Of course, I'll do my best to embarrass your investors. I'll name every one of them."

Garrick got up from the barstool, sloshing the ice in his drink. He took one last pull from the glass. "John!" he called to the goon. "My guest is leaving now. Could you show her out, please?"

"Of course, sir."

"Hold on, buster. May I use the lady's room?" Suzanne slipped from the thug's grasp and stepped into Garrick's library, where they used to make love on the sofa and talk for hours about their future together. She knew Garrick's old habit of placing his mobile phone on the bookshelf in the

314

library. She grabbed his phone and slipped into the bathroom.

She figured Garrick would not have changed his phone's pin number: the unimaginative AYN. But when she entered the pin, Garrick's phone failed to unlock. She tried again, with the same result. *For God's sake,* Suzanne thought. *What was the damned pin?* She tried again, typing ATLAS, trying both upper and lowercase. Again, failure.

She sweated, resisting the onset of a mild panic attack, and tried again, typing variations of GALT, without success. Then she had a notion. He wouldn't, would he? She typed her name. SUZY. The mobile opened. She attached a military-grade high-speed wire from her phone to his and waited for Garrick's data to transfer to a new, unlocked mobile. Ten minutes later the data transfer was complete. Suzanne was now in possession of a clone of Garrick's phone.

She washed the sweat off her face, quickly reapplied her makeup, and brushed her hair. She placed the clone in her handbag and hid Garrick's phone under the sleeve of her coat. She breezed from the bathroom and set his phone back to its place on the bookshelf. She stepped toward the front door, refreshed and ready to get the hell out of Garrick's life.

As she walked out the front door, Suzanne pointed her middle finger to the sky and walked through the gate. She turned around and saw Garrick standing by the door, glaring at her. What was he thinking? His pin was her name. Unbelievable. Did the poor bastard still love her after all?

"Oh well," she whispered to herself. Mission accomplished. She had just created an unobstructed window into Garrick's hidden life. She believed, all right. She trusted. She trusted the power of deception. She trusted the rage of Carson McCready. Message Agent X under Garrick's name, and X wouldn't have a clue. Garrick would be a ghost, scratching and clawing for

315

his freedom in hell, and yet the creature of the underworld, once known as Garrick Cripps, would still live in the eyes of the undead. An illusion. A feat of magic. But Suzanne was a scientist and a rationalist with little tolerance for magic. She'd leave such sentimental notions to the true believers.

Carson McCready was not a true believer. Perhaps Carson the father, the son, and the soldier had been a sentimental man when it came to his son or to Laura. But now, Suzanne guessed, the former Navy SEAL would have no use for any unnecessary feelings.

~

Suzanne got into her car and drove down the mountain as fast as possible. When she pulled into the main village of Morro Bay, she parked in a public lot near the beach. She took a breath and felt content to watch the silent surf from within the warmth of her S-Class. She felt tired and started to drift off. She fell asleep and woke twenty minutes later.

There was no use in waiting longer. Garrick would not call and try to apologize. What love was there had been destroyed by lies, false promises, and fakery. More likely he'd send one of the goons into town to follow her and kill her when the time was right.

She started the car and drifted into the weekday traffic of Morro Bay, winding her way to the Coast Highway heading south toward Santa Barbara. She drove through the fog that enveloped the highway, looking frequently at the rearview mirror. Visibility was poor, and she concentrated on keeping the car within the lines as best she could.

Her Bluetooth lit up with an incoming call. She hit the answer button and heard a man's voice. "You'd better pull over, Suzanne. Driving conditions suck."

"Who is this?"

"Your tool. Forget me already? It's Cunningham."

"Darryl?"

"There's a road a quarter-mile ahead. Take the right and drive into the gravel lot. There's a restaurant. I'll meet you there."

Suzanne pulled into the lot and parked. She found a table inside near the fireplace and removed her gloves. She felt the warmth, and relaxed until the server came. Then she ordered a hot drink and waited.

She heard the door chimes clang behind her. She turned around and saw Darryl Cunningham's six-five frame ambling toward her. He sat down without a word. The wooden chair creaked against his weight. The server came and he ordered a black coffee.

When both were settled, Suzanne said, "You were following me because . . . ?"

Cunningham held his gaze at the steaming coffee then finally looked up. "Where's my damned money?"

"I don't have it. That little shitstorm in San Diego got in the way. At this point I'm as fucked as you are, big guy. But not as fucked as those poor people in the stadium."

"I got put on leave. Medical leave. Shrink says I'm not emotionally well after what happened."

"You mean the bomb?"

"Might have had something to do with me screaming at Director Fletcher's assistant on the phone. Told her that her boss was a motherfucking liar and a killer, and one day he'd pay. I lost a tail earlier. I shouldn't be here. But this is as good as any place at the moment." Cunningham looked her up and down. "You look exhausted. Are you okay?"

"I shouldn't be okay, but I am."

"Why did you go to Garrick's?"

"You followed me to his house?"

"I've been tracking you for almost forty-eight hours, Suzanne. I've got nowhere else to be. So where is my money?"

"Eurynomos was supposed to pay you. He didn't?"

Cunningham glared at her. "Why am I not surprised? What did Garrick say?"

Suzanne gazed at her coffee mug, thinking about how to answer. "Honestly, Darryl, it doesn't matter. I need to apologize. You didn't deserve this. I'm sorry. I was a nasty bitch to you. But you weren't exactly Mr. Perfect. You tried to make a pact with the devil, and the devil fucked you over. What did you expect?"

"Are you the devil, Suzanne?"

The server showed up with a pad and pencil. "Can I get you two anything else?"

Suzanne looked at the young woman. "Do I look like the devil?"

"Are you talking to me, ma'am?" the server replied.

"Yes. Do I?" Suzanne repeated.

"Not exactly, no. But he does," the young woman said, gesturing toward Cunningham.

"Thank you, sweetie. That will be all," Suzanne said.

The young woman smiled and walked away. "Let me know if you need anything, folks."

Suzanne turned to Cunningham. "I made a lot of mistakes in my life, and Garrick was my worst. That's what I went to tell him. I know my apology doesn't help. But at least you're still alive, Agent Cunningham."

"Ex-Agent Cunningham. But as long as we're being contrite, I am going to tell you something, and I hope we can be on the same page."

"Tell me what?"

"Have you heard the name Amy Watson?"

Suzanne looked puzzled.

"Never mind. She was the Justice Department agent who put a target on my back when she suspected I was colluding with you people. She was right, of course, but now she's on the same target list as me. You and me, we know too much, and we're on the same wrong side, and now it looks like you're on Garrick's shit list too. That means we're both on the bad side of the conspiracy *and* the law, which makes us best friends forever."

"You're sure about that?"

"As sure as I can be. Where are you going? What are you going to do?" Cunningham said.

"You don't seem that upset about your money we promised."

"Just as well. I feel less guilty. Truth is, I'm lost. I thought we could have a pity party together. I wanted to see you again."

"Your timing isn't great, Cunningham."

"Well, our date can wait. I need to ask you a question."

"I don't like questions."

"More like a favor. I'm part of an impromptu team of unofficial investigators trying to prove Carson McCready's innocence. I owe it to myself, personally, to make this right. So I hate to ask, but could you go back and tell Garrick you're sorry? Tell him you've lost your way. You still believe in the cause and want to be with him, and so on."

"Why would I do that?"

"He's got to be stopped, Suzanne. This has gotten way out of hand. You can be more effective on the inside."

"You want me to embrace the movement after all?"

"I didn't say that. But are you okay with a thousand innocent people being murdered for the sake of the perfect capitalist state? I like capitalism. But I like the Constitution more. I feel guilty as hell, and I won't let this shit go unanswered."

"Of course I'm not okay with it. Fuck Garrick and his movement. I'm done. But I'm not a spy, if that's what you're asking."

"I know. It would be difficult. But we've got an unusual opportunity to be on the inside of this plot as it goes forward. You would be more valuable to the investigation than you ever were to him."

Suzanne stared into her coffee cup and looked up at the man apparently asking her for help in earnest. "Darryl?"

"What?"

"I don't want that. I want to go home. I want to go back to who I was before all this. Before Garrick. Before William. Before you, even. I want a damned dog, Cunningham. I want a puppy, and I want to walk him to work through my neighborhood in Boulder and let the little guy piss on big trees. It's a lovely neighborhood and the people are friendly and kind. I want to see my mother and father. They're getting old. Before it's too late, I want a life like that. I don't want to be a beautiful bitch with perfect skin and expensive tastes. I don't want to be a damned spy. Have I earned at least that? What do you want, Darryl? To chase down Garrick Cripps for the rest of your life?"

Cunningham removed his top coat and loosened his tie. Even now, he wore the uniform of a proper FBI agent. "Damn, Suzanne."

"That's all you have to say?"

"Fucking A right, I want all that too. If it were up to me, I wouldn't mind being the guy who could share that life with you. I'm ready to stop. Ready to quit being a cop or even an ex-cop. I'm getting too damned old for this shit anyway. Watson was about to take early retirement herself. I'd just as soon leave the rest to Jason Treadwell and all the other hotshot kids to take up where we left off. Maybe they could do it better than us. We didn't do so good, all in all. But . . ."

"But what, Cunningham?"

"I'd feel like shit giving up now."

"That's the thing," Suzanne said. "I wouldn't. I'd feel great. I'll change my identity if I have to. I won't let Garrick ruin my life more than he already has."

"I don't know what to say. Part of me doesn't believe you because you snookered me."

"I had a job to do."

"I took the bait, and I feel like a fool. I should have busted you then."

"Maybe. But would that have stopped Garrick? No, go do what you have to do, Darryl. If someday you decide you're done, find me. You're FBI, or at least you were. You're good at finding people. Just remember. Two rings. Wait two minutes exactly. Then, if I'm still alive, I'll call you back."

36

LOVELY ELY

Lemon Grove was in Carson's rearview mirror. By nightfall California was behind him, and he was almost halfway through Utah. He tired of Utah quickly. He got off the 15 and headed west to Nevada. The Great Basin Highway would take him north into the void. Darkness was looming, and the empty black road was no place for a night drive.

He hoped to get to Ely by nine p.m. The trip would be longer, but with fewer people and hassles. Less chance for trouble. Time to get out of trouble. Get out of town to think. Carson would go to Montana now. Figure out his next move. Consider what Amy Watson had told him. Find Laura. He called his mother. "Mom, tell nobody where I am or that you talked to me, okay?"

"What's going on with you, Carson?"

"Nothing, Mom. Just getting out of Dodge for a bit. I need to clear my head. Thinking about visiting cousin Chuck in Montana."

"Oh, he'd love to see you, honey. After everything that's happened. My God, Carson. I just can't bear it. Poor Michael.

Your father. I miss them so."

"I know, Mom. I should never have let him come."

"Carson, don't say that. Never think that. Promise me."

"Can't help it, Mom."

"Just be careful. I can't lose you too. I just can't, son. Don't be doing anything drastic. I know how you can get."

"Nothing drastic. Promise."

He drove several hours through the big emptiness until he arrived at Ely. He checked into a Motel 6 under a false name and placed an extra twenty under the clerk's nose, which persuaded her not to ask for his credit card or driver's license. He needed a drink. There was a good Chinese a block away. After dinner Carson returned to the front desk and told the clerk, "There's another fifty if you can find me a bottle of Irish whiskey."

"That might not be doable. Liquor store's closed." She looked at the fifty. "I'll see what I can do."

Within twenty minutes a young guy showed up at Carson's door carrying a bag. Carson opened the door and saw a short Latino kid. A kid about Michael's age.

"Hey, man. I'm Emilio, Rosie's brother. From the front desk. Here's your whiskey, man."

Carson put the fifty in the kid's hand.

"My sister will get in big trouble if her boss finds out."

Carson pulled out another twenty and handed it to the kid. He still looked unsatisfied, but Carson was done. The cheap whiskey had already cost him seventy bucks. "All I got, brother. Have a good night. And thanks a million." He shut the door tight and locked the deadbolt.

He lay against the queen bed's headboard with as many pillows as he could find. Diego lay beside him. He wrote on a yellow notepad and drank the whiskey from the bathroom's plastic cup. He got a buzz and needed to think. Think this through.

Montana felt right. Montana was a feeling, not anything thought out. It had been a gut decision to leave. A gut decision to tell his mother that he was going to see cousin Chuck. She deserved to know, and she knew to never, ever disclose his whereabouts to any soul.

At the top of the yellow pad, he wrote Laura's name in large letters and drew a vertical line down the center of the notepad. He stared at the blank yellow pad for several minutes.

Carson had many reasons to forget this strange, devastating chapter in his life. More reasons than he could count to run to Montana and never be found again. But why had the cops let Carson leave? The FBI hadn't pursued him, and he couldn't fathom why. The government was imprisoning his own teammates, innocent men, and it would have been just as easy and plausible to whisk Carson away too.

After failing to get through to Laura, he had called her mother. "She's gone, Carson. I can't say where. I'm so sorry," Hilda said.

He had poked around at the university, but there was no record of the supposed lab she worked at. On paper she was listed as a full professor. But office staff told him she had been "on leave" for several months.

He scribbled on the yellow pad, brainstorming. He freshened his drink. He believed Laura was trying to survive in her own way, and that probably meant isolating herself. The signs were bad. Laura was running and, Carson presumed, didn't want to be found. Did Garrick threaten her, or worse?

Carson was almost through the bottle, jotting notes and ideas, calculating his next move. He needed to get online, and his disposable phone wasn't capable of it. He punched in the number for the front desk. Rosie picked up.

"Hey, it's me in room eleven."

"Yes, Mr. Carpenter, how can I help you?"

"Thanks again for arranging that whiskey run. I have another job for your brother."

"What do you need?"

"Access to a computer. I need to get online."

"There's one at the front desk here."

"No public computers. I need some privacy if that's possible. There's another fifty in it for you and your brother."

"I'll try, Mr. Carpenter. Could take a while. You're not in trouble, are you? You wouldn't get us in trouble, right?"

"I'm not in trouble, Miss. It's all good. Just want to be left alone."

~

Two days after the bombing, Laura flew to Puerto Villamil in the Galápagos Islands of Ecuador, a twenty-hour plane and boat trip from the East Coast.

She spoke to exactly three people: the taxi driver who transported her to the beachfront casita, the man who checked her in at the front desk, and the same waiter each night at the beachfront restaurant. She avoided eye contact with everyone else. She wanted to be at the beach. She wanted Charles Darwin to transport her back to the very beginning of evolutionary biology. She would explore the Galápagos. She needed her own silent world, where she could be mesmerized by brilliant blue water, brown herons, sea lion pups, and the multiplex of sounds of the natural world.

But feelings of guilt plagued her. She was running away, bailing on Carson when he needed her most. The Pentagon

325

was now on lockdown, suspending work on all cyber projects until national security conditions settled down. She had panicked, feeling like low-hanging fruit and waiting for federal agents to come knocking.

She walked to dinner at the resort's restaurant and sat on the porch under the canvas awning, feeling the cool evening breeze and enjoying a fresh margarita. She had thought about leaving her tablet at home but brought it with her anyway. She was told that the restaurant had Wi-Fi. She had installed masking software to hide her identity and location, which provided some comfort. But, against her better judgment, she powered up the device to check for messages.

Nothing unusual. Colleagues wishing her well. A couple of emails from friends. A professor from the University of Michigan seeking feedback on a paper. Then there was one message from several days ago, well down the list. She didn't recognize the server or the email service. It looked suspicious but had somehow got through her spam filter. She ran the message through her antivirus software. There was nothing visibly dangerous about it, but she told herself not to open it.

The message could be from Carson, but it could also be a trap. She didn't want to think about danger when she was in the Galápagos, reading Darwin. Thinking about species and survival, the weeding out of the weak and the survival of the strong. If she were to act rationally, Laura would close the tablet. She would enjoy her margarita and the brilliant blue ocean and the sounds of the sea and the beach teeming with birds and seals.

But instinct overcame her rational mind, and she opened the message.

Dear Laura, 9on't be alarmed. It's me. When

you opened the message, I received an encrypted code indicating the message was opened. DO NOT reply. Read and then delete this message immediately. I will receive another encrypted code showing the message was read. Assuming that you are still in possession of your computing devices, I must take the risk that you and you alone opened and read this message.

I will try to be brief. I hope I can persuade you to join m3 and fight back against this terror. I spoke to our person, the investigator who has been dismissed from her job. She's on our side. She believes that the democratically elected government of the United States has been dangerously compromised. We do not know whom to trust. Current officeholders cannot be relied upon to execute the laws of the land and provide constitutional protections to the citizens of the United States.

I'm headed toward M6ntana. You know I like a good beer. I have a cousin on a ranch. I won't say exactly where, not just yet.

Above all, I miss you. Hope you are well.
Do what you wish with this information.
All my lovely,
Soledad

⌒

Laura downed the margarita, enjoyed a quiet meal, and went to bed early. She re-read "Soledad's" letter, finding it more curious each time. No doubt it was Carson, referring to their favorite hideout as teenagers. He'd written what amounted to an elementary code. The strange typos. Montana spelled as M6ntana. "All my lovely?" What was that? Reminding her he liked beer? Clearly he wanted to tell her something without spelling it out.

The next morning she packed her bags. Two days later she landed in Las Vegas, where she rented a car and drove north toward St. George, Utah, stopping to check with hotels near the freeway. The question was always the same: "Has a Carson McCready checked in? I'm supposed to meet him here." And always, the answer was the same: "No Carson McCready here. Sorry, can't help you."

The search was tedious, and the road empty. Long stretches of thinking about her past and the future. Random thoughts. Crazy thoughts. Was there a future with Carson? Montana was probably a wonderful place. She'd heard good things. Montanans were rugged individualists, right? Like Carson. Montanans were not moralizers and religious freaks. They were live-and-let-live types. Like California without the smog and traffic.

But Montana wasn't an anything-goes kind of place either, not like California. Couldn't be too selfish to survive in a place like that. Humans trying to eke out a life in a rugged land. A culture of cooperation evolves in a place like that. Going it alone can get you killed. Get you pushed out to die in the cold. A place that required tolerance. Accepted quirkiness.

She remembered the dog. Carson would have his dog, Diego, with him. A yellow Lab. Carson loved that dog. He would be staying at hotels or motels that allowed dogs. Big dogs. She changed her query. Carson McCready, a man with a big yellow Lab. Is he checked in here? Nope. Haven't seen him or the dog. You might try Motel 6. They allow big dogs.

That triggered something. The strangely placed numbers

328

that appeared like typos. She inspected the letter again. She remembered the number six. The weird way he wrote M6ntana. What did M6 mean? Motel 6, like the other hotel staff suggested? There would be a dozen Motel 6s along the way.

She reached for her phone, then remembered she'd dumped it. She found a road map of the west stowed in the rental car's glove compartment. Carson could have started out on the 15 North through Vegas. But would he stay on the 15? Maybe he'd cut over to Nevada and go north on the deserted highway that passed through small towns a few hundred miles apart. That's where Carson would go.

The numbers. The hidden code. The nine and three triggered something. She looked again at Carson's letter. Was Carson pointing to state Highway 93? The Great Basin Highway—one of the most remote highways in the continental United States. Carson was a drinker—"you know I love a good beer." That, too, hinted at Nevada, not Utah. He would get off the 15, cut west, then head north on the 93.

She broke from Utah and swooped onto the empty Nevada road. Nothing but mountains and sky, lonely roads, and small towns a hundred miles apart. And one of them was lovely. A Motel 6 on the 93 in Lovely Ely, Nevada.

37

THERE'S A PLACE I WANT TO TAKE YOU

Agent X told the man what to do. The man needed nothing more. No words were exchanged about his availability and whether or not he could fit the job into his schedule. Agent X was his only client. Simple directions, simple expectations. Handsome rewards. Always was with Agent X. Where does a former Army Ranger end up? He goes into law enforcement. Maybe writes a bestselling book. Or retires and plays golf. Some guys are legit. But not all of them.

The man was mostly legit. Agent X was special and had unique requests. The man couldn't give a damn about Agent X's agenda. Agent X revealed nothing unnecessary for the mission. But the man had a sense that Agent X had big money behind him, actually bigger than big. Endless money for endless work. The man would ride this gravy train for as long as it lasted.

"The name is Carson McCready. Follow him. Find him. Then do what you do, when the time is right," Agent X told him.

The time was getting right. Just about perfectly right. An

ideal scenario, actually. Carson got off the 15 in Utah and turned left to Nevada. Nevada was good. A big empty place with dark, lonely roads. When Carson stopped to take a piss, the man would pull over, map in hand, and ask for help. The man heard Carson was a helping sort of guy. Heard he was a pretty tough guy in his day, but the man had known plenty of tough guys in his day. Take any tough guy, an unsuspecting tough guy, and the guy's done before it starts. Down on the side of the road. Into the bushes. Then the kill. A silent kill. Too bad about the dog. The man would rather not kill the dog. But the dog would die. No place for a guy to be down on the side of the road, bleeding on the gravel shoulder. A good place to die in the woods. He'd drag Carson into the woods and the woods would take him. The creatures, the weather. They'd finish the job. That's how it would go.

The man would survive. He knew how to survive, and he knew how to kill. Carson was a nice guy. Just another Navy washout who worked at the county jail. Agent X had told him so. The kind of ordinary guy who was incapable of killing and unfit to survive.

~

Carson could do nothing more with the borrowed computer. Either Laura would get the message or she wouldn't. Even if she did, he didn't know if she would come.

While waiting for Emilio to pick up the laptop, Carson took Diego out for a quick walk before it got too late. They walked around the back of the motel to a strip of grass, where Diego did his business. The air was cool and fresh. Even in June, temperatures cooled down quickly this far north. A freak storm could leave a couple of inches of snow at this time of year. He and Diego walked up the side road behind the Motel 6, then over to the small city park across the street. Carson brought Diego's baseball bat and hit a few tennis balls, one of their usual games. He needed Diego tired out to help calm him down for a night in the motel.

Diego fetched a few balls before Carson called it an evening. Emilio might already be there, waiting. As he was walking, Carson noticed a late model black SUV with tinted windows and California plates parked in the gravel lot behind the motel. The vehicle was familiar. Carson had noticed one just like it stopped at a gas station in Caliente, just over a hundred miles south of Ely. He had seen the same SUV through his rearview mirror as he had driven northward. The driver had kept a steady distance from Carson's BMW. Carson punched the gas and got up to ninety-five. The rig kept pace at a constant quarter-mile behind.

As they walked by the SUV, Diego pricked up his ears. Rig was way too nice for Motel 6. Guy must have a dog. Vehicles like that don't stay at Motel 6 unless they have a dog. For no apparent reason, Diego let out a sharp bark. Carson let his senses run. He had a gut feeling and it wasn't good.

~

The man had followed Carson to this Motel 6 in Ely, Nevada, because the target never stopped by the side of the road to piss, never giving the man a chance to kill him and then drag the body into the woods.

But this was okay. Or just as good. His SUV was out back in the dark, blended into the night. The man walked toward the front but remained out of the light on the opposite end of the motel from the front desk, only fifty feet from room

332

eleven. He had watched the Latino kid park out front, stop at the front desk, then walk in the man's direction. A little spring in the kid's step, like he had something going on. The man pulled out a cigarette and called to the kid. "Hey, brother, got a light? Forgot mine in the bar."

The kid came over. Trusting kid. Nothing ever happened in Ely. "Sure, man."

The kid lit the man's cigarette. The man said thanks. "Gotta have a smoke before bedtime, right?"

"*De nada*, sir. Have a good night."

"Wait," the man said. "Wanna make a few extra bucks?"

"Can't right now, kinda busy."

"Easy money, kid. I'm here to surprise an old buddy of mine. Just knock at his door and I'll be right behind you and we'll get his goat. Hundred bucks. Easy."

"Maybe, but—"

The man pulled out a crisp Benjamin and gave it to the kid. The kid looked at the bill like he'd seen the second coming. "Sure, I can do that," the kid said. "Just knock on the door and you'll be behind me, right?"

"Like I said, easy money."

~

Carson heard the knock. That would be Emilio. Interesting kid, Rosie's little brother. Parents had probably brought them up from Mexico when they were babies. Rosie had an accent, but the kid didn't. Now stuck in Ely, Nevada. Emilio must have worked a half dozen different jobs, various gigs to put together a living wage. Emilio had skills and motivation. He'd give the enterprising kid another tip.

Carson got up. Diego started going crazy, barking and

growling. Carson's first thought was to get him to hush. Diego wasn't a growler. He was a lover. The growl was out of the blue, uncharacteristic. Carson stopped short. Emilio was a good kid, right? He wouldn't rob him. The kind of kid who loved his sister—he wasn't out to attract any trouble for Rosie at work. Diego growled again.

Carson spoke through the door. "Emilio, one second. Be right there."

He slid toward the front window and took the tiniest peek possible through the crack in the curtains. Just enough to see the man in black standing behind the kid. Enough to see the man holding something in his hand behind his back. A big guy. A big guy with a concealed weapon.

Carson thought quickly. His gut was right. The thing was happening now, and it would just happen again if he didn't let it happen right now. No more searching on the borrowed computer tonight. No downtime with the whiskey hoping to hear from Laura. That would be too easy. Easy wasn't in the program. He'd have to fight. No cops. No authorities. The guy had followed him, hunted him down, and was there to kill. The guy was a chicken-shit bastard, hiding behind an innocent kid, a two-bit assassin now here to perform a routine, professional kill.

Carson forecasted three attempted kills. The guy would shoot the kid in the back of the head. He'd push his way into the room, then he'd point the barrel at Carson's head. He'd silently kill Diego to hush him. Then he'd kill his target. The bare whisper of a silenced weapon, and he'd vanish. Elapsed time: three to five seconds.

Carson assessed the room and immediately grabbed Diego's baseball bat. He wasn't going to make this easy for the guy. Carson needed to disrupt and get in a blow. He'd create the tiniest distraction, the slightest hesitation, an infinitesimal break in the guy's neural connections. He needed a fraction of a chance to hurt the guy and slow him down.

Carson grabbed a pillowcase and cut slits for his eyes. He got a felt pen from his duffle. He scribbled nonsense as fast as he could on the pillowcase and pulled it over his head. He put Diego in the bathroom and shut the door. Pulled a beanie over his head onto the pillowcase. Counted to three and clicked off the room lights. Then he grabbed the bat and kicked open the door.

~

The man saw the lights go out, then the ghost creature burst through the door. The kid ran off, diverting his attention just a fraction, so that he saw the whirl of a wooden stick slicing through the air a second too late. Tiny shards of light exploded in the blackness, a blur of white and black and the stick accelerating in the quarterlight. The barely visible stick slammed into his head and warm blood dripped on his face, blinding his eyes. But where was the weapon? He looked for the gun through the blood in his eyes and it was in his hand but he couldn't feel his hand and his fingers were dead and numb and then the weapon disappeared from his dead hand and he heard its heavy metal thump on the concrete.

He backed away from the crazy ghost creature whirling the stick and then threw a hard punch that landed on the creature's throat. The creature was choking, and the man wound up for another punch to the throat, a kill punch that would bring the guy down, just like it brought all men down. The kill punch found air. The choking, whirling ghost was too quick and the man too slow, bleeding from the head,

335

and then through the blood he saw the stick-thing slashing through space, and this creature's blow did not hit the air. The man crumbled and watched the crazy ghost pull back the stick once more for a final crushing blow to his head, and that was the last living thing the man saw. Then there were voices a thousand miles away, and then the pain, an inhuman suffering. A guttural scream. An image of his wife, his life, and then of the bastard Agent X and his yellow teeth. And then he saw hell. His own private hell that he always knew would come.

~

In Carson's world twenty seconds was forever. About as long as a protracted Oscar speech. Or the time it takes from setting up to a target and making a golf swing. Time for a SEAL to play dead in a watery cave. The modern human body isn't built for intense violence of over twenty seconds. It takes less than eighteen seconds to turn the tables on an assassin. Less than two seconds to kill him and leave him bleeding on the ground.

Carson saw the kid watching from the shadows, shaking and sniveling. Carson removed the pillowcase and walked to the kid, helping him stand. Carson looked around. Nothing. Nobody came out of the motel. The parking lot was nearly empty. The vacancy sign flashed into the dead, frosty night. No sirens, no authorities marching over to take command. Just Carson, the big guy on the ground bleeding on the dust, and Emilio, shaking under a tree. Carson held the kid.

"You okay? You saved my life. He was gonna kill me and then he was gonna kill you," Emilio said.

Carson pulled out the hundred he was going to give the

kid. "You earned this. You saw nothing here, okay? If your sister asks, you saw nothing."

"Okay, I never saw nothing."

Carson wanted to tell the kid the truth. He wanted to give him a speech that would scare the shit out of him. If the kid were scared, he might live. Emilio would do what was necessary, and he'd find a way to survive the angry mob that would inevitably come after immigrants with brown skin and dark eyes.

Think about your sister and think about you. Say anything to anybody and there'll be another guy just like this guy coming to town and he'll kill you. He'll kill Rosie and he'll kill you. Do you understand me? I'm sorry to tell you this. It's gonna be bad. You'll see what I mean. It's starting now. This, what you saw here tonight—it's the beginning.

Carson wanted to shake the kid. At that moment he loved the kid like he loved his own son. This kid was here and now, and he wanted to teach the kid how to survive, just like he'd teach Michael how to survive if he were still alive.

But the lad wouldn't understand. Carson couldn't tell him the truth. He'd give him hope, instead.

"You'll be okay, kid. You know that, right? You're smart, and you work hard. I'm counting on a great future for you, okay? And take good care of yourself and Rosie. Now I need to take our big friend here for a little jaunt. Then I'm gonna have a good night's sleep. And then I'm gonna get up early, gas up, have a good breakfast, and be on my way. Someday maybe we'll meet again. We're on the same team, Emilio. Don't forget that."

Carson removed everything from the assassin's pockets, grabbed the guy's keys, and shoved him into his room. He brought the black SUV around from the back and lifted

337

the heavy bastard into the rig. He drove the rig back to its original parking spot, left the guy with his keys on the dash, and walked away. The guy would never be moving again, poor fucker. Carson, a civilian, hadn't wanted to kill the man. But he had had no choice. The man had come to kill him. Carson was justified in killing the man. If a guy came around again, sometime in the future when things were bad, then Carson would kill the bastard without remorse. From now on there would be no blindsides. Carson's eyes were open wide. Ready for the bad and ready for worse, much worse.

~

At daylight he loaded Diego into his car and drove to the nearest gas station. There would be no hurry. In Ely nobody hurried, and neither would Carson. He sauntered into the gas station and paid in cash. He returned to the car, the pump still filling the tank with premium. Damned Beemer, he thought. He topped off the tank, looking at Diego in the back seat, grateful to his bones that he was unharmed.

He nosed into the diner's parking lot and sat at a booth, looking out the window for an unobstructed view of the dusty Beemer with Diego safely inside. He bought the local paper and read about an incident last night at the Motel 6. The local sheriff had talked to the night manager and her younger brother. Talked to a few guests. Nobody had seen or heard anything. No bodies were found, no evidence of anything except for a black SUV with a phony registration and forged California plates in the back parking lot. Carson's heart skipped a beat. No body found.

He took his eyes from the paper and looked around the diner and through the window without moving his head. He noticed a woman with long sandy blonde hair in a silky scarf getting out of a late model sedan. She looked like a movie star just passing through. Like she belonged anywhere but Ely, Nevada. Wearing blue jeans and a sky-blue western shirt, she crunched through the gravel lot to the front entrance and then entered, jangling the bells on the opening door. She took the scarf off and said something to the hostess, who seated her in the booth down the aisle from Carson's. It was Laura. She hadn't looked up yet, just minding her own business. She looked wary, out of her element. The waitress brought her coffee and a menu. A moment or two passed. Laura set down the menu, keeping her head still and letting her eyes wander around the room. Then she looked sideways, directly at Carson. Her icy exterior melted.

"I was wondering when you'd show up," Carson said.

Laura turned her head toward him. Her worry lines melted into a slight smile. She cleared her throat, took a sip of ice water, and set it gently on her table. She got up and sat next to him in the booth. "I guessed right. You hinted you'd pass through here and you're here. Where the hell have you been?"

"Could ask you the same thing."

"Where are you going?"

"Montana. Me and Diego."

"I can see you're going somewhere."

"There's room for you."

"I've got a car."

"Sell the car, store the car. Leave it."

"What's in Montana?"

"Mountains, rivers. There's a place I want to take you."

"Oh? And where would that be, mister?"

"A cabin at a country inn, near the Yellowstone River, in

339

the Paradise Valley, the prettiest place in America. Off the beaten track, in the pines. You'd never find it without me. No tourists. Just people living, getting together, having some fun."

"What would we do there?"

"We'd stay in the cabin. We'd have a warm meal and some good wine. There'll be a band, a small one. And we'll dance. You okay with that?"

"Shouldn't we be doing something?"

"And what would that be?"

"My God, Carson. Michael. Your lovely boy. You brought him to me, and I can see nothing but that haunting image. His smile. The way he moved. He was you. You were him. Now that I've found you, I need to find Garrick. I need to track him down, cut off his balls, and watch him bleed out while he's watching a video of your football game. I'll put toothpicks in his eyes to prop them open, so he can't shut them when he watches the children die under the rubble."

"I need some time."

"For what?"

"To dance with you. I need you, Laura. I can't do this without you. Let's make love and let's just be. For a short while. I need to just be. Our peace won't last. The time will come."

"Then what?"

"Resistance. Maybe war. Civil war. It could get to that."

~

Laura Cavendish left with Carson and Diego. The three drove off into the empty—with nothing in the empty but sage, mountains, sky, and wild things. What if Darwin had landed here instead of an island in South America? Would this great place have changed Darwin's thinking? A harsh place. A

340

brutish place, warning that liberty came with a price—not of death, as some would have it, but from the will to love. The big sky a medium for a vast and exquisite painting, an allusion to humanity to love and survive or to die coldly, helplessly, darkly. Once you knew how to look, which was to not look at all but to sense it, a green flash writ larger than the known universe burst into a brilliant and endless painting across the pastel sky.

Was she hallucinating? Why did she feel that this flash was something new, bigger and more powerful than a million green flashes, and that she was the first human to ever see what love looked like in a painting across the sky?

"Stop the car, Carson, please. Do it now."

Carson pulled over to the gravel shoulder separating the highway from the vast landscape to the east.

Laura got out, walked for a few hundred yards into the sagebrush, dropped to her knees, looked into the sky, and cried her heart out.

A half-hour later, she got back in the car. "I'm ready now. Let's go."

Carson said nothing and asked nothing. He could see the future of the world, just as Laura saw an earthly beauty that overwhelmed her. There would be light after this. The most beautiful light one could imagine, and Laura saw it for an instant.

But, first, there would be darkness. Carson knew it. The inevitability. The anger. Even revenge. The need to clear the toxins that have and would destroy the things that made life worthwhile. His son. Just like Carson could not tell Emilio what a SEAL's eyes could see in the darkness, Carson would say nothing to Laura. Not now. Laura saw something in the sky that was beautiful and precious. To Carson, the protector,

341

what brought Laura to tears was worth a fight—the biggest one of his life—before greed and avarice could take their ultimate toll.

If Carson didn't believe that, he'd give up now and run away. If he didn't trust his instincts, he'd be like one of those algorithms Laura talked about, and he'd give up after calculating no purpose in continuing the fight.

Carson McCready was not a bot. He was not an algorithm that responded to its environment in a purely strategic way. This was no game. No zero sum. He would act, because the cost of doing nothing would be incomprehensible.

38

HE CALLS IT LIBERTY

Cousin Chuck's ranch was isolated, pretty, and tranquil, providing sanctuary to a dozen horses; several dogs and cats; various goats, sheep, and ponies; and three guests: Carson, Laura, and Diego.

Carson and Laura helped with chores—feeding hay to the horses, filling steel troughs with water, raking sticks, burning overgrown brush, and preparing dinners and lunches for Chuck, his wife, and their two children. The girl tried to teach Carson about riding until he fell off a horse and put a painful dent in his lower back. And when Carson wasn't doing chores, he was thinking.

If he were rational, like the professional warrior he'd been, Carson would first bolster his defensive position. Keep Chuck and his family safe. Set up a secure communications network. Work with Amy Watson and her team to create a bulletproof plan for his first capture-and-kill mission to disable and depose of the conspiracy's general, Garrick Cripps. He'd follow up with systematic monitoring and planning for the next target and the one after that. He'd designate his successor to lead the

343

resistance were he to be captured or killed.

Yet he contemplated peace. Longed for it even. Just blending into the Montana landscape, feeding cows and horses, pruning bushes, watering plants, and disappearing with Laura in peace and solitude.

As a SEAL, his instinct had always been to act, never content to let his environment dictate who he was or what he should do. His ability to act—no, his innate need to act—was the one trait that explained most of the decisions Carson had made in this life. Working with felons at a high-security prison—after he'd supposedly retired—was just the latest example.

The images in his mind nagged at him. The little blonde girl, her head spinning through the blackened air. Black Terrell pleading for White Terrell's body to rise. The men on his crew, each of whom Carson loved, all now either dead or disappeared. His son. His son. His only son, laughing and smiling and then nothing but a burned body and a set of teeth that permitted validation of the precious human being he'd been.

Carson rarely became angry. Anger required too much mental energy that he'd rather devote to getting things done. As a master chief he rarely raised his voice, also to save physical energy. Deal with the problem. No need to yell and scream about it—to prove what? That he could yell and scream?

But now he felt extraordinary anger, and wanted more than anything to scream his despair to the unmovable mountains surrounding him. He quietly shoveled horse shit and raged at the thought that his own son had been caught up in some libertarian bullshit perpetuated by a lunatic. He alternated between blaming himself for exposing Michael to the mess and condemning Garrick Cripps to die—horribly, violently, brutishly.

A law-abiding citizen who still believed that justice would prevail would say Carson was being irrational. Take it down a notch, Chief. You're innocent. Trust the FBI and the legal authorities to do the right thing.

But Carson was clear-eyed. He saw what was happening all around him. The innate ability of humans to think and reason on their own had taken the train to Loony Tunes, USA. No amount of the perpetrators' bald-face gaslighting— that Islamic terrorists were to blame—could convince him otherwise.

Lying to his face, and to the face of his country, pissed him off. Garrick Cripps and his conspiracy's sense of entitlement pissed him off even more. Amy Watson was right. At that moment the burden of confronting the perpetrators was his to own. She called it destiny. He had no name for it. Only his profound urge to act—or stay in paradise forever.

One day, nearly a month after they'd come to Montana, Carson approached Laura as she was mending the fence in the backyard.

"Honey, look at this." Laura pointed to a dark hole in the grass. "I saw a huge marmot scamper into that hole. I wonder how many are down there."

"I need to talk to Suzanne Dreyfus."

Laura dropped the wire cutters on the grass and held her hand to her face to block the sun. "Why, for God's sake?"

"She'll know where to find Garrick."

"She might. But I've lost touch with her. Why now?"

Carson gently kicked the fence post with a heavy work boot. "Do I have to spell it out, Laura? I want to meet Garrick for a cup of tea."

"I thought we'd just be together for a while. It's barely

been a month since we left California."

"I've been thinking, and as long as he's out there planning another San Diego in Houston or Toledo or wherever, I can't sit here pretending we're living in paradise, happily ever after. I don't want to leave this place. I've been dreaming of something this good for a long time. Ever since I left the Navy. But I've done a lot of shit I didn't want to do. This is one of those pieces of shit."

"I won't try to stop you. I learned that a long time ago."

"I could say the same about you."

"I'm here now, aren't I? I chose to be here with you, and I don't want you to leave."

Carson pulled Laura toward him. He hugged her gently. "Will you give me Suzanne's number?"

"I don't have it. Just a personal email address. Carson, let me contact her. I'll know how to approach her without alarming her."

"What do you mean?"

"We have to be careful with Suzanne. We don't know whose side she's really on."

~

To: suzannedreyfus45@gmail.com
From: SEALCarson@protonmail.me
Re: Events
Suzanne,

It's me, Laura. Remember? I'm sure you do because you begged me to take a leave of absence from my university position to work with the Pentagon. I know Garrick. You know Garrick. You know as well as I do that Garrick was the *mastermind behind the murder of more than a thousand moms, dads, and kids in San Diego. Maybe you even had something to do with that?*

You won't be able to find me, so no point in wasting your time trying. I'll get right to it with a few questions, to which I'd appreciate your prompt and honest reply, assuming you are capable of either virtue.

1. Where is Garrick?
2. Do you still love him?
3. Are you a staunch believer in Garrick's cause?
4. Will you help me find him?

I'm with a man, Carson McCready, and I'm writing on his behalf too. I don't believe you know him, though you probably know of him. I grew up with Carson. He headed up the telemarketing operation at the county jail, but perhaps you knew that? Carson would like to speak with you by phone. Please talk to him and be straight with him. You owe him that much. No, strike that. You owe the world that much.
Laura

~

Two days later, Suzanne responded. It was dusk, and Laura went to the bedroom to show it to Carson, who was lying on the bed reading a book about wild horses.

"She answered," Laura said.

"Have you read it?"

"Yes. Listen to this." She opened the email and started reading in a hushed voice.

347

Dear Laura,

As to your questions:

1. Where is Garrick? On his yacht near Nassau.

2. Do you still love him? None of your business.

3. Are you a true believer in Garrick's cause? Garrick and I are different people.

4. Will you help us find him? Have Carson call me on the number I've provided.

Suzanne

Laura sat on the bed next to Carson and turned to him. "What do you think?"

"Remember those mysterious texts warning us about a pending cyberattack?"

"Yeah, sure."

"That could have been Suzanne, right?"

"Strong possibility," Laura said.

"I still don't trust her. She could be lying. She dodged your question on whether she was still a true believer. She split from Garrick. Okay, so what? That doesn't mean she's abandoned the movement."

"I don't trust her either, Carson. But she could be our only way to get to Garrick."

~

The following day, Carson snuck away behind the barn. The conversation lasted ten minutes.

"I think you know who I am," he whispered into the phone.

"I do."

"You know why I'm calling."

"I thought you'd be dead by now," Suzanne said.

"Why would you think that?"

"He sent someone to kill you."

Carson let the comment pass, though he wondered how she would know that. "How are you doing?" he replied.

"Why do you care?"

"Why? I have a hunch. You sent me those crazy messages about the conspiracy, didn't you, Suzanne?"

"I don't know what you're talking about."

"I don't believe you."

"The best I can say is I'm not dead yet. I try not to be afraid," Suzanne said.

"Sorry, I can't help you with that."

"I don't need your help. I try not to give or ask for help from anyone. I don't want to depend on anybody."

"I need to find Garrick."

The line was silent for several seconds. Carson waited.

"Don't hang up," he said.

"I haven't."

"I suspect you know him better than anyone. I'm hoping you can help me find him."

"He's protected in the open. He's getting what he wanted, and more."

"Where, exactly?"

"His yacht in the Bahamas. He calls it *Liberty*."

"Would he be alone?"

"He'll be entertaining guests. He'll have come out of the cave he's been operating in for years. He'll be celebrating with like-minded people."

"Celebrating what, for fuck's sake?"

"That he killed for an ideology," Suzanne said.

"He'll be with his co-conspirators, I presume."

"Groupies is more like it. I won't be there."

"So you used to be Garrick's co-conspirator, but you've had a change of heart? Is that what you're saying?"

The line was silent. Then she said, "I'll tell you what I told Laura. Garrick and I are different people. What would you like to know, Carson?"

"You said he'll be on his yacht. I need to know who will be there."

"Maybe William Wharton, his partner in crime. And I mean that literally. A few politicians. Maybe the current director of the FBI. An Austrian by the name of Mueller. Perhaps his chief of staff. And a guy known as Agent X."

"Mueller's chief of staff?"

"No. The president's. POTUS himself."

"This goes that high?"

"No doubt in my mind."

"Who in the hell is Agent X?"

"I've never met him. I suspect he's a former FBI official. Garrick relies on him for a lot of things."

"What's that mean?"

The line was silent.

"Suzanne? Who in the fuck is Agent X?"

"He executed Garrick's orders on Liberation Day."

"What?"

"He carried out the order to bomb the stadium, Carson."

"Did you know about the bombing?"

"Not until it was too late. I had never believed Garrick would go this far. I was wrong."

"How do you know all this?"

"I could tell you William is in love with me and he tries to protect me, that he slips me information but pretends he's still one hundred percent behind Garrick. But that would be a lie. Let's just say I have certain skills related to espionage.

350

Leave it at that."

"What happened between you and Garrick?"

"Look, Carson. It's a long story that neither of us has time for. I was never really totally aligned with Garrick's ideology, nor his behavior. I loved him, and I lost him."

"Anyone else?"

"Yes. There is, actually. He's not someone you'd think about, but he's been in this all along. Almost from the beginning. He's the senior US senator from the state of Kentucky. I think you know him."

Carson froze. "How would you know that?"

"I did some research. Lots of people would love to get their hands on you, Carson McCready. Graybill included."

"When will this get together happen? What's my window?"

"Late August. They'll be there a week."

"Long party."

"Guests will come and go. Big shots planning their next moves. These people do not fuck around."

"Have you been to this yacht?"

"Many times."

"I'll find the specs and layout. Which cabin is Garrick's?"

"Bottom deck. VIP cabin. He calls it the master cabin. But he might give it up for the chief of staff or the senator."

"What about the captain?"

"He's a good guy."

"He'll radio for help. I can't let that happen."

"He'll sleep in the first crew cabin. A few steps forward and aft of the crew lounge. If he's not on the main deck in his captain's chair."

"Good. This stays between us. Keep William out of the loop, okay?"

"Don't hurt him, Carson. Promise me that."

"May I ask why?"

"I told you. William is a damned fool, but he trusts me and still cares for me."

"Can you trust him?"

"I never really know who to trust. I'm not even certain William will be there."

"Where are his quarters, usually?"

"William sleeps in the guest cabin forward and starboard of the VIP cabin."

"Look, Suzanne. Hurting William isn't my objective. But your friend chose to play revolution against the United States. He exposed himself to trouble. He's not safe. Nobody is. By the way, that includes everyone."

"Does that include Laura?"

"Laura has never planned a revolution against the United States government. William has. And Garrick. I'm not sure about you."

"Is that a threat?"

"No, just a reminder. If I were you, I wouldn't join any more movements you aren't willing to die for. And by the way, Laura is tougher than she looks."

"She never struck me as tough. Laura was young, and Garrick was a predator. Never underestimate him."

~

The next day, the fifth of August, Carson asked Laura to take a ride.

"Where we going?"

"Let's head out. I want to show you something."

"Did you talk to Suzanne?"

"Yes. Let's go."

Diego hopped in the back of the Gator, and they rode down a bumpy dirt road for thirty minutes, climbing almost five hundred feet until they reached the end of the road overlooking a deep bluff.

"What's out there, Carson?"

Carson pointed south and west. "That's Yellowstone over that way." Then he pointed north. "There's Livingston, and over there is Bozeman. You'd never imagine cities and towns in this empty country, would you? Tens of thousands of people out there."

Laura sucked in the fresh air. "Do any of those people out there know what's happening?"

"You mean do they read newspapers and watch the news?"

"Yeah. What do they know?"

"I don't know what they know. Or don't care to know. But even if they don't know shit, they have an opinion. You know how it goes. Same old, same old. Another violent event that kills innocents. An Islamic attack on America. Big deal. Same story, same enemy. I heard the administration is already planning a retaliatory strike against Iran."

"I heard that too."

"And so it goes. Nothing has changed. What we did was for nothing. In fact we made it worse by stopping Nessie and thinking we did something special. It's bigger than us. Will people even notice when Walmart owns the General Accounting Office? Or that McDonald's runs lunch programs in schools? Or that a consortium of Boeing and General Dynamics runs the Department of Defense?"

"I doubt it. Politicians being politicians and corporations being greedy. Like you said, what's new? We pay our taxes. But all that Washington crap doesn't really affect us, and all politicians suck. That's how people think. We're helpless, so why even bother?" Laura said.

Carson took a deep breath. "I'm leaving for a while, honey. I'd like to meet Garrick Cripps."

"Is Suzanne helping you? What did she say?"

"She was helpful, actually. She's not a pleasant person."

"She can be charming. When she wants to be."

"I can't tell what she's all about, frankly. I don't completely trust her."

"I hope she was honest with you, at least."

"Time will tell."

"What are you and Garrick going to chat about?"

"This and that. Why he did it. Assuming he did it. Why he believes what he believes. Why he killed my son."

"I'm coming with you."

"You can't. I won't let you. Let it go, Laura."

"I need to be there."

"No, you don't. They'll kill you, and it's certain they'll try to kill me."

"Carson, stop and think. Let's go with the original plan. We'll find the right people to help us. Like Agent Watson. We'll work with them to do what we can, what's workable. Not necessarily what we desire but what we can actually do."

"I know the risks. I don't want help. It's better this way. Stay here with Chuck and the family. Help them. You help me by helping them and taking care of Diego. Are we good?"

Laura scanned the horizon and said nothing.

"Out loud, darling. Are we good?"

"Don't worry about us. We'll be fine. When you see Garrick, give him my best."

Carson hugged Laura close. "I'll send him your undying devotion, dear. I'll leave at dawn. I'm heading to Virginia and then Nassau. For the next five days, maybe longer, I don't exist."

39

PAYS TO BE A WINNER

Carson drove non-stop for two days until he reached Little Creek. He'd been to the Virginia SEAL base a few dozen times over the years and lodged off-base at the same Holiday Inn on Shore Drive. He calculated the supplies he'd need to pull off the mission. He considered scraping up gear from local military surplus outlets, but that would take a day or two to complete, shrinking his window of opportunity. He needed gear and a boat. Above all, he needed a favor.

On Tuesday morning he woke, dressed, and drove to a nearby café. On the way he stopped at a convenience store and purchased a new burner. He sat in the back of the café, facing the front door, staying alert while glancing at the menu. He ordered black coffee, eggs over medium, and fried potatoes. He pulled a yellow piece of paper from his back pocket and set it next to his plate. He tore the plastic off the burner and set the phone next to the piece of paper. Scooped a forkful of eggs and potatoes into his mouth, savoring the flavors until he chewed it down. He slugged the last few drops of his coffee and picked up the burner while pressing the yellow paper flat onto the table so he could read the number. He carefully dialed and let the phone ring out on the other end. On the fifth ring, a man picked up.

"Bruce here."

"Would this be Master Chief Winton Bruce?"

"Who's this?"

"Carson."

Carson waited for a reply.

"Carson fucking McCready? Hold on a second."

Carson waited, smiling at the server as she came by to refill his coffee. He heard voices on the other end of the line but couldn't make out what they were saying. Five minutes passed, then Winton got back on the line.

"Sorry, bud. Had to find a quiet place to talk. How in the hell are you?"

"Wint, it's been too long. I'm actually surprised you're still around."

"I'm out in two years. That's the plan. You're ahead of the game. You always were, you bastard. Where are you?" Winton said.

"Having breakfast. Let's meet at the pub in Lynnhaven. Can you get away?"

"You're here?"

"Yep. I need to talk to you."

"I check out here at two. See you then."

It had been five years since Carson had seen Winton Bruce. They came up together in SEAL training and got to be friends and drinking buddies. Their wives had also been friends, and the couples would get together on weekends for backyard barbeques and beer. Winton and Carson got promoted at roughly the same rate. Shortly after Carson became a platoon leader based in Coronado, Winton slid into

356

the same job based in Little Creek.

When Carson walked into the pub, he saw Winton sitting in a booth with a mug of beer. Winton stood, and the two men hugged and patted each other on the back. Carson felt awkward, not having kept in touch with his old friend since leaving the Navy. The server brought Carson a mug of beer, and the men raised their glasses.

"If you ain't cheating, you ain't trying," Winton said.

Carson recognized the SEAL slang and returned the toast. "Pays to be a winner."

"How you been, you white bastard. You never deserved that promotion to chief. You know that, right?" Winton said.

"I'll admit, guilty as charged."

"What the hell happened in San Diego? I'm hearing you're some kind of fugitive. What the fuck, Carson?"

Carson was scribbling on the rumpled piece of paper he'd put on the table, considering how much he should tell Winton, even though he had once been a close friend. "I got caught in the middle of the most fucked-up thing you could imagine. I've got a girlfriend."

"Is that right? How are Kathryn and Michael? Kid must be in high school by now."

"Michael's gone, Wint."

"What'd you just say? Michael's what?"

"The motherfuckers killed him. They killed my friends. And a thousand people I never knew. Folks who just came to a charity football game to root for us. I missed it, Wint. I should have seen through the fuzziness, but I missed it. The clues were in my face. Deep down I wanted to pretend I was wrong. I wanted to forget everything we learned about combat. I'm paying the price."

Uncharacteristically Winton reached over the table to

touch Carson's arm. "Then why are you here talking to an ugly Black bastard like me?"

"Yeah, right. The girls loved you, Wint. You were my hero."

"Carson, I'd love to chit-chat all fucking day. But I've got to ask. Why in the fuck are you in Little Creek? This is the last place you should be."

"I need a favor, Winton. I had nobody else to ask."

Winton set the beer mug on the varnished wooden table. He pulled a pack of Camels from his shirt pocket and stuck a cigarette in his mouth, pretending to inhale it. "Don't look at me that way. I can't smoke, and this is my therapy."

"How are Jenny and the kids?" Carson said.

"Better than we deserve, bud. We're doing great."

"That makes me happy. For you.

"Now I feel guilty."

"You won't after I ask the favor," Carson said.

"I'm listening."

"I need some gear. I can't say why. Just trust me."

"What kind of gear?"

Carson pushed the scrunched-up piece of paper toward Winton and tried to flatten it on the table. "I have a list."

Winton took the piece of paper from Carson's hands and inspected the list. "Let's see here. Jesus, Carson. What is this?"

Carson grabbed the list. "Looks like your eyes are busted, so I'll read it to you. One LAR V Draeger rebreather, one pair of Voit UDT Duck Feet swim fins, one drysuit, a P226, two black balaclavas, a tactical vest, five carabiners, a water bladder, one escape and evasion kit, one black Navy knife . . ."

"Hold on there, buster. Why the LAR V?"

"I need a no-bubble rebreather, okay? End of story."

"That P226. That's old school. The guys pack the Glocks now."

"I won't carry a Glock. The SIG is more reliable."

"You're making this difficult, McCready."

"Can I continue, Winton?"

"I'm still listening."

"I need one 25-meter aluminum roll-up rope ladder and grappling hook."

"No launcher?"

"Absolutely not. The roll-up is silent."

"I suppose you need a boat too."

"I will need a boat, as a matter of fact."

"How long is your trip?"

"Long enough."

"Okay, looks like you're going to climb aboard a large boat, a ship, and you're an uninvited guest."

"Actually, it's a yacht. My source says it's a Christiansen. Hundred and sixty-four feet, twenty-nine-foot beam, vacuum-infused composite hull, max speed sixteen knots. You get the picture."

"Your target is loaded."

"Something like that."

"I heard about that builder. They made Tiger's boat, right?"

"Yep."

"I take it you're not climbing Tiger's boat."

"Nope."

"Then whose boat are you climbing? Never mind, don't tell me," Winton said.

"Good call. Does this mean you can get me this list?"

"I need another beer," Winton said. He waited until the server put down two more mugs. "You realize how dangerous this is, Carson. You're on a rubber boat hoping to God your target boat isn't traveling. You've also got to hope for calm weather, or the turbulence will sink you. You've got sixty-seventy pounds of gear on your back, and you need dead-on accuracy firing that grappling hook and rope launcher. We practice this shit in teams. You're going solo. How often have you solo climbed a ship under hostile conditions?"

"Never."

"You need a decent boat and someone who can drive it."

"I was hoping you'd take note of my dilemma."

"Where's your launch point?"

"Miami vicinity."

"To where?"

"Open water near Nassau."

"Why not launch there?"

"Too risky. Nobody needs to know I'm coming."

"What am I thinking, Carson? I can't help you with this shit. I'd like to retire with full pension. Without going to prison."

"I know. You shouldn't."

"Does this have anything to do with San Diego?"

"Yes."

"I need more than that."

"Wint, I'm going after the guy who killed Michael and a stadium full of moms, kids, dads, and grandmas. Is that enough?"

"Just one guy responsible for all that? How would you know?"

"Long fucking story. Trust me when I tell you the fate of the whole goddamned country is at stake. You don't know it. The Navy doesn't know it. Nobody knows it yet, except for a handful of rich people who've been close to the conspiracy for decades. FBI knows it but they're acting dumb because they're in on it. Maybe CIA knows it but they haven't said shit."

"You're sounding like a crazy conspiracy theorist, Carson.

360

Are you listening to yourself?"

"I know. I sound crazy. You know me. Am I crazy?"

"Dammit, Carson. Okay, I'll help you, but this is how it's going to work. Get to Nassau. I don't care how. Drop this insane idea of trolling on a rubber raft for fifty miles and climbing a ship by yourself. Few SEALs in our day were more skilled than you or had more endurance. But look at yourself. When's the last time you did any heavy lifting underwater? Take it from a guy still in the game. You haven't trained for three years. I guarantee you've lost enough skill and endurance to make this a suicide mission. So, in answer to your question, yes, you are crazy."

"Okay, I'll get to Nassau. Then what?"

"I'll arrange for an individual to meet you with your gear and a suitable boat. That individual will drive you out to the ship and back. What you do in between is your business."

"How skilled will this person be? I don't need a taxi driver."

"I won't send you an amateur, Carson. The idea is to give you a fighting chance to survive."

"You thinking ex-SEAL?"

"Or close to it. I'll need to pay him—or her."

"How much?"

"Two grand, minimum."

"That's doable. But I've got one question. Can this individual be trusted?"

"I hope so."

"Hope isn't good enough, Wint."

"Look, buddy. I said I'll arrange for someone to help you. I know of some people. Former special ops running side-gigs to make a few extra bucks. Reliable and competent, and they follow chain of command. Just remember, they're freelancers. Don't expect them to be your friend or believe in what you're doing. I can't say it's risk free, but you're in no position to be picky."

"No argument there. I'll deal with it."

"When are you leaving?" Winton said.

"When can you arrange the gear and the meet?"

"Give me twenty-four. I'll have the individual contact you when you get to Nassau. Get a room near the airport and wait. One more thing. Have you thought about an extraction plan if it all goes to shit?"

"Swim like fucking hell and hope for the best."

40

"WE ARE THE GODS OF LIBERTY"

Carson landed at Lynden International on a busy Wednesday afternoon. He stepped out of the airport with a black duffle that contained sunglasses, sunscreen, a baseball cap, a change of underwear, socks, a toothbrush, and a razor, though he hadn't shaved in four days. While waiting for a cab, he put on the hat and sunglasses to block the shockingly bright sun. He was already sweating droplets and he was thirsty as hell.

A cab pulled up to the curb and the driver, who resembled a young Bob Marley, got out to help Carson with his luggage.

"Welcome to the island, sir," he said, looking skeptically at Carson's black leather bag. "That's all you've got, man?"

"I travel light, but thanks for asking."

Carson could see Marley glance at him through the rearview mirror, hoping to chit-chat.

"What brings you to the island, man?" Marley said

"A little R and R, buddy. Just what the doctor ordered, you know?"

"I'm feeling you on that one, my friend. Any special plans while you're here?"

363

"Thought I'd do a little diving. Drink some rum. Hang by the pool."

"Now you're talking, my good man. That's exactly what I would do. Nice little bar back that way on Bay Street. Good rum and lots of it, man."

Marley smiled and held his fingers to his lips, as if holding a spliff. "I'm not a big drinker myself. Prefer other refreshments, you know?"

"I'm good for a shot of rum, then off to bed. Boring, I know."

"Boring is good, man. Keeps a dude out of trouble. I feel you, brother."

The drive to the run-down resort only took ten minutes. As Carson got out of the cab, Marley handed him his duffle and a business card. "In case you get stranded, call me. I'll help you out, man."

Carson inspected the card. "You know, I'll do that. Expect my call in about thirty-six hours. I'm going to need a ride around midnight. Can you be here?"

"This isn't no drug deal, right? I'm done with that shit, man."

Carson laughed. "No worries, buddy. I'm meeting my guide. We're going scuba diving."

Carson checked in, found his room, and shut the curtains. He yanked a cold bottle of water from the fridge and downed half of it, then laid down to take a nap.

For his purposes, Carson preferred a cheap room at a Motel 6 or Travelodge over a resort of any price or dimensions. Nothing but resorts in Nassau, it seemed. But then again most visitors to the island weren't a former Navy SEAL there to find a man on a fifty-million-dollar yacht who was planning to bring down the United States government. If having tea with

364

Garrick Cripps wasn't his whole purpose for being there, then reading a big novel, drinking a bottle of rum, and smoking a giant spliff sounded pretty damned good to Carson at that moment.

As soon as he lay down on the bed, Carson dozed off in what became a luscious nap. He dreamed about his phone ringing. It rang for minutes before he picked it up and heard a voice imploring him to wake up, and then he woke up for real to his phone ringing. He answered it out of breath and heard Laura's voice urgently telling him to wake up and listen.

"Carson? I've got something for you."

"Laura, are you okay? What's going on?"

"That little gathering looks serious."

"Wait, darling, back up. What are you talking about?"

"I hacked into Garrick's ship. I got *Liberty*'s hull number from the Florida Wildlife Conservation Commission, where the boat was registered. I programmed Baby to locate that hull number and retrace its path over the past two weeks. Suzanne wasn't lying. He's in the Bahamas. I know exactly where he is."

"You've been busy."

"The boat hasn't moved in several days."

"Where is it?"

"You're probably on the upper coast of the island where the resorts are, right?"

"Correct. Found a small resort for seventy-five bucks a night in the north."

"All right. *Liberty* is anchored on the opposite side. It's mostly beach, brushland, and a few empty roads. You know where Bonehead National Park is?" Laura said.

"Yeah, sure. There's an observatory and a parking lot."

"The yacht is half a mile from the coastline. The water is calm there."

Carson was struggling to wake up. He downed a bottle of water while Laura talked. He reached to the end table and grabbed a tourist guide to the main island. "I'm looking at the map now. Yeah, there's a dirt road to the beach, and it looks like it could be isolated at certain times."

"If I were you, I'd come in from the airport side. It's a fifteen-minute drive straight south from Lynden International to Bonefish. The other way has more turns. More like twenty minutes."

"Nice work, Laura."

"You're welcome."

"Sorry I've been silent. I'm dead tired and trying to rest up. I'm supposed to meet my driver later today and plan logistics. I'm aiming to launch tomorrow night."

"A driver?"

"Babe, I shouldn't be talking to you about this. The less you know the better."

"Too late for that now, buster."

"An old friend helped me set this up. He's arranging for someone to drive the boat to the yacht. Former special ops, he said."

"Is this really worth it, Carson? This sounds more dangerous than I ever imagined."

"This is a cakewalk. This is nothing, trust me."

"I want to show you something. I hacked into the video feed on the yacht. Surveillance cameras are everywhere on that ship, and they're set up for remote access, which means they're linked to a network. And you know about networks."

"They're hackable."

"Correct. I'm looking at the top deck where they've been having these lavish dinners and meetings. That yacht is unbelievable, Carson. Absolutely gorgeous. But there was one problem—I hadn't been able to hack the audio feed. But I've been fiddling with Baby's algorithm and cracked the audio code this morning. Carson, this is pure gold."

"You're a wizard. Could you show me a live feed right now?"

"Sure, I'll stream it to your phone. Hold on. Are you getting it?"

"Yeah, let's watch this," Carson said.

Laura streamed one of the cameras on the main deck. Wait staff were milling about, appearing to be setting a large dinner table for several guests. This was real time on the infamous *Liberty*, but the minutes moved slowly in the half-light between afternoon naps and cocktail hour. Nothing much to see, really. Carson heard distant voices.

"This is what you're so excited about?" he said.

"I know. Mostly boring yacht stuff. But I'm thrilled we can hear what they're talking about. If you want, I'll keep an eye out and call you if anything happens."

"Do that, babe, because right now I can barely keep my eyes open."

~

Laura grabbed a beer and took her laptop to the back deck of the ranch house, anxious to pick up more details from the yacht scene to pass on to Carson. She wasn't thrilled that he had left her in Montana, but she thought of his departure as his last mission—to settle scores with Garrick Cripps and be done with the terrible past.

In truth Laura didn't know what Carson was capable of. In the years since they had parted ways, his world had become alien to hers. She had always seen him as a laid-back, generous

367

soul, who wouldn't harm any living thing. Intellectually she understood that he had become a full-fledged, decorated Navy SEAL, but she still couldn't wrap her head around her high school boyfriend actually harming a human being, enemy or not. The Carson she knew would have figured out a way to avoid conflict. All of which added to her confusion about what exactly Carson intended to accomplish on this crazy trip to the Bahamas. Whatever his intentions, Laura realized, she had never stopped loving him. Now that she had packed up her life to be with him in Montana, she'd do anything in her power not to lose him before their life together began in earnest.

And so she kept a close eye on the yacht as it lay off the coast of Nassau. She refused to stop watching, lest she miss an important detail that might keep Carson safe. Dusk was coming fast on the ranch, and the family would be sitting down to dinner soon. She closed her eyes, inhaling the fresh mountain air, smelling the pines, luxuriating in the peaceful setting.

Laura forced herself to get up. She turned around toward the kitchen window, looking to see if Chuck's wife, Alice, had started to prepare dinner. The kitchen lights were off. Laura turned back to her meditations. Then sounds of male voices interrupted her reverie. Where were the voices coming from? She glanced at the laptop and refreshed the stream coming from the main deck of the yacht.

Several men in fine dark suits surrounded the dinner table. Each man was looking at the head of the table. Garrick Cripps was holding court, congratulating everyone for the "magnificent work" in San Diego. His sonorous voice was unmistakable. Mostly he congratulated himself on recruiting former FBI agents, including someone called Agent X.

"Let us mark that moment when the Freedom Society changed the course of world history," Garrick said.

He went on, "San Diego was the beginning. Over the next few days we'll designate additional CPD events, remembering our motto: Creep, Penetrate, and Destroy. Let's formally begin the proceedings by recognizing the men at this very table who embody everything that John Galt stood for as an individual. Around this table we are blessed with ten John Galts, geniuses all, icons of self-interest born to build, create, and sustain a government-free society until the end of time."

Garrick's voice boomed. "We are the Gods of Liberty. We are the guardians of humanity, and we shall exert our collective will to do what's necessary to maintain our freedom forever."

The scene was shocking in its absurdity. Laura had never witnessed anything like this, a cultish gathering of obviously wealthy, powerful men, all of whom seemed like doe-eyed children worshipping at Cripps's alter, hanging onto his every utterance.

Drunk with power and blood, the men spoke emphatically and half-drunkenly, as if reenacting a Skull and Bones ritual at Yale.

"Hear! Hear! To Garrick Cripps! Long live our King!"

Cripps rose. "Socialism snivels on its deathbed. But we must never lapse, lest we lose our liberties and our way of life beneath the altar of—what? Let me hear it, gentlemen."

"The nanny state!" the men howled.

"Fake freedom that socialism promises its weakest citizens," Cripps yelled. "Criminals, immigrants, anarchists, communists. Do-gooders of all colors and stripes. The Society stands as hardened soldiers against the pathetic treachery of the weak. We are patriots, tasked with a sacred duty to stop the onslaught of self-imposed slavery."

369

Laura called Carson immediately. "Wake up, mister. Nap time is over. Don't talk. I'm sending you the live stream from the yacht. Watch and listen, okay?"

"All right. I'm awake. Give me a sec." Carson grabbed his tablet from the duffle, powered it up, and opened the link Laura had just sent. "Okay, got it. I'm watching it now."

Carson immediately recognized several men at the table, including William Fletcher, the director of the Federal Bureau of Investigation, drinking wine and grinning.

Fletcher raised his glass. "To Garrick Cripps and his *Liberation Manifesto*, the unrivaled genius who has single-handedly brought our movement into the twenty-first century."

The lights on the yacht dimmed. In unison, the men—all in black suits and red ties—raised their glasses and spoke as members of a secret cult of identically minded people. They chanted about the virtues of capitalism, mechanically repeating the motto three times.

When the men around the long rectangular table finished the chant in praise of capitalism and its icons, Garrick lifted his glass in the air. "To Lord Atlas! May he be watching over us all, for we are his missionaries, tasked with spreading freedom far and wide and forever."

Carson could only see the backsides of the others turned to the opposite side of the yacht. He noticed one man whose back was turned to him wearing a military dress uniform. The black-and-white video feed got fuzzier, and Carson couldn't identify the individual's branch of service.

Garrick turned to the man in uniform and raised his glass. "In case any of you haven't met one of the country's most decorated Navy SEALs, whom we have recruited to work with us from now on, please say hello to our new head of international security."

370

The new security chief stood and turned toward the man on his left. Carson could see the left side of the security guy's chest and a black Trident insignia pinned to his uniform. A SEAL all right. But Carson couldn't see his face. Nor could he see William Wharton, who apparently was absent from the lofty proceedings, as Suzanne had guessed he might be.

Carson watched for another minute, then closed the feed. "Laura, I've seen enough. Talk to me. What do you make of it?"

"I don't know. It's the weirdest fucking thing I've ever seen. Grown men acting that way?"

"I know."

"Carson, are you planning to attend this dinner party, or what?"

"Don't worry about it. I'll let you know when I let you know. I'm sorry, babe. I can't say anything more—for your own sake. Please trust me."

"I do trust you. I hope you know that. I worry though. I don't know what you are capable of. I don't know this side of you. I want you to be safe. I want you to come home to me."

"You're right. You don't know who I've become. Take that as a positive. Better that you don't know. You know the real me, and I hope that's why you love me. No worries, okay?"

"All right. I'm good with that. For now. Anything else?"

"Yeah. I'm wondering who the fuck Lord Atlas is."

~

Carson hung up with Laura, knowing the peril ahead. He had lied when he told her it would be a cakewalk. His intel was fuzzy, and the chance of failure was far greater than zero.

He immersed himself in direct-action sensibility, a familiar

371

state of mind that had rarely let him down. He could never allow his emotions to surface. It had to be that way because emotional distancing was his best defense for staying alive and completing the mission.

He painted a picture of the operation's main purpose in his mind. Climb aboard the yacht, find the SEAL's cabin in the middle of the night, and tear the Budweiser off his lapel. Then he'd cut a hole in the man's chest and stuff the medal into the hole of his heart, letting the bastard bleed out and die as a traitor, woefully unfit to call the Trident his own.

41

THIS BUD'S FOR YOU

Carson's boat pilot finally called him later that day. When he answered the call, he realized she was a woman—a rarity in special ops—but he refused to utter any nonsense about her gender or qualifications.

"Carson McCready. I'm Luna. I'm here to help you in every way possible, in any way you need. I've got your gear and the boat."

"Luna. Beautiful name. You come well recommended by my good friend, Winton Bruce."

"Can't say I know him personally. I know of him, sir, and of his reputation."

"Who do you work for?"

"I'm an independent contractor, sir."

"Winton said you're affiliated with a group of some sort."

"I get referrals from our service bureau. That's all, sir," Luna said.

"Tell me about the boat."

"It's a fifteen-foot Zodiac."

"Can you be more specific?"

373

"The F470 Combat Rubber Raiding Craft."

"All right. Excellent work. I'll send you the location of the launch site now. Let's be ready to launch at 0100 hours. No sooner, no later. No sitting around. Can you promise me that, Luna?"

"Absolutely, sir. I'm here to help you succeed, whatever your mission might be."

For the rest of the day, Carson remained in his room, darkened with shutters and blinds that he hadn't opened since checking in. He played the mission plan step by step in his mind and repeated the process several times. The specs of the yacht. The location of the cabins and the likely occupants of each. He'd cut the Zodiac's engines two hundred meters from the yacht. He'd paddle from that point to the boat's midsection. He'd launch the rubberized grappling hook, then the collapsible ladder. He'd pin the Zodiac to the yacht and climb to the bottom deck.

Carson took a brief nap. Before he fell asleep, he called Bob Marley and arranged for a pickup at eleven p.m. He'd arrive at the launch point with plenty of time to spare.

~

Lying low in the bushes about thirty yards from the launch site, Carson saw a late model Jeep drive up to the shoreline with the Zodiac in tow at 12:30 p.m. A nearly full moon revealed a young woman with dark hair emerging from the passenger's side of the rig. She stepped to the back bumper, lit with backup lights, and untied the rigging holding the ropes to the trailer. A huge muscled man, at least the size of Black Terrell, came out of the driver's side to help her. They unloaded the boat, and he carried it single-handedly to the shore. They removed the rest of the gear from the Jeep's back end, including the fifty-five-horse-power motor. Carson watched the woman, whom he presumed was Luna, fill the motor's tank from a five-gallon plastic container that was strapped to the trailer. The pair worked quickly and in unison, saying few words to each other.

When they had set up the boat and gathered the gear next to it, the big man looked at his watch.

"Is this guy coming or not? He should be here by now," the man said.

"He'll be here. Don't worry."

"Will he have the money?"

"He wired the money," Luna said.

"Call me when it's done, okay?"

"Go on ahead. I'll call for a ride when I'm ready."

Carson felt relieved watching the man get in the Jeep and drive off at 12:45 a.m. He represented a potential complication of the mission Carson didn't want to deal with. When the Jeep had driven out of sight, Carson continued to wait and watched Luna's behavior. He inched in silence toward her as she sat on the drybags, appearing to be texting someone. She put the phone away in a pocket of her tactical vest resting between her legs. From the same pocket, she pulled a handgun and attached a titanium suppressor on the barrel. She worked cleanly and quickly. By then Carson was about twenty feet behind her. He moved out from the bush and in a half-second grabbed the weapon from her hands. She struggled to hold on, but Carson twisted the gun from her hands while squeezing and pulling her left ear. She gave up and turned around.

Carson holstered the weapon. "Are you ready to go?" Carson said.

"What the fuck are you doing?"

"Just checking your reflexes. That was slow. You'd be dead by now if I were an enemy. But I'm not your enemy, am I, Luna?"

She rubbed her ear. Carson could see she was strong. A tall, strong woman. But way out of her league. Or so it seemed. "You're not my enemy. I'm on your side."

"I am glad you brought the SIG."

"That's what you asked for."

"Winton told you about the money, I assume."

"I've never met him. I told you that. I'm a former Marine, now an independent contractor. I work for rent and tuition."

"College? Well, good for you, Luna. Where are you from?"

"Atlanta."

"Georgia Tech? Is that your school? I hear it's got a great art program," he said, knowing that art was hardly what Tech was known for.

"Right. I'm studying to be a graphic designer."

"Actually, I lied. Last time I checked, Georgia Tech was all about science and engineering."

"And graphic design. Last time I checked. Sir, are we doing this or not?"

"Are you going to ask me what the mission is?"

"Do I need to know the details?" Luna asked.

"No, I suppose you don't. You'll do what I tell you to do. But most people would want to know regardless."

"Tell me what you want."

"What did your handlers tell you?"

"Something about boarding a yacht called *Liberty*. You needed gear and a boat, correct?"

"You sure it was *Liberty*?" Carson asked.

"Absolutely."

Her answer triggered a sharp warning. He had taken care not to provide Winton with the yacht's identity, nor its call sign. "Doesn't all this strike you as strange? All this SEAL gear. Do you do this sort of thing often?"

"I left the service a year ago. I don't do this shit out of habit. I need the money."

"Where is your friend?"

"What friend?"

"The guy in the Jeep who dumped you and all this shit on the beach. The big guy."

"How do you know that?" Luna said.

"You were stupid. I'm not."

"That's my boyfriend."

"He came with you from Atlanta?"

"Yeah. We're on vacation. When I'm done with you. Sir."

"Let me see your phone," Carson said.

"I can't do that. It's private."

"You got any ID?"

"Hell, no. I left it at the hotel."

"Give me your phone."

"Why?"

He pulled the SIG from his holster and held it to her temple. "Sorry, but I'm a careful man. Give me your damned phone, Luna. Then we can be friends."

Carson grabbed the phone and opened the text messages. "All right, Luna. What's this? 'Deal with him sooner rather than later.' And you say, 'Not a problem, sir.'" Carson paused. "Who's texting you?"

"The guy I work for. He runs the agency that got me this job. Who else?"

"Okay, Luna, assuming that's your real name. I'd rather not kill you. But I know you're a liar who's trying to get

377

me killed."

"You're crazy," she said.

"The text. Your made-up facts. Everything about you says, in fact, that I'm not crazy."

"You really think you're going to get away with this?"

"Get away with what?"

"Whatever you're doing."

"Who are you working for?"

"I'm just an operator for hire. What's your problem?"

"You're my problem."

"Please! It's nothing personal. The agency tells me what to do. Please!"

Carson stood holding the SIG and pointed the barrel at her. Before she could scream, he shot Luna in the head. He lifted her body onto the Zodiac and threw the drybags stuffed with gear into the boat. He texted the number on her phone: *It's done.*

A minute later, someone returned the text. *Excellent work. Funds to be transferred immediately. Now toss your phone and dump the body. The client will be in bed by the time you get to the ship.*

Carson tore off his sneakers, wondering who the "client" might be—other than Cripps himself. He slipped on rubber boots and rested the tactical vest on his shoulders. He secured his knife and placed the SIG, along with Luna's phone, in the vest's chest pocket. He pulled out his phone, checked the GPS coordinates of the yacht, and hastened to open water.

He threw Luna's body overboard and watched her sink under the heavy weight of her armored vest. He looked at his watch. The time was 01:30 a.m. He could see stars in the sky, but all else was pitch-black and dead silent. The sea was calm, but he felt the wind kicking up. He readied the launcher and the ladder and re-started the motor.

Within a quarter-mile from the yacht, he cut the engine. He rowed the Zodiac for another twenty minutes. Luna was thoughtful to bring all the gear he'd requested. Most likely for her own use and to maintain a modicum of credibility on her mission to kill him. But on whose behalf? According to her, she freelanced for an independent contractor that hired former special ops for off-book jobs. Not implausible, considering that freelancers probably carried out the stadium bombing as well. And certainly plausible because Carson had already eliminated a would-be assassin at the Motel 6 in Ely. A bad thought. Had Cripps's gang gotten to Winton too?

He couldn't afford to dwell upon extraneous details that had limited utility for completing the job that had taken him thousands of miles of driving plus a boat ride into the dark waters of the Caribbean.

From the drybag he removed his helmet, including the four-tubed night-vision goggles attached to it. He put on the helmet and adjusted the focus on the NGVs. He looked out to the horizon through the goggles and recognized the contours of *Liberty*, floating to the rhythm of the ocean's gentle movement like a mother rocking her baby.

Other than the yacht's deck lights, he noticed no sign of life. The ship sat still in the darkness. He continued to row, one cycle at a time, taking long breaths between strokes, listening to his breathing and feeling his heart rate. The starlight guided him closer to the yacht. At thirty feet, he stopped rowing until the Zodiac slowed to a near stop. He changed his mind. Seeing the ship up close, he noticed that *Liberty*'s bow was blinded from the ports of the main deck at the captain's chair. He could hide underneath and climb from there. He turned and pulled twice gently toward the bow, allowing the boat to drift. He stuck one hand over the rubber railing to stop the craft from bumping into the yacht. He tied down to the yacht's anchor line and waited a moment for the sound of any movements above. If anyone was on the lookout for Luna, Carson couldn't tell. *Liberty* appeared to be dead silent.

Carson removed the wind-up pole from its case and stood it up with the grappling hook attached. He stood on the Zodiac's bottom, found his balance on the rippling water, and wound the rope ladder upward until the grappling hook reached the fiberglass molding above the bow. He pulled on the hook until its razor-sharp teeth clawed securely into the fiberglass. He unattached the pole from the ladder and brought it down to the raft, disassembled it, and rested the pole on the Zodiac. Again he listened for any sounds or movements. Holding the handgun, he climbed up the ladder. It took him ten seconds to get to the top of the bow. He lay lat on his belly on the ship and crawled toward the brass railings, forward of the captain's perch. He peeked into the portholes, confirming his suspicion that the perch would be empty.

His watch said 2:15 p.m. From the time of boarding the *Liberty*, he'd given himself just ten minutes to complete the mission—more than enough time to kill his targets and head back to land.

As he entered the doorway to the com room on the port side of the yacht, Carson could feel his mind and body in transition, as if his personality were shifting into a new balance. Like an out-of-body experience as his mind sharpened into a terrible focus, driven by a mysterious force that seemed to change his self-concept and alter his behavioral code. The force placed blinders on his eyes, compelling him to drive onward and forward. Carson felt himself breaking through the barrier of normalcy. He had entered the kill zone, and there was no turning back.

He climbed to the helm of the ship and opened the communications and control panels. Modern ships were insanely vulnerable. He disabled the five switches and wires that controlled coms, video, audio, lighting, and engines. The ship went completely dark and powerless.

Carson kept moving down the steps to the middle deck. He cocked the handgun and flipped the safety switch. In the kill zone, there was little time to sort the targets. The fifteen-round clip had fourteen rounds remaining. He required at least twelve rounds to complete the mission. Carson had a second clip ready to go, but he didn't want to kill the captain and crew.

He worked from forward to aft through the cabins, letting the chips fall where they may. With the image of the ship's layout in his mind, he got to his knees and gently opened the door to the first cabin past the captain's quarters. He got to his feet and found a man lying on his stomach snoring into a puffy white pillow. A small Nazi flag rested on the nightstand next to the bed. He presumed, correctly, that this was the Austrian Suzanne had told him about. He grabbed the extra pillow and thrust it over the Austrian's head. He pulled the trigger and heard the pillow go poof upon the impact of the silenced weapon.

He crept to the next guest cabin and the next one after that, repeating the same method, modifying the procedure depending on the angle of attack, distance from door to bed, the target's sleeping position, and so on. He killed the first five terrorists with nine rounds remaining.

Carson reached near the end of the guest cabins, with just two remaining—one more guest room and the VIP cabin. Two must-kill targets were left: Garrick Cripps and the unknown

SEAL. He slipped through the door of the last guest cabin. The man was lying on his back, appearing to be half-asleep, his fucking Glock sans silencer on the nightstand, making it imperative that Carson either get to the gun or kill him before he could reach the weapon. With the advantage of the NVGs lighting his target in the darkness, Carson crouched down to the ground and aimed the SIG at the man's forehead.

The man moved on the bed. He opened his eyes in terror and tried to grab the Glock. Recognizing the SEAL's face, Carson knifed his arm to the nightstand and swept the gun to the floor. "It pays to be a winner, right, asshole?"

Carson didn't wait for an answer. He knew the answer. The SEAL was definitely not the most decorated SEAL alive. Not even close. The rich kid from Kentucky was a murderer who'd been disgraced by his peers in his own platoon.

Carson shot Davis Glover between his eyes.

The VIP cabin was next. He opened the door on his hands and knees and crept into the room. A man was sleeping on his side, snoring, his back facing the door. Carson inched toward the bed to see the target and recognized him immediately. He was not Garrick Cripps. "Fucking Graybill," Carson hissed, referring to the senator from Kentucky, Carson's chief pain in the ass for the past three years. Carson resisted the urge to kill Graybill immediately, so the senator could look his killer in the eyes. He silenced Graybill through the heart instead, then moved in silence onto the final cabin.

He'd make quick work of Garrick Cripps and complete the operation. He tried to suppress the urge. The need for it to be over. To get out of the kill zone and rebalance. To return to himself, Carson McCready, a decent human being. But he wasn't done. Fuck the urge. Stay focused. This thing isn't over, he told himself.

Now, however, he didn't know Garrick's location on the ship. Suzanne's intel had been off. He wasn't in the VIP cabin, which meant Garrick was hiding in what he thought would be a secure location. A feeling of terror swept over Carson's consciousness. The feeling of the other shoe still to drop. Another familiar sense that confronted his will and wit on every operation he'd been part of as a SEAL.

He slowed his breathing and positioned himself behind the VIP cabin door, listening for any sounds and movements. He'd be patient. He had cut the ship's communications, reinforcing his confidence that the mission was secure and still winnable. The ship's captain was a wildcard, and he still didn't want to kill the captain or the crew. But where in the hell were they?

He heard a click from a distance of about twenty feet. He turned to the engine room, which was about sixteen feet from the VIP cabin in the stern. Carson stepped toward the stern and stopped by the side of the doorway to the engine room. He had seven rounds left. He considered that Garrick would have a weapon. Carson also considered that the room would be void of light, giving him a major advantage over any man waiting in the darkness, terrified at the thought that he was about to die. Carson opened the door, got on his knees, and scanned the room. Nothing moved. He heard something. The sound of a man breathing but not having the lung capacity to breathe in silence.

"Garrick Cripps. I know you're here."

The breathing sound stopped. Carson waited, his knees still on the floor.

"Welcome to *Liberty*," the voice said. "I was expecting Luna."

"Are you Garrick Cripps?"

"Who wants to know?"

"Don't worry about who I am. Luna had to get back to school. I thought you and I could talk."

"Talk? The time for that is long past, don't you think, Chief?"

"So you know who I am."

"Master Chief Carson McCready. Yeah, I figured. Luna was supposed to kill you."

"How'd you know I'd be coming for you?"

"Suzanne told me once that you'd hunt me down and kill me. Your kid was unfortunate collateral damage. I'd say I'm sorry, but that wouldn't do any good. Do you know the lovely Suzanne?"

"Yes, as a matter of fact."

"You have no idea what she's capable of," Garrick said.

Carson secured the NVGs to his face. "The cyberattack wasn't enough? You gave up on that way too easily."

"I woke up, Chief. The setup was too delicious to waste. You, the disgruntled former SEAL and your do-gooding telemarketing boys. Right out of central casting for a trip to Guantanamo. Looks like I was right. You're a wanted man, and the American people are really pissed off that the government let that tragic event in San Diego happen. Just awful, wasn't it?"

"Explain something to me, professor. How'd you come to believe your own government, the one Americans created, was out to crush its own people? Hell with Russia. North Korea. Your own goddamned country is your enemy number one, and yet . . . Never mind, you're wasting my time," Carson said.

"And yet what?"

"You do vote, right? I was in a cave in Afghanistan, but I still voted."

"Who in the fuck says I vote? That's a waste of time. You don't know that, Chief? The government has always told you what to do, how to behave, how to live your life. You were born free, but you're now blind. You don't know real freedom because the bastards captured you. And you let them by joining the military. Only fools join the military because it's like walking into a jail cell on your own volition, locking yourself up, and tossing the key for life. I chose to be a free man. I refuse to subjugate myself to any authority. Capitalism is my authority. I bucked the socialists off my back. I live on my terms, not some bureaucrat's in Washington."

"I can see you've thought a lot about your freedom. Congratulations. You use big words and fancy philosophical arguments, but I don't think you've thought this through."

"No thinking required, dumbass. Freedom is absolute. There are no buts or qualifications to being free. You either are free or you aren't."

"Do the damned math, professor. Multiply you by a couple of million like you equals the apocalypse. The end of civilization. That's just common sense. Even freedom has rules and an entrance fee. You must pay to play. Civilization offers no free lunches. Respect the laws of nature, or nature will come at you—harder, meaner, and more deadly than anything you've ever known."

"You know nothing about freedom. You're a soldier. You do what you're told."

"I learned something about freedom surfing big waves. I learned the same lesson as a SEAL. I'm free, all right. Free to be an idiot. I like the idea of survival. You do know about survival, right, Garrick? I mean, have you really learned how to survive? A little hint: throw your social Darwinism bullshit out the window. If you're really serious about survival, that is.

When the shit hits and you're looking into the abyss, survival comes down to you and nature's laws. Nothing else. Try to whine and complain about big, bad tyranny when you're looking death in the eyes. Try it. See where that gets you."

"What's your fucking point, Chief? I've got a one-hundred-sixty-foot yacht called *Liberty*. Who are you? What have you got to show the world that you're a man to be reckoned with? You made it back to the real world, but all I see is a poor fuck in a soldier costume."

"You hired a tactical team to plant the bomb that killed a thousand innocents. A kid's severed head flew over my head. She had short, sun-kissed blonde hair. Like she spent a lot of time at the beach. I could see her ghastly scream frozen on her lifeless face. You merely exercised your freedom to kill that child, right? Never mind. Don't answer. Fuck you. You have no right to even answer that question.

"You asked me who I am. You mocked me for not having the wealth and power that you command as a 'true believer.' But right here, right now, I might as well be God. You're an Ayn Rand freak. I was more interested in Thomas Hobbes. I'm the end of the line for you. I'm the mean, nasty, and brutish 'but' of your life and your fucked-up idea of freedom. It ends, now."

"You can't kill me, Chief. I'm bulletproof."

"Oh? How's that going to work?"

"Sweet Laura Cavendish is under surveillance as we speak. Ever heard of Agent X?"

"No. Why, should I have?"

"He's got a team ready to go. A nice little life you two have in Montana—that's about to end. If I die, she dies."

Carson let a few moments pass without a word. His watch said 2:25 a.m. but he stayed with the slowed tempo of the operation, dispensing the chatter as a psychological tool. Disarm Garrick's mind. Get him to relax for a split second until he made a mistake. Carson continued to focus his vision through the NVGs. He sensed movement. A piece of clothing twitched through a slit in the pipes that attached the engine to the turbines.

Guessing that Garrick was bluffing about Laura, Carson formulated an impromptu plan but it wasn't risk free. He aimed his weapon through the slit at the piece of clothing. He fired and heard a loud groan and the sound of metal ricocheting on the floor. He sprang from his knees to his feet and hustled toward the sound. He found Garrick Cripps slunk on the floor of the engine room, holding his arm. Blood soaked through Garrick's nightshirt, dying the white cotton into a deep shade of purple.

Without hesitation he stuck the black knife into the black heart of Garrick Cripps. As Garrick was bleeding out, Carson twisted the serrated blade into his chest. He touched his lapel and took a moment to grieve in silence, then he said, "That's for Michael McCready. A fifteen-year-old kid. My son." He twisted again. "And that's for my dead father, who taught me about men like you before I was old enough to get it. Now I get it."

Carson removed the Trident pin, a.k.a. the Budweiser, from his chest pocket—the one he'd earned twenty-five years ago when he officially became a Navy SEAL. He held the medal in his hand, kissed it goodbye, and stuck it into the hole the knife blade had cut into Garrick's chest.

"This Bud's for you, motherfucker."

Carson turned around abruptly at a noise coming from the entrance to the engine room. He got up and opened the hatch. A man was standing directly in front of him, pointing

387

a handgun at his face.

"A little early for a Budweiser, McCready," the man said.

The man wasn't a killer. Carson recognized the face. He knew immediately the man had never killed another man face-to-face. Even if he were a former FBI official, long retired, now in the business of executing children and their mothers in the service of greed. So this was Agent X? He commanded from afar, taking orders from Garrick and handing down those orders to operators, like Luna, who did the actual work of taking lives. Fifteen-year-old-lives, like his son, Michael.

The man was a civilian, though he thought of himself as a player. But, like with most civilians, there was hesitation. The need to comprehend their own sense of utter surprise. They find their prey and are so, so proud. Success! They silently pat themselves on the back. They become obsessed with the need to play with their prey, like a cat catching a mouse, before thinking about pulling the trigger. No sooner than the man had uttered his cute, introductory remarks to Carson at the hatch, he was bleeding out on the deck.

~

When Carson hit the shore at his launch point, it was nearly five a.m. He found his phone buried under some energy bars and sat on a dry bag full of gear he'd tossed on the sand. He tore open a chocolate bar, took two large bites, and sucked down several ounces of water from the bladder attached to his vest. He lay flat for several moments, unable to move. He was hungry and he was worried, despite telling himself to stay calm. Laura was okay. He knew that. But he forced himself to sit up and dial her. It rang out with no answer. Carson realized it was 3 a.m. Montana time and Laura was probably deep in sleep.

He removed Garrick's phone from his vest. Carson searched for any messages from a would-be killer, no doubt a hired operator, waiting for instructions regarding Laura. He scrolled down to a message from someone identified in the phone as Ranch Hand, who last texted Garrick just an hour ago at approximately four a.m.—some ninety minutes after Carson had left Garrick bleeding out in the engine room.

Ranch Hand: *Ready and waiting at the site. Say the word.*

Garrick: *Stand the fuck by! Do nothing I don't personally authorize. Clear?*

Ranch Hand: *Remember our deal or it's over.*

Garrick sent Ranch Hand another text at half four. *Stand down and clear out. Great news to tell when we see each other.*

Tell me now, Ranch Hand texted back.

Garrick: *Luna got him.*

McCready?

Confirmed.

Then it hit Carson. "What the fuck?" he said. He'd killed Garrick at approximately 2:35 a.m. and a man he presumed was Agent X just minutes later, and 120 minutes afterward, "Garrick" was ordering this Ranch Hand operator—who was apparently poised to harm Laura—to stand down.

Carson was exhausted and his brain fuzzy from poor hydration. Who had told the operator to stand down? It wasn't Garrick. The Trident pin through Garrick's heart rendered his death a certainty. If not Garrick, who?

Carson jammed Garrick's phone back into his pocket. He continued to rehydrate and forced himself to nibble on the energy bar. He lay against the rubber Zodiac. He stretched his legs out and a sharp stab of pain reared up from the horse buck a few weeks ago. His phone lit and buzzed. It was

Laura. She was okay, and Garrick Cripps was not, thank God. He exhaled.

"Carson, talk to me."

He considered how much to tell her about someone called Ranch Hand. "I'm here, babe. It's over."

"And?"

"I'm exhausted. I'll fill you in later, okay? I should get a new burner."

"I love you. I want you back here, McCready."

He tried to suppress any alarm in his voice. "Are you okay?"

"We're fine. Staying busy at the ranch. Trying to keep up with your cousin Chuck."

"Good. I'm glad to hear that. Keep on the look out for any trouble. Remember that spot I showed you at the edge of the ranch. It's a good little spot. Don't go anywhere without that shotgun and Diego, okay?"

"Should I be worried, Carson?"

"No, no. Better to be safe. Double check with Chuck if you have any questions about the shotgun. He'll show you what to do."

"Your cousin was asking about you. Wondering what was going on."

"What did you tell him?"

"Just that you had some loose ends to take care of in California."

"That's perfect. I don't want him worried either."

"Carson, what's wrong? You're coming home soon, right?"

"Yeah, honey. I'll be there as soon as I can."

"You sound tired. I'll let you get settled. Then call me."

"Sure, I'll call you. I love you with all my heart. You know that, right?"

"I love you too. We'll talk later. Call me with your new

burner when you get back to the States."

"Be safe."

Carson placed the SIG and the remaining clips into his vest. He stuffed his knife, underwear, socks, and anything else he might need into the drybag. He leaned back against the boat and felt real hunger for the first time in several hours.

When he was ready, he texted Marley for a ride back to the hotel. He waited, with too much time to think. He should move out, quickly. But there was no team of comrades at the pickup site to whisk him to safety. There was only Marley.

He loved Laura with all his heart, and there was nothing else he wanted more than to spend the rest of his life with her. Go back to Montana, maybe buy a little place with a bit of land to look out into a sky bigger than the Pacific Ocean.

But part of him didn't want to go back. Laura would be okay. She was a good woman. Any man worthy of her would love and care for her.

Could Carson still say he was a good man? Before he had killed under the sanction of the United States of America as a Navy SEAL. Now he killed lawlessly in a lawless nation. A nation of laws had been seized by tribes of men. Men whose sense of privilege was unbounded by common decency and the common good.

Where was America? Where did she go? Carson wanted to think she was waiting, back in God's country, back in Montana, ready to come out again when all was safe. Americans had built a democracy to protect freedom. Now that freedom and reliance on laws and not men had disappeared almost overnight, under siege by forces of greed and unlimited power striving to serve the few at the expense of the many.

Garrick had despised the weak. He believed that caring for them was the road to serfdom. When people are hopeless and powerless, that's the road to mass poverty of mind and spirit when there is no choice. When there is no freedom. When the few take from the many, bleeding the many dry until they have nothing but useless hope and a shadow of the America that once was. When folks looked out for the welfare of neighbors they didn't even know. When folks were called citizens.

Curious word, Carson thought. Who was a citizen? He Googled the word: *A native or naturalized member of a state or nation who owes allegiance to its government and is entitled to its protection.* The right and security of citizenship weren't free. You pledged allegiance. You paid your taxes. Nothing was free. Citizenship came with the cost of responsibility. That was SEAL mentality to the hilt. An organism consisting of many individual parts. To survive you became one of the many, and the many became one living thing.

Carson chuckled to himself while recognizing the tragic irony. Garrick hated freeloaders as the enemies of freedom, and yet that's exactly what he had been. A freeloader. He got the security and protection of the very government he despised and strove to eliminate—and replace. But what would he replace it with? What's left without government? Who could then claim the rights of citizenship when Americans woke up and discovered nobody voted because voting was irrelevant? A year from that day, people would remember what they had. Ten years from that day, people would have forgotten a thing called democracy, a place called America, having settled into a new world called Libertyland, and a tiny few would wonder: *what happened? What have we done? What have we lost?*

Carson had ripped his precious Trident off his chest. He was now a stateless being, having the ultimate freedom to kill without guilt and perhaps without consequence. A lone wolf who would dwell in the kill zone forever, and call himself free. Carson McCready. Red-blooded American killer. The King of Libertyland.

Carson laughed. He could actually become the king Garrick had always wanted to be. That would be so easy. The knee-jerk propaganda was ingrained into the dark side of American culture. The details of liberty were hard. Reality, not words, was hard. His father dwelled in the details of liberty to help those who who'd seen injustice. He had to form an argument, well-reasoned and based in reality not conspiracies. Justice was hard. His father had to know his shit about the law and human nature. He had to work fifteen hours a day to protect the unprotected. He got little in return, even from his own son.

As a highly-decorated Navy SEAL, Carson could fall back on the automatic. Where he didn't have to think. Where he was entitled to simplicity. Where he could easily assume the role and repeat the lines. Be the standardized man of destiny. Like Davis Glover who had turned on his own people to play the role of the undefined patriot. Carson didn't do well with the ill-defined. He examined words and their meanings. He examined the way of patriotism and he solved the riddle and that showed him the path, and that path turned away from hate and greed to a greater path of trust, love, hope, and dreams.

42

RESISTANCE

The driving distance from Miami to Red Lodge, Montana, is roughly twenty-five hundred miles, which works out to about thirty-seven hours of driving time for normal drivers. Carson drove up to Kansas, then even farther north to South Dakota, and then he shot west toward Red Lodge, where he would arrive at the county road from town to Chuck's ranch, another thirty-minute drive. He left Miami on a Sunday. Two and a half days later, he called Laura from Rapid City and told her he'd be home late the next day.

By coming home Carson had resisted his unyielding urge to go forward alone, a lone wolf attacking his prey one by one and allowing his rage to fire the killer within him. His sense of retribution was deep and volatile. Michael's killing accounted for most of his rage. And yet there was more to it than the loss of his son. By the time he got to Montana, Carson remembered, and understood more fully, what was at stake. He remembered the day he had taken the SEAL oath of honor—the final completion of SEAL Qualification Training. A day of sublime pleasure. The pinnacle of his training, the day marking his achievement as a full-fledged, battle-ready SEAL, would be better called Survival Qualification Day. Pinning his Trident to his chest. Sharing the moment with his graduating team of peers at the beach in Coronado. The sun was at high mast. He faced the Pacific and felt the ocean breeze on his face. Even then it was only the beginning, because the day meant nothing until he became part of a team.

He could feel the same sense from his teammates. The formalities of graduation were brief and perfunctory. Graduation was a day to stop, congratulate, and assess. A day of calm. A day to rest for the next day and start preparing for a new phase of training, ultimately leading to his first deployment as a SEAL months after that. Whatever pride of accomplishment Carson had felt at graduation was certainly anticlimactic. At that juncture reciting the SEAL ethos and pinning on the Trident were just words and a piece of metal. Was he really worthy of either when the shit hit the fan?

"In the worst of conditions," the SEAL ethos read, "the legacy of my teammates steadies my resolve and silently guides my every deed. I will not fail."

What did those words really mean? He'd heard the words many times before, but never really understood them until the initial moments of his first mission to Afghanistan as a newly minted SEAL. Within seconds of his platoon landing in Taliban territory, under fire from the moment the men stepped out of the chopper, Carson intrinsically realized, in real time, the most vital lesson of all. He and every member of his team were woven together, each man responsible to a higher authority: the ethos of a SEAL to abandon selfishness for the sake of something larger than oneself. During those initial moments of lawlessness and deadly anarchy, each man suspended his sense of personal survival for the sake of a larger living organism.

But it was never easy. The fucking hardest lesson he'd ever learned—to trust other human beings so much that you're willing to sacrifice your hard-wired instinct to survive individually. That is until you realize that without your team, and without everyone on the team making the same realization, you'd certainly die a Hobbesian death.

He'd repeated it to himself, again and again, until the violent first stage of the mission was completed. And he repeated it now as he passed through Red Lodge and drove toward the ranch.

I will not fail.

I will not fail my team. My family. My country.

Carson kept driving. He knew Laura was right—this wasn't over, and he loved her more for her willingness to fight with him in order to prevent the unthinkable. He knew for certain more trouble would come. But from whom? Not knowing the answer to that basic question left him angry and bewildered. His experience as a SEAL went only so far, and he felt out of his depth. The mission on the yacht had gone smoothly. His targets were easy, and he had pounced on them without a moment's hesitation or fear.

He had killed them all.

Yet his doubts survived. Had he killed the leader of an extremist faction of libertarians or his body-double? Garrick was too smart. He would never have left himself that exposed. Or had his hubris overwhelmed his brilliance? Carson had accomplished his mission, and yet he'd just entered a black hole. Where would the conspiracy re-surface? Who would lead the movement without Garrick in charge? Carson and Laura alone could never mount an effective counter-attack on an unseen and unknown enemy.

And there were things that had nagged him the entire trip that he couldn't wrap his mind around. How had Garrick supposedly communicated with an operator standing by at the ranch when Garrick was already dead? He assumed that Garrick had paid someone to hire Luna as a hit-woman. But he couldn't help but wonder if his old friend, Winton Bruce, had played a hand in that deception.

Some fifty miles from Red Lodge, Carson pulled over and stopped the car next to the road. He clicked the trunk open, got out, and found the dry bag. He found Garrick's phone stuffed into the bottom of the bag underneath his gear. He powered up the phone and looked for the text exchange between Garrick and the operator: *Stand down and clear out. Great news to tell when we see each other.*

The wind outside howled and dust kicked up from a semi passing him on the road. But he couldn't wait. He had to know. Using Garrick's phone he found Suzanne Dreyfus's contact information and hit dial.

The phone rang numerous times. He clicked off, waited a minute, then dialed again.

Finally she answered. "Garrick?"

"Garrick is dead."

"Carson?"

"Alive and well. You set me up, Suzanne."

The line was silent for several moments. "I had to. I'm sorry. It had to be you."

"The recruiter was yours, right?"

"Yes."

"And Petit."

"Correct."

"What about Heller and Alvarez?"

"No. I mean, they had nothing to do with me. But Garrick

397

and William have, or had, a company that convinced Alvarez to start the telemarketing deal. All with an eye to privatizing the county jail. You were my own private contribution."

"Why me?"

"You were perfect."

"I should hunt you down like all the others."

"Maybe you should. I wouldn't blame you."

"But I won't."

"Why not?"

"I'm calling you from Garrick's phone."

"I see that."

"Garrick was already dead when someone told the operator at the ranch to back off. So I know it wasn't Garrick. And I killed every other bastard on that yacht. Leaves me with one possibility."

"And what would that be?"

"It was you, Suzanne. You sending me the texts about the cyberattack. Setting me up with that job. Knowing Laura, and that she and I were close. It was you all along. Why?"

"I'm going to tell you a secret, Carson."

"I'm listening."

"*The Liberation Manifesto*. You've heard of it?"

"Yes."

"I wrote it. I gave it to Garrick for his fortieth birthday. I meant it to be a fun gift. I thought the whole libertarian thing was so over the top. He gave me all these books, you know. The pseudo-intellectual bastards take themselves so seriously. I made fun of it. *The Liberation Manifesto* is one big sad fucking joke, Carson."

"Sounds like you're covering your tracks."

"I'm confessing, dammit. I thought through the implications of pure libertarianism. Now I know how

398

dangerous it was. The evil joke was on me. All because I was either too clever or I loved Garrick too much. Probably both."

"I should come after you. Everything went according to plan, right? Everything except the kids. Everything except my son. But it happened. And the rest is clear now."

"Clear? How?"

"You're a selfish bitch, Suzanne. You know and I know that. But you saved Laura, didn't you? You kept the operator from killing her and everyone at the ranch."

Suzanne said nothing.

"What are you thinking now?" Carson said.

"Be good to her, Carson. She's the best thing you've ever had. But do me one favor, okay?"

"And that would be?"

"Don't ever, ever let her write you a manifesto. If she does, throw the damned thing away, kiss her lovingly, and ask her to marry you. Everything else is bullshit. Promise me that."

~

Carson drove through the front gate to the ranch, passing the shade from the trees that lined the long gravel driveway to the house. It was nearly dusk.

At the end of the driveway, he could see Laura's silhouette amid the shade of the trees and the sun setting behind her. As he got closer, Laura's likeness turned into vivid color. She was wearing jeans and her favorite baby blue western shirt. He stopped and got out of the car next to the gate leading to the house. She came to him as he opened the car door. She squeezed her body close, enveloping him in her arms. She said nothing and he responded with silence, gripping her tightly, then kissed her. Within a minute Diego ran through the gate, smiling and yipping as he crashed into Carson, nearly tipping him over. He got on his knees. "Hi there, good dog. I missed you too."

He stood to face Laura. He could see tears welling up in her green eyes. "You made it. Thanks for staying alive."

"I just realized something. I'm taking a real breath of air for the first time in ten days."

"How's it feel?"

"Like I'm finally alive, and I'd like to stay that way for a little while."

She took his hand and led him to the small wooden deck at the back of the ranch house, surrounded by flowers and plants. Chuck and his wife, Alice, were smiling, reaching out to touch their cousin Carson as he walked toward them. They were dressed like they were going to church. The boy's shirt was tucked and his jeans pressed. Alice wore a flowered dress, and Chuck's brown hair was combed and slicked. Carson didn't suppose the family knew his reason for being gone, but they seemed to understand he had had to leave for something important to him and others.

Carson looked at the family, and then at Laura. He told himself to relax, to give away as little emotion as possible, but he felt like breaking down and crying.

And yet this was how he had envisioned coming home. He didn't wish to fight again, not with anybody. He wanted to be alone with Laura and his dog. To sit outside by a fire and just be. To be in love with life. To feel the freedom to love. That hope was Carson's true north. His Libertyland.

And yet Carson knew exactly what he was up against. He now understood the ability of some to amass power and to deceive. A kingdom of strange languages and human-like creatures who dwelled in an incomprehensible reality. An underworld that drove men like Garrick to kill children and their parents. Provocateurs, players, who wrote manifestos that even they didn't take seriously, except to bank the proceeds and feed outlandish causes and extreme ideologies.

Laura handed Carson a glass of champagne and moved closer to him. He took Laura's hand and squeezed it. She would know that unstated code, revealing his pain at having to choose. Act as if everything were fine. Return to normalcy. Accept what is. Pretend America was still America and always would be.

But Carson could see the future and doing nothing small would do something big, leaving the powerful the freedom to take from the poor and steal from the many. As a man, Carson refused to be sorry. He'd do anything in his power not to be sorry. Not for a damned thing.

Laura squeezed his hand in return. Twice. An unstated code to buckle up, Chief. We'll remember. We'll always remember.

A NOTE FROM THE AUTHOR

If you enjoyed this book, I would be very grateful if you could write a review and publish it at your point of purchase. Your review, even a brief one, will help other readers to decide if they'll enjoy my work.

If you want to be notified of new releases from me and other AIA Publishing authors, please sign up to the AIA Publishing email list. In return you'll get a free ebook of short stories and book excerpts by AIAP authors. You'll find the sign-up button on the right-hand side under the photo at www.aiapublishing.com. Of course, your information will never be shared, and the publisher won't inundate you with emails, just let you know of new releases.

ACKNOWLEDGMENTS

I'd like to thank several people who've provided invaluable insights for *Libertyland,* including Andy Ross, Mark Weinstein, Kendra Harpster, and Fran Lebowitz.

ABOUT THE AUTHOR

Peter Sacks is an author, journalist, and social critic. He is the author of notable books such as *Tearing Down the Gates: Confronting the Class Divide in American Education*, which won the book of the year award from the Association of American Colleges and Universities, and *Standardized Minds: The High Price of America's Testing Culture and What We Can Do to Change It.* He has been nominated twice for the Pulitzer Prize and is a frequent keynote speaker at colleges and universities. Sacks has contributed articles and essays to many national publications, as well as making appearances on radio and television programs.

OTHER BOOKS BY THIS AUTHOR

Generation X Goes to College: An Eye-Opening Account of Teaching in Postmodern America (Open Court).

Standardized Minds: The High Price of America's Testing Culture (Perseus).

Tearing Down the Gates: Confronting the Class Divide in American Education (University of California Press).

Affirmative Action for the Rich, contributor (The Century Foundation).

Printed in the USA
CPSIA information can be obtained
at www.ICGtesting.com
LVHW042332260424
778560LV00001B/70

9 781922 329578